complicated
you

Thank you for even
reading one page of
my book! I hope you
enjoy ☺

This book contains references to suicide, eating disorders and self-harm.

Florence would love to interact with you on social media, so please give her a follow and say hello!
Instagram: @florencewilliams1
TikTok: @flosfiction

ISBN: 978-1-3999-2405-4
First Edition: June 2022

Cover design by Sophia Nicolella

For every book sold, Florence will donate to Samaritans, registered charity 219432.

For my mum, dad and sister who taught me

that a problem shared is a problem halved.

Thank you for being there when it felt like

I was carrying the weight of the entire world

on my shoulders. I love you always.

PART ONE

Chapter One

"Have you left the house yet?" my dad predictably asks down the phone.

"Not yet. I'm just putting the last box in my car." I sigh, balancing my phone in the crook of my neck. I yank the door of my black Ford Fiesta open and throw the box inside.

"Okay. I'm sorry we can't be there to wave you off."

"It's okay, honestly. I know you couldn't take leave and there was no point Mum missing work just to say goodbye. I'll be home at Christmas."

"Okay, love," he says. "And don't go forgetting our plan. This is your second year of university, take it extremely seriously. Job applications are right around the corner—"

"—and I don't want to give a law firm any reason to

reject me. A poor transcript makes for a poor future," I recite Dad's usual spiel.

"That's my girl."

I roll my eyes, grateful that it's just a phone call and he can't see the look on my face. "I'd better go. I'll text you when I get there."

I hang up and hop into the driver's seat, punching my new address into the navigation system. I pull away from my family home, feeling a familiar pit in my stomach at the thought of returning to campus.

It's not that I hate university, I just don't *love* it. The thing about university is, you're told it will be the best three years of your life. You're told that you'll make amazing friends, be immersed in some of the best academic lectures and have a pretty busy social schedule. So far, my monochrome experience has been nothing like the technicolour dream I was sold.

At the beginning of my first year, I made a conscious effort to go with my housemates to all the parties I could, saying yes to every single night out and trying to make friends with complete strangers... but all the parties felt the same.

The same cheesy pop music played in the same student nightclubs, filled with the same people. Every. Single. Week. And I never found anyone I clicked with, so after a while, I just stopped going.

A sea of red brake lights stirs me from my thoughts as I approach a mass of traffic slowing into a single lane, all navigating around orange traffic cones. These lane closures have been disrupting the same stretch of the motorway for almost a year now, and I'm not exactly sure what they're for. The road looks the same every time I drive past, no repairs or improvements in sight. But at least I know that by this point, I'm less than an hour from campus.

I turn my music up to a ridiculously high volume, singing along to my OneRepublic playlist the rest of the way, tapping my fingers to the beat of *Run*.

My car is the only place I'd ever listen to music this loudly—I don't even play music in my apartment unless I'm wearing headphones—so I figure I should make the most of this time alone.

The campus clocktower quickly comes into view when I finally pull off the motorway. I try to ignore the sense of panic rising from my stomach to my throat as I reach my apartment building.

Once I'm parked up, I grab as many boxes as my hands can manage and shuffle to the main entrance. I'm panting by the time I reach my apartment.

Jesus, I'm unfit.

When I step inside, my flatmate, Jake, is standing in the hallway with a cardboard box full of kitchen pans. He silently nods at me as he makes his way to the kitchen. I dump my stuff on the bed and head towards him.

"Hi," I say quietly, leaning against the doorframe, staring as he empties the box of pans onto the kitchen counter. He looks down at them deep in thought.

He appears slightly bigger than I remember him being last year. His maroon t-shirt hugs his defined arms, and his chest sticks out much further than before, making it look like he's permanently sucking in a huge breath. I can't decide if this new look suits his baby face.

"Hey. How was your summer?" he asks, brushing a hand through his thick, dark blonde hair.

"It was okay. I worked for most of it, so nothing special." I give him a small smile and walk towards one of the stools tucked under the kitchen counter.

"Of course you did!" a girl's voice chimes from the other side of the room.

I turn my head to see my other flatmate, Kady, lying across the couch. She has a book in one hand and a can of Diet Coke in the other. Her dark braids flow to her waist and across her pale pink top. She looks serene, as if she's spent her whole summer relaxing abroad.

"I hate to make you jealous, but I went to Greece for

a month with the volleyball team. We took a boat around some of the Greek islands. It was unreal!"

"I've never been to Greece before, I bet it was beautiful," I reply.

"No way! You have to go at some point. You spend too much time working, girl." Kady smiles and lies back down, reopening her book.

"I know, I know." I sigh playfully.

"I can't say my summer was as exciting as Kady's," Jake chips in, waving a spatula in his hand and then setting it down in the nearest drawer. "I went to rugby camp. It was pretty intense. Coach wants us on top form for the start of this season."

Well, I guess that explains the added muscle.

"Anyway, I'm gunna go grab the box of cutlery from my room. See you in a bit." He holds out one hand and gives us an awkward wave before leaving the communal space.

I go back to my room, grabbing my keys and making my way back to the car to get the rest of my belongings.

Chapter Two

The harsh sound of my morning alarm stirs me from my sleep. I groan and reach for my phone to turn it off as the noise grows louder and louder.

Even though I continued unpacking until late last night, I can't sleep in. I need to go into town today and see my boss.

Resignedly, I roll out of bed and tidy the white linen bedsheets before showering and changing into mom jeans and a baggy t-shirt. I grab my khaki overshirt, purse and car keys before darting out of the door.

As I descend the stairs, Alice, my third, final—and somewhat intimidating—housemate pushes through the heavy building door with Jake trailing behind. They're both bright red and completely out of breath.

"Hey guys," I say as I reach the bottom step.

Alice snaps her head towards me. "Oh. Hey, Zoe," she says with an air of disinterest.

"Good run?"

"Yeah. Jake actually got up on time and decided to come with me." She glances smugly in his direction.

"I didn't exactly have a choice. You knocked on my door at seven this morning! Plus, coach has us on a crazy fitness regime since summer camp," Jake replies, once again finding a way to mention the fact he's on the rugby team. He loves to subtly brag. I'm yet to see him walk on campus *without* wearing his team jersey.

"Kady said you wanted to come with us to the sports fair this afternoon. She's not kidding, right? You actually want to come?" Alice asks, tilting her head towards me.

"Uh, yes. I'm coming."

"You? Joining a sports team?" Jake asks, eyebrows raised.

"Uh huh." I nod, lowering my head to the floor.

I know that I need to join some sort of sports team this year if I want to get a good graduate job, it's part of Dad's '*big plan*'. I wish it was just about grades. Whenever I've attended a law fair on campus, the only thing any firm seems to care about is how many clubs you're a part of, or how much you've embraced '*university life*'. Go figure.

"Well, good luck if I don't see you before the fair," Jake says, following Alice into our apartment.

I continue down the stairs and walk to my car, switching off the radio and rolling down the window to let in the warm September air.

When I get to town, I park in the dreary multi-storey car park, duck out through a fire-exit door and make my way across the high street to work, overtaking dawdling shoppers as I go.

My eyes quickly spot the familiar bright pink *Jacks* logo plastered across the storefront. My manager, Emily, is in the window trying to reattach a mannequin's head to its body. I knock on the glass, startling her.

She puts her hand to her chest and closes her eyes, taking a deep breath. Her panic quickly transforms into a smile when she recognises me.

"You nearly gave me a heart attack!" She laughs, climbing out of the window display. "I was wondering when you were going to show up. Don't fancy working today, do you? I hate changing these damn mannequin outfits. You always do a better job," she says, wiping her hand across her forehead for dramatic effect.

"Absolutely not, thank you. I would rather stick pins in my eyes," I reply with a sarcastic smile.

"Fine. I guess I'll have to do it myself." She sighs. "Well, go ahead to the staff room. Your paperwork is already printed out on my desk for you to sign. Make sure to check the uniform list as well, you'll need to pick some new outfits for this season."

"Sure," I reply, internalising my groan. I *really* don't want to pick out new clothes.

"Oh, and Zoe—" Emily calls. I turn on my heels. "It's good to have you back."

I nod instinctively, unable to meet her eyes, and walk to the stock room, leaving Emily to get back to wrestling the mannequin.

The familiar damp smell of the underground cave hits me as soon as I enter the back office. It's a cramped space with no windows or air flow—definitely not one for the claustrophobic.

I run down the stairs and open the door to the stock room, where piles of clothes are neatly folded across metal shelving.

My contract is printed and waiting on Emily's desk, so I reach for a pen to fill out the remaining details and sign my name. As promised, she's also left a list of uniform options for me, she's even scribbled handwritten stars next to the outfits she wants me to try.

I look for the pieces folded in the stock room, searching by name for the right ones. After sifting through the first row of shelves, I head to the second unit and practically jump out of my skin as I turn the corner.

A guy with a mop of dark brown hair is sat on the floor with his back against the wall. His knees are to his chest and he's scribbling something on a stock list with a highlighter. The pen lid is in his mouth, and I try not to stare too intently at his lips as he chews the plastic.

He must be our new stockroom hire. Although, he's not decked out in the standard, preppy, overpriced Jacks clothing that every other member of staff has to wear. Instead, he's sporting a baggy grey t-shirt, black skinny jeans and a pair of lace-up Vans. His style suits him completely, but—with a face like his—I'm pretty sure he'd suit anything.

He doesn't notice me staring at him. I can hear the faint beat of music seeping out of his earbuds, so it's no wonder he hasn't clocked me. He's nodding his head to the music, humming along to whatever he's listening to. I pull my bottom lip into my mouth to stop myself from grinning at the sight.

Not wanting to risk being caught ogling at the guy, I

eventually lean down and tap one of his knees.

"You're the new stock room assistant?" I ask as nonchalantly as possible, heading towards the dresses folded on the shelf next to him

"Sorry, I was in a world of my own. What did you say?" he asks, taking one bud from his ear. He smiles at me, his hazel eyes lingering on my face.

Jesus, his stare is lethal. So is the sound of his voice. My heart has just started beating a million miles an hour. What is he doing to me?

Get it together, Zoe.

"I umm... I asked if you're the new stockroom assistant? I'm Zoe, by the way," I eventually stutter.

"Yeah, that's me. I'm Ryan. Really nice to meet you." He beams and holds out a hand.

I bend down awkwardly to where he's sitting and reach for his hand, immediately dropping the clothes that were tucked under my elbow. Cursing to myself, I hastily plunge to the floor to pick them up.

Ryan lets out a tiny chuckle, but I don't dare look at him.

"You too," I mumble, standing up and turning to make my way out of the stockroom as fast as I can.

"Wait!" he calls out just as I get to the door. I turn around to find him holding out a dress. "You dropped this." He smiles. "I think you'd suit it."

I open my mouth to reply, but as I look up at him and his lopsided grin, my brain freezes.

He's much taller than me, but I suppose that isn't hard given I'm only five-foot-one. I reckon he's older than me by a few years too, I'd say he's in his early twenties. He's also slender yet pretty muscular, although not in an outrageous way like Jake is.

My eyes wander down to the semicolon tattoo he has just above his right elbow and, as he catches me staring at the design, he runs a hand though his mop of hair. He then shakes his head slightly, ruffling his hair with his hands before patting it back in place.

"Well, it was nice to meet you. I'm sure I'll see you on shift soon."

"Yeah, you too," I mutter, spinning on my heels and walking out of the stockroom.

Chapter Three

I'm standing in the dressing room, looking down at the piles of clothes on the wooden bench. Everything feels out of place; my heart is in my mouth, my stomach is in my throat, my head is spinning.

I *hate* trying on clothes.

For one, these dressing rooms really suck. They don't have a lock on them, or even a real door for that matter. I only have a tweed curtain separating me from the shop floor.

And second, I don't like what I see in the mirror, especially with these unflattering Jacks mirrors making me look twice my width and half my height.

I know I don't have the body to work here. I only got the job because my sister worked for the same brand whilst she was at university. The girls that work here are skinny, preppy types with super long blonde hair and an all-year tan. I'm short with curvy hips and thick legs, not to mention muscular shoulders and a round stomach.

I try on the first outfit, a dusty pink V-neck t-shirt with the Jacks logo printed on the front paired with blue skinny jeans. I immediately decide against it when I see how unflattering the tight, low waist jeans are in the mirror.

After trying on several dresses, which seem to cling to my body in their own unflattering way, I pick up the plain navy dungaree-dress that Ryan said would suit me.

Surprisingly, it doesn't look completely terrible.

I quickly change, gather my things and walk towards Emily by the till, dropping the dress on the counter.

She eyes my new uniform, raising a brow. "Look who's finally branched out with a new style." She smiles approvingly. "Did you get this from the stockroom?"

I nod slowly.

"Oh, so you met Mr Walker then? What did you think?"

"Who?"

"Ryan." She chuckles.

"Oh, umm, I don't know... I mean, he doesn't look like the typical Jacks hire, but I guess that could be a good thing?" I shrug.

Emily laughs, shaking her head as she lifts the uniform logbook from under the desk and starts writing on it. "You can say that again. He's in a band with my brother and needed a job. They know each other from music college. Couldn't say no to the little sods, could I?"

So, I was right. Ryan must be around twenty-two, the same age as Emily and her twin brother, Tyler.

I have the urge to ask more questions about Ryan but resist as the growl in my stomach reminds me that I haven't eaten anything for a while.

For the past couple of hours, I've been trying my damned best not to think about the sports fair. But I can't. I literally can't think of anything other than the stupid fair.

What am I thinking, joining a sports team?

I can't handle the pressure, *who am I kidding?*

This university is crazy about sports, it seems everyone is part of a squad. Just like Jake, every student likes to strut around campus in their team jerseys, wearing the logo like a badge of honour, letting everyone know they belong. It's so cliquey it makes me nauseous.

A knock at the door startles me.

"Ready?" Alice pops her head round my door.

"Yup." I jump off the bed and throw on my white and lilac Nike Airforce Ones.

"Good. We can't be late, Kady's working the volleyball table," she says impatiently as we walk into the hallway where Kady is leaning against the wall, waiting for us.

She's smiling brightly, wearing the university volleyball jersey and tight leggings. Her long braids are tied into a high ponytail, and they swish as she walks towards us. She looks like one of those perfect Instagram influencers, even in her heinous university kit.

"Ready to recruit those freshers!" she says with a laugh as we make our way towards to door.

We turn onto the university road and walk towards the iconic redbrick buildings at the centre of the campus. The famous clocktower is in plain sight the whole way and I'm reminded of why I love this place so much. It often feels like a world of its own, a self-contained bubble away from the busy city.

"So, which team are you signing up for, Zoe?" Alice asks curiously, looking at me out of the corner of her eyes. "I didn't expect you to join a club this year, let alone a competition team," she presses with a disbelieving—and slightly mocking—laugh.

"I think it's a great idea," Kady adds with a warm smile.

"I'm thinking about trying out for cheerleading," I tell them quietly, biting my lip.

"Cheerleading?!" Alice gasps.

"Um, yeah. I mean, I danced at school and used to do gymnastics, so I figured it's my best chance. And besides, they only do a few competitions a year, which is much better than the gymnastics or dance squads. Apparently, they compete every weekend."

"Well, I think that's great, Zo. You'll have so much fun I'm sure," Kady warmly adds, nudging me softly with her elbow. I meet her eyes and return the smile.

"Are you sticking to the track team this year?" I ask Alice, trying to shift the attention from me.

"Yeah," she answers vaguely before turning to Kady and going into a deep discussion about last year's sports socials, which—for obvious reasons—means I can't join in. Not that it bothers me. I've sort of gotten used to them being a pretty tight knit duo. At least it allows me to go back to staring at the pretty campus architecture and avoiding small talk.

I say goodbye to the pair of them as soon as we enter the giant sports hall, and I begin scanning the huge, busy space for the cheerleading table.

Eventually, I locate it, unsure how I missed the bright thing covered in trophies and gold bows in the first place.

Before I can talk myself out of my decision, I take a deep breath and go directly to the first cheerleader I see with a clipboard in hand.

"Would you like to sign up for cheerleading try-outs?" The girl beams at me.

She has straight brown hair, styled into a neat half-up, half-down ponytail with a giant gold bow on top of her head. The rest of her silky hair falls down to her waist. She's wearing the full cheerleading uniform: a short, figure-hugging navy skirt and a matching, equally tight, navy long sleeve cheer top with *Panthers* plastered across it in red and gold writing.

I grimace, nearly deciding to back out due to the outfit alone.

This so isn't me.

I'm not the type of girl to pull off a tight mini skirt, nor a giant glittery bow and obnoxiously large smile. I swear I only smile when I'm at Jacks, getting paid to be cheerful.

I nod at the girl, reminding myself that I need to do this if I want to secure my dream job. Taking the pen from the girl's perfectly manicured hand, I sign up for the first try-out session tomorrow evening, giving myself as little time as possible to back out.

I decide not to look for Kady or Alice after signing up. Instead, I take the opportunity to call my sister on the walk back to the apartment.

"Hey sis. How's uni? Are you enjoying being back?" Hannah asks before I can even say hello.

I fill her in on my day, including signing up for cheerleading. She doesn't hide her excitement, gushing over the fact that I'm finally stepping out of my comfort zone. She's one to talk, but I don't tell her that.

"How are the socials? There must be loads going on considering it's welcome week," she probes.

"I wouldn't know," I answer honestly. "Although, if I pass try-outs tomorrow, I imagine there will be some sort of team party."

"That's great! Make sure you're having fun, okay?" she says.

"Sure, sure," I reply. Before hanging up, I promise to call her again next week.

As soon as I put my phone back in my pocket, it buzzes.

Kady: I lost you at the fair!
Kady: Come to the Guild for a drink?

Kady: All the sports teams are here—it'll be fun! ☺

The last thing I want to do is spend my night at the campus bar, especially with try-outs tomorrow.

I ignore the texts and push through my apartment door, walking to my bed and flopping down on the mattress.

I'll just tell Kady that I fell asleep early and didn't see her message.

I decide to spend the night watching a film on my laptop instead, hitting play on the same movie I watched last night, *Endless Love*.

Is it normal to happily watch the same film over and over again? I've never met anyone else who does the same thing, but that doesn't stop me. It's comforting... safe.

Just as I nestle into my duvet, one of the bedroom doors across the hall slams and footsteps make their way towards my room. I tense as I wait for whoever it is to knock on my door.

Relief floods through me when I hear them head out of the apartment. It must be Jake, probably going to the Guild for the sports social with his rugby team... or perhaps he's proving to be the better housemate by going to meet up with Kady and Alice.

Chapter Four

I'm not entirely sure how I managed to get through today. Even the mountain of class reading I had wasn't enough to stop me clock watching. Every hour, every minute, every second dragged at an unbearable rate.

Until it was time to get ready for cheer try-outs.

I thought the time would never come. But now I'm here, parked up in the car park, looking out at the dreary night, staring at the sports hall entrance.

My body feels heavy. I can't move. It's like I'm pinned to the seat of my car by some kind of powerful, magnetic force.

What was I thinking?

I can't do this. I can't join a sports team. There's no way I'll fit in with the cheer squad. I'll stand out for some reason or another. It'll be because I'm too boring or too curvy or I'll be clueless when it comes to the stunts. I'll be hopeless. And I'll be laughed out of the building.

Just as my heart feels like it's about to explode out of my chest, I grip the steering wheel, clutching it until my knuckles go white.

"Breathe, Zoe," I tell myself.

And then, I do just that. I breathe in and breathe out.

As my mind unravels and the brain fog clears, I slowly climb out of my car and amble towards the sports hall.

I look towards the revolving doorway and notice Kady push through. She must've finished volleyball training or something.

She hasn't noticed me. She's too distracted by whatever music is playing through her bright pink headphones.

What is it with people playing music so loud that they have no clue of their surroundings? Isn't that dangerous?

And I don't understand this new trend of wearing obnoxiously large headphones to the gym. Don't they fall off her head as she runs? They look so heavy and uncomfortable. What happened to just wearing the standard earphones that come free with your phone?

Kady finally notices me as she raises her head. She's smiling brightly at me. I breathe a sigh of relief; she doesn't seem ready to scold me for missing last night's drinks.

"Cheer try-outs?" she asks, tilting her head and pulling her headphones off her ears, resting them on her neck.

"Yeah. Today's the day." I smile awkwardly.

"Nervous?" she asks. I nod my head and she immediately reaches her hand out, gripping my forearm. "Don't be. You'll do great. Tell me all about it when you get home, okay?"

"Sure." I smile, attempting to gulp down the air that seems to be trapped in my throat.

Kady turns and begins to walk towards the main road. She can't have taken more than a few steps when I hear her shouting my name. I turn around to see her running back to me.

"Jake is going to cook the whole apartment dinner tonight. You'll come, right? That way, you can either celebrate or commiserate with us," she says, slightly out of breath.

"Umm... maybe. I'll have to see what time I get back from try-outs," I reply.

Kady frowns. "But we've not had chance to eat as a group since we've come back. And we missed you last night." There's no hint of malice or sarcasm in her voice like I'd feared, just affection.

Now I feel bad.

"I know, it's just—" I begin to formulate an excuse, but Kady cuts me off.

"Zoe, you know we want to hang out with you, right?"

"Huh?"

"Me, Jake and Alice. We want to hang out with you, but you always seem to hide in your room. I mean, I get that you want to focus on your law degree and job applications, but it's university. I thought things would be different this year. I thought you'd be more comfortable around us now? I don't know. I just think you should be having fun, relaxing every now and then. I really miss hanging out with you."

"I know... I... I don't know. I guess you're right." I sigh, feeling like the worst housemate in the world. Although, I'm not entirely sure I believe Kady when she says Alice misses me—not that I'm going to admit that.

"So, you'll come to dinner?" She smiles so bright it lights up the dreary sky around us. It's a smile that's hard to say no to.

I nod and agree to the dinner, even though the thought of it only adds to the knot in my stomach. I'd feel terrible if I bailed twice. Kady doesn't deserve that. The least I can do is make an effort with the person that always shows me so much kindness, despite my reticence.

Kady wishes me luck and we say goodbye. I watch as she makes her way to the bicycle rack just outside of the sports hall, unlocking the chain on her pink bike and climbing onto the seat. I continue to watch her cycle away and disappear around the corner.

It's pitch black by the time I leave try-outs. I feel a clammy film of sweat stuck to my skin as I wipe my hand across my face.

I knew the session would be tough, but I didn't expect to feel this exhausted.

I climb into my car and open the window slightly, letting the mild air cool my face. As I pull out of the car park and follow the winding route out of campus, a smile creeps across my face.

Try-outs didn't go badly at all. In fact, I'd even go so far as to say they were great. I picked up the stunts easily and never once dropped the tiny girl that I had to throw in the air. I definitely wasn't the best, but I wasn't the worst either. And I know my tumbling impressed the coach.

I performed every back flip and standing tuck she requested. I could do the longest tumble sequence out of any girl at try-outs. Everyone in the room cheered as I tumbled, they weren't bitchy at all. They were encouraging and friendly and kind.

It was great.

By some weird twist of fate, I'm actually hoping I get onto the team. More than I'd like to admit.

The drive back to the apartment takes longer than expected. The main road I usually take is blocked with rows of police cars, so I turn off and take a side street to avoid the standstill traffic.

When I eventually pull into the car park and step out of the car, my body aches all over. Who knew cheerleading was so physically demanding?

After taking a long time to hobble up the flight of stairs, I open the door and limp to the kitchen.

"Have you seen Kady?" Jake asks as soon as I get through the door.

"I saw her as I went into the sports hall, about two hours ago. She was on her way back here I thought." I take a seat on the couch opposite Alice.

"No, she's not come back." She sighs. "Typical, she bails on the one group meal we decide to have." She laughs, rolling her eyes.

"She's probably with that lacrosse boy she kissed last night," Jake replies, and both Jake and Alice burst into knowing laughter.

"Do you need a hand with anything in the kitchen?" I ask, changing the subject quickly. I don't like the idea of gossiping about Kady if she's not here.

Jake shakes his head at me, so I go into the hall and try to call Kady. I'm desperate to find out where she is, for my own selfish reasons. She's the easiest to talk to out of all my flatmates, and I'm not sure I can sustain a whole dinner conversation with just Jake and Alice.

Her phone goes straight to voicemail. I text her and ask her to call me back.

"Let's just eat without her and leave her a plate. I'm starved," Alice suggests, taking a seat at the kitchen counter.

"Smells delicious." I smile at Jake.

We sit at the table in silence and begin to shovel food into our mouths. I can't work out if it's a product of pure hunger, or if we're pretending to be too engrossed in our food to have to force a conversation.

The awkward tension is temporarily broken by my phone buzzing on the table, making us all startle. I check it to see if it's Kady and instead discover it's an email from the cheer squad.

"You look like you've just seen a ghost," Jake laughs. "Care to share with the rest of the class?"

"Sorry. It was just a text from my mum," I lie and put my phone back on the table with the screen facing down.

I stare at the space laid out for Kady—an empty cup and full plate of food. I can't help but wonder where she's got to. She didn't actually say she was heading straight home when I saw her, so maybe she did go out and just lost track of time, which sucks because I was actually looking forward to seeing her tonight. She would have asked how try-outs were and wanted to know all the details. I know she would have been excited to hear how well it went.

After I finish eating, I wash my plate in the sink and excuse myself whilst the others get comfortable on the couch to watch a movie. I tell them I have work early in the morning and, much to my relief, they don't insist I join them anyway.

I go back to my room, close the door behind me and unlock my phone with shaking hands. My fingers find the email icon and I open my unread message.

Thank you for trying out for the Panthers competition squad. As you know, try-outs this year were immensely competitive. However, we are pleased to inform you...

I made the team.

Actually, I made the *first* team.

I can't help the smile that spreads across my face. I'm not a substitute or reserve, but a first team performer. I'll be on the squad for every competition, *and* I'll also be performing at a huge annual fireworks event.

The coach was telling everyone about the event at try-outs. It's the first time the cheer squad showcase a new routine on campus. We'll perform during the half-time of an American football game in front of hundreds of spectators. The night is finished off with a gigantic firework display and after party.

I didn't think I'd care so much about something like this, but the sense of excitement tearing through my body makes it clear that I do.

I don't need a mirror in my room to know I'm flapping around, giggling to myself.

I'm excited. I'm actually excited?

What is going on?

I text my sister immediately to tell her the good news.

Rereading the email, I realise there's an initiation party tomorrow night to celebrate with the whole team. The bar we're going to, Circo, is a notorious hang out for all the campus sports teams, hence why I think I've only been once before.

I sigh. I know I should go. I don't want to be the odd one out of the team before we've even had our first practice. Maybe it'll even be good for me.

Chapter Five

The first thing I notice as I walk into the kitchen this morning is the untouched plate of lasagne left out for Kady. I didn't hear her come home last night. The front door is close to my bedroom, so I usually hear everyone coming and going. But I didn't hear Kady.

I put the plate in the fridge and check my phone for texts or calls from her.

Nothing.

Trying to push my thoughts to the back of my mind, I make my usual cup of coffee. God knows I need it.

It was tough getting out of bed, my body felt like it was pinned to the mattress. I couldn't resist snoozing my alarm.

My muscles ache twice as bad as yesterday, and I know I'm walking with a limp. Not only that, but the stunting we practiced at try-outs has left me with faint purple bruises all up my arms.

When I run into Jacks with two minutes to spare before my shift, I immediately head to the staff room and throw my bag into a locker. Ryan is sat at the small table, texting on his phone and eating an apple. He looks up and grins at me.

"Late night, was it?" He laughs, taking another bite of his apple.

My face feels hot, and my heart starts beating faster as I continue to feel his eyes on me, watching my every flushed move.

"I was studying and lost track of time," I huff, jamming my bag into the locker and forcing it shut.

"You don't look like you've *just* been studying all night. Why are you limping?"

Another wave of heat floods my face. "Sports injury," I mumble.

"Likely story." He chuckles again.

"Get your mind out of the gutter, Ryan."

"You'd only know mine was there if yours was too," he replies with a smug grin.

Feeling embarrassed, and not wanting to admit my hobble is a result of cheerleading, I head out of the staff room before Ryan has the chance to ask me anything else.

I move towards the pile of clothes outside of the stockroom, taking them out to the shop floor.

Ryan emerges behind me, carrying another pile of clothes. Ignoring his presence, I make my way towards Emily, who is stood at the till reading a catalogue of some kind. She looks up as she hears our footsteps against the creaky wooden floorboards.

"Thanks for bringing those up. Could you hang them and put them out on the floor for me?" she asks.

"Sure." I reach into the bag of hangers next to the till and grab a shirt to hang. Ryan reaches for a hanger too, but Emily quickly stops him, holding her hands up.

"Not you. You're banished to the stock room in that outfit, Mr!" she says, moving out from behind the till and swatting a hand at him. She presses her hands to the back of his shoulders and wheels him to the back office. They both can't stop laughing and bantering as they go.

I now understand how he gets away with wearing his own clothes to work. Emily and Ryan seem really close, not in a romantic way or anything, but they seem super chummy, like siblings or something.

As Ryan walks—well, gets pushed—away, I notice another tattoo on the back of his arm. I can't quite make out what the design is supposed to be, possibly an Egyptian eye, but whatever it is, it looks cool.

I spend the next few hours ignoring the burning desire to go to the stockroom and talk to Ryan. Instead, I focus my attention on serving the tonne of customers clogging the tiny store. I totally lose track of time until I see Ryan drift across the shop floor with a guitar bag swung across his lean shoulders.

"See you later, Zoe. I'm done for the day." He waves as he walks towards the street and out of sight.

"You'll catch a fly in your mouth if you continue to ogle at him like that." Emily laughs, pointing at my face.

"Shut up," I mutter, snapping my lips shut.

"So, you don't think he's cute?" she pries.

I look at the floor, hiding my face from her. I shake my head.

"Liar." She smirks. "Everyone fancies Ryan."

I roll my eyes. "Including you?"

"Eww, gross! *No!* I can't believe you just said that!" Emily gasps dramatically. "I'm very much in love with my boyfriend, thank you very much. But you, on the other hand, are very much single."

"Thanks for reminding me." I sigh, elbowing her playfully. "I don't have time for a relationship."

Emily groans. "Blah, blah, blah. You do. You're just too wrapped up in the legal career crap, which is fine, but come *on,* Zoe, you're at university! You should be having more fun! Why not go on a couple of dates?"

What is it with everyone telling me to have more fun?

"I couldn't think of anything worse than going on random dates." I pause. "But you'll be pleased to know that I'm going out tonight. To a sports social."

"*Ooo*, maybe you'll find a hunky rugby player!" Emily laughs. I just groan and roll my eyes. "And I suppose it's a good thing you're not planning on dating Ryan. I wouldn't want that for you."

"Why?" I ask, failing to stop the word from leaving my mouth.

"He doesn't really do the whole girlfriend thing. At least, I've never seen him get serious with a girl. He has a lot going on." Emily shrugs and walks towards the till, which is now surrounded by impatient customers.

I look down at the pile of clothes on the table in front of me, wondering what on earth Emily could mean.

Perhaps Ryan has a busy music schedule? I wonder if his band are any good. Emily hardly mentions her brother, let alone his band. I've not met Tyler in the year I've known her, so God only knows what his band is like.

I guess it doesn't matter how good they are when Ryan looks the way he does. He could get any girl on the planet with a face like his. He's probably just a player and doesn't date because he doesn't want to be tied down by a girlfriend.

Either way, it's none of my business.

When I get back to the apartment after work, I immediately rush to get ready for my cheer initiation night out.

The apartment was strangely quiet when I got back. I noticed Alice had left a note in the kitchen for Kady, asking her to call one of us as soon as she got in. I guess the others haven't heard from her all day either.

I don't know how I'm supposed to handle a situation like this, whether I should begin to panic or not. I'm used to all of us being on our own schedules and hardly seeing each other for days, but it's strange that Kady bailed on plans that she created herself. She's never been like this in the past.

But then again, it is university after all, *and* it's the first weekend back. Students pull all-nighters partying all the time. She probably went out, crashed at one of her teammates' houses and stayed there hungover today.

I quickly try to call her again. It goes straight to voicemail. Sighing, I turn my focus to applying my makeup.

I decide to try and make an effort tonight, so I go for more than just my usual concealer and mascara by adding a layer of foundation, a bit of bronzer and the mauve lipstick my sister gave me for my birthday last year. I figure nice make-up might distract from the ridiculous outfit I have to wear.

The whole team have been given navy blue t-shirts with bright gold and red writing plastered all over it. It's one hundred percent obnoxious and, of course, lets everyone know that I'm a first team cheerleader. I've also been given a signature gold bow to clip onto my head. I'm going to look *ridiculous*.

Figuring I'll put the bow on once I actually arrive at Circo, I stuff it into my bag. No need to humiliate myself on the walk.

I head out of the apartment and into the night without giving a second thought to what the hell I'm getting myself into.

Chapter Six

As I get closer to the sports bar, my heart starts beating faster and I can feel my hands shaking. I picture all the things that could go wrong.

This is why I hide in my room at any opportunity. This horrible feeling in the pit of my stomach, telling me I'm going to fail.

I put one foot in front of the other and reach the street where the bar is situated, right in the middle of the small student village.

As I look towards Circo, I can see a bunch of students lingering outside. They already look completely wasted. I walk around them, grimacing as one of the guys vomits on the pavement. Lovely.

The bouncer on the door checks my ID, and I walk through a white metal gate straight into a beer garden.

Several brown wooden picnic benches are scattered around, filled with students sat in groups, all drinking and laughing away to one another.

I head up the metal stairway and into the main bar area. The floor feels sticky under my Dr Martens, as if someone has spilled an entire bucket of sugary alcohol on the floor.

Pop music blares through the speakers of the dimly lit bar, and the place is completely packed. It has to be one of the cheesiest sports bars I've ever been to, they even have blue and red lights flashing through the place. If it wasn't for the strong smell of alcohol and huddles of tipsy students, I'd think I was at a high school disco.

Pushing through the crowd and heading towards the back of the room, I spot a sea of gold bows. I take off my denim jacket and wrap it around my waist to reveal my cheer t-shirt and clip the gold bow into place. As I get closer to the team, Kim (our cheer captain) waves at me.

"There's our number one tumbler!" she chimes, handing me a shot glass filled with light gold liquid.

I take the tiny cup without saying anything, downing the contents in one go and shuddering as the alcohol burns my throat. *Tequila.*

Kim smiles widely and hands me a large red cup. I sniff the rim. Whatever is inside smells sweet, but I don't recognise the drink. I take a sip and the sugary cocktail softens the traces of tequila clinging to my throat.

By the time I look up from my cup, Kim has already disappeared, cornering a late arrival with the tray of shots. Feeling awkward, I turn my attention to the TV in the corner and pretend to watch the basketball game playing on the giant screen.

"Hey, I'm Nadine," the girl next to me says with what sounds like an American accent. Her smile is so wide I think it might cut her face in half.

"Hey. Were you in my group yesterday? At try-outs? I'm Zoe." I turn to face her.

"Yeah, I was! You're a really great tumbler. How long have you been cheerleading for?" she asks, taking a sip of her drink and staring intently at me. Her confidence is even more arresting than her beautiful appearance—if that's even possible.

"I haven't cheered before. I did gymnastics at school, but that's it." I shrug.

"No *freaking* way! I can't believe you've never cheered before, you're amazing!" she says, grabbing one of my wrists and squeezing it. "God, I wish I had your talent!" She exhales dramatically.

"Are you new to the squad too?"

"Yeah. I tore my ACL in my first year of uni, so I'm

only just trying out in my final year. Typical," she groans.

"Ouch." I grimace. "Sounds painful. Did you cheer before uni?"

Nadine nods her head, her long jet-black bob swaying as she moves. "A little in middle school when I lived in America, but I had to give it up when my dad got a new job over here. I don't get why none of the schools in England do cheer. I've had to wait for what feels like *decades* to finally be able to join a squad again."

"Yeah, I think it's just a university thing here." I smile. "So cool that you're from America. Where abouts?"

"I grew up in Boston, but I'm actually from Korea. My parents moved to America when I was born."

I raise my eyebrows. "Wow. Your life is so much more interesting than mine." I laugh. "Where's home for you now?"

"Buckinghamshire."

"Quite the opposite to America then!"

She smiles widely. "Uh huh! What about you?"

"Tewkesbury," I answer.

Nadine furrows her brows, tilting her head slightly. "Where?"

"Exactly." I roll my eyes theatrically and we both giggle.

Kim calls Nadine's name and she's forced to take

another shot of alcohol. She tips her head back to take it but doesn't shudder like I would. Instead, she raises her hands in the air and shimmies her body, which makes a group of guys wolf whistle as they walk past.

"Right girls, it's time for your initiation game!" Kim announces with a squeal.

She leads the squad to a sectioned-off area of the bar, where a space has been set up for us. We're told to pair up and, to my immense relief, Nadine instantly stands next to me.

Each pair is passed a rope and told to tie it around their ankles for a three-legged race. Nadine giggles and bends down to wrap our legs together.

I groan. "This is the type of crap we played when we were kids. How is this an initiation game?" I whisper to Nadine.

She laughs, throwing her head back. "You're telling me you would do a three-legged race from one end of a bar to the other and then down a whole table of shots, using only your mouth, when you were in school?" She sniggers, pointing to the huge table filled with shot glasses at the finish line. "What type of school did you go to?"

I laugh and bring my hand to my head, shaking it. "Okay, definitely not! But just so you know, I'm going to suck at this."

"Well, I'm glad there will be something you suck at."
She laughs. "Anyway, who cares? The punishment will be
more shots, I'm not complaining!"

To no surprise, we come last after I manage to trip
over Nadine's feet a thousand times. She didn't seem to
care though; she was too busy finding my fumbles
hilarious.

Kim passes us our *'punishment'*—a tray of bright
green shots. The rest of the team chant as we pick them
up, downing each one as quickly as possible.

The additional alcohol makes me feel instantly dizzy.
I need some air. Fast.

I untie my leg from Nadine's and sneak back down the
metal stairs to the beer garden.

I inhale deeply as fresh air hits my face.

Snatching the bow off my head, I slump on one of the
empty picnic tables, dangling my feet off the edge and
fiddling with the bow.

"A cheerleader? Really?" a voice chuckles behind me.
I dart around and lock my gaze with a dazzling pair of
hazel eyes.

"Ryan? What are you doing here?"

"I had a gig in the basement of this place." He cocks
his head towards a black guitar bag swung across his

shoulder. He shrugs it off and leans it against the bench before taking a seat next to me.

I feel the sleeve of his black hoodie brush against my bare arm, sending a wave of chills down my spine.

"But you avoided my question," he says, smirking.

"No, I didn't. You didn't actually ask me a question. You just stated the obvious."

He sighs and rolls his eyes with a huge grin across his face. "Okay, let me rephrase for Little Miss Pedantic. Are you a cheerleader?" His eyes flit from my t-shirt down to the pair of Dr Martens I'm wearing. He struggles to suppress a laugh.

"No. Well, sort of, I suppose." I shrug. "I had try-outs yesterday and made the team." I look down to the gravel floor, knowing my cheeks must have turned the same shade of red as the writing splattered across my top. As I look down, I notice Ryan is wearing black Dr Martens too, but his are shoes, not boots.

"Ah. I was going to ask if you'd recovered from your injury. But looking at those bruises on your arm, it doesn't appear so." As he speaks, he lifts my arm, pretending to inspect the bruising.

I inhale sharply at his warm touch. His fingertips feel like fire, like a match that just set off fireworks in my body.

I open my mouth to speak, but no words come out.

"Must've been a serious training session. You didn't drop anyone I hope," he adds.

"Uh... l-luckily no, I didn't drop anyone. We just get bruises sometimes from the impact of catching the flyer," I eventually stutter. Why the hell am I explaining the dynamics of cheerleading to a guy like Ryan?

He raises his eyebrows and nods at my words. "Congrats though. I didn't have you pegged as the cheerleading type. Do you enjoy it?"

I shrug. "I don't know yet, but I'll be sure to let you know after my first practice."

He lets go of my arm and pulls the sleeves of his hoodie down over his hands. The absence of his touch makes me notice the cold too. I take my jacket from around my waist and put it back on, happy to be hiding this ridiculous top and my bruises.

"How come you want to cheer then? If you've never even tried it before?"

"Umm, I needed to get on a competition team this year to help with graduate job applications."

"Ah, and what is it you want to do when you graduate?" He raises an eyebrow and bites the side of his lip.

"Become a lawyer." I shift in my seat, playing with

the hem of my jacket.

"And whose idea was that?" he asks, studying my face.

"What do you mean? Whose idea?"

"As in, did you wake up one day and decide you wanted to be a lawyer, or did you get pushed in that direction by some helicopter parent?"

"I decided it. My parents aren't helicopters. They're great." I look up so our eyes meet. "I chose law because I want to make them proud. What's so bad about that?"

"Sorry, I don't mean to pry. I'm just trying to figure you out... what makes you happy..." He brushes a hand through his mop of hair and then shakes his head, his fingers ruffling the strands. "You didn't seem that thrilled when you said you were a cheerleader, and you didn't look happy when you said you wanted to be a lawyer, so I just assumed it wasn't your choice."

"It's not that," I answer honestly. "I just hadn't thought about it in that way before."

"What way?"

"I didn't think about happiness when making those choices," I admit.

"That's kind of sad." He frowns. "But I'm sure your cheerleading adventures will provide you with plenty of excitement!" he adds, his sarcasm not lost on me.

I roll my eyes at him and nudge his shoulder.

"You should probably get back to them in there, right? I don't want to keep you from making friends or showing off your dazzling bow!" He grins menacingly, reaching out to grab my bow. I playfully swot his hand away.

"No, it's okay," I begin, laughing a little. "I was actually going to walk back to my apartment now. I think I've had more than enough socialising for one night."

I hop down from the picnic table and feel Ryan reach out to take hold of my elbow, causing me to turn back.

"You're not walking back alone, are you? You're going to meet your boyfriend or something, right?" His tone is suddenly serious. He looks down at me, concern dancing across his face.

"I don't have a boyfriend." Or friends for that matter, but I'm not going to admit that. "I like walking alone. It gives me time to listen to my music." I shrug, pulling my phone from my pocket and stuffing my bow into my bag.

"You can't walk back alone, it's late. I'll give you a ride. I'll even let you choose what music we listen to in the car."

"But didn't you drink? If you had a gig?" I ask.

"Nope. Completely sober." He pauses. "I don't really like to drink when we perform."

"You don't?" I couldn't imagine performing on stage completely sober, I'd need the Dutch courage.

"Not really, it can mess with my vocal cords. I'll sometimes have a couple, but it's rare."

"You sing?" I ask, making no effort to hide my surprise.

"Uh huh." He looks down at his shoes for a moment, kicking the dirt. "Now, are you coming or what?"

I nod resignedly and try to follow him towards the exit, battling my tipsy state and the influx of people around us.

We squeeze through the mass of people now hanging in the courtyard. It's so busy, I struggle to keep up with Ryan. He glances back, noticing my battle, and reaches his hand out. I hesitate.

He gives me an impatient stare, so I quickly interlock my fingers with his.

Yep. His touch just set off another round of fireworks inside me.

He pulls me through the crowd easily, and I try to ignore the tingling flames shooting up my arm.

"Are you a student too?" I ask him once we get onto the street. Emily already told me he graduated a while ago, but I have no idea what else to ask him. I can't focus properly with his hand over mine.

"No. I graduated from music college in London last year. I moved here afterwards with the band." He doesn't look at me as he answers, he's too busy navigating a path for us through more crowds on the street.

"Did you study for a degree or something different?"

"I got a bachelor's degree in commercial music," he answers matter-of-factly.

We stop at the edge of the road, waiting for cars to pass so we can cross to the quieter side of the street. Is it weird that I'm grateful for the mass of cars zooming along the street for giving me a few extra seconds with Ryan?

"You're in a band with Tyler, right?" I ask.

Ryan answers with a nod.

"So, you work at Jacks to fill the gap?" I press, curiosity burning with all the questions that have now formed in my brain.

"Yeah. I only work the hours I need to, to pay the bills. I have a YouTube channel too. It's monetised, but nowhere near enough to live off. Any money I make from music is a plus, as opposed to essential. I don't do it for the cash, I do it because it makes me happy."

He lets go of my hand and puts his in the large pockets of his hoodie. I ignore the empty feeling that suddenly hits my body at the loss of his touch, the Catherine wheel in my heart fizzling out.

"Although, it would be great to be paid enough to play music full time and get out of working in retail," he continues. There's an emotion in his voice that I can't quite put my finger on... passion, or hope maybe?

"So, you don't aspire to become a famous musician and travel the world then?" I probe, grinning at him. I could definitely picture Ryan on tour, selling out arenas filled with wild, die-hard fans.

"Travel, yes. Fame, no. I don't think I could handle that pressure. I would love to tour, to see the world doing something I love, but I don't think you need fame to be successful."

"Huh." I exhale.

The look on my face seems to make him curious.

"What?" he asks, watching me closely.

"You're just a surprise, that's all. I figured most musicians would be caught up on their fame potential."

"Not this guy." He smirks. "My car is just here by the way." He points towards a giant black Jeep Wrangler.

"Woah. This is quite the car," I gasp as we get closer to the huge four-by-four. No one drives cars like this around here, the city traffic is far too hectic.

Ryan bows his head, his cheeks flushing a little. I can't work out if it's due to the cold air, or if I've embarrassed him.

"It's my dad's old car. I grew up in Cornwall and we all had pretty big cars. We needed them for our surfboards and stuff." He shrugs, as if trying to justify himself.

"Cornwall. I bet that was a fun place to grow up."

Ryan chuckles under his breath. "Yeah, it was a pretty good."

"Do you miss home?"

"Not really." His smile immediately falters. "It doesn't really feel like home anymore."

Ryan unlocks the car, throwing his guitar in the boot. He glides into the driver's side before I have the chance to ask him any more questions.

It takes a physical effort to jump up to the passenger seat, battling my short height and the alcohol coursing through my body.

Once I'm successfully in the car, my gaze shifts behind me. A beat-up skateboard is next to a worn-looking notepad that's left open on the back seat. I can't make out any of the writing scrawled across the lined pages, but I'd like to assume they're song lyrics.

"Go on, put some music on," he instructs, holding out an auxiliary lead.

"It's okay, I don't want to play anything," I tell him, being careful not to look in his direction as I buckle my seatbelt.

"But you said you wanted to listen to music?"

"I did, but now I'm okay. Thank you though."

He shrugs and plugs the cable into his phone, picking his own playlist to listen to.

"You like Bastille?" I ask, surprised when I hear the familiar vocals fill the car.

"Yeah, they're a big influence on my band's music. You like them too?" He looks at me with eager eyes.

"Sure." I shrug.

He stares at me as I turn the sound system up.

"Do you not like talking about music or something?" he asks, turning the volume back down using a button on the steering wheel.

I pause, gesturing for Ryan to turn left out of the parking area, buying myself some time to think about my answer. "It's not that I don't like it, I just get a little uncomfortable."

"Why?"

I exhale. "It's just... I hate how judgmental people get about personal music taste. I always remember kids at school would pick fun at what other people listened to. I hated that. Songs mean different things to different people. Who are we to judge somebody else's taste? A song could have a deeper meaning to someone that we just don't know about. Who cares if it's mainstream or sung by a cheesy boy band? It's a free country."

Ryan looks at me and I suddenly feel embarrassed. I don't meet his eyes, instead focusing on the road and gesturing for him to take the next turning.

"I take it you're not going to tell me your favourite bands then?" he asks menacingly.

"Sure, I will... just to prove you wrong." I sigh dramatically. "OneRepublic and Amber Run."

"Gun to your head, which is your all-time favourite?"

"That's *such* an unfair question," I groan.

"Why?"

"Because they mean different things to me." I glance at Ryan. He couldn't hide his huge grin if he tried. "I love OneRepublic because they've been such a strong part of my growing up. From school to now, they've always been there, you know? And Amber Run, well, have you heard their lyrics? *Jeez.* So powerful."

Ryan nods, laughing along in passionate agreement. "So, gun to your head you'd die."

"Exactly!" I laugh. "I really don't have a favourite band. I listen to different music depending on how I feel at the time. If I resonate with the lyrics of a song, I'll play it on repeat like a million times."

Ryan looks at me before staring back at the road. He opens his mouth to say something but decides against it.

I grab his phone and flick through his playlist in an attempt to busy myself. The tension in this car suddenly feels like it's at an all-time high.

I settle on *Wings* by Birdy.

As soon as Ryan hears what I've picked, his hazel eyes turn towards me for a moment.

"You like this song?" he asks.

"Yeah. It's one of my favourites."

"Mine too," he whispers.

We sit in silence as we listen to the song, absorbing the lyrics.

When we finally pull up to my apartment, I jump out, forgetting how high up the Jeep is, stumbling a little as I land on the pavement. I quickly thank Ryan for the ride and race towards my building, praying he didn't see my misstep.

"Zoe?" he calls out as I reach the door of my building. I turn to face him. "Are you working tomorrow?" he asks, and I nod slowly in response. "We should hang out after your shift if you're free?"

My stomach lurches. Ryan wants to hang out with *me*?

"Sure," I reply, feeling a flush of excitement dance across my face as I step into the building.

Chapter Seven

I thought Ryan would be working today and we could leave together to '*hang out*'. But I haven't seen him. He doesn't have my number, so I have no way of knowing if he's planning on bailing.

Would he have checked the rota for my shift time? Maybe. But who knows how his brain works? I bet he's forgotten about hanging out, our plans weren't exactly concrete.

If he has forgotten, it's no big deal, I have plenty of studying to get on with anyway.

Okay, I really need to chill out.

Ugh, I wish there were customers to distract me. I really need to keep myself busy. Although, it's not like I can blame everyone for avoiding the shops on an unseasonably beautiful day like today.

In an effort to keep busy, I grab some clothes from the stock room and carry them to the shop floor, dumping the pile on the counter as soon as I reach it.

I turn around, brushing fly-away strands of hair from my sticky face when I recognise a tall figure at the other end of the shop. I blink in case my eyes are playing tricks on me.

Nope. He's actually here.

Ryan is leaning against a shelf of folded t-shirts, laughing with Emily about something. The laugh softens his features and makes the corners of his eyes crinkle. I can't help but feel a warm sensation in my stomach just looking at him.

As soon as he sees me, he smiles and walks in my direction. I don't risk a glance at Emily, I have no idea what he's told her about our plans.

"Emily said you can finish early. You ready?" He tilts his head and smiles at me.

"No, she didn't." I've never been allowed to finish work early in the year that I've worked here. I don't see how today can be any different, even if it is quiet.

"Cross my heart," Ryan replies, holding his hand to his chest. "She said she was thinking of sending someone home because it's been so dead, so I volunteered you."

I stare at Ryan, still unsure whether he's joking or

not. I tear my eyes from his face and glance at Emily. She's looking at me and gestures with her hands for me to leave the shop floor. I wonder how he pulled that off...

"Oh, okay. What are we going to do?" I ask and then suddenly panic, wondering if he expected me to think of something. I don't know how these situations work.

"I thought we could link up with the rest of the band at the park. We've got beer, food and music, of course." He grins and I force myself to smile back at him.

I hadn't expected this to be a group thing. I thought maybe we would hang out alone, not necessarily as a date, but... I don't know. I guess maybe I thought he would want to get to know me, that's all. But why would he? Why would a guy like Ryan Walker be interested in spending time with just me?

I try not to think about how utterly terrifying hanging out with a group of total strangers will be.

I'll just focus on the fact that I'm escaping work early to sit in the sun. And maybe I'll even get to hear Ryan play his guitar.

Yeah, this will be fine. Totally fine. Right?

"Earth to Zoe," Ryan says, waving a hand in front of my face.

"Sorry. Sounds good. I'll go get my stuff." I spin on my heels to grab my bag from the locker.

Once we step out of the store, Ryan pulls out a pair of thick, black sunglasses from his back pocket. It's hard not to stare at a face like his on a normal day, and those sunglasses have just made it a million times harder.

The park is packed with groups of people having picnics and barbecues across the huge lawn.

Suddenly, the familiar sensation of knots in my stomach takes over my body. My hands start shaking as we walk towards a group sat underneath a large oak tree. I shove my hands deep into the pockets of my dungaree-dress and take a couple of deep breaths to try and calm myself.

I can't tell if Ryan senses my internal panic, but he grabs the back of my arm and gives it a gentle, reassuring squeeze.

"You must be Zoe! I'm Tyler, Emily's brother," a caramel-haired guy says as soon as we reach the group. He pushes a guitar off of his lap and stands up to hug me. Weirdly, he doesn't look as much like Emily as I'd expected. Not for a twin anyway.

Ryan introduces me to his other two bandmates, Claire and Adam, before taking a seat next to Tyler on the picnic blanket. He pats the space next to him.

I plonk down and Ryan leans across the blanket to pass me a beer. My head is still groggy from last night's drinking, so I shake my head, reaching for a ginger ale. Ryan does the same.

"You're not drinking?" I ask.

"No. I'm driving," he replies, lifting his head towards the sun.

"Oh, cool." I pause, trying to regain control of the butterflies in my tummy. "So, what's the name of your band?" I ask quietly, leaning into Ryan.

"The Lanes," he answers, shuffling a little closer. "I'd tell you where the name came from, but I actually have no idea. There's no deep, poetic story that there probably should be." He chuckles.

"Do I get to hear one of your songs?"

"Not unless you come to an official band practice or gig."

"Is that an invite?" I smirk, feeling a little more at ease from his smile alone.

"Always."

"Well, maybe I can find some time in my extremely busy schedule. I'll have to see though." I sigh playfully.

"I would be honoured." Ryan smacks his hand to his heart with a mock gasp. "A competition cheerleader taking time out of their day for *me*? Wow, I've made it."

"Shut up," I groan, nudging him with my shoulder, simultaneously trying to prevent a laugh from tumbling out of my mouth.

"If you come to a gig, I'll have to steal you for the afterparty," Claire says warmly. "It'll be nice having a girl to party with instead of just having these morons."

"That's if she can tolerate you after today." Ryan laughs.

"I don't think it's me you have to worry about," she retorts, winking at him. "Stop being a prat. Go get your guitar."

Ryan waves his middle finger at Claire before going to retrieve his guitar from under the tree.

"What shall we play?" Tyler asks as soon as Ryan comes back.

"I know," Ryan replies, sitting down next to me with a knowing grin.

Still looking at me, he begins to play a sweet tune. I instantly recognise the OneRepublic song. It's got to be one of my all-time favourites.

As he starts to sing the opening lyrics of *I Lived*, my heart does a back flip. I thought the fireworks in my body at his touch were something, but *this* is on another level. Have I just visibly turned to jelly in front of his entire band?

His voice is so soft, so velvety.

Jeez, my body is screaming as I listen.

I thought he'd be good, but I had no idea he would be *this* good. His voice is so flawless it knocks the wind right out of me.

The others join in and I close my eyes, sinking deep into their harmonies. Usually, I would feel totally self-conscious in such a public setting, but I get completely lost in the song. I even start quietly singing along too, unable to resist.

When I finally open my eyes, I catch Ryan staring at me along with the rest of the band.

"You never told me you were a singer, Zo," he says softly, his overfamiliarity causing my stomach to churn in the best way.

"Oh no, I'm not," I try to deflect. "Unless you count singing in the car by myself," I add with an awkward laugh, causing the rest of the band chuckle.

"Fuck, your voice is epic. With pipes like that you should consider a career change," Ryan says.

"Yeah, you could put one of us out of a job!" Tyler adds, grabbing his beer and raising it towards me.

Ryan absentmindedly strums a couple of chords on the guitar, and I lose myself in this unfamiliar, peaceful feeling. I feel safe somehow, like his voice is wrapping me up in a thick duvet and holding me in a firm embrace.

Adam is lying down, scrolling through his phone

when he suddenly bolts upright, disturbing the peace.

"Guys, have you seen the latest news alert?" he asks.

Everyone reaches for their phones to see what he is talking about. I realise I haven't even checked mine since the start of my shift this morning.

"There's been an accident. A girl at the university has been killed," he adds, staring at his phone.

"What?" I dig to the bottom of my bag and pull out my phone.

My stomach drops and the sharp taste of bile rises to my throat.

I have hundreds of missed calls and text messages from Jake and Alice.

I know what's coming, I just know it.

Hot tears spike the back of my eyes as I open the messages from my flatmates, pleading for me to come home or call them back.

They confirm my worst fear. Kady never made it home.

She was hit by a bus on her cycle ride back to the apartment.

Kady never made it home.

Kady never made it home.

Memories flash through my mind of police cars blocking the road outside our apartment building as I came back from try-outs the other day.

I drop the drink in my hand. It falls onto the picnic blanket, spilling everywhere.

The park is spinning.

I think Ryan is saying my name, asking me what is wrong, but I can't hear properly. I know everyone is looking at me, waiting for me to talk, but I can't.

I hand Ryan my phone to look at the messages. I can't speak. I can't stop the rising feeling in my stomach. I turn away from the group and throw up on the grass.

Ryan moves towards me, rubbing my back, trying to soothe me as I wipe my mouth. Still numb, I sense him lifting me to my feet, wrapping an arm around my waist as he guides me out of the park.

I feel totally detached from my body as Ryan helps me out of his car and pulls me towards my building. The feeling is so strange, watching myself being guided towards my apartment by this guy I barely know.

I have no idea if Ryan is talking to me. My ears are muffled, as though someone has cupped their hands around them, curbing my senses. My entire face feels hot and clammy too.

When we get to the front door, Ryan takes the keys out of my trembling hand, swiping my pass and walking with me through the door. He checks the apartment number on my key chain before leading me up the flight of stairs. His hand doesn't leave the arch of my back as he guides me.

I pause outside the kitchen door and shake my head, trying to snap myself back to reality.

When I walk in, Jake is sat on the couch, but I can't see his face. Alice is stood by the window. She glares at me as soon as I walk in. Her eyes are red; they narrow to slits as she looks between me and Ryan.

"Where have you been?" she demands, arms crossed. I jump at her tone. It's only when Ryan reaches from behind to squeeze my hands that I realise they're shaking.

"At work, sorry. I came back as soon as I saw your texts."

"Well, we were out all day and night looking for her," she says flatly.

Jake doesn't look in our direction. He sits on the couch in silence with his head bowed to the floor.

The room is silent. My heart feels like it's been ripped out of my chest and an ache begins to burn in its place.

"I had no idea," I finally whisper. Tears roll down my

cheeks and I swallow to try and hold them back. I hate that I didn't know how worried they were, or that they went looking for her. If I'd have known, I would've been with them in a heartbeat.

"You never do, Zoe. You're so wrapped up in your own world that you don't see what's going on around you," Alice yells. "And don't cry, *you* don't get to cry."

Jake looks up at Alice with a horrified expression, but he doesn't say anything.

I suck in a sharp breath to ease the stabbing pain that courses through my body.

Suddenly, I feel Ryan's hands on my shoulders, pulling me to him. "I think that's enough. I know you're angry, and I'm sorry for your loss, but there's no need to take it out on Zoe," he says firmly.

He leads me out of the kitchen. "Which one is your room?" he asks. I point in response, and he guides me towards it, still holding my shoulders reassuringly.

He unlocks the door and takes a step inside. I sit on the bed, trying to focus on the plain white wall in front of me.

"Alice is right. I should have been here," I say quietly, trying to gulp back the tears. Ryan takes a seat next to me.

"Do *not* blame yourself," he says through gritted teeth. "She was out of line. She's grieving and took it out on you. It was a shitty thing to say. I would have told her where to go if the situation was different."

I look down at his hands as he clenches and unclenches his fists. We sit in silence, both trying to steady our breathing.

"Did you know they were out looking for her?" he finally asks, and I shake my head. "Exactly. So how were you going to be here if they didn't even tell you?"

He puts his arm around me. I lean closer, resting my head on his shoulder. I take a deep breath, inhaling a familiar scent. His t-shirt smells like the laundry detergent my parents use at home, and the fresh cotton scent provides a little comfort to the deep ache in my chest.

"Promise me you won't listen to anything she said? You have every right to cry and grieve." He squeezes my shoulder and then pulls away from our hug, using his hands to cup my damp face.

I nod slowly, our faces mere inches from each other. We lock eyes, and I allow myself to swim in the warmth of his hazel irises.

"Zoe, remember that grief affects everyone in different ways, and to take a measure is cruel. It's not up to Alice to decide whether or not you have the right to react a certain way. Grief is not a competition," he says, wiping his thumb across my cheek to catch a falling tear.

"You're really good at this." I laugh feebly, bowing my head and using my palms to wipe my face. His arms move around me, pulling me to his chest. I feel his cheek rest on top of my head.

We sit like this for a while and I stare out of the window, watching as the sun sets, turning the sky a beautiful pink colour. I think of Kady as I look at the bright, colourful sky, wishing I could turn back time.

I'm unable to tear my eyes away from the window as I watch the darkness swallow the colours until the sky is nothing more than a black void.

Chapter Eight

My heavy eyes slowly blink open. The room is pitch black.

I lean over to my desk and turn on the lamp. I scan the room quickly. There's a yellow post-it note stuck to the desk.

Zo, got your number from Jake.
I'll call you tomorrow. Ryan x

I turn the lamp off and drift back to sleep, trying to push the images of Kady and sound of police sirens out of my mind.

Chapter Nine

I wake up to hot bile rising from my stomach to my throat. I run to the bathroom, throwing up in the sink. My body burns from the sudden shooting pain of throwing up on an empty stomach.

I walk back to my room, climb into bed and shut my eyes once again. I wait for sleep to suppress my aching chest and the heavy guilt I feel across every inch of my body.

Chapter Ten

My head is pounding. It feels as if someone is thumping it against a brick wall. I don't want to open my eyes, but the banging is killing me.

I blink and realise the thumping isn't in my head, it's coming from the bedroom door. I don't respond, I bet it'll be Alice looking to start round two.

My phone starts buzzing on the nightstand and an unknown number flashes across the screen. I hit ignore and check my messages to find the same number has messaged me multiple times. It's Ryan.

My phone starts to buzz again, and I answer.

"Hello?" I croak. My throat is so dry, I can barely speak.

"Open the door. I'm outside your room."

I climb out of bed and wipe my eyes, standing still for

a moment, trying to balance myself after getting headrush from jumping up too quickly. When I unlock my door, Ryan is stood there with a serious expression across his face; his lips are pursed, and his brows are furrowed.

He steps into my room and looks around. "Did I wake you?" he asks, looking me up and down.

He swings a backpack off his shoulder and drops it to the floor before walking over to my desk and handing me a cup of water. He must have left it there for me when I fell asleep last night. I gulp the whole glass down, suddenly realising how thirsty I am.

I run my tongue over my lips and pick up my phone again, pulling it free of the charging cable and checking the screen. My eyes widen. It's Tuesday afternoon. *What the hell?* I've slept for two days and missed all of my classes.

"I'm sorry to just show up here, Zoe. I called you yesterday, and when you didn't answer, I figured you might need some space. But then I didn't hear from you again today and I got worried." His eyes scan my face. His forehead is crinkled as he watches me, and I feel guilty for having worried him so much. Guilty, but also strangely happy knowing that he cares enough to come back and check on me.

"It's honestly okay, I'm glad you're here." I run my

hands through my greasy hair and catch a glimpse of myself in the mirror. I look like I've been dragged through a hedge backwards.

"Uh—I'm just going to take a shower," I say without meeting his eyes. I grab my towel, a fresh t-shirt and sweats from the dresser.

"Take your time, I'll be here when you get out," he says, taking a seat on the bed.

I rush to the bathroom and shower as fast as possible. I wash my hair, trying to scrub away the pain of past two days.

The ache in my chest makes me want to vomit, but I have nothing in my system to throw up. Instead, I stand facing the rushing jet of water and close my eyes. I let the pain flow over me. I cover my face with my hands, trying to muffle the sound of my sobs.

The pain has crashed down on me like a tonne of bricks. It's the exact same, heavy pain I felt on Sunday when I found out that Kady died. It hasn't lessened in the slightest.

For a brief moment, when I first woke up, I forgot all about the accident. But now, being reminded all over again, kills me more than I can bear.

How is this reality?

How am I now living in a world without Kady in it?

It doesn't feel real.

It doesn't make sense.

I fight to regain control of my emotions and step out of the shower, drying myself and changing into my baggy clothes.

When I get back to my room, Ryan has made my bed and is sat comfortably on it, leaning against the headboard. He gives me a once over, trying to read the emotions drawn on my face as I try just as hard to hide them.

"I got you some supplies." He gestures towards his backpack, which is now on the bed alongside various bags of snacks. "I figured if you haven't eaten, then comfort food is the way to go." He smiles innocently and I feel my heartbeat quicken tenfold.

I'm not sure if I feel comfortable enough to eat in front of him, but I can't deny how sweet the gesture is. I thank him and sit down on the bed.

"Do you want to talk about it?" he asks. I shake my head, keeping my eyes fixed on my legs crossed beneath me. I tug distractedly at the drawstring on my sweats.

"Okay. Well, just so you know, I've told Emily so you didn't have to. I hope you don't mind. She's given you the rest of the week off and more if you need it. She said don't worry about work, she will still pay you your hours."

"I haven't even thought about work... or classes." I begin to panic and wipe a hand across my forehead. My parents are going to be furious if they find out I skipped class. I haven't missed a lecture since I started university, and now I've ruined my perfect attendance record before my second year has properly begun.

"Don't worry about any of that right now, Zo," Ryan whispers, pulling me closer to him. I sink into him, leaning my head against his chest.

"Why are you being so kind to me?" I ask quietly. We hardly know each other, and I figured after hearing how my flatmates feel about me, he would've left the other night and never came back.

"Because I know how all-consuming grief can be," he whispers, keeping his arms wrapped around me. "I lost my dad a couple of years ago."

I want to ask him so many questions, but I don't want to say the wrong thing and upset him. He has shown me so much kindness in such a short space of time. I don't want to ruin things between us, so I just whisper, "I'm so sorry," and give his leg a comforting squeeze.

We decide to watch a film, and I let Ryan pick something. He purposely avoids anything emotional, instead putting on some anime, which I would usually hate, but I actually don't mind it right now.

Ryan nudges the snacks in my direction, and I try to pick at some despite my nerves, but as soon as I do, my stomach starts churning. My face feels hot, and my hands start to sweat. It's unbearable.

I excuse myself to go to the bathroom and turn on the taps, hoping the sound of the rushing water will mask the noise as I throw up.

There's a strange sense of comfort in the sudden physical pain that takes over my body as I bring up the tiny amount of food I've eaten. It overtakes the numb ache in my chest for a split second.

I sit next to the toilet and take a few deep breaths before washing my face under the running taps. I put toothpaste in my mouth and then slowly walk back to my room, hoping Ryan doesn't notice my bloodshot eyes.

Keeping my gaze firmly locked to the floor, I move to sit on the bed. Ryan puts his arm around me, rubbing circles with his hand on my back, seemingly unaware of what just happened.

We stay like this, cuddled together with his arm snaked around me, throughout the whole film. I don't move an inch, not wanting him to wriggle out of our embrace at any moment. His touch might set off a hundred fireworks in my stomach, but it's the safest and most comforted I've felt over the past two days.

When the film ends, Ryan closes the laptop lid. "Can I pick you up tomorrow and bring you to band practice?" he asks. "Only if you feel up to it, of course."

"That would be nice."

I know I need to get out of this room, so hanging out with Ryan and his band feels like a good idea. The last thing I want to do is go to campus, where I'll be reminded of Kady everywhere I look. And I want to see the band again. I felt so comfortable with them at the park, and I yearn for that warm feeling again.

"I'll pick you up at eleven." Ryan leans into me, giving me a gentle hug. I inhale his fresh cotton scent.

As soon as he leaves, I sit on the bed, staring at the leftover snacks.

Before I know what I'm doing, I open every packet of cookies and chocolate, inhaling every ounce of food, hardly stopping for breath. I feel my stomach bloat and every inch of my body expand. I look at myself in the mirror and dart to the bathroom.

I turn on the taps.

When the nausea doesn't initially come, I slide my fingers down my throat, feeling smug when the food rises—the pain covering me like a blanket.

I sit next to the toilet for a couple of minutes, waiting for my breathing to calm and for my eyes to stop watering.

I slowly get up, wash my face with cold water and go back to my room, lying down on my bed until the pain in my stomach subsides.

When the physical pain dissipates, guilt washes over me.

Kady should still be here, not me.

She had everything going for her. She was beautiful, kind and brilliant at anything she set her mind to. She was the social secretary of the volleyball team. She had more course friends than I could count. Everyone loved her.

She belonged and now she's gone.

I wish I could swap places with her. Hardly anyone would miss me.

Staring at the ceiling, I wipe the tears pooling my eyes. My phone starts to vibrate, so I reach across the desk for it and look at the screen. It's my sister.

I take a deep breath before answering to stabilise my voice.

"Hello?" is all I can manage to say.

"Zoe, we heard what happened. Are you okay?" she's speaking fast, worry clear in her voice.

"Yes, I'm okay," I respond flatly. "Are you with Mum and Dad? Can I talk to them?"

"I'm not, I'm at my house. Have they not called you?"

"Not yet."

"Don't worry, I'm sure they will soon. You know what they're like sometimes."

"Yeah, I guess," I respond vaguely.

Hannah tells me to call her if I need anything and reminds me that I can always come home for a while if I need to.

The last place I want to be is home right now, it would be too much, and I know my parents wouldn't approve if I took more time out of class. I just need some time to adjust to this new reality.

Chapter Eleven

I leave the apartment twenty minutes before Ryan is due to pick me up. I craved some fresh air after spending so much time in my room.

Sitting cross-legged on the bench, I play with the shoelaces of my lilac and white Airforce Ones whilst staring at the tiny scatter of clouds overhead, watching the direction they drift in. It's another beautiful September day, although slightly cooler than last week.

A car pulls into the car park, and I instantly recognise Ryan's giant Wrangler. I hop off the bench and go to the passenger's side.

"Hey kid. You're looking better today." His tone is bright and warm, but I grimace at the nickname he's chosen for me. *Kid?* I'm only three years younger than him, what the hell?

"I figured I should at least attempt to look human today," I say, trying to joke away my distain.

"How are you feeling?" He looks at me as he turns the car stereo down.

I pause for a moment, thinking about how best to answer him. I'm used to telling people that I'm fine, keeping my emotions close to my chest. But for some reason, with Ryan, my instincts tell me to say exactly what's on my mind.

"Numb... and exhausted," I admit.

"Did you manage to get much sleep after I left?"

"Yes, quite a lot actually," I reply, gazing out of the window as Ryan drives along the main road.

This is the street where it happened, where Kady was killed. The road is now devoid of police cars and tape, but the hole in my chest tears a little wider at the sight. Everything looks completely normal, as if no life was lost. Cars continue to race past as usual, and I feel a bubbling anger churning in my stomach.

"I used to be the same... when my dad died," Ryan says quietly, interrupting my thoughts. I look up at him, expecting to see a sad expression on his face, but he looks totally calm, staring at the road ahead.

"How did he—you know—pass... if you don't mind me asking?" I keep my eyes locked on his face, searching for any possible sign of discomfort, ready to change the subject if needs be.

"I'm not sure if you ever caught it on the news, but do you remember hearing about a train that crashed in Thailand a couple of years ago?" he asks. I nod my head slowly, keeping a close watch as he tightens his grip on the steering wheel. "Well, my dad was on it. He'd been working away at a photography festival out there."

I vaguely remember seeing details of the wreck all over the news channels, the desperate attempt to recover the bodies.

"No one survived, did they?" I ask, feeling a knot in my stomach at the pain he must have felt. I wonder how his family found out about it. I hope they didn't make the connection when they saw it on the news, that would've been even more heart-breaking.

"No. It took fucking ages to be able to bring his body home as well. I think that was the hardest part—how long it took to get closure. I felt so incomplete after the investigation. It was just put down as an accident and the whole thing was brushed off. No one was held accountable." He takes a deep breath but doesn't take his eyes off the road as he talks. "It's been especially hard for my mum; I feel like he took her with him, you know? She's so empty without him."

"And what about you?" I ask, my chest aching.

"It was fucking hard at first." He shrugs. "I was away from home, studying at college, but the band pulled me through. They were great, and I just sort of threw myself into my music." He runs a hand through his thick hair and shakes his head so the strands fall back into place.

"I'm looking forward to hearing you guys play today." I smile, figuring he may want a change of subject.

"Yeah, me too." He looks at me gratefully, giving my knee a squeeze. "The band are keen to see you again by the way. They really liked you."

Ryan slows the car and somehow manages to effortlessly slide the Jeep into a space that looked far too small for it.

"This is it." He points towards a Victorian terraced house with a bright red door.

"Is this your place? Or do you just practice here?" I ask, staring up at the house as I climb out of the car.

"Both. We all moved in here together at the start of the year and use the space downstairs to practice, which makes things a lot easier."

"How come you guys don't live in London anymore? If that's where you all went to college?"

Ryan shrugs. "Too expensive. We can make music anywhere. And Tyler wanted to live closer to his family."

"That's nice... that you were all happy to move for him."

"Of course we were. We're family." Ryan grins and puts his key into the front door.

As I step into the light hallway, I kick off my Nikes and add them to the collection of shoes already piled by the door.

"Right, let's go downstairs," Ryan says, opening a door to reveal a staircase leading from the kitchen.

I follow him down the small, dark stairs into a large basement that must span the whole area of the house. The band are already there, setting up for practice.

"Look who it is!" Tyler beams at me, putting his guitar down. He jumps off the couch and immediately comes to hug me.

Ryan fetches his guitar, and they all shift over to the practice space. I move to perch on the arm of the colourful fabric couch to watch.

They begin warming up, fiddling around with their instruments, making their own soft sounds.

After a while, they decide to run through their songs. I can't even begin to describe the chills that shiver down my arms as I hear the beginning of one of their original songs.

Ryan closes his eyes as the band play, listening

intently to the music before opening his mouth and letting his soft, velvety voice fill the space.

I didn't really notice it at the picnic, but his voice is much raspier than I expected. I can hear the depth and strength of his vocals so much better here. His voice is captivating, unmistakeable—and yes, it's setting off fireworks in my body.

The whole band's performance is incredible, they have an authentic indie sound that makes me think of my favourite artists. I've got chills just being in the room listening to them. How is it possible to have such a physical reaction to live music?

I take in every lyric that flows from Ryan's mouth, absorbing every word. He sings as though he really means it, as if every phrase has a clear purpose. And in that moment, I realise he's written the lyrics. The song is filled with so much raw emotion, exposing the internal struggles he faced after losing his dad.

You're everywhere I look
Yet somehow nowhere at all
Hell, do I miss the times
You'd catch me when I'd fall

So where are you now?

I still scan every crowd
In search of you
In search of you

I'm empty and lost
Stuck on a track, no going back
Plunged into darkness
Blinded by your loss

So where are you now?
I still scan every crowd
In search of you
In search of you

I hope you're up there
Somewhere, looking down
Do I make you proud?
Or does heaven not exist at all?

I thought I would feel awkward watching them play, but I feel so transfixed by their intimate performance that I allow the music to take me away from the present. My body begins to sway to the slow rhythm of the song. I'm lost in his voice, lost in *him*.

"Did you write that?" I ask when they finish playing.

Ryan nods cautiously. "It was incredible, I've never heard anything like that before."

"I wrote it fairly recently. It's not perfect, but we should be able to play it at our next gig." He shrugs, seemingly unaware of his talent.

Ryan looks over at the rest of the band. They nod knowingly, transitioning into another song.

I can't tear my eyes away as they continue through their set list. I'm mesmerised by Ryan. I didn't think their music could reach any deeper inside of me, but as they sing each song... I drown. I feel every word to my core.

I now understand why Ryan uses music to cope with the pain of losing his father. As I sit here, becoming totally absorbed by their songs, I too feel the pain in my chest subside. If only for a short while.

Chapter Twelve

I start to feel more human after spending most of the day at Ryan's house. For the first time since I found out about Kady, I don't want to simply sleep to forget the pain.

"Can we stay down here for a bit?" I ask Ryan once the rest of the band head upstairs for dinner. I don't want to leave this sanctuary before I absolutely have to.

He nods and takes a seat on the couch, watching me as I wander over to their instruments.

I mindlessly glide my fingers across the keys of a piano sitting in the corner of the room, stroking the soft surface of each one. Although, I don't dare press down and disturb the silence.

I wander across to Adam's drums and draw circles on the cymbals, tracing the faint ridges with my fingertips and enjoying the sensation of the cold metal on my skin.

I spot several guitars hung on the adjacent wall and pause when I reach Ryan's.

As I run my fingers down the strings, it feels as though I'm touching an extension of him. It's as though the music he shared with me earlier created a bond between us, an attachment. As I move my fingers, I feel the magnetic pull to him even though it's not his body I'm actually touching.

He must feel it too. He appears behind me, and I feel the warmth of his hand on the back of my arm. I inhale sharply, his hand reigniting the fireworks in my core.

He's standing right behind me, his body only inches from mine. I can feel his breath on the back of my neck. My whole body is whizzing, exploding from the heated tension, and I desperately fight the urge to turn around and crash my lips to his.

"Do you know how to play?" he whispers into my ear. I gulp and shake my head. "Liar," he coos. "You also said you weren't a singer, so I don't believe you."

I feel him watch my hand as it moves silently down the neck of his guitar. He inhales sharply as he watches my fingers linger on the strings.

Moving forward, he presses the front of his body into the back of mine, wrapping one arm around my waist and raising his hand to the neck of the guitar. He runs a finger across the back of my hand, tracing circles over my skin.

Without warning, he snatches his fingers from my hand, as if suddenly noticing the intimacy between us. My body shrinks as we break contact, as if someone just poured water over every spark.

What was that about?

He grabs the guitar from the wall and walks over to the couch. He mumbles for me to grab Tyler's guitar and join him.

I do as I'm told and follow him, frustration brewing at my inability to read his mind.

He looks up without meeting my eyes and points to Tyler's guitar, silently motioning for me to play something.

"Honestly, I don't play. I mean... I had lessons at school, but that was years ago."

Ryan's face softens as he hears the panic in my voice. He smiles encouragingly. "Can you remember anything you used to play?"

"Sure, I think so. I learnt this one chord progression that my music teacher said features on a lot of pop songs, but honestly, I don't think I'd be able to play it very well." I look at Ryan, hoping he can see the fear in my eyes and won't push me to play.

"Show me the chords," he instructs.

I awkwardly show him the individual chords, placing my fingers on the neck of the guitar without actually strumming the strings and making a noise. I'm sure if I swipe my hand across the strings, it'll sound terrible.

"You know, you don't have to be perfect at everything, Zoe. We're only doing this for fun. You shouldn't be afraid to play, especially in front of me." He smiles, cocking his head to the side. "Do you trust me?"

"Of course," I mumble. "But I did just spend the last few hours listening to your band practice. Can you blame a girl for not wanting to embarrass herself after that?" I force a laugh.

"Okay, fine. No guitar." He waves his hands in a truce. Yet, a second later, a smirk forms across his lips and despite his statement, he starts to play his guitar.

I roll my eyes at him. He's enjoying this.

He continues to play, and before long the loose notes and chords transform into a tune I recognise. He's playing a cover of an old Bastille song. I look at his hands and realise he's using the same chord progression I just showed him.

After a little while, I grow more comfortable. He doesn't look at me as he plays, which helps release some of the pressure. I open my mouth to quietly sing along.

My eyes are closed, listening intently to the sweet sounds Ryan is drawing from the guitar.

My voice eventually grows a little louder, a little more confident. Ryan starts to join in, effortlessly singing in perfect harmony.

When I open my eyes, he is still looking down at his guitar, lost in his own little world. Music has such a power over him, and it makes me feel brave enough to try to strum along too. I loosely remember teaching myself to play this song when it first came out, so it's not completely unfamiliar.

As I play, I realise I don't sound as bad as I feared, only stumbling with the chords a couple of times.

In the midst of the song, Ryan looks up with a huge grin spread across his face. I shake my head, stifling a laugh as I sing.

I'm surprised by how natural, how easy it feels playing with him. I've never even listened to music with other people before, let alone actually performed. But this feels safe, comforting.

When the song finishes, I put Tyler's guitar down on the floor and sit cross-legged, staring at a smug-looking Ryan.

"Would you ever consider playing with the band?" he asks eagerly, scooting closer to me on the couch.

"No way! That would terrify me. I'm not good enough," I answer, shaking my head.

"Fuck, your diffidence amazes me, Zo. I know so many people from music college who'd kill to have a voice like yours, myself included."

"You can't be serious," I scoff, rolling my eyes.

"Honestly…" Ryan says, moving so close that his legs touch my knees. "I don't get it."

"Get what?"

"I just don't get why you don't have more confidence in yourself," he whispers, searching my eyes.

I have no idea how I'm supposed to respond to that, so we sit in silence for a moment as I try to figure out what the hell I'm supposed to say back.

Finally, it's Ryan who breaks the silence. "What is it about performing that you wouldn't like?"

"I just don't think I could handle the pressure, the opinions of other people. Plus, I'd be too worried about messing up."

"But how is it different to a cheerleading competition, performing in front of a huge audience?"

I bite my lip. "Because to me, music is so much more personal compared to a choreographed cheer performance alongside twenty other girls. Music just feels too private to share. I feel like our song choices are an extension of our souls—as silly as that sounds—and I don't want to bare my soul to a room full of strangers. The thought alone scares the crap out of me."

Ryan smiles, but he doesn't immediately respond. He looks a little lost in thought, staring into the distance.

He eventually shakes his head and smiles, but his expression doesn't seem to convey happiness, it looks disbelieving. "If I had a voice like yours, I would want everyone to hear it. But it's okay, we've got time, kid." He winks at me, and I roll my eyes.

The faint sound of Ryan's phone vibrating disturbs the room. As the noise gets louder, he pulls his phone out of his pocket, checking the caller ID.

"Sorry, it's my—uh—I just need to take this," he says and heads out of the basement in a flash. I don't even have time to question him, he's out of the door way too quick.

Please don't be some ridiculously hot supermodel girlfriend.

Alone now, I look around the large basement and my eyes land on a collage of picture frames on the wall by the practice area. I get up and wander over to them.

From a distance they seem like artsy black and white photographs of famous musicians, but as I get closer, I actually realise these monochrome photographs are all of The Lanes, playing various gigs and festivals. My eyes are drawn to one which looks like it was taken at a festival in the summer.

In the picture, Ryan is wearing his usual plain, oversized t-shirt, but with a pair of baggier jeans rolled at the ankles. He's performing to a large audience, completely in his element, waving a hand in the air and singing into the microphone.

Seeing these images makes me even more excited to go to one of their gigs. I bet he's a hundred times more mesmerising on stage. If that's even possible. But then again, maybe I *don't* want to see him at a gig. I'm sure he must get tonnes of female attention... and I'm starting to realise that I don't think I could witness that.

A knock on the basement door makes me jump. I turn to see Claire pop her head around the door.

"Hey," I quickly say, heading towards her.

"Hey. I'm just making some focaccia with Adam; it'll be ready in a minute. You must be starving," she says, walking into the basement and closing the door behind her.

She hovers expectantly, leaning against the arm of the adjacent sofa.

"That sounds great," I gulp. I shift uncomfortably at the thought of eating but try to give her a polite smile. I'm pretty sure I can make some excuse to escape to my flat before the food is ready.

Claire smiles and searches my face for a moment. "So... how's things with Ryan? He's never brought a girl back here before, you know."

"Oh no, I'm pretty sure we're just friends," I answer truthfully. I have no idea where I stand with Ryan if I'm being honest with myself. There's no denying the tension I feel between us whenever he's near me, but I've tried not to let myself run away with the idea. I know I'm nowhere near good enough for a guy like him.

"Really? But you guys seem so compatible." Claire pauses. "Huh," she adds.

"I mean, he calls me kid."

The door swings open, revealing a smiling Ryan. Claire jumps off the couch and quickly makes her excuses, turning back up the stairs to find Adam.

"Here." Ryan pushes an acoustic guitar towards me.

I hadn't even noticed he was carrying anything down the stairs, my mind was still back in the conversation with Claire. I take the guitar and stare at it, confused.

Ryan registers the look on my face and adds, "I want you to take this home with you. Use it, don't use it—it's up to you. But just in case you feel like practicing or taking your mind off the heavy stuff, I figured it might help."

My heart soars at the thought of taking a piece of this

haven back to my apartment. I look down at the instrument and my eyes begin to water.

"Don't you need it?" I manage to whisper.

"No. It's just a spare I keep in my room. I'm sure you'll put it to better use." He shrugs casually.

"Thank you so much," I choke, putting the guitar down and pulling him into a tight embrace. He wraps his arms around my waist, and I breathe in the comforting smell of fresh cotton.

Chapter Thirteen

Bright light streams over my face. My tired eyes flutter open, immediately finding the offending crack between the curtains that's pouring sunlight into my room, disturbing my otherwise perfect sleep.

I sit up and lean across the desk for my phone, checking the lock screen for the time. Midday.

I've been asleep for fourteen hours.

How the hell did I sleep through my alarm? Did I forget to put one on? Surely, I've slept enough already this week. Why am I still so tired?

I didn't feel particularly exhausted after band practice yesterday, but as soon as I got back to my room, all I wanted to do was sleep.

I suppose I can afford the lazy morning, it's not like I'm majorly behind on my studying. I only missed the routine introductory lectures this week, and I'm ahead with the required reading for the first few weeks of class.

I stay in bed, sitting up and leaning against the headboard, not wanting to get up. I don't have anywhere I need to be right now; I have the week off work thanks to Ryan. Cheer practice is scheduled for later this afternoon, but that's still hours away.

Grabbing my laptop, I put on an old series of *Gilmore Girls* that I must have watched a million times. Before too long, my phone buzzes and I look down to see a text from Ryan. I snatch my phone and immediately unlock the screen.

Ryan: Work sucks without you.

I smile to myself before replying.

Me: Why? Because now you actually have to get some work done?!

Ryan: Hilarious. Hope you're good today. Speak later!

Just as I am about to climb out of bed to go to the

kitchen, I hear Jake's voice suddenly boom from down the hall, calling for Alice. They briefly congregate in the hallway before heading out of the apartment. I wait in my room for a couple of minutes, just in case one of them comes back.

Once the apartment is completely clear, I walk to the kitchen in a haze, still groggy from oversleeping. I make a big mug of coffee and just stand there for a moment, surveying the empty room. Everything looks exactly the same, but nothing *feels* the same.

Before my mind can catch up with my feet, I walk out of the kitchen and across to Kady's room. I stand outside of her bedroom door for a moment and take a couple of deep breaths.

I turn the handle; the room is unlocked.

I let the door swing open.

I don't dare move my feet, keeping them firmly planted outside of her bedroom. It would be wrong to go inside.

My heart sinks as I take in her room. Everything is still in its place, exactly how she left it. Her bed is messy, the purple duvet sprawled in the position it must've been in when she last slept in it. Lilac and pink fluffy pillows are scattered across the mattress and floor.

Her wardrobe doors are open with a few t-shirts

thrown to the floor, as if she was rushing to try on outfits before she went out. Her makeup is dotted all around the bottom of her full-length mirror. I can still smell her rose scented perfume too.

An image of her sitting on the carpet, applying her makeup whilst she listens to her favourite Beyoncé song flashes through my head.

It feels as if she's just popped out to the shops or to volleyball practice, it doesn't feel like she's been permanently pulled from this world. Although, the throbbing pain in my chest reminds me that I won't see her walk through the front door ever again.

I shut her door and hurry back to my room, taking a moment to try and suppress the rising nausea. Once again, I find myself yearning for physical pain to replace the heartache.

I sit back on the bed and lean against the wall to steady myself. Closing my eyes and pulling my knees to my chest, I try my best to calm down. But I can't sit still for long.

My instincts get the better of me; I run to the kitchen, grabbing every box of cereal bars and snacks I have in my cupboard, bringing them back to my room and consuming them like I'm in a race against time.

Without even having to think, I take myself to the

bathroom, stick my fingers down my throat and relieve my stomach.

I hang my head as I try to catch my breath.

Mechanically, I go to the taps, wash my hands, brush my teeth and drag myself back to my room. When I walk through the door, my eyes immediately land on the guitar Ryan gave me. It leans against the far wall, inviting me to pick it up. I reach for it, grabbing it by the neck and taking it to my bed.

As I have the apartment to myself, I decide to play around with some chord progressions, getting used to the instrument. I try to remember a few songs I learnt in high school.

After a while, I pull up some tutorials on my laptop, feeling brave enough to learn something more complicated.

I play until my fingers feel sore and the pain in my heart retreats. I don't stop until a low battery warning flashes on my laptop, forcing me out of the moment and back to reality.

Jolting to attention, I realise how long I've been playing. I have ten minutes to get to cheer practice. *Shit.*

I scramble off the bed and throw on my gym kit and hoodie, grabbing a bottle of water from the kitchen. I rush to the car, start my engine and head towards campus.

Despite only having a few minutes before practice starts, I take my time on the road. I drive carefully the entire way there, taking a slight detour to avoid the road where Kady was taken.

It's growing dark by the time I pull up at the sports centre. I try to push the memory of the last time I was here as far to the back of my mind as possible, walking quickly to practice.

"Hey!" a strong, melodious voice calls out to me from behind. I turn around to see Nadine running to catch up with me. She wipes a perfectly manicured hand with bright red nail polish across her forehead when she reaches me.

"Hey." I smile back, trying to act as bright as possible as we march towards the gymnastics hall.

"How's your week been? I tried to find you again at initiation night, but I think you'd left... or I was too drunk to remember seeing you," Nadine says, giggling.

"Sorry, I did leave. I had work early the next day so couldn't stay late. How was your week?" I ask, pushing through the gymnasium door.

"Yeah, really good thanks! Although did you hear about that girl from our uni that got killed in a wreck? I think she was in the year below me." She fiddles with her bobbed hair as she talks, trying to force it into a low ponytail.

"She was my flatmate," I manage to say in a broken whisper. A flood of emotions rush over me just hearing myself say the words out loud. I take a sip of water from my bottle.

"Are you okay?" Nadine's eyes are wide, shock coursing through her irises. I nod, unable to speak. "You know I'm always here if ever you need anything, okay? Let's swap numbers. We should hang out some time anyway." She holds out her hand for my phone.

I pass it to her, and she dials her number. Once she's saved my information, we dump our phones in our bags and walk onto the sprung floor where the rest of the team are congregated for practice.

Kim flies through the doors, a large iced coffee in hand. "Girls! As you know, we have our firework event coming up next month. The training schedule has already been emailed to you," Kim begins. I panic, realising I haven't checked my university emails all week.

I lean closer to Nadine. "What's the training schedule? I haven't checked my emails," I whisper.

She looks at me with an understanding smile and gives my wrist a squeeze. She quietly lets me know that we have choreography camp all weekend to learn the routine, and our practice hours have doubled every week leading up to the event.

I suddenly feel grateful that Ryan got me out of working this weekend, it means I don't have to worry about swapping shifts last minute. I also feel surprisingly good about the added training hours, God knows I need the distraction.

Four hours later, I'm walking out of the sports hall with Nadine. We're still trying to catch our breath. My arms and legs ache, and once again, I know I'm going to be bruised after that intense session.

"Those stunts were tough. There's no way we're going to be able to pull those off for the firework event." I turn to Nadine, shaking my head.

"I know! *And* we're going to be so nervous on the actual performance. Did you hear Kim say a thousand people show up to watch? *A thousand people!* And it's broadcast on national TV!" Nadine responds brightly, waving her hands for dramatic effect.

My phone starts ringing, so I say goodbye to Nadine and check the caller ID. It's Ryan. I quickly swipe to answer.

"Hey," he says breathlessly. If I didn't know any better, I'd say he sounds worried. "What are you up to? I never heard from you after cheer practice, is everything okay?"

"Oh. Yeah... sorry, my bad. Kim extended the session by two hours so I'm only just getting out now," I explain as I unlock my car. It feels so alien having someone other than my family check up on me.

"I see. Uh, can I come over? Or do you have plans?"

"Now?"

"Yeah, if you're free?" His voice cracks slightly at the end of his question.

"Sure. I'll text you when I'm back at the apartment," I say, hanging up and feeling a wave of uncontrollable excitement.

Chapter Fourteen

On my way home from cheer practice, I allow myself a glance at the corner where Kady's accident happened. I don't know why, but I'm fixated on it. I just hadn't expected everything to look so... *normal.*

I pull into the supermarket nearby, and head directly to the flowers by the entrance. There aren't many fresh bunches left, but I pick the brightest ones they have, settling on some red gerbera daisies.

Ambling through the quiet aisles, I pick up a variety of snacks, including a tub of ice cream and some blocks of chocolate. I also reach for one of the free plastic spoons they have next to the cashier, which are supposed to be for the lunch meal deals they sell, but the disinterest on the cashier's face suggests that she couldn't care less if I took one.

"Girls' night in?" she asks me as she scans my items.

"Something like that." I force a smile at her and tap my card on the reader before returning to the car and dumping the food on the passenger's seat.

The car lights flash as I lock the car with the button on my keys. I walk in the direction of the main road, flowers in hand.

Once I reach the site of the accident, I stand still, looking at the empty pavement, taking in every detail of where Kady must have taken her last breath.

God, I desperately hope she didn't suffer.

Kneeling down, I place the flowers against a lamppost, breathing in the early autumn air whilst I replay the last conversation I had with her in my head.

I don't ever want to forget the sound of her voice.

I dab my eyes with the sleeve of my hoodie and continue to stare at the pavement.

"I'm sorry it was you and not me," I finally say to the wind, unable to ignore the crushing weight of guilt on my chest.

When I get to the apartment, I lock myself in my bedroom and open the now softened ice cream. I pull the plastic spoon from my pocket and sit on my bed, grateful

I had the foresight to grab one from the supermarket so I could avoid the communal kitchen.

Inhaling the comforting smell of chocolate, I begin scooping from the tub. The smooth, cold ice cream cools the burn in my chest, extinguishing the fire in my body and rapidly filling my empty stomach.

I text Ryan, telling him to come over. I then grab a towel from my wardrobe and dart for the bathroom. Before I undress, I turn on the shower and kneel at the toilet, sticking my fingers down my throat.

The pain makes me smile.

I lean my head against the bathroom wall and wait until my body calms.

When my throat finally stops burning, I jump in the shower and wash my hair before changing into a grey sweatshirt and black yoga leggings.

Just as I dispose of the ice cream carton, the apartment bell rings and I rush to the door, figuring its Ryan. I buzz him up and swing the door open, feeling a rush of excitement as I watch him climb up the stairs.

I laugh as he approaches. He's wearing a grey hoodie and black skinny jeans.

"I guess you got the uniform memo." I point to our practically matching outfits.

Ryan looks me up and down, laughing. "You wear it

better though, Zo." He winks, pulling me in for a hug. "It's good to see you."

"You too." I breathe in his fresh cotton scent, letting it absolve all my earlier pain.

After a few moments, we wriggle free of our embrace, and I lead him to my bedroom. He shuts the door behind him, removing his backpack from his shoulders and opening the zipper. He pulls out some sort of thin magazines.

"I brought you a few of my old guitar books." He hands the stack to me. "I thought you might want to borrow them for a bit, learn some new songs or whatever." He shrugs.

"These are great, thank you." I flick through the pages, already itching to try some out. "You know, I actually spent my morning learning new songs."

"You did? That's amazing." He pulls me in for another hug when I nod. "I'm proud of you, you know? You're handling things so much better than I would," he whispers into my hair.

I gulp, feeling a sudden wave of guilt. I wonder what he would say if he knew what I was up to just moments ago.

As he relaxes his grip, I move over to the desk and pick up my laptop and the guitar. "I guess I can show you?" I offer, which makes his face light up. His grin is so adorable that I have to pull my lips over my teeth to hide my smile.

I sit on the bed and begin to play a melody. I feel his eyes burning into me, but I try to keep my focus on my hands. He starts humming along to the tune, tapping his hand on his knee to the rhythm. I love seeing how excited he is by my musical progress, not to mention how engrossed he gets in any song, no matter how simple.

"You learnt that today?" he asks once I stop playing. I nod and put the guitar down. "Okay, you have to play at our next gig."

I immediately put my hand in the air to silence him, shaking my head. "No way. I only just started messing around with the guitar again. Plus, playing is just an outlet. I'm not ready to add the pressure of performing. Baby steps, please!"

"Okay, okay!" He waves his hands dramatically, smiling. "But you'll come to our gig next weekend, right?"

"Uh huh." I nod, trying my best to act casual. "I was actually thinking of asking my friend from cheer to come along, if that's okay?"

"Of course it's okay. That would be awesome. How was cheer tonight by the way? Can you now confirm you enjoy it, Little Miss Pedantic?"

I nudge him playfully. "Yes, it was good. We're going pretty full out with training. We have a show coming up next month."

His hazel eyes brighten. "What show?"

As I begin to tell him the details of the firework performance, he sits further back on the bed, leaning against the headboard. He looks so at home in my room, so comfortable. I think I could get used to this.

"Okay. I'm coming. And I'll bring the band too," he says.

My stomach churns at the thought of him in the crowd; watching the performance... watching *me*.

I startle myself awake, sweat dampening my face. I shift my body and quickly identify the source of the heat. My legs are wrapped around Ryan's and I'm lying on his chest as he grips me close to his body. We must've fallen asleep during the movie we put on.

I check the time on my phone. It's three in the morning.

As I blink at the screen, Ryan stirs next to me, recoiling from the bright light.

"Hey," he croaks, groggy from sleep. "What time is it?" he asks, wiping his eyes. I turn my phone towards him and once his eyes adjust to the brightness of the screen, they go wide in shock. "I should get going." He quickly bolts upright, untangling himself from me.

"It's okay. You can just stay, if you want? There's no point driving home this late," I suggest quietly, really not wanting him to leave.

"I guess if I go now, I won't be able to get back to sleep. I don't want to fuck up my sleeping pattern." He shrugs casually. I didn't think musicians were particularly fussed about their 'sleeping pattern' but I'm not going to say that to him.

He starts to pull off his jeans and I look away until his legs are under the duvet. I hop out of the bed, opening the window slightly and pulling the curtains shut. I take off my jumper and peel off my yoga pants, swapping them for my checked pyjama shorts. I move quickly, hoping Ryan isn't looking at me whilst I change.

In bed, I lie on my side with my back to him and try to fall to sleep, but every inch of my body is tense; it feels electric, all too aware of how close he is to me.

I squeeze my eyes shut, but I know there's no way sleep will take over. All I can think is that if I turn around, my lips would be just a millimetre from Ryan's. The thought is excruciating.

A few moments pass, and I hear Ryan's breathing deepen. I figure he must be asleep, but he wriggles and cups my hand with his, interlacing our fingers.

His warm arm reaches around my waist, pulling me closer to him. I wonder if he's moving in his sleep and this action is unconscious, but I don't dare speak. I don't dare disturb this moment.

His whole body is pushed against the back of mine and my heart is racing. I feel his breath on my neck and my body ignites as his lips slowly brush against my skin. *Did he just kiss me?*

Chapter Fifteen

I've been awake for the past twenty minutes, but I've barely moved. I've not wanted to. I've not wanted to burst this blissful bubble with Ryan. If I could, I would stay wrapped in our embrace forever.

But his phone has other ideas. It won't stop vibrating from the inside pocket of his jeans, which are discarded somewhere on the floor. I feel Ryan stir next to me, the noise waking him.

Finally, the vibrating stops. Whoever is calling seems to have given up.

"Morning," Ryan breathes, rubbing my shoulder.

I turn over to face him. We stare at each other in silence for a moment, unsure of what to say.

Staring into my eyes, he gently brushes a piece of my

fly-away hair behind my ear and cups my face in his hand. I wriggle closer to him, putting my arm around his waist.

He opens his mouth to say something, but once again the sound of his phone interrupts the moment. I silently curse whoever is calling him. They have terrible timing.

Ryan sits up, reaching down to the floor for his phone. He scrolls the messages before jumping out of bed and quickly getting dressed. He doesn't look at me as he moves, and a worried feeling sweeps through me.

"I have to go, but I'll call you, okay?" he promises. I don't even have time to flash a fake smile before he's out of the door.

I can't help but wonder what made him leave so quickly. Maybe another girl was texting him or something. I've never actually asked whether he's dating anyone. I have no idea what his history with women is like. The only thing I have to go off of is Emily's warning not to date him, but she didn't exactly explain why.

I wonder if he regrets staying over. It's not like anything happened besides the tiny kiss on my neck and that oddly intense moment we had this morning, but I suppose he might be feeling weird about it. He might just see me as a friend and panicked that he's giving me the wrong impression.

Ugh, who knows?

I internally sigh. I'm not going to think about him. He promised he would call, and I have studying to do anyway.

But first, I need a fix of my favourite liquid. Coffee.

I walk straight to the kitchen and startle a little when I see Alice sat at the breakfast bar, swirling a spoon in her cereal bowl. My desperate need for coffee overtakes anything else, and I walk straight past her towards the coffee machine.

"Hey," I say as I brush past. I know I should at least be polite and act like the bigger person.

"Hey. I'm glad it's you, I've been meaning to talk to you," she says, looking up from her bowl with a sad look on her face.

"I was just talking to Kady's sister on the phone." Her voice cracks slightly as the words leave her mouth. "They're coming this weekend to clear out her room." She wipes a tear from her eyes and looks down at the breakfast bar.

"Oh," is all I can manage to say, feeling a lump rising to my throat.

"They said her funeral will be on Wednesday. They only want a small service for her close friends and family, but they said you are welcome to go."

I decide to ignore her snide comment. I'd say I'm doing so in order to be the more civilised of the pair of us, but in reality, I'm terrified of the confrontation.

"It's a good thing they can finally have the funeral," I reply instead.

"Yeah, it is. Do you think you could drive us there?" she asks. I nod, biting my tongue, focussing on making my coffee.

Alice finally gets up to go to her room and I retreat to mine, deciding to call Ryan. I feel strange being the one to call him, especially after he promised he would call me, but I think he would want to know about Kady's funeral.

The call goes straight to voicemail. I try to brush it off, telling myself he might just be busy. He can't be at work today, I checked the rota on my phone this morning, but I don't know what other commitments he has.

I grab my laptop from the desk and take it to bed with me. I resume watching my rerun of *Gilmore Girls* in the hope it will distract me from Ryan's silence.

When I finally start to relax and stop checking my phone every two minutes, I hear it vibrate on the desk. My heart leaps and I jump to unlock it as fast as possible.

My stomach drops when I see Nadine's name flash across the screen instead of Ryan's.

Nadine: Coffee before cheer tomorrow? Xx

A smile creeps across my face as soon as I read the text.

Okay, now I feel bad for being disappointed that Nadine text me and not Ryan.

I reply quickly, solidifying a plan to meet for coffee in the morning.

Chapter Sixteen

I can't stop thinking about Ryan. I still haven't heard from him.

My worry kept me up all night, causing me to restlessly toss and turn. One minute, I was panicked that something bad had happened to him, the next I feared he simply regretted spending the night in my bed.

I wound myself up as I sat in my room, overthinking and overanalysing his lack of contact. As the time dragged on without hearing from him, I felt a gaping loneliness inside of me that I'd never experienced before. The pain kept getting worse and worse. I got so frustrated to the point that I had to *physically* do something about it.

I relied on my stash of food to pull me through. I gulped down as much as I could until my stomach felt ready to burst.

After all the food was gone, I stuck my head over the toilet, finding pleasure in the food resurfacing. I revelled in the throbbing pain in my throat, got high on it, as it took away my fears.

I thought I would feel better this morning, but I don't. I just wish Ryan would let me know that everything is okay. I'm having flash backs to when we hadn't heard from Kady. The memory, mixed with Ryan's silence, is torturing me.

He knows what I'm going through, so why wouldn't he just let me know that he's okay, even if we are just friends?

I realise I barely know Ryan, but I'm sure he's a decent enough person to call me like he promised. So maybe something awful has actually happened to him...

Deciding to learn from the past and be proactive, I text Emily to ask if Ryan is working today. Maybe he picked up my weekend shifts to cover for me and Emily just didn't update the rota. That would explain why he hasn't checked his phone.

I hit send on the text to Emily as I leave my apartment, jumping into my car and heading straight for campus to meet Nadine.

When I get to uni, I walk to the coffee shop and

suddenly feel a wave of butterflies float through my stomach. I know I'm not exactly the best at making new friends, so I just hope I don't mess this up somehow. I really like Nadine.

By the time I get inside, she's already sat at a table. She looks up from her phone when she sees me and waves brightly, pushing a coffee cup towards me.

"Thank you," I say, sitting on the empty chair.

"Don't sweat it, you can get them next time." She beams. Her words do something to me, I relax slightly. *Next time.* She already wants there to be a next time?

"So, how are things with you? We never got to talk properly after cheer practice the other day. I'm so sorry about your flatmate. I'm here if you need anything, okay?" she says with a sympathetic smile.

"I'm okay, actually. I guess time is helping. Plus, all these training sessions are keeping me busy," I say, forcing a laugh.

"How have the rest of your housemates been? Are you guys close?" She fiddles with her pink Chanel card holder on the table, spinning it around in her tiny, manicured hands. The pristine, post-box red nail polish shimmers under the coffee shop lights and I wonder how she keeps them looking so perfect, not a chip in sight.

I sigh deeply. "I wouldn't say we're super close. We

haven't spent a lot of time together since the accident—not that we usually spend time together anyway—but we're just dealing with it in our own individual ways, I guess." I shrug.

Nadine nods slowly as I speak. Her mouth is pressed into a thin line as she studies my face. "I see… I'm the same with my roommate, so I wouldn't worry. She recently got a new boyfriend, now I hardly see her." She rolls her eyes.

"It's like having the whole place to yourself though, right?"

"Yeah, I suppose it is. I don't have to worry about constantly cleaning up her mess in the kitchen. I have a hard time cleaning up my own." She laughs, and I can't help but join in, her laughter contagious.

I continue to listen to Nadine complain about her flatmate's new boyfriend. She tells me about the time she got so fed up with him, she dunked his toothbrush in the toilet bowl. I laugh so hard I get stomach cramps. It feels so alien, so good.

"Are you free next weekend?" I ask, wiping tears of laughter from my eyes. She pauses, caught off guard by my sudden question. Is it too soon to ask her to come to the gig with me? Would that be weird considering we've only hung out this one time outside of cheer?

"Yeah, I am. I was going to go to the library to finish an assignment at some point, but I have nothing else planned. How come?"

"My friend invited me to his gig—he's in a band—and I said I would go. I was wondering if you'd want to come? Don't worry if it's not your thing," I say, feeling a lot less confident now the words have left my mouth.

"That sounds great! Count me in!" She grins, clasping her hands together eagerly. "Are they a band from campus?"

"No, I met the lead singer at work. He works for the same clothing brand as I do."

"Is he just a friend?" Nadine tilts her head. Her eyes are suddenly brighter, eager to hear some gossip.

"I think so, yeah. It's kind of complicated... I think... I mean, I'm probably just overthinking everything." I look down, picking at the paper sleeve on my coffee cup.

Nadine leans closer. "Spill."

I let out a small, uncomfortable laugh and she cusses at my reticence, only making me laugh harder.

"Fine." I sigh. "We only recently became friends. His name is Ryan. I first met him a couple of weeks ago. He seems really cool. He's been so supportive, you know, with everything I have going on. I'm just trying to read his signals. One minute he's wanting to see me every day, and now, I haven't heard from him after he said he would call."

Nadine smiles encouragingly, so I feel comfortable enough to continue to ramble to her, explaining everything; from hanging out with the band and finding out about Kady, to him staying over at my place the other night.

"Maybe he's trying to play it cool?" she suggests.

I shrug. "I honestly don't know him well enough to even guess. It's just worrying me, you know? Not hearing from him reminds me of..." I don't even need to finish my sentence and Nadine nods her head, reaching for my hand across the table. It feels so good to rant to someone about this.

Talking of Ryan reminds me to check my phone to see if Emily has replied to me.

I swipe to find two messages sent thirty minutes ago.

Emily: He's not working today.
Emily: Tyler said he went home to his mum's.
Emily: Everything ok?

I feel a lump in my throat and a wave of anger bubble in my stomach.

Nadine looks at me as my eyes gloss over. "You

okay?" she asks.

I shake my head, unable to speak. I know that if I open my mouth right now, tears will spill over. Instead, I push my phone towards her and let her read the message.

Despite knowing Ryan is safe, I can't help but feel betrayed. He knows exactly what I went through just the other week, the panic I experienced when I didn't hear from Kady. I can't believe he would say nothing and just let me imagine the worst.

"What an asshole!" Nadine exclaims with a huff, crossing her arms and leaning back in her chair. "Honestly, that is *not* cool. He should know better. Frankly, I think it's worse if it's just a friendship he wants." She huffs again, crossing her legs to match her arms.

"What do you mean?"

"If he was your friend, he would respect your feelings and not play mind games. Especially whilst you're grieving. Behaviour like that is reserved for assholes who are too immature to express their romantic feelings," she states matter-of-factly. "He clearly has feelings for you, otherwise he wouldn't be this hot and cold. You deserve better, Zoe."

I know that I should accept her warning that his behaviour is toxic, but I can't help fixating on the other part of her theory: that he might like me. In reality, the betrayal should outweigh my hopes that Ryan could want to be more than friends, but it doesn't. It's nowhere close to the exhilarating feeling soaring through me.

"Now, I know from the way your eyes just lit up that you're going to ignore my advice, but hey, no judgement from me," Nadine says, waving her hands in the air. "Admittedly, I'd be the same if I liked someone. Just promise to be careful, okay? I'm here whatever happens."

She smiles brightly and leans her elbows on the table. "Plus, if he hurts you, I'll throw something at him on stage." She grins widely, standing up from the table. "Right, girl. We've got a cheer routine to learn, come on."

I follow suit, standing up from the table and trying to supress a giggle. Nadine links her arm through mine as we walk towards the gymnasium.

I could get used to this. I could really get used to this whole friendship thing.

Chapter
Seventeen

It's been five days since Ryan disappeared. But thanks to Nadine and her distraction techniques, I've gotten used to his silence.

After our weekend of cheer training, Nadine made me promise to spend every day with her in the lead up to the funeral. We hung out at the library in between classes and watched movies at her apartment every evening. I haven't touched my guitar. I've ignored Ryan's advice to use music to help. Because it doesn't. It just reminds me of him.

I know it's not Ryan's absence that is entirely responsible for the debilitating pain in my chest. It's the fast-approaching funeral. Tomorrow is the day we say goodbye to Kady forever.

I've never been to a funeral before, let alone for someone my own age. I can't imagine what it'll be like.

As I mindlessly re-watch the same movie I sat through with Nadine yesterday, my phone starts ringing. It'll be my sister wanting to check in before the funeral, so I answer without looking.

"I'm fine, Hannah. I swear!" I say into the speaker.

"Zoe?" My heart sinks to the pit of my stomach. I look at the screen to check the caller ID. Ryan.

"Um... yeah?" is all I can manage to croak out. Why didn't I check the name before answering? I'm not prepared for this conversation right now, or any conversation for that matter.

"Are you okay? Whose Hannah? What's happened?" he rushes.

"My sister," I snap.

"But you're okay?"

"I'm fine, Ryan. Perfect. Why wouldn't I be?" My tone isn't subtle in the slightest, but I'm past caring.

"I'm so sorry I haven't called or text. I left my phone in my room here and had to go home in a hurry."

"I thought something had happened to you."

I jump off the bed, pacing up and down the room, trying to focus on my steps as opposed to the voice on the other end of the line.

"I honestly didn't think. I'm so sorry, Zo. I'm stupid. *So* stupid. The worst, in fact. I'm not used to having to think about telling anyone else where I am." I can hear his breathing pick up on the other end of the phone. "I mean, I don't usually tell my friends where I'm going. I should have realised you were different."

What is he getting at? Is he telling me he should have told me because he sees me as more than a friend, or because of what happened with Kady?

"Can I come over?" he asks.

"Uh... I don't think that's a good idea, sorry. It's just, the funeral is tomorrow and I'm pretty tired. I want to get some rest."

Kady's life and memory deserves my full attention right now. I don't want any confusion over Ryan to take over, and talking to him on the phone is scrambling my mind.

"Okay, kid. Good luck tomorrow, I'll be thinking of you." He hangs up and, even though he called me that stupid pet name again, his kind words make me feel a little guilty for being so hard on him.

Maybe I should have let him come over. Besides his disappearing act, he really has been there for me. He gave me a guitar, kept me company when I was down and pulled me through the dark early days of grief. Why was I so quick to be hard on him? I've never had someone care about me so much, why did I push him away?

I let out a deep breath, tossing my phone onto the desk and clutching my head in my hands.

My eyes flit across my room to the wardrobe. I walk towards it, opening the doors and rummaging through the bottom shelf. Finally, I find the remaining bars of chocolate and biscuits stashed in the far corner.

I take them to bed and consume them as quickly as possible, not stopping to take a breath as the sweet, dense food fills my stomach.

Images of Kady flood my mind as I close my eyes, waiting for the nausea to take over. Like clockwork, it only takes a couple of minutes until my stomach feels unsettled.

When I get inside the bathroom, I lock the door and turn the taps on, sitting down next to the toilet.

The pain of gagging overtakes every other feeling in my body. I lean over the toilet and allow my stomach to empty. It takes a while for everything to come back up, straining my throat more than I've experienced before. When it's over, I let the pain wrap around me and I clutch my trembling stomach with my hands.

Before I try to get up and go back to my room, I wait

for my breathing to slow down, but it won't settle. Instead, I feel tears overspill from my eyes. I hold my hand over my mouth, not wanting my housemates to hear me cry.

I'm angry at myself for getting so upset. I don't have a right to feel this pain and loss and loneliness.

I'm selfish.

There were people in Kady's life, like her parents, her family and her close friends, that are entitled to be consumed by grief.

I have no right to feel this way at all.

I wipe my mouth and get up off the floor. Unable to meet my own gaze in the mirror, I head straight back to my bedroom and climb into bed.

I lean over for my phone on the desk and dial Ryan's number. To my relief, he answers on the second ring.

"Hey, you okay?" Ryan asks.

"Yeah, I umm... I'm sorry for being short with you. I'm just really nervous for tomorrow," I admit, wiping my eyes and hoping he can't hear the tears in my voice.

"Oh, please don't apologise, Zo. I get it, I really do," he says softly. His voice sends a comforting wave through my body. I close my eyes and nestle my head into my pillow.

"You're right though," I whisper.

"About what?"

"You are the worst." I grin and I can hear him chuckle down the other end of the phone.

He is the worst. The worst for making me feel all these things I've never felt before, for making me addicted to hearing his voice, for making me miss him so much whilst he's been away.

"Will you just stay on the phone with me for a bit?" I ask, not wanting our conversation to end. "Tell me about your day."

Ryan launches into a story about his morning surfing and skateboarding with his friends before the long drive home. He tells me how bad the traffic was on the way back here and how long the journey takes him. My eyes feel heavy, and I sense myself drifting peacefully to sleep, lost in the sound of my favourite voice.

Chapter Eighteen

No amount of concealer will hide the dark circles under my eyes this morning. I look a mess. My throat is tender, my eyes are bloodshot. I try to brush my hair to smooth the manic waves, but every time the brush touches my scalp, I wince in pain. My entire body feels sore.

I button up my black shift dress, slip on my Dr Martens and head towards the kitchen.

Aiming straight for the coffee machine, I reach for a mug and pour myself a double shot. I add a splash of cold water so I can drink it immediately, God knows I need the caffeine right now.

"Are you ready to go?" Alice pokes her head around the door.

I nod and down the rest of the cup, placing my empty mug in the sink.

"Jake is already on his way. He decided to take his own car as he went to the gym first," Alice tells me as we walk out of the building.

My phone buzzes and I glance down to read the message.

Ryan: Good luck, Zo. Thinking of you today xxx

I smile and text Ryan back straight away, moving my fingers rapidly as I type.

Me: Good luck for the funeral or the car ride with Alice?

Ryan: Ha! Both. But you probably need more luck with the latter xxx

"I wonder what the service will be like." I turn to Alice as we jump into my car. I can't think of anything else to say to fill the awkward silence between us.

"Sad, probably." She looks out of the passenger window and stays silent, unable to look in my direction. I don't mind the quiet, it's way better than a forced conversation.

When we pull up to the cemetery car park, groups of unfamiliar people congregate at the far end of the lot, surrounding the doors of the crematorium.

We scan the group for Jake, spotting him at the other end of the car park, far away from everyone else. We walk towards him, and the three of us huddle together under my umbrella, shielding ourselves from the miserable drizzle.

"Do you recognise anyone else here?" Alice eventually asks.

Jake nods. "I saw a couple of the volleyball girls and they said a few of the team were coming today. They're just over there." He points to a group of tall girls gathered closely with the rest of the funeral party.

We resume people watching in silence, scanning the unfamiliar crowd. The congregation of people move towards the main entrance, and we join them, shifting towards the small building.

Once inside, we wait for everyone else to fill the seats before finding spaces next to each other on the back row.

I'm not sure what I expected from a funeral ceremony, but

it was difficult. My heart shattered all over again when we saw Kady's coffin being brought into the church. It was a light oak colour, covered in a huge wreath of bright pink and purple flowers, mostly roses, her favourite.

Seeing who was carrying the coffin made my heart ache more than I could bear. Her two teenage brothers were at the front of the casket, with their dad and three other young boys following behind.

It was hard. Seeing how young they were. They were too young to be carrying a casket into a funeral.

Kady's mum, Ruth, slowly followed behind them. She wore a dark purple wool coat and flat black shoes with a purple hat resting on top of her dark curly hair. She was leaning into another relative also wearing the same colour dress. I noticed that everyone walking down the aisle wore a dark shade of purple instead of black, opting for a darker version of one of Kady's favourite colours.

As Ruth walked to the front of the room, one of her hands clutched her stomach and the other pressed a handkerchief to her face. She looked like she was trying to physically keep her body together, holding herself tightly so she wouldn't shatter into a million pieces. Her dark eyes focussed on the coffin during the entire precession, not looking away for even a second.

It was a strange feeling, attending the family funeral.

It made me realise that they barely knew the Kady we did at university. The eulogies echoed her personality, of course, but all of the memories and stories reflected a younger version of Kady as a child. They didn't show her as the independent, fierce, strong woman she was at university.

I suppose that's what happens when you live away from home, you grow and make memories away from your old life. Despite the phone calls Kady made to her parents each day, they never really knew who she hung out with on campus, or what she did outside of class besides volleyball practice.

The worst part of the whole thing was when the dark curtain finally closed around Kady's casket until it was out of sight. They played her favourite Beyoncé song, and the upbeat pop music painfully juxtaposed the heartache we all felt. I know I won't ever be able to listen to that song again without being reminded of today.

"I don't think I could stay for the wake. I don't feel like we belong here," Alice says quietly as we huddle outside of the crematorium.

"We don't have to," Jake says, running a hand through his hair and rubbing his exhausted eyes.

"Why don't we go to the Guild? We could gather everyone she knew at university and have our own

137

celebration of her life on campus," I suggest.

I'm not surprised when their mouths hang open as they look at me. I don't blame them. I know I never usually want to socialise. But today is not my day, it's Kady's.

"You know, that sounds perfect." Jake softly smiles and fiddles with his black tie. Alice doesn't say much, her lips form a tight, forced smile in return.

Chapter Nineteen

By the time we drop our cars back to the apartment and walk to campus, the Guild is packed full of people. I knew Kady was popular, but I didn't realise she was *this* popular.

The only people I know in this room are my housemates—who have now wandered off to join their respective sports teams—oh, and Kim. But I'm kind of hiding from her. I don't want her to know I'm Kady's flatmate, it'll just lead to gossip on the cheer squad.

I walk out of the double doors, into the courtyard, and sit on the edge of the mermaid water feature. I pull out my phone to call Ryan.

"Hey, I was hoping you would call. How was it?" he asks.

"It was okay. We're back on campus now, having a drink at the Guild with some of Kady's friends." I pause. "Do you want to come hang?"

"You know, I'm actually walking past your campus right now. I went to the music shop in the village. Are you sure her friends won't mind me crashing though?"

"There are so many people here, no one would notice. Plus, it would be great to see you." I feel a smile play across my face. I hate how much I've missed him.

I hang up and go back inside to order us both a drink.

Ryan is already at the mermaid fountain by the time I get out of the building. He's sat casually on the stone ledge, looking down at his phone with his skateboard propped up next to him. He's wearing a dark green hoodie with a black denim jacket and black skinny jeans.

Why does he have to look *so* good all the time? Literally, all the time.

I hate what my heart does just watching him.

Fireworks, chill.

He looks up from his phone just as I step outside, smiling as he walks towards me. I hold out the bottle of beer I got him, but he pulls me in for a bear hug before taking it. I sigh heavily as I breathe in his cotton scent.

"Do you have psychic powers?" he says, taking a sip of his drink.

"Huh?" I tilt my head.

He raises the bottle. "It's my favourite beer."

"Oh." I feel my cheeks flame for some reason. "You're welcome."

We sit down on the fountain ledge, and he looks at me, smiling expectantly. I assume he's waiting for me to continue talking, to tell him about the funeral, but my brain freezes as I look more closely at his face. He's freshly shaved, showing off his razor-sharp jaw line, and his cheeks are slightly rosy from the cool air. He really does look good. But maybe that's because I haven't seen him in a few days...

Who am I kidding? He looks good. I just hate him for turning me to mush.

"H-how was everything at home?" I finally stutter.

He quickly drops eye contact, fiddling with the paper label on his beer bottle. "Fine, yeah. My mum's been a bit unwell, so I went to check on her." He shrugs, taking another gulp of his beer.

"Is she okay?" I probe.

He pauses for a moment before answering. "It's complicated. She's still struggling with the loss of my dad, and she's not really got anyone at home besides my aunt. My brother is..." he trails off, looking past me towards the trees lining the campus road.

"I didn't know you had a brother," I say encouragingly, hoping to ease his discomfort.

He clears his throat and frowns. "Yeah, he's older than me by a couple of years. We're not that close, not anymore anyway." He pauses. "Enough about me. How have you been today?"

He grabs my hand and squeezes it. He doesn't pull it away like he usually does. Instead, he interlocks his fingers with mine and places our hands on my lap.

He draws circles on my palm with his thumb, and my insides dance at his touch. I just hope my face doesn't give me away.

"You know I'm here for you too, right?" I say, meaning every word.

"I know, kid." He pulls his hand free of mine, running it through his hair and then shaking his head so his dark fringe falls back into position. He doesn't place his hand back in mine.

I close my eyes and take a few deep breaths, trying to suppress the stinging rejection.

"Have you been playing the guitar?" he asks.

"I haven't played as much as I would like. My schedule's been pretty hectic with cheer." I shrug. There's no way I could tell him that the real reason I haven't played is because I've missed him way too much, and just looking at the guitar makes me think of him.

Ryan's soft lips form a flat line, a crinkle becomes visible between his brows. "That's good, keeping you busy I guess," he says with an air of indifference, still frowning and twirling the ring on his thumb with his fingers.

I hate that I can't tell what he's thinking. He can't be that pissed that I've not been playing, surely?

"What's up?" I eventually ask. He furrows his eyebrows again, thinking deeply.

His cool attitude makes me shiver involuntarily. He pulls off his jacket, passing it to me. I open my mouth to protest, but he raises a hand to silence me. I put the warm jacket on and inhale the familiar scent, allowing it to comfort me as I wait for him to answer my question.

"I just thought playing guitar made you happy, that's all. You're really good at it." He looks at me so intensely, his hazel irises burning my cheeks. I have to look away in order to think straight.

"It does," I say, but his frown doesn't soften. I cock my head to the side and mimic his expression. "I don't understand. What have I done?"

"Nothing, Zo. I was thinking about what you said the other night, when I bumped into you after my gig, you said you didn't think about your happiness when deciding your career. I'm just wondering, when you make decisions in your life, what do you prioritise?" He looks directly at me, searching my face for an answer.

I take a sip of my drink to buy me more thinking time.

"Uh." I exhale. "I think maybe I prioritise stability and making my family proud, I guess."

"That's it?" He raises his eyebrows. I shrug, unsure of what to say. "Wouldn't you rather wake up every day doing something that excites you? That creates a fire in your belly?"

A fire in my belly?

"I think that's very unrealistic. Not every job is perfect every second of every day." I pause. "We aren't that different you know, you and me." I point back and forth in the space between us. "You get your enjoyment from music, but you still have to go to Jacks. I'm sure you don't always find those early morning stockroom shifts enjoyable."

Ryan chuckles, shaking his head. "Who wouldn't enjoy getting up at six in the morning to fold hundreds of t-shirts in a dingy stockroom?" He laughs. "You have a good point though; I'll give you that. But I just got the feeling that you did everything, like cheer and becoming a lawyer, for everyone else. Have you actually thought about what makes *you* happy?"

"Making my parents proud makes me happy," I

respond automatically.

"All I am saying is, just make sure that, when making everyone else happy, you don't forget about yourself." He stands up from the fountain ledge, picking up his skateboard and tucking it under one of his arms.

I quickly follow his lead and he holds out his spare hand for me to take. His fingers wrap around mine and the warmth radiating from the touch sets me alight. Again.

Damn you, fireworks.

"Come on, I'll walk you home," he offers. We move to the main road hand in hand. I feel a little giddy by this gesture. Giddy, but confused.

Just make sure that, when making everyone else happy, you don't forget about yourself.

"Do I seem unhappy to you?" I finally ask, turning to look at Ryan.

"Well, not unhappy... but I wouldn't exactly say happy, either."

"I mean, you did meet me around the time my flatmate passed away." I nudge him and he shrugs, clearly standing by his earlier statement. "I don't think I'm that different to other people though. Most people I know want a stable career, to be married by thirty and have children."

"Ah yes... the social norms!" Ryan exclaims, shaking

his head.

"It's hard not to listen to them though, especially as a woman. We're expected to want those things. It's hard differentiating between what I want and what I'm made to feel I should want, you know?"

"Yeah, I totally get it. It's hard finding your own voice when there are so many pressures around you." He pauses. "But the most important thing is that you actually evaluate the choices you make in life to determine the real reason you're doing them."

I nod. "Yeah. I guess you're right."

"Always am." He winks.

"That was deep." I exhale. "No giving me a break, even on the day of a funeral, huh?" I nudge him playfully, causing a smirk to form across his mouth. His eyes linger on my face for a little while and he bites down slowly on his bottom lip.

We finally reach my apartment, and Ryan turns to me, stopping just outside of the main door. I ask if he wants to come in, but he shakes his head, saying he has to go to work early tomorrow.

My stomach drops in disappointment. It's not even that late and he already wants to disappear again. I get the feeling he doesn't want a repeat of the other night.

"I'll see you at my gig this weekend though, right?"

I nod silently and he smiles.

"Good. See you later, kid," he replies, ruffling my hair with his hand.

Is he serious right now?

He drops his skateboard on the floor and rides down the street, disappearing around the corner. If I wasn't so stung, I'm sure I'd find watching him skate pretty attractive.

When I get to my room, I change into my pyjamas and lie on my bed, staring at the ceiling. My eyes brim with frustrated tears. I wipe them away, trying to supress the aching feeling in my chest and the draw to climb out of bed and head in the direction of the food cupboard.

Just as I'm beginning to fall to sleep, I hear keys unlock the apartment door. I sit up, waiting for whoever it is to go to the kitchen. I figure I should go and see my flatmates after the day we've all had.

"She's so ridiculous though!" I hear Alice shriek as soon as she enters the apartment. "She abandons us again for that stupid boy when today was about Kady!"

I creep to my bedroom door to eavesdrop. I wonder what drama went down at the Guild this time.

I hear Jake shush Alice, trying to silence her. "Be quiet, she might hear you!" he says.

Wait.

They're talking about me?

I press my ear to the door.

"I don't care! I can't stand her and I'm sick of pretending otherwise. I never wanted to live with her this year, Kady forced me into it." Alice huffs.

I feel a sharp pain through my chest and fresh tears prick my eyes.

Alice was with her athletics friends all night, how is my being with Ryan any different?

I don't get what her problem is.

And why didn't Jake stick up for me?

I walk back to my bed and grab my headphones, turning up the volume as far as it'll go to block everything out; today, Ryan, my housemates, everything.

Chapter Twenty

I thought Emily would be on my case about my lacklustre customer service today, but she didn't say a word. I spent most of the day absentmindedly staring out of the shop window instead of paying attention to the goings on inside the store. I assume she let me off the hook as it was my first day back since Kady died.

"Okay, you're not going to the gig tonight with this frown on your face!" Emily smiles, looking at me through the dressing room mirror. I roll my eyes at her and force the biggest smile my muscles will allow.

We decided to get ready for the gig together after we closed the store, bringing our make-up bags and curling irons to the customer dressing rooms. Emily has her own music playing through the store's speakers too, her favourite R&B songs blaring loud. I feel like I'm at a nightclub, not my place of work with my manager.

I sigh as I open my eyeshadow palette, choosing a bronze colour to apply to my lids. I know I need to lighten up before tonight, but my head is scrambled.

I've hardly slept these past few days. Thoughts of Kady and Alice and Ryan jumbled through my mind like one giant tidal wave.

"What are you going to wear tonight?" I try to divert the conversation.

"I have a black jumpsuit, but I'm going to wear my white Converse. Where are your clothes? You're not wearing your work uniform, are you?"

"No, I forgot to bring them up. I'll just go change now," I tell Emily, hopping up and making my way to the staff door.

"Grab the drink!" she yells back.

When I get downstairs, I pull on my glittery oversized t-shirt and tuck it into my black high-waisted jeans. I throw my work uniform into my locker along with my makeup bag before lacing up my Dr Martens platform boots.

After grabbing Emily's bottle of vodka from the staff fridge, I find some cups to drink out of, balancing it all in my arms as I make my way back to the shop floor.

"Woah, look at you!" Emily beams at me as she throws her bags behind the cashier desk. I ignore her compliment and pass her the bottle of vodka and three glasses.

We hear a knock on the shop door and turn to find Nadine waving at us from outside. She looks stunning in a black and gold crop top with tight jeans, showing off her perfect figure. Both Emily and Nadine look like supermodels with their washboard stomachs and long legs. I feel so out of place next to them.

As I unlock the shop door and Nadine walks in, I quickly introduce her to Emily and watch them both gush over how pretty the other is and how excited they are to party tonight. They click so instantly you'd think they've known each other for years, not mere seconds.

"Can we take shots now?" Emily darts straight for the vodka bottle on the till.

"Hell *yes*," Nadine replies with a devilish grin.

Emily pours the shots, and we knock them back.

I shiver. "Ugh, that's strong."

"Tonight is going to be fun!" Nadine chimes, flapping her hands around excitedly. "Are you nervous to see Ryan?" she asks. I immediately shoot her a warning glare. But it's too late.

"Why would you be nervous?" Emily demands. "Did

I miss something?"

"No, no," I assure her, waving my hands.

"I think he likes her, but she thinks they're just friends," Nadine says with a sigh. She glances in my direction, and I flash her another pleading look. "Zoe, stop freaking out. Emily would be the best person to ask about this situation. You know him quite well, right?" She turns to face Emily.

"Uh huh, he's like my brother," she replies sweetly. "Zoe, Nadine's right. I'm not going to tell anyone, especially not Ryan. He might be like a brother, but girl code comes first!"

Nadine raises her empty glass to cheers Emily. "So, you think he likes her?"

"I think so, and my brother Tyler said the same thing." She pauses. "But we've never known him to have a girlfriend or anything before."

"As in, because he doesn't date or because he keeps them a secret?" Nadine asks. I actually love the fact she's asking all the questions I'm too afraid to.

"I dunno." Emily shrugs. "A bit of both. He's never had anything serious enough to let us know about it, but I know he gets a lot of attention."

I lower my eyes to the floor, not wanting Emily to see my reaction.

"Well, if he's a bust, we'll just have to find you someone else!" Nadine laughs, placing her hands on my shoulders and running her fingers through the tips of my curly hair. "And maybe someone for me too."

I'm relieved when Emily and Nadine delve into a conversation about their relationship statuses, no longer prying into mine. I learn that Nadine is completely single after getting out of a messy situation with a guy last year. She seems over it, which I'm glad about. He sounds like an asshole.

"Shit, we better go. We'll miss the start of the gig if we don't hurry," Emily says, quickly pouring each of us one last shot of vodka before we head out.

As we stand outside the giant brick music venue, my nerves take over. My heart starts racing. My palms start sweating. My chest feels tight. My breathing quickens.

It's going to be fine.

We follow Emily, who skips the massive queue outside and goes straight to the front, giving the staff our names. I hand my ID to the bouncer, trying to steady my trembling hands. We're let through and Nadine hooks a comforting arm through mine as we walk inside.

The club is already full of people milling about next to the bar, loud pop music blaring through the speakers. The huge stage is completely empty, minus the band's equipment, and I scan the room for them.

"They'll be backstage," Emily says, leaning into my ear. I nod and try my best to act as if I wasn't trying to look for Ryan.

"Thanks for inviting me! This is going to be amazing!" Nadine says brightly as she starts to guide us towards the busy bar. I groan in protest, not wanting to spend all night trying to get served by overwhelmed bar staff.

"No, follow me. We get free drinks in the VIP area," Emily explains as she walks across the empty dance floor, towards a metal staircase in the corner. She says something to the hostess manning the area and the girl lets us through.

Emily leads us up to a pretty narrow viewing balcony with only enough room to fit a row of black leather VIP booths between the brick wall and the railings. From here we have a perfect view of everything.

I walk over to the railings and stare out at the empty stage, picturing Ryan performing. Excitement finally overtakes my nerves at the thought of hearing his voice again.

The pretty blonde hostess walks towards us with some kind of electronic tablet, asking us for drink orders. Emily orders for us, and Nadine wriggles excitedly in her seat.

Once the hostess leaves, Emily excuses herself to go to the bathroom and Nadine immediately leans across the table with wide, eager eyes.

"Are you excited to see Ryan?" she asks, beaming.

"I feel nervous," I admit, fluttering my eyelids away from her.

I look around the venue and realise how packed the place is, so many people have come out to watch The Lanes. There's no way Ryan's going to speak to me tonight. He'll be way too preoccupied. I just hope it's not with another girl.

"So, you really don't know where you stand with him?" Nadine asks.

I shake my head. "Not at all."

I'm relieved when Emily returns to the table. Within a few seconds, the blonde waitress also reappears, carrying a tray full of drinks.

I pick up a tiny shot glass and tilt my head back, allowing the brown liquid to trickle down my throat. The bitter taste makes me shudder, it's so much worse than the vodka.

Grabbing one of the cocktails from the table, I take a gulp to wash away the horrible alcohol clinging to my mouth, the sweet vodka lemonade flushing out the tequila.

"The warmup act will be coming on any second. We should go downstairs and get a good spot in the crowd," Emily says.

As soon as I stand up, I feel lightheaded as the alcohol courses through my body. I look at Emily and Nadine, who both appear as disorientated as me.

We stumble down the metal stairs whilst the warmup act walks onto the stage, fearlessly pushing our way into the middle of the crowd, securing a space as close to the front as we can manage.

The warmup band are good, but I can't focus. I keep looking around in case I spot Ryan somewhere.

"I need another drink," I shout to the others over the music.

Emily smirks at me, lifting a metal hip flask from the inside of her jumpsuit. I can't believe she snuck her own alcohol in when we get free drinks all night. Although, the thought of stumbling back up those metal stairs to place an order makes me feel grateful she had the foresight to bring her own supply.

I giggle as she unscrews the cap and knocks some back before passing it to me. I smell the top and instantly recognise the pungent alcohol. Vodka.

I take a drink and pass it to Nadine, who takes an even bigger gulp. I can't stop laughing at her as she confidently knocks back the strong spirit.

We turn to face the stage and I sway gently to the unfamiliar music, all the while continuing to scan the edges of the stage.

Finally, I spot Tyler at the side, hanging behind a thick black curtain separating the backstage from the crowd. I nudge Emily and point towards him. She waves her hands frantically in the air to get her brother's attention. He eventually notices us and waves back with a grin.

Tyler turns away for a second and pulls Ryan out of the dark backstage, closer to the curtain's edge. His eyes scan the crowd in the direction Tyler is pointing and I wait until his eyes finally land on me. He looks good, no... *incredible* in slim black jeans and an oversized denim shirt. The sleeves of his shirt are rolled up to reveal his small scattering of tattoos.

He looks directly at me with a huge grin on his face and winks. I feel a rush of butterflies as I smile back, the corners of my mouth stretching from ear to ear.

He mouths, "*You look great!*" giving me a thumbs up signal.

I bring my hand to my mouth to hide my smile and shrug slightly. The alcohol makes me feel confident enough to mouth, "*You too!*" back at him.

Oblivious to my silent conversation with Ryan, Emily wraps her arm over my shoulder and pushes the hip flask towards me. I look up at Ryan, he's chuckling as he watches me take a long drink of alcohol and shudder at the bitter taste.

"And you're telling me he doesn't like you?" Nadine leans into my ear, smirking. I laugh and shake my head. "Have more faith in yourself, girl," she continues. "By the way, the guy stood next to him is *hot*. You never told me Ryan had hot bandmates."

"That's Emily's brother."

"No *way*," Nadine gasps. "Emily! You never told me your brother was hot."

Emily turns to face us, mock horror on her face. "Gross. I thought Zoe crushing on my adopted brother was bad enough."

"I'm not crushing on Ryan," I groan. Both Emily and Nadine turn to face me and theatrically roll their eyes at the same time.

The crowd suddenly erupts, and I realise we just

missed the warmup act introducing The Lanes. Everyone is buzzing as the band rush onto the stage.

I can't tear my eyes off of Ryan as he confidently takes his central spot, talking to the audience, psyching them up for the show. The crowd are lapping up every single word and I feel a strange sense of pride as I watch him move with so much confidence. He's a natural.

The band begin to play the introduction to their first song. Nadine and Emily are both gripping my hands, and they immediately begin moving their bodies in time to the song, swaying effortlessly to the rhythm.

Despite the alcohol pulsing through my body, my feet remain frozen in place and all I can manage is a tiny, rigid sway. I suddenly feel conscious of the fact that I've never properly danced in a club or at a concert with anyone before. I have no idea what to do and my body stiffens as I feel Ryan's eyes on me.

As if sensing my panic, Emily pulls out her hip flask once again and ushers me to take another gulp. I oblige, taking a bigger drink than before and passing it back to her. Both Nadine and Emily take one of my hands again and I copy their moves, slowly rocking my hips to the beat of the music.

I close my eyes.

I take in the music, letting it run through my body,

losing myself in Ryan's voice.

I finally forget where I am, unlocking my hands from my friends' and lifting them in the air as I twist and sway.

"He can't stop looking at you," Nadine shouts into my ear. I snap my eyes open, feeling a rush of excitement pulse through me.

My eyes land on Ryan who, as Nadine said, has his eyes locked on me as he sings. I can't help but stare back. I continue to dance and even start to sing along to the chorus, remembering some of their songs from practice last week.

Ryan is smiling as he sings, his beautiful velvet voice filling the room. It pierces right through me, straight to my very core. I relax into the music, locking eyes with him as if we're the only ones in the huge venue.

I tear my eyes away from his gaze, only for a second, but long enough to see a group of girls with longing expressions, staring at Ryan as he stares at me. They momentarily follow his gaze in my direction and their eyes turn to venom as they find the source of his gaze.

I've never been in this situation before. Usually, I'm the girl who is invisible, unnoticed. Not that my feelings of insignificance bother me, far from it. It always felt comforting to know no one was looking at me or watching my every move. But I can't help but feel a little giddy, lapping up Ryan's attention and enjoying having the eyes of the hottest guy on me.

The alcohol has hit me properly now, but I don't feel out of control.

I feel good.

I feel free.

I'm high on my lack of inhibitions. Ryan and the music are taking me so far from reality that I don't ever want to come down.

Chapter Twenty-One

At the end of the set the crowd go wild, begging the band to play an encore. Ryan is smiling so hard—it makes my whole body melt. He's in his element. His stage presence is magnetic. His passion so obvious.

This is the fire he spoke about; this is the fire he wants me to have with my own career.

He was right. I *need* to feel it.

I never knew it would feel this exhilarating to watch Ryan jump around on stage, belting out his lyrics and singing along with the audience. The way he nodded his head and danced to the beat of his own songs, completely lost in his own world, makes me want him even more.

Tonight has made me realise just how much I like

Ryan. If I'm honest with myself, I think I've felt that way for a while. I just know it's not realistic. Whilst seeing him on stage sparks something in the very core of my heart, it also makes me realise how undeserving I am. He can do better than me. I know it. He probably knows it.

I'm so deep in my own thoughts, I don't notice when the venue turns into a nightclub. I didn't see the band walk off stage, nor did I notice the crew clearing the set and replacing the instruments with a large mixing desk.

"Let's go find them," Emily yells over the music.

As Nadine and I follow her off the dance floor, I suddenly feel a hand on my wrist. I swing around to find the source of contact.

"What did you think?" Ryan smiles at me with a confidence that suddenly makes me hungry to close the gap between us.

I turn around and wrap my arms around him. He returns my eager embrace and lifts me off the floor, his arms around my waist.

"Ryan, you were so amazing! Honestly, incredible," I gush into his neck, still embracing him tightly. I can hear him faintly chuckle as he grips me tighter.

My mouth is against his ear, and I fight the temptation to plant a kiss there, even though my whole body is itching to be as close to him as possible.

As Ryan lowers me to the floor, he holds both of my hands and I steal a look over his shoulder to see the same group of girls that were giving me daggers during his set. I immediately shift my eyes away from them to look at the floor, but a huge smile grows across my lips.

I eventually look up at Ryan, who isn't paying any attention to the girls whatsoever. Instead, his eyes are studying my face with a smug look that turns my insides to slush.

"Come on, let's go upstairs." He cocks his head towards the metal staircase. I respond with a nod, practically floating when he keeps one of my hands tightly intertwined with his.

By the time we get upstairs, the others are already sat in one of the VIP booths with a huge bottle of vodka in the middle of the table. Nadine is next to Tyler. He has an arm wrapped around the back of the booth where she's sitting. She beams up at me as she shuffles closer to him, making room for me and Ryan to sit down.

"Hey, I'm Ryan, you must be Nadine," Ryan says, shooting out his hand towards her.

"That's me. You guys were so good. I can't believe I've never seen you play before."

"Thanks, that means a lot," Ryan replies with a huge grin.

"That has to be one of our best shows yet. Don't you think?" Tyler adds.

"I reckon it had something to do with the audience," Ryan replies, turning to give me a knowing wink. I bow my head to try and hide a giggle.

"You mean, because your big sister was in the audience for once?" Emily says from across the table. Tyler rolls his eyes at her and shakes his head.

Emily turns away to nestle into the guy next to her. I immediately recognise him; it's her boyfriend, Sam. I'm glad he finally made it out of work to meet us. By the looks of things, so is Emily.

Adam pours a round of drinks for everyone. I sit this one out, realising Ryan must be totally sober in comparison.

Ryan downs his drink and pulls me closer, snaking an arm around me. My legs are completely pressed against his. I lean into him but try not to get ahead of myself as a giddy feeling sweeps over me.

I need to chill. We're just friends. He won't want more.

"You look fucking beautiful tonight, Zo," Ryan whispers into my ear, his head lingering close to my face. His fingers trace the back of my neck, drawing circles around and around, teasing me.

After a moment, I feel his mouth move to kiss my ear lobe. It's just how I imagined kissing him downstairs. The touch of his lips sends adrenaline sparking through my body. My hand instinctively grabs at his thigh, and I hear him let out a tiny moan.

I open my eyes and glance around the table, suddenly aware of our surroundings, but no one is looking our way. I keep my hand on Ryan's thigh, slowly running it up and down as he strokes the hair on the nape of my neck.

Holy *crap*, my body is on fire.

His head is only inches from mine, and I know if I turn to look at him, I won't be able to control the urge to kiss him. I reach for a cold drink, taking a sip to help calm me down.

We sit in a comfortable silence as we watch our friends, all in their own little worlds. Emily is kissing her boyfriend, whilst Tyler and Nadine latch onto each other's every word. Despite Ryan telling me Claire and Adam are only friends, I have to admit, they also look pretty cosy, leaning into each other and looking at something on Claire's phone.

"I love this song," I breathe as the DJ plays a remix of *Wings* by Birdy. I gently sway to the song in my seat, thinking about how we listened to it in Ryan's car after the cheer initiation night. I wonder if he remembers.

Ryan jumps out of the booth and stands up, holding a hand out for me. "Let's dance," he says, smiling. He leans over the table to take another shot before pulling me away and down the metal stairs to the dance floor.

I try to ignore all the eyes that are on Ryan as we make our way to the middle of the dance floor. He's completely oblivious to the attention, only concentrating on one pair of eyes... mine.

We face each other and he wraps one hand around my waist, pulling me closer to him. I put both of my hands around his neck, clutching at the collar of his thick denim shirt. I bite my bottom lip as I continue to stare at his face. He looks back at me with fierce eyes.

We both confidently move to the song, keeping our hands on each other the whole time. I can't believe how easy it feels with him. I raise my hands in the air and he runs his fingers up and down the side of my waist.

The fireworks in my body make me lower my hands. I push my fingers through his mop of hair, and he pulls me closer to him, my body pressing against his.

He uses his hand to tilt my chin up so our eyes meet and leans his head a little closer.

I know what's coming. I can feel it. And I want it so fucking badly.

Finally, he brings his lips to mine, kissing me with

gentle force and cupping my head in his hands. The shape of his soft lips match perfectly with mine.

He runs his hands down the back of my hair, and I open my mouth to let his tongue glide across mine. We move in perfect harmony.

Chapter Twenty-Two

I can't resist the smile that lights up my face when Ryan pulls away from our kiss.

But as our eyes meet, I see an emotion flash across his eyes that I can't read. His expression brings me crashing back to Earth, my heart plummeting to my stomach.

"I can't be your boyfriend," he says into my ear.

For a moment, I stand still; confused and dazed and still panting from our kiss. Maybe I didn't hear him correctly over the music.

Luckily, I have the confidence of the alcohol pulsing through my body, helping me to recompose myself. "I never asked you to be," I say flatly.

"I just don't know how to act around you, Zo." He wipes his hand across his forehead, looking at me blankly.

The alcohol takes over and I step closer to him, gripping his shirt in my hands and drawing him towards me. "You should act however you want to act."

He smiles, placing a hand on my shoulder and pushing us apart. "I am, kid."

Ouch.

He takes another step away from me and rubs his thumb and index finger along his bottom lip. He laughs awkwardly, shaking his head, as if having an internal conversation with himself.

I don't bother to ask what he's thinking. The confident exterior I was trying to maintain for the sake of my pride and self-worth shatters into a million pieces on the dance floor.

Well, I feel totally crushed. I don't understand how he has the ability to make me feel like I'm the only girl in the world one moment, and a silly child the next. My head is going to explode. I need to get away from him.

I walk off the dance floor and back up to the table. He doesn't even try to stop me.

I repeat his words over and over in my mind.

I am, kid.

Does he mean he's acting how he wants to by kissing

me? Or that he's acting how he wants by pulling away?

I've had too many drinks to think clearly, but instead of trying to sober up and get some clarity, I pour myself a shot of vodka and sit next to Nadine with a huff.

"Are you okay?" she whispers, eyeing me. I press my lips in a firm line and shake my head. "Where's Ryan?" she asks, looking over my shoulder. I shrug without saying a word.

"He's probably gone to talk to his management, they came over here looking for him just now," Claire says, standing up from her seat across the booth and sitting in the empty space on the other side of me.

I don't reply, focussing instead on trying to hide my emotions.

"Did he tell you he's been signed?" Claire presses, completely unaware of my mood. I give her a vacant stare, letting her know I have no idea what she's on about. "He's releasing a solo album and should be going on tour over summer," she gushes excitedly.

What the hell?

It's not the fact that he's going solo that shocks me. He has so much talent it's unsurprising he got signed by a label. It's the fact he kept it from me. Why hasn't he told me this big news? Surely, that would be one of the first things you'd tell a friend.

"But what about your band?" I eventually ask.

Tyler leans across Nadine to join our conversation, explaining that Ryan's had a lot of attention recently from different labels. The band seem really excited for him to venture out on his own. I'm surprised by how much they support him, but I guess they are friends before bandmates.

"He definitely deserves a break after all the shit he's dealt with," Claire adds.

"You mean his dad?" I ask.

She nods. "Sure. He's gone through a lot, and I think music helps him so much." Claire looks at me as if she's searching my face for something, but I just stare at her blankly, still trying to control my burning emotions.

She eventually sighs and adds, "Don't let how distant he acts sometimes get to you too much, Zoe. I know he can be difficult to read, but his intentions are good, I promise." She places a hand on my knee.

I find it hard to believe Claire, the feeling of rejection is still too raw. My eyes sting from trying to fight back the tears I'm desperate to shed. I turn to face Nadine who registers my emotions.

"Shall we go?" Nadine mouths. I shake my head. I don't want her to leave, she's having so much fun with Tyler.

I stand up. "I'm going to go. I don't feel well. I think it's all the alcohol," I say.

Nadine offers to come with me again, but I decline, promising to call her tomorrow. I know the band will have an afterparty at their house and I don't want her to miss out on my account.

I quickly say goodbye to everyone and dart away from the table before anyone has time to protest. I run down the metal staircase just as I feel the tears begin to fall down my cheeks.

I'm glad Ryan is still nowhere to be seen. I know I'd just find him clinging onto a prettier, skinnier, *better* girl.

Why did he have to kiss me if he didn't really mean it? It doesn't make sense. If he wanted to just be friends, why even take the risk of ruining it for one tiny moment?

I walk outside, letting the bitter evening air fill my nostrils. I walk straight over to the line of black taxis and climb into one, giving the driver my address. I text Nadine to have a good night before switching off my phone.

Chapter Twenty-Three

"I'm sorry," I mumble for what feels like the millionth time today as I scramble to pick myself up off the sprung floor.

I haven't landed my tumble once this cheer practice, and I know Kim must be freaking out. Our big firework performance is this weekend. We don't have time for my mistakes.

I've been given a moment in the routine to perform a solo tumble sequence. It's a huge deal and a massive opportunity, but I can't land it. I keep falling on my ass every time I try to stick the last twist.

"It's okay, Zoe. This is the first day you haven't executed this. I know you can do it. You know you can do it. We've got all week to get this right, it's only Monday. Plus, we can always simplify it if we need to, but I know we don't need to. You've performed it perfectly every single practice before today," Kim says softly. I was not expecting that response at all. I was waiting for her to scold me.

"Okay," I grumble, defeated. I wipe my sweaty hands across my shorts.

"We've been practicing for three hours straight. You're probably just tired and in your own head," she continues.

I nod and turn to look at the rest of the squad sitting at the edge of the mat, using my tumble practice as an opportunity for a break. The session today has been *killer*.

I look straight at Nadine, who has her eyes fixed on us. She smiles sympathetically.

"I think you just need a break. A proper break. Go take a seat with the other girls. We can go again in a little while," Kim says.

I walk over to Nadine and take a seat on the floor next to her.

"Your phone has been vibrating every two seconds," she says.

I pull my phone from my bag just as it starts to ring. Ryan's name flashes across the screen and I quickly hit decline. He called me just as frequently yesterday, but I couldn't face him, not so soon. It's only been two days since the gig. I need more time.

"Do you wanna talk about it?" Nadine asks, staring at my phone's lock screen, eyeing the number of missed calls.

I shrug. *Do* I want to talk about it? I have no idea.

"Kim?" Nadine yells across the gymnastics hall, causing the room to fall silent. "Would it be okay if we went to get a drink?"

Kim pauses for a moment before nodding sharply. "Sure. Everyone, take thirty minutes! Be back here by seven," she instructs.

Nadine puts her arm through mine and practically marches us out of the sports hall and into the chilly night.

"Spill," she demands.

I sigh. "Okay, so... Ryan kissed me at the gig."

Nadine lets out a squeal, flapping her hands excitedly.

"No, no," I say, waving my hands in the air. "Don't get excited. He kissed me, pulled away and then said he couldn't be my boyfriend... and then he called me *kid*."

Nadine groans. "What is with this guy?" she asks as we make our way into the coffee shop.

I'm grateful that this place is always open late.

Caffeine is vital if I have a hope in hell of executing these tumbles.

I order both our drinks and meet Nadine at a table.

"So yeah, he called me a few times yesterday and again today. I don't know what he wants, but I'm not ready to face him yet. I feel so embarrassed," I say, smacking my hands to my forehead.

Nadine immediately pulls my hands from my face and wraps her fingers through mine. "Zoe. Stop this. *You* have nothing to be embarrassed about. It's him that should be embarrassed."

"You think?"

"Yes! Zoe, look at me." I do as she says. "You are amazing, and if he can't see that then it's his loss."

I laugh gently. "It's just so ridiculous how we're literally sat in the same place, having the same conversation about him. When will I learn?" I groan.

Nadine chuckles, shaking her head. "Never. Because you like him. And he likes you too. He's just being an idiot." She briefly pauses. "I wasn't sure whether to tell you this because I don't want to get your hopes up, but when he came back to the table at the gig, he kept asking where you were. He was pissed you left. And when we got back to their house for the afterparty, he just shut himself in his room. Tyler said he's normally the last one to go to bed, but this time he didn't even stick around for one drink."

"Then why behave the way he did?" I ask, more confused than before.

"I dunno. It's like he's trying not to like you, but then he just can't help it?"

I take a sip of my coffee and place the cup back on the table. "I guess I don't actually know that much about him. He's kind of a closed book."

"And until he learns to grow up and open up to you, I think you have to be careful."

"You're right." I sigh. "So, tell me about Tyler. All I know is you went to the afterparty and stayed overnight with him. Have you exchanged numbers?"

"Yeah, he asked for my number and he's picking me up from practice tonight just to drop me home. How sweet is that? And then he wants to take me on a date tomorrow," she gushes, her eyes gleaming.

"Ah, that's nice! What are you going to do for your date?"

"He said it's a surprise. He's planned everything." Nadine claps her hands in front of her mouth and a grin spreads across her face.

"That's amazing," I say, trying to give my biggest smile and hoping Nadine doesn't notice how forced it is.

It's not that I'm not happy for her, I'm beyond happy. They seem like a great match. I just can't shake the burning jealousy. Why can't it be this simple with Ryan? Why doesn't he want me the way Tyler wants Nadine? Is he embarrassed? Ashamed?

"Come on, we'd best get back to practice so you can execute these tumbles, girl! You got this."

Chapter
Twenty-Four

I face my full-length mirror and carefully apply red lipstick, trying to control my trembling hands so I don't smudge it all over my face. It doesn't help that I just threw up, now my breath is so ragged, my whole body is shaking.

Kim gave us all clear instructions on how we should apply our makeup for the big firework event tonight. I've spent the past two hours putting on gold eyeshadow and jet-black eyeliner, trying to make each eye match perfectly.

The music seeping through my earphones is keeping me sane as I finish getting ready, pinning my gold bow in place. I turn the playlist up loud enough so I can't hear myself think. The OneRepublic songs try their best to drown out any thoughts I have about seeing Ryan today.

I can't believe that after a week of ignoring his calls and texts, he's actually coming to our event tonight. I only know this because Nadine told me he's coming. She got the info from Tyler after spending almost every day with him this week.

I'm not sure if I'm excited or angry about seeing Ryan. I haven't actually wanted to ignore him. Every time he calls, I'm itching to answer, but I've forced myself to be strong.

Although, how strong will I be if he's actually standing in front of me?

All I know is, I can't get pulled back in again. I can't become consumed by him. I'll only get hurt.

Once I finally admitted to myself how much I really do like him, I've not been able to ignore it. Fireworks erupt from my stomach every time I just think his name in my head. It's too much. Especially when he goes from kissing me to calling me kid in the blink of an eye.

He's like one of those rollercoasters you get at theme parks—you know, the ones that are indoors and pitched black so you can't see where you're going. One minute you're exhilarated, climbing high. The next you're plummeting to the ground at lightning speed.

And I think I want to get off.

I remove my sweats and change into black spandex shorts, staring in the mirror at how unflattering the tiny, tight shorts are on my chunky legs. I put on the bright red team t-shirt, carefully easing it over my head so as not to disrupt the perfectly positioned gold bow. Why I didn't just put the t-shirt on before pinning the bow in place, I don't know.

Even without spending the morning with my head over the toilet, my body feels so fragile. Nerves float through every limb and I feel as if I could snap at any moment. Will I still feel this delicate when we perform? There's no way I'll be able to hold my stunt girl in the air and execute all my tumbles if I can't shake this feeling. It'll be the first time in Panther's history that a stunt drops at firework night.

I see Nadine's name flash across my phone screen. I grab my denim jacket and meet her downstairs, rushing through the door and jumping into the back of Tyler's pristine, electric blue Honda Civic.

"Thanks for picking me up." I smile at them as I climb into the car.

"How do you feel?" Nadine turns around in the front seat to face me.

"Nervous... and excited, I guess. It's gunna be a huge event." I exhale.

"You'll be amazing. We're all buzzing to watch you guys!" Tyler smiles and squeezes Nadine's leg. It's weird seeing how quickly they've slotted into a relationship. I won't even entertain thoughts of Ryan and how I wish we could get to a place like this. I won't let thoughts of him ruin tonight. I won't.

I don't respond to Tyler's comment, I just look out of the car window, focussing on the trees lining the road.

Tyler drives through the north campus gate, taking us as close to the American football pitch as possible.

"Your campus is *nice*," he exclaims, looking at the tall clock tower and Victorian red brick buildings with an open mouth as he pulls to a stop.

I always forget how impressive the campus is when you first see it. I had the exact same reaction when I stepped off the train at University Station for my first campus tour. I knew I would go here, whatever it took.

We hop out of the car. Tyler climbs out too, rushing to Nadine's side and holding her hand. He walks us towards the sports fields, pointing at each building in awe as we pass. He chats away freely, Nadine clinging onto every word.

We say goodbye to Tyler once we reach the football field. I look away as he gives Nadine a deep kiss. She giggles and pulls away, hooking her arm through mine as we descend the steps towards a cluster of gold bows and red tops.

"Hey girls, you look stunning!" Kim walks over to us, giving us a hug. She looks unbelievable. Her tanned legs go on for days and her shorts hug her petite figure perfectly. Her long brown hair looks glossier than ever; each ringlet has been curled with such precision, every single one looks identical to the other.

We spend the next hour drilling our stunt routine and marking the dance moves in an effort to warm up on this chilly autumn night. The chill is made so much worse by our ridiculously small sports shorts. I want to personally murder whoever made this uniform a tradition.

"Okay girls, remember we have to stick together during the first half of the game, cheering on the side-lines. But after our performance, you are free to do as you please!" Kim announces with a squeal as we walk to our side-line position.

I take my spot next to Nadine and glance around the pitch. I hadn't noticed how quickly the field began to fill with spectators. The hill is completely packed full of people all dressed in red, blue and gold with paint on their faces and huge Panthers banners.

"Have you spotted them yet?" Nadine asks as she scans the crowd. I shake my head. I don't want to know where the band are, I don't want to get distracted during the performance. I just want to focus on not messing up.

"Tyler said he would wear a red hoodie so I could spot him," Nadine informs me.

I chuckle. "Everyone's wearing red hoodies. It's the team colour!"

She smacks her hand to her forehead, laughing, but she doesn't give up on finding the band. Her eyes are wild as they dart across at the mass of fans in the distance.

The commentator announces over the speakers that the game is about to begin. I barely understand the rules of American football, so I don't really watch the game, neither does Nadine. She fidgets next to me, fighting the temptation to go to her bag and check her messages from Tyler. Kim would flip out if Nadine dared move from her side-line position.

We cheer for the footballers when instructed by Kim and follow her lead for reactions to the game. When I've had enough of watching, I call over to Kim and ask her if I can warm up a little more, feeling my body stiffen from the chilly air.

"No fair! Why do you get to escape this awful game and I don't?" Nadine sulks, sticking out her bottom lip.

"Because you don't tumble."

"Smart ass. I hope you fall on your head." Nadine

glares at me as I walk away from the group.

"Enjoy the game," I call out to her, grinning. She tries to stifle a chuckle, but when I give her my middle finger, she lets out a cackle, earning a warning glare from Kim.

Once free of my painful cheer duties, I start stretching and jogging around on the spot, hoping to shake out my jitters. As soon as I limber up, I stand holding one leg in the air in a heel stretch.

"Nervous?" someone asks. I turn and notice one of the substitute football players watching me stretch. I blush, dropping my leg back to the floor as he hugs his white helmet to his chest, smiling.

"Yeah, my heart is racing," I admit, blowing out a breath.

"I bet you'll do great. If you don't, you can just spend the night partying to forget about it," he replies with a cheeky grin, revealing his perfect teeth.

"Girls!" Kim yells. I snap my head in her direction. I say goodbye to the player and jog towards the rest of my team. "Girls, it's almost time! Good luck! We can do this; we've all worked so hard!" she squeals.

I find Nadine and we grab hands, giving each other a quick hug. The commentator announces our team and we run to the middle of the field, waving as the crowd erupts.

Chapter
Twenty-Five

Our performance was perfect. Every stunt went brilliantly—no mistakes or falls—and every dance move was exactly as choreographed. It felt amazing.

My tumble section was flawless, if I do say so myself. I thought I would hate all the attention, but it was actually pretty exhilarating.

We all left the pitch on a high, we couldn't stop hugging each other.

I finally understand the buzz of being on a sports team. I'll never judge my housemates for their obsession with competition squads again.

As I look up at the brilliant, starry night, I tell Kady that this is for her.

"Let's go find the band!" Nadine suggests eagerly.

I agree, not even caring about seeing Ryan anymore. I feel so confident, so high on adrenaline, I could handle anything. We go over to the side-line to grab our clothes, only to see the band already there, waiting for us.

Nadine rushes over to them and gives Tyler a huge hug. I follow slowly, pretending to be preoccupied with putting my hoodie and jacket on, taking my time to do up each button before padding over to them.

"My God, Zoe, you were incredible! I had no idea you could move like that!" Tyler beams, pulling me in for a hug as soon as I get close enough.

Ryan rushes forward as Tyler lets go of me and wraps his arms around me. "Fuck, you smashed it, Zo. It was epic. You're such a performer," he says into my hair, squeezing me quickly and then pulling away.

As soon as he lets go, he looks at me as if he is going to say something but meets my gaze and decides against it. He walks over to Adam and doesn't look back in my direction.

I ignore his behaviour, focussing instead on Nadine. She spends almost the entirety of the second half of the football game giving a play-by-play account of our routine, even though the band were there to witness the performance for themselves. They don't seem to mind one bit though.

Tyler keeps a hand on her shoulder as she talks, focussed intently on every single word she says. It's nauseatingly cute. He's so focussed on her; I doubt he even notices when our team win the game.

"Yo, tumble girl!" someone shouts by the now crowded dugout. It's the player I was talking to earlier.

I smile brightly as he gestures for me to go over to him. I leave the band, feeling their eyes burn the back of my head as I go.

"Here," the footballer says, reaching into a huge cardboard box, pulling out two bottles of prosecco. I look at him, confused, and he adds, "Did Kim not tell you? Each participant gets a bottle. I figured you and your other cheer friend would want yours." He points towards Nadine who is looking in our direction—along with the rest of the band. All of them quickly and awkwardly look away as soon as they see us turn towards them. Only Ryan keeps his eyes fixed on me.

"I'm Dan by the way," the footballer introduces himself, holding out a free hand.

"Nice to meet you. I'm Zoe." I shake his hand. "Thanks for letting me skip that queue." I laugh, nodding towards the large line of muddy American footballers mingling with cheerleaders, all waiting for their own bottles of alcohol.

"Don't sweat it. It's the least I could do for the star performer." He beams. I begin to walk away and as I reach the band, I hear Dan shout, "See you at the Guild!" before turning back to the rest of his teammates.

"Did he buy you that?" Ryan asks flatly as soon as I start unwrapping the foil on one of the bottles.

"No, he's handing out the free drink we get for performing," Nadine interjects, reaching across for hers. I give her a quick smile for saving me and she winks.

We open the bottles and take a huge gulp before passing them around the group. When one of the bottles gets to Ryan, he frowns at it before downing a swig. As he pulls the bottle from his lips, I instinctively smile at him. He playfully rolls his eyes back at me.

I'd been trying to give him as little attention as possible tonight because I don't want him to think he can get away with his crappy behaviour. But as soon as I see a slight frown on his face, my resolve turns to putty. I can't seem to shake the fact that I want to see him happy.

It doesn't take us long to finish the bottles. Claire and Adam go to one of the pop-up bars, getting us more drinks in time for the beginning of the firework display. Whilst we wait, numerous people walk past congratulating me and Nadine on our performance, sending us into fits of tipsy giggles.

"So, you guys are gunna be famous on campus now, right?" Tyler laughs, rolling his eyes. We both grin back at him.

"And beyond. We were on national TV, don't forget," Nadine retorts.

Tyler waves his hands and starts bowing in front of us. I give him a playful kick in the shin.

"You're dead, Jones." He smirks, grasping his hand around my waist and lifting me over his shoulder. I let out a scream as I feel him tickle me.

He eventually lowers me to my feet. I press my hands to my knees, taking a few seconds to regain my breath, eventually standing up straight with an aching stomach from all the laughter.

I turn towards Ryan, who's still pretty quiet. He has an empty expression on his face, looking into the distance with his hands in the pockets of his black denim jacket, not paying the three of us any attention.

Scooting closer to him, I try my best to bring him out of his daydream. He looks up and gives me a small, disingenuous smile. "You really were amazing tonight, Zo." He gives me a nudge with his elbow, still looking at the floor. He looks sad. I can't figure out why and I hate it.

I give his bicep a squeeze. His face softens slightly, and I confidently pull him in for a hug.

Claire and Adam come over and pass us our drinks. Neither Ryan nor I pull out of our hug as we take them in our spare hands.

Overhead, the fireworks start shooting and popping. Ryan spins me around so I can face the display. He keeps one arm around me, and I rest my head against his chest, looking up towards the glowing sky.

He leans down and plants a kiss on the top of my head, squeezing my shoulder with his hand at the same time. The action doesn't feel romantic or soppy, it feels almost apologetic. But, of course, it's enough for another set of fireworks to whizz inside my tummy. They're big enough to rival the ones overhead.

The display is incredible, so many bright colours float around in the sky. Every time a pink or purple one explodes, I think of Kady.

I've only ever seen firework displays like this at a distance, from my bedroom window at home on bonfire night or New Years. They look so much bigger and brighter up close, so much more magical. I jump and gasp at every one, pointing to all the pretty colours.

Ryan laughs at my reaction and pulls me tighter to him. He rests his chin on the top of my head and squeezes his arms around my chest.

Once the display comes to an end, the crowd starts to slowly disperse. Ryan doesn't remove his grip on me, instead we remain standing exactly as we are. I can't say I'm complaining one bit.

The rest of the band shuffle closer to us, looking between me and Nadine expectantly.

"What's happening at the Guild tonight?" Adam asks.

"Yeah, we overheard loads of people talking about it in the queue for the bar, and your football friend mentioned something, didn't he?" Claire adds. I feel Ryan tense next to me at the mention of Dan, but he doesn't say anything.

"Oh, it's the afterparty. You guys should come... but no pressure if it's not your thing." I shrug, trying to act casual.

"Count me in." Tyler winks at Nadine.

The others also agree to join us. I try to hide my smile when it becomes obvious that Ryan is coming too. He keeps an arm swung across my shoulder as we walk off the football pitch and towards the red brick archway back to the main campus.

The university roads are full of students walking in the same direction, all drinking and chanting in big groups as they head towards the bar.

When we get to the metal barriers and queue to get into the Guild, there are already hundreds of students stood outside in the courtyard, smoking and sitting on the ledge of the copper mermaid fountain, which looks a brighter shade of green thanks to the night lights illuminating it.

Inside, the main bar has been transformed into some sort of nightclub. All the seating has gone, and there's a DJ on a small stage in the corner next to a huge dance floor. Students hold up their cups as they sway and dance to the cheesy pop music.

I don't even have to look at the band to know it's not their type of venue, or their type of music. Nadine doesn't seem impressed either.

"You know, there are two other floors. Let's go downstairs, it's *so* much better in the basement," Nadine calls over the music and points towards the door.

I grab hold of Nadine's wrist as we push through a huge cluster of American football players loitering on the stairwell.

"Great performance, Zoe!" a few of the guys shout to me as we move. I've never seen them before in my life, I have no idea how they know my name. I blush and look behind me for the others.

Ryan catches up with me at the bottom of the stairs,

placing a hand on the small of my back as he eyes the group of guys.

Nadine pushes open the large red double doors to the basement floor and just like the upstairs area, it's packed.

"Let's go to the bar!" I shout to Ryan over the R&B music.

He follows me to the back of the room and, thankfully, there's no queue given almost everyone seems to be in the middle of the dance floor. I can understand why, this music is so much easier to dance to compared to what they were playing upstairs. The rest of the band seem happier too, bobbing along as we walk.

"I'm sorry if this place isn't your type of thing," I say to Ryan.

As we approach the bar, the girl serving looks Ryan up and down, nudging her co-worker. They both giggle like schoolgirls as they stare at him. I can't say I blame them.

After ordering our drinks, Ryan turns to me, wrapping his arm around my waist. "Don't apologise, I'm having fun," he assures me with a smile so bright it crinkles the corners of his eyes.

He tries to get his card out of his wallet to pay, but I beat him to it, tapping my card on the reader. He scowls at me but nonetheless picks up the tray of mixers and bottle of vodka.

The rest of the band are stood around a table near the bar, swaying to the music and watching the crowd on the dance floor. Once we reach them, we all take a couple of shots and mix ourselves longer drinks. The burn of the alcohol rushes through my body and reignites the high I felt after the performance.

"Let's dance!" Claire says, swaying in her seat. Adam snags the bottle from the table, taking it to the dance floor.

Ryan holds out his hand for me as we follow Claire towards the centre of the crowd. Nadine is right beside me with slightly bloodshot eyes and a huge grin on her face as she looks down at my fingers interlocked with Ryan's.

I love that she doesn't judge my decisions, even though they always seem to bite me in the ass the next day. I can't believe she's happy to be there for me regardless, no matter how self-inflicted my anguish is.

The band dance so easily to the music. I guess they're so used to performing that they have no problem dancing to the rhythm of any song. We all laugh and tipsily bob around as the alcohol makes us more relaxed.

I close my eyes and let the music take over my body.

I feel Ryan next to me, so I lean my head back, shimmying against him. He runs his hands up and down my waist and I feel the same electricity I always do whenever he touches me. I keep my eyes closed as we move, never wanting this moment to end, never wanting to be snapped back to reality by his impending, inevitable rejection.

When the song finishes, I open my eyes. Nadine meets my gaze just as one of her favourite songs comes on. Her eyes go wide as the girl group's voices fill the room. She squeals and grabs my hand, spinning me towards her. I ignore the cry my body makes at the loss of Ryan's touch.

We both sway our hips, dancing together in the same way we did at the band's gig. Who knew I could easily catch on to this dancing in a nightclub thing?

Our moment is interrupted when I suddenly feel a pair of rough hands around my waist. It takes me a moment to react. I thought they were Ryan's, but looking at Nadine's wide eyes, not to mention how rough and desperate these alien hands feel on my body, I know it can't be him.

I snap my head round, my heart pounding in my chest as I realise it's Dan. I pull away and immediately try to grab for Ryan's hand, but there are so many bodies around us, I feel like I'm about to drown.

Chapter
Twenty-Six

I'm using all the power in my body to resist the sea of
dancing bodies churning in every direction around me,
but Dan's sloppy hands are still all over my waist, gripping
me, squeezing my skin. I feel sick.

Finally, Ryan's hand connects with mine and he
yanks me with such a force that I'm by his side in a flash.
His jaw clenches as he stands next to me, watching Dan
like a hawk, ready to pounce.

Dan reaches out again, completely unaware of Ryan's
presence. He manages to stumble and put his arm around
my waist, almost pulling me back to him.

"Come here," he slurs. *Ugh*, he's absolutely wasted.

Panic rises in my chest. I steal a backwards glance

towards Ryan. He immediately moves out from behind me and steps in front, blocking me from Dan. He squares up to him, pushing his chest out.

"Back the fuck off," he growls. "*Now.*"

I edge closer to Ryan to make sure that if Dan tries to retaliate, I can pull Ryan away, or at least try to, I know in reality my efforts would be futile.

Dan recoils as he looks up at Ryan. I can't blame the guy; I would if I were him. Despite being an American footballer, Dan's practically half Ryan's size, and nowhere near as muscular.

Dan holds his hands up and stumbles away through the dance floor, murmuring that he was only trying to have fun. I let out a huge breath and smile at a scowling Ryan. I catch his eye and his shoulders relax a fraction as he wraps his arms around my shoulders and pulls me to his chest.

"Are you okay?" he asks. I nod, trying to diffuse his anger by taking his hands. He doesn't react to my touch. He's too busy watching Dan leave the basement.

I start dancing, feigning confidence in an effort to try to distract him. I'm not entirely sure what's come over me. All I know is that I don't want this night to be ruined by an idiotic football player.

Eventually, Ryan looks down at my hips moving to

the rhythm of the music. He smiles, shaking his head and swiping his thumb across his lips. His hands find my waist and he pulls me closer. I feel the tension leave his body as he moves with me, our bodies touching.

He holds his hand up, momentarily stopping still to pull something from the inside pocket of his jacket. A hip flask.

"I'm gunna need this after that fucking asshole," he begins, taking a huge swig of his drink. He pushes it towards me, and I take a long sip. "Are you sure you're okay though?" he asks, tucking the flask back into his pocket.

"Positive. I absolutely love it when creepy drunk guys grope me," I laugh, but Ryan just scowls. I roll my eyes, sighing. "Yes, I'm sure. I'm with you."

He beams and snatches me close to him again. It doesn't take us long to get lost in the music. We dance, laugh and completely empty his hip flask. We move closer and closer together, forgetting everyone else around us. I feel the music pulse through me, causing me to float on a high.

He brings one of his hands to my neck, removing any space between us.

A wave of familiarity passes through me. I know what's coming and I can't fight it, no matter what rejection is around the corner.

He leans down, biting his full lips and bringing them to mine. My mouth opens and my tongue glides across his. I run my hands through his hair, tugging at the thick strands. He gasps into my mouth and nips at my bottom lip. His hands move all over my body. His touch feels desperate somehow, pleading.

I want more. I *need* more.

But I know he won't ever give it to me.

I pull away sharply, pushing his chest with my hands. "I can't do this," I admit, shaking my head and backing away.

"Can we at least talk about it?" he shouts over the music, his eyes scanning my face. I nod and let him lead me away from the busy dance floor to the courtyard.

We find a corner by the edge of the mermaid fountain, it's the same spot we sat at the last time we were here, after Kady's funeral. Only this time the patio is brimming with people and the sound of thumping music coming from the bar can still be heard out here.

"Is everything okay?" Ryan asks, his brilliant hazel eyes now full of concern.

Why is he so worried? I'm not the one that rejected him the last time we were in this situation. *He* rejected me. And he continues to do so. Time and time again. How

201

has he forgotten that?

All I know is—I'm tired of it. I don't want to hide my feelings anymore and I'm fed up with pretending like his hot and cold attitude doesn't affect me.

"No. I can't do this, Ryan. You can't kiss me one minute, reject me the next and then kiss me again." I raise my hands in the air. "I'm sorry if I'm not good enough for you or whatever, but please, just *stop*." I feel a lump in my throat as it catches the last few words that tumble out of my mouth. I swallow it down. He's not getting the better of me this time. "You're messing with my head," I whisper.

"Don't *ever* say you're not good enough," he barks, looking to the floor.

I don't respond, terrified my tears will spill over and reveal my true feelings to the one person I need to guard them from the most. I swallow again, but the lump feels like it's permanently lodged in place.

"I'm sorry, Zoe. I really am. I just suck at this."

"A-at what?"

"At this." He waves his hands in the space between us. "I struggle to let people in."

I pause for a moment. I hate this weird place we're in, but bending to his will isn't good for me.

"No, you don't. You have the band. They're like

family to you. Why is it so difficult with me?" I demand. I'm surprised to hear the strength in my voice.

"You're different, you know you are. I want more with you." His hazel eyes meet mine, pleading with me to understand.

"More?" I whisper.

"Yes, more. Fúck, I want it all with you." He exhales. "I always told myself that I wouldn't get into anything serious with anyone, but then tonight I realised how stupid I've been. You're everything I could ever want, Zoe. If not more. And I know I'm going to lose you if I don't drop this shit." He shifts uncomfortably, running a hand through his hair and looking at the floor. "After my dad died, my mum broke. She totally fell apart without him. She's still completely shattered, and I can't stand to see her that way." He looks at me. "I didn't want to become like that. Or do that to someone else."

I inhale a sharp, cold breath.

Finally, I feel like I am beginning to understand.

"No one has control over life and death, Ryan. What happened to your family was a tragic accident." I try to comfort him, holding out my hand and taking his.

"I know, I know, and I realised today how stupid I've been to fight my feelings for you. I want to be with you. You have to believe me."

His words knock the breath out of me, and I stay frozen for a moment. I try to blink, but I'm scared if my eyes close for even a millisecond, I'll realise this was all in my head, that he didn't say the six words I've been dying to hear ever since I met him.

"I thought you didn't want me." I bite my lip to stifle my emotions. It doesn't work, I feel a warm tear escape from my eye.

Ryan puts a hand on my cheek, wiping it away with his thumb and tilting my head towards his. "I want you so bad, Zo, and I have for a while now. I've just been an idiot." He sighs. "The way you talk about music, your voice, everything. Fuck, you already mean so much to me." He shakes his head, never taking his eyes off me. "Do you know what I want?" he asks.

I tilt my head, waiting for him to continue.

"I want to experience life with you. I want us to feel young, forget what we're going through, and just be happy. Together."

I'm completely lost for words. I just stare at him, unable to move, blink or breathe.

"I'm sorry I made you feel shit tonight. Will you just give me a chance to show you I'm willing to make this work?" he asks.

Still unable to speak, I close the gap between us,

bringing my lips up to his, hoping my kiss answers his question. He wraps his arms around me, pulling me closer to him. He runs one hand through my hair, and I let out a small sigh.

"Can we get out of here?" he asks.

I nod and he takes my hand, leading us towards the campus gate.

"Do you mind if we go back to your place, not mine?" I ask Ryan as we walk towards to main road. I don't want to be anywhere near my apartment, especially with Ryan. I have successfully avoided Alice since the funeral, and I want to keep it that way.

He agrees and orders a cab on his phone.

I realise I should probably text Nadine to tell her that I'm going home with Ryan. A couple of seconds later I get her reply.

Nadine: No FREAKING way. Finally!
Nadine: I want to hear everything tomorrow.
Nadine: Be safe ;)

Me: OMG stop!

Nadine: Never. See you in their kitchen tomorrow morning ;) xx

I laugh to myself and put my phone back in my pocket.

"You know, you're the first girl I've ever wanted to date." Ryan turns to me as we stand outside the university gates. We lean against the small stone wall lining the road, looking out at the cars roaring past.

"Likely story." I scoff and roll my eyes.

He laughs. "No, seriously. I mean it."

"So, nothing happened with anyone after your gig?" I can't stop myself before the question tumbles out of my mouth.

"Not at all. Why would you think that?" he asks with a frown.

I shrug. "Just curious."

"No way. Don't get me wrong, I used to mess around before, but I haven't been able to think about or even look at anyone else since I met you." He reaches to tuck a loose strand of my hair behind my ear. "You really don't see how drawn I am to you, do you?" He shakes his head, smiling.

My silence answers his question.

He sighs, frowning as he runs his hand down my spine. "I suppose that's my fault," he mutters.

Car headlights come towards us, and Ryan checks the

car's number plate before opening the door for me. I slide across the cold seat with him following behind.

Ryan wraps his arm around me, and my giant gold bow hits his cheek. He lets out a chuckle as he unclips it from the top of my head, throwing it onto my lap. I had completely forgotten I was wearing that damn bow until now. I feel mortified knowing we had such a serious conversation in the courtyard whilst I looked like that.

I lean my head on Ryan's chest and rest my hand on his leg, drawing little circles with my hand. My mind is running a million miles an hour, but I can't help but smile, finally knowing how Ryan feels.

"I can't wait to get you home," Ryan breathes into my ear whilst kissing my neck.

"Okay, but if we're going to do this, I want one thing," I say confidently.

I feel him stiffen beneath me. "Shoot."

I clear my throat and sit up straight. "I want you to stop calling me kid."

Ryan snickers and shakes his head. "Okay," he finally agrees, pulling me back against his chest.

"What was with that anyway?"

"I dunno." He shrugs. "I'm an asshole."

"*Were* an asshole. Because if you're still an asshole then you can go home alone."

Ryan laughs. "Yes, yes, Little Miss Pedantic. I *was* an asshole."

When we pull up to the house, Ryan unlocks the door and takes my hand, pulling me inside.

He grabs my waist and pushes me back against the door, holding my face in his palms.

A rush of energy pulses through my body at his every touch; I'm on fire once again. He pulls me in for a kiss and I latch onto him.

My hands move under his shirt. I gasp at how muscular his body feels under my fingertips. I've never touched his bare skin before; I've only ever clung onto his shirt. Feeling him like this makes me desperate for more.

I close my eyes, leaning my head back, panting. He moves his lips from my mouth, down to my neck and back up towards my ear. I let out a moan and run my hands through his hair and then to his waist, bringing him close to me.

"I only want you," he whispers into my ear, sending another shock through my body.

My heart is racing, but not in the way I'm used to. This time, there's no nasty ache or pain in my chest, I only feel an agonising desire to bring him as close to me as physically possible.

"Then have me," I say.

He fiercely crashes his lips to mine, his tongue pushing into my mouth as he snatches me away from the door.

We try to move towards the stairs without pulling apart from each other, but we fumble and break away, laughing as we walk up the stairs to his room.

His bedroom is exactly how I imagined: band posters cover the walls, stacks of records pile up on his desk. He even has a couple of skateboards resting against the far wall by the window. His guitar lays on his bed with pieces of paper scattered everywhere.

He leans over to clear the bed before sitting down in the middle of it, leaning against the headboard. He smiles at me, his hazel eyes glistening as he gestures for me to join him.

I slowly sit down, crossing my legs to face him. He smirks, rolling his eyes at my sheepishness and pulls me towards him. Sitting upright, he wraps my legs around his waist and looks at me as he runs his thumb across my lips.

He starts kissing me softly. My hands roam through his mop of hair, pulling the strands away from his face as my body rocks on top of his. I find the buttons on his shirt and undo them. I slide his shirt off, my fingertips tracing his stomach. He breaks away from our kiss to gently remove my jacket and hoodie.

When he tugs at my t-shirt, I stop him before he can pull it off. "Do you mind if I keep this on?" I ask so quietly I'm surprised he can hear me.

"Of course you can." He smiles and kisses me on the lips. "Is this okay?" He places a hand on my back, underneath my shirt. I nod. "Promise me you'll tell me if anything I do makes you uncomfortable?"

I nod again.

As he kisses me, he cautiously runs his hand across my back, finding my lace bra. As he moves his hand to the front of my body, he pulls away from our kiss, locking eyes with me to seek permission. I smile and nod, reassuring him that it's okay.

It's not that I don't want him touching me. I just don't want him to *see* what he's touching.

He undoes his black jeans and peels them off his legs, throwing them to the floor. I manage to pull off my shorts at the same time. As soon as I've tossed them away, he lies above me, kissing my lips, pulling the navy duvet over us as he moves.

"Are you sure you want this?" Ryan asks.

I bring my hand to the back of his head to pull him closer to me. "I've never been more sure of anything."

Chapter
Twenty-Seven

I'm woken by sunlight beaming across the room. I blink a few times to try and focus my heavy eyes. Ryan is lying on his back with his arms snaked around me. My cheek rests on his bare chest. As I unwrap my leg from his body, I can't help but smile, remembering last night.

I look at the time on my phone and realise that I've only had a few hours of sleep. Despite the lack of rest and my pounding hangover, I feel great. I just hope Ryan feels the same way about me in the light of day.

"Morning beautiful," he croaks. Relief floods through me when I clock him smiling down at me. He runs his hand over my head and leans down to kiss me.

"You're not working today, are you?" he asks.

I shake my head and shuffle closer to him, leaning into his warm chest. I trace lines across his bare back with my fingers.

He closes his eyes for a moment, taking a deep breath. "Good, because I want to spend the day with you."

As we lie in comfortable silence, he gently strokes my hair, kissing the top of my head. I feel a wave of pleasure flow down my spine at his touch. I feel so relaxed, I don't want to move. But my stomach grumbles loudly, intruding our peace and earning a chuckle from Ryan.

"Breakfast?" he asks, but neither of us attempt to move.

I shake my head. "I'm okay, thank you," I whisper. My heart begins to race at the thought of eating with him and I feel my body clench.

Ryan sits up. His eyes narrow, pointing at my torso. "Your stomach says otherwise."

He gets out of bed, throwing on a t-shirt and a pair of black gym shorts that he finds on the floor. He ruffles his hair, running a hand through it and shaking his head so the strands fall back into place. He holds out a hand for me. I put my sweaty palm in his as he pulls me out of bed.

When we walk into the kitchen, Nadine is sat on a bar stool, swinging her legs with her head in her hands. Tyler is at the cooker with his back to us, frying some bacon.

The smell fills my nostrils and my stomach grumbles again.

Nadine lifts her head, looking me up and down with a smirk on her face. I roll my eyes at her and sit at the counter, unable to keep a straight face.

As I take a seat, she leans into me and whispers, "Good?"

I nod my head and grin at her. She beams back and gives my hand a gentle squeeze.

Completely oblivious, Ryan goes to the fridge, pulling out a big bottle of orange juice. He reaches for four glasses, filling them up and sliding two across the counter for us. He then offers us a cup of coffee, which I eagerly accept and watch as he moves around the kitchen. I can't take my eyes off of him. I can't believe we're finally here, enjoying a blissfully simple morning together. Who would've thought?

"Zoe, do you want breakfast? I've made enough," Tyler calls over to me without turning around.

I shake my head and open my mouth to decline, but Ryan quickly interjects. "Yes, she would," he says, giving me a stern look.

So much for a blissfully simple morning.

I decide not to argue with him. I don't want to draw attention to myself. I stay silent as Ryan asks Nadine about the rest of the night at the Guild. She launches into an animated story of their crazy night, but I can't focus on anything other than the fact I'm going to have to eat in front of them in just a few minutes.

I can't remember the last time I ate properly without it coming back up. It was probably the meal I had with my flatmates. I think back to that dinner, how we were all sat eating away whilst Kady was led on the tarmac, taking her last breath...

Tyler slides a plate across to each one of us and I feel Ryan's eyes on me as he leans against the kitchen counter. I thank Tyler and rub my sweaty palms against my thighs. Nadine instantly picks up her food, eating the sandwich without a care in the world.

I grip my knees, trying to control my shaking hands before picking up my food. I bring the sandwich to my face, but my chest starts to tighten, and my body goes rigid. I already feel nauseous before any food has entered my system. This usually happens once I've consumed an obscene amount of food, not before.

I jump up from the stool, quickly excusing myself.

I race into the bathroom and sit down on the cold tile floor, wrapping my arms around my knees and resting my head on them. Hot tears prick my eyes. I try to focus on taking deep breaths to control my shaking body.

I don't know why I couldn't just eat like a normal person. What is wrong with me?

The sound of the bathroom handle turning causes me to look up just in time to see Ryan's head pop around the door. I could've sworn I locked it.

He takes one look at me and rushes down to where I'm sat. "What's wrong?" he asks, wiping a tear from my cheek. His eyes are wild as they search my face for answers.

"I-I don't know," I stutter, choking on my tears. "I'm sorry... I couldn't eat." I lean into his chest so I don't have to look at him. This is far too humiliating.

I feel his t-shirt dampen with my tears, but he doesn't say anything in response. He gently rubs my back, soothing me like a baby whilst I continue to choke on my breath.

After a few minutes of silence, once I have regained my composure, I wipe my eyes. "Wow, that was embarrassing," I say with a laugh. Ryan gives me a sympathetic smile.

"What happened, Zo?" he asks softly, still stroking my hair.

"I don't know. My hands just went clammy, and my chest tightened. I felt like I couldn't breathe. I don't know why."

"It sounds like you had a panic attack," he says flatly. I stiffen, unsure how to respond. He doesn't wait for me to speak. "Does this happen often?" he presses.

I sigh, staring at the wall. "Not very often, not before... before Kady. Now it happens more." I shrug. I leave out the part where I usually consume a tonne of food and puke in the toilet when it does.

"More? Like once a week?" Ryan probes.

I shake my head. "Every couple of days. Usually, I don't feel sick before I eat though, just afterwards." My eyes start to tear up again with embarrassment.

"Hey, don't cry. It happens. My mum gets panic attacks all the time, it's completely normal. I've had them before too."

"It's definitely worse when I'm eating in front of people, I've noticed that," I admit.

"Okay, well I'll get you something small and you can eat up here alone. You need to eat something as the hunger won't be helping the anxiety or your energy levels."

"But what will the others think?" I panic. "Won't that look weird?"

He shakes his head. "No, I'll just tell them you were too hungover to eat downstairs. They won't suspect a thing. Sound good?"

I nod, trying my best to turn the corners of my mouth into a smile, but I know it must look as fake as it feels.

"Then, eventually, we'll build up your confidence so maybe we can eat together? Small steps." He winks at me as he jumps up from the floor.

Once he goes downstairs, I pull myself up and walk into his room, curling up in the duvet and bringing the sheets to my face, inhaling his scent.

After a minute or so, there's a knock at the door and Ryan tells me he's going to shower quickly whilst I eat.

When I open the door, he's already disappeared, and a slice of toast sits in his place. My stomach growls as I pick up the plate and close the door.

After I've eaten, I go straight downstairs to wait for Ryan in the hall, not wanting to stay in his room alone in case the nausea hits. I want to distract myself; whatever happens, I don't want to throw up this time.

As soon as he emerges from the bathroom, looking far too hot with wet hair and dressed in all black clothes, I show him the empty plate. He beams as he pads down the stairs and takes it into the kitchen for me.

"Do you think you could drop me home to change?" I ask just before he pivots down the hall.

"Sure!" he shouts back enthusiastically.

Chapter Twenty-Eight

The drive back to my apartment doesn't take long and Ryan waits for me in the car as I go upstairs to shower. When I walk into the apartment, it's quiet and I figure everyone is out. I go straight to my room, grabbing my towel and taking it to the bathroom.

As soon as I open the bathroom door, I startle. Alice is stood at the mirror applying her makeup. She turns to face me, holding a tube of lip gloss in her hands.

"Sorry, I didn't realise someone was in here," I mumble, backing out of the room slowly.

"It's fine." Alice sighs. "You're always with your *boyfriend*, so I figured I didn't need to lock the door anymore," she almost spits the words, shrugging her shoulders. She turns back to the mirror to brush her lips with even more sticky, bubble-gum pink gloss.

"No, I'm not actually. I've been at cheer training," I say quickly, feeling myself get defensive. I try to give my best poker face, but Alice just smirks at my reaction.

"Whatever." She shrugs.

"Look, I'm sorry if you think I haven't been around since Kady's accident. I've just been non-stop training for cheer," I explain and inhale deeply. "We had our performance last night. It's been helping me keep my mind off of..." I feel my voice catch in my throat.

God, I hope I don't start crying. I always seem to cry during confrontation.

"I *am* sorry I haven't been around, Alice. I don't want you to feel alone, or like I've abandoned you. I'm always here," I continue, but she holds up her hand to silence me.

"You think I need *you*?" She huffs, her eyes fill with anger. "Why don't you get it, Zoe? I don't care that you're gone. In fact, it's easier. But look at you—" She waves her arms up and down. "You say that you're grieving and hurt, but you're not acting like it. You're so wrapped up in your own world." She pauses for a beat. "You don't care that she's gone because you never cared about any of us in the first place."

After delivering her final blow, she grabs her makeup

bag and pushes past me out of the bathroom. I'm left staring at the wall, unable to move as the tears silently spill over my eyes.

Deep down, I knew it was Kady that brought us together. Without her, Alice has no reason to tolerate me. I think that's what I've been struggling with the most, the guilt that it was Kady who was taken. She was the one who was at the centre of everything, with a tonne of friends. It would've been easier if it was me. No one would've missed me.

A few minutes pass before I move towards the shower. When I get in, I let the hot water burn my back. No matter how much I focus on calming down, I can't stop the bile rising in my throat. The only way to get rid of the pain aching in my chest is to empty my stomach. It's impossible to breathe and I need a small ounce of relief.

As my breakfast pours down the shower drain, my heart races and my throat tightens. I keep taking short breaths in between gulps of salty tears to try and calm myself down. I wash my hair twice and scrub my body, biding time until I feel somewhat normal again.

But it doesn't work.

I realise the only way to calm down is if I just let my tears flow until there are none left.

Once the shower finally turns cold, I jump out and

run back to my room in my towel. I can see my phone light up on the bed, so I rush to grab it and answer Ryan's call.

"Hello?" I croak.

"What's happened?" Ryan demands, hearing my sobs.

"N-nothing. Sorry, I won't be long."

"I'm coming up, buzz me in."

I can hear him get out of the car, so I quickly throw on a t-shirt and pyjama shorts before running into the hallway to buzz open the apartment block. I leave the door to my apartment wedged open and walk back into my room. I don't want to wait for him in the hallway in case I bump into Alice.

In a matter of seconds, Ryan bursts into my bedroom. He closes the door but doesn't move towards me. Instead, he stays glued to his spot, his eyes fixed on my face, searching for something. As soon as I look back at him, my tears begin to flow again.

"Zoe, we don't have to do this. If this isn't what you want anymore, that's okay," he begins with a panicked whisper.

"No, no. It's nothing t-to do with last night. Why would you think that?" I hiccup and wipe my sore eyes.

"I, umm, I don't know. Sorry, I'm new at this." He smiles uncomfortably, taking a step closer to me. "What is it?"

I give him a play-by-play of my encounter with Alice in the bathroom. His eyes scan my bedroom whilst he listens to me, his attention finally landing on my duffle bag tossed in the corner. He grabs it and unzips it before going through my wardrobe.

"What are you doing?" I ask, scared he'll find my stash of food.

Luckily, he pays the bottom shelf no attention, instead pulling clothes from the rail.

"Packing. You're not staying here," he spits. "I'm not having her talk to you like that, it's bullshit. You're coming to stay with me." He's taking deep breaths, trying to contain his anger.

"Ryan, honestly, it's fine. I can't move in with you, we haven't even gone out on a proper date yet!" I pause when I see disappointment flash across his face. "Not that I wouldn't want to," I quickly add. "I just don't want to burden you with all this drama, that's all."

He stops throwing clothes into my bag and walks towards me. Finally, his shoulders relax, and his face softens into a small smile. I pull at the belt loop on his jeans and bring him down to sit next to me on the bed. I put my arms around his torso whilst he picks me up to sit on his lap. I cling onto him like a koala, nestling my face into his neck.

"You'd never be a burden," he says into my hair.

We sit in silence for a few minutes as he tenderly strokes my hair. Even though my eyes sting from all the tears, his touch helps me relax.

"Come on, get dressed and pack a bag." He gently taps me on the back. "It doesn't have to be forever, just for a while, until your roommate chills out."

I quickly pack my things into a bag, feeling an odd rush of excitement at the thought of waking up to Ryan every morning.

Once we get into his car, he drives in the direction of his house. I lean my head on the seatbelt, gazing out of the window.

I sigh. It's such a relief to finally be on the same page as him. No more fear of rejection, no more games. I don't know what I would've done without him coming into my flat just now, getting me out of that horrible situation and into the safety of his world.

He reaches out for my hand. "What are you thinking about?" he asks.

I wrap both of my hands around his, giving it a squeeze. "Just how glad I am to have you," I answer honestly. "Thanks for letting me stay with you."

"You got it, babe." He grins at me, placing his free

hand in my lap. Finally, a new nickname I can get on board with.

The ache in my chest feels a little smaller than it did an hour ago. It's manageable. Despite my run in with Alice, I feel happy. His touch soothes me into complete contentment.

"Wait here," Ryan commands once we pull up to his house.

I don't have time to protest, he's already inside with my bags and running back out to the car with his guitar before I have time to open my mouth.

"Where are we going?" I ask.

"I want to take you somewhere important to me."

Chapter
Twenty-Nine

Ryan doesn't tell me where we're going, no matter how many times I ask him. I watch eagerly out of the window as we make our way up a long, beautiful driveway. Large conifer hedges line the path, blocking any view I could have of our final destination.

Eventually, an old manor house comes into view. The stone building is surrounded by a lush green lawn with perfectly mowed stripes cut into it. Green ivy climbs up the brick work and across the ground floor windows. It looks like something from a village postcard. I wonder who lives here.

My eyes land on a wooden signpost outside of the mahogany front door, next to large planters filled with lavender. The white writing on the sign reads *Priory House.*

Ryan drives to the side of the house and parks in a visitor parking bay. He shuts off the car engine, turning to me and taking one of my hands in both of his. "I come here every week to play music, and I wanted to bring you along."

"Okay?" I reply slowly, just as confused as I was before we arrived.

"It's a hospital. For people recovering from mental health illnesses," he says, biting his lip. He looks down. His clammy fingers brush the back of my hand, drawing circles on my skin.

"Why do you play here?" I ask, unsure of what else to say.

"I run a music therapy session. I mean, that's what they call it, but it's not really an official therapy session. I just play with patients who like to use music as an outlet on their path to recovery." He shrugs and exhales. "It seems to help them a lot and that's all that matters, I suppose." He pulls his hands away from mine and glances out of the car window towards the huge front door.

"How did you find this place?" I ask.

"Claire, actually. My head was all over the shop after my dad died. She suggested I look up a therapist or something." He pauses for a moment, letting out a small sigh whilst continuing to stare out of the window. "I wasn't, like, admitted here full time or anything. I just came for weekly appointments. My therapist suggested I bring my guitar here and play in a quiet space.

"Eventually, some of the patients caught wind of what I was doing and wanted to join. I guess it naturally evolved into a scheduled weekly thing, and I wanted to carry it on after recovery."

I take a few seconds to absorb this information. I can't believe how honest he is being with me, completely unprompted. I feel like last night changed so much between us. He finally wants to let me in, to let me know the real him.

"It's great that you do this, Ry. I can't imagine what the people here are going through, but they must appreciate you being here for them." I reach over and squeeze his knee with my hand. As he looks back at me, I see an unfamiliar emotion flash across his face.

I follow Ryan's lead as he quietly gets out of the car and makes his way into the building. Inside, the place looks somewhat clinical with white walls, a large reception area and rows of empty waiting room chairs.

"Ryan, dear," a plump middle-aged woman with a thick midlands accent beams up at him from the reception desk. "It's lovely to see you." She pulls a clipboard out from below the desk, placing it on the counter.

"Hi, Susanne." Ryan smiles as he swings his guitar bag behind his back and reaches for the clipboard and pen to sign in.

"And who do we have here?" Susanne smiles up at me. Her inquisitive voice is so high pitched it makes my hungover brain throb. I rub my forehead, smiling at her.

"This is Zoe, she's coming to the class today." Ryan tilts his head towards me as he pulls the pen cap off with his mouth.

"Oh, how wonderful!" Susanne exclaims, smiling widely.

Once Ryan has finished scribbling on the clipboard, he pushes the paperwork towards Susanne. I notice he's added my details to the sign-in sheet and even put my phone number down. I smile as I realise that he must have my information memorised.

"Well, it's lovely to meet you, darling. Go on through. Do you have your card, Ryan?"

"Sure do. Catch you later!" He waves as he turns to the door.

Ryan swipes a key card from his pocket. It emits a loud buzzing noise, making me feel as if I'm being released from a prison cell... or being locked into one.

He swings the door open, holding it for me to walk through.

I didn't know what to expect, but the fluorescent lights and sage colour walls make the hallway seem bigger and airier than I imagined. With the abstract pictures of trees dotted across the walls, the space feels peaceful and calming. Nothing like a prison.

We walk down the quiet passage towards a set of thick wooden doors. Ryan once again swipes his key card to let us into the room.

Inside the room, it feels a lot darker than the airy hallway. The windows just above the panelling are frosted and a row of trees sit right outside, blocking the sun from penetrating through.

The room looks and smells like one of the town halls I used to go to for after-school dance classes when I was a kid. All that's missing is a ballet barre against the wall. It does, however, have a tiny podium stage and stacks of black assembly chairs lining one side.

I quietly follow Ryan to the small stage as he places his guitar down.

"You don't have to follow me, you know." He chuckles.

"I know... I just don't know what to do with myself," I admit with a nervous laugh.

"You could start unstacking the chairs whilst I tune my guitar?" he suggests.

Feeling grateful for the distraction, I get straight to my task, ignoring the rising tightness in my chest.

Ryan unpacks his guitar and sits on the edge of the stage to tune it. I feel relaxed as soon as he starts playing some melodies and humming along.

"What do you do in the sessions?" I ask, my nerves and curiosity getting the better of me.

"Mostly sing in a group really, like a choir, I guess. Some of them have guitars and stuff too, but I like to let them lead it. You don't have to join in, only do what you're comfortable with."

He places his guitar down on the stage and gestures for me to come closer to him. His legs are dangling off the edge and he wraps them around me as I step closer, removing all space between us. Even sat on the stage, he's still taller than me. I look up to his face, meeting his eyes.

"You look scared, babe. Don't be. No one here sings because they want to be the next Beyoncé. They all come here for the same reason we play music—"

"—because it's an escape from what's going on in our heads?" I add.

"Exactly!" He makes no effort to hide the huge grin that's spread across his face.

He leans down to kiss me, but the kiss isn't a peck like I was expecting. It's deep. Passionate. And enough to make my head spin.

After a few moments, we hear footsteps and voices outside the door. I quickly spin around, fearful that a group of strangers might have just witnessed our kiss. Ryan smirks, seeming to read my thoughts, and jumps off the stage to let the group in.

I exhale, realising the wooden door was locked.

Everyone cheerfully bustles into the class. No one looks particularly unwell like I had expected, their illnesses are completely invisible to the eye.

I immediately kick myself for my train of thought, feeling completely ignorant for somehow assuming I'd be able to tell if someone was suffering this way. I suppose that's why they call mental illness a silent killer.

They all grab a chair and huddle in a semi-circle around the stage to face Ryan.

I've been glued in place this whole time, not wanting to move from the edge of the stage. A few curious pairs of eyes look my way and I try to give them a small smile, hoping they don't mistake my awkwardness for hostility.

"This is Zoe," Ryan eventually introduces me as he perches on the stage. "She will be joining us for the session to see what this is all about."

I move to sit on one of the spare chairs at the back of the group, not wanting to be exposed at the front.

Ryan asks if anyone has any preference over which song to play first. A girl at the back of the group slowly raises her hand. She can't be much older than me, I'd guess she's in her mid-twenties. Her long brown hair is braided into two French plaits and her nails are painted a bright purple colour, matching her baggy jumper.

"*Adventure of a Lifetime*," she requests. Ryan smiles at her encouragingly, making her hunched shoulders relax.

One of my favourite things about Ryan is his ability to instantly put anyone at ease. It's probably why they asked him to run this class in the first place. He's never judged me for the songs I like to listen to or learn on the guitar, he just appreciates any interest in music. He gets adorably excited over it. And it makes me all the more attracted to him... if that's even possible.

"Great! And why have you picked this song?" he asks.

She brings her hand to her mouth and runs her fingers across her lips. "Because, well, I don't know about anyone else here, but I constantly feel like I'm a prisoner in my own head."

There's a slight murmur of agreement in the room.

"Go on," Ryan encourages with a smile.

"Umm... all the negativity and hateful stuff I tell

myself weighs so heavy that, sometimes, I don't think I'll ever be able to break free from it." She talks quickly before shrugging and rubbing her palms against her knees.

"And how did hearing this song make you feel?" Ryan continues.

"I felt... happy, I guess. I wanted so badly to feel as free as they seem in this song. I couldn't help but sing along and forget that literally the other day, I didn't want to be alive anymore." She looks up to Ryan and an intense silence fills the air for a moment.

"Thank you for sharing that with us, Becky." Ryan beams. "It's one of the reasons I actually added this song to the list. We all like to play music to forget certain things, right? But as you said, it can also motivate us and give us the push that we sometimes struggle to give ourselves." He looks directly at me as he talks, his eyes studying my face. "Okay, so how do you want to play it then?" Ryan asks, turning his focus back to Becky.

"You do the first verse, I'll do the second and then we all join in?" she suggests.

Again, Ryan makes his encouragement perfectly clear by smiling and nodding. Becky's shoulders relax once more, her mouth turning up into a smile.

A shuffling noise echoes through the room as they all open their music folders. Ryan pulls out his own song sheet and hops off the stage to pass it to me. He winks as he hands over the paper and I feel warmth seep into my cheeks.

I want to tell him that I don't need the sheet, that I know the lyrics already, but I don't want to draw attention to myself.

Everyone stands up from their seats and Becky moves to the front to be closer to Ryan. She rolls up the sleeves to her plum-coloured jumper, revealing bandages covering her arms all the way from her wrists to her elbows.

I try not to stare, attempting to focus on the music sheet in front of me as Ryan begins to play.

Chapter Thirty

Singing with the group was exhilarating. I felt free, exactly how Becky said she wanted to feel. We all forgot where we were in that hour as we clapped and sang along. Some of the group even started to dance together, smiling and laughing the entire time. It was a wonderful chaos of sound.

It felt safe. Like home.

No one wanted to leave when Ryan called the end of the session. He was completely mesmerising, the way he encouraged every single person to let themselves go, to embrace the music. I think my confidence may have improved a tiny ounce just by being in the room with him.

During the session, each person told a story, explaining why they chose a particular song and what it meant to them in their recovery. I couldn't believe how bravely they laid everything out on the table. I even found myself connecting to some of their stories in little ways.

One guy, Bradley, explained how his depression could be felt in his stomach. On bad days, his stomach would hurt so badly that he could barely move. The cramps would pin him to his bed for days. It was so unbearably physical for him.

It made me think about my chest and the hole I've felt since losing Kady. But I know I'm different to Bradley. I know that in a few weeks, once I'm past the shock of a world without Kady in it, I will be back to normal.

"How did you find that?" Ryan turns to me once the room is empty.

"Like one giant hug," I say with a laugh. It was an emotional rollercoaster, but I never wanted it to end.

I stack up the chairs and put them back in their usual spot at the side of the room. The space, once enlightened by music, returns to its dark slumber.

"Well, that's the whole idea I suppose. To feel supported," Ryan says, packing away his guitar.

I let out a yawn and he puts his arm around my shoulder, giving it a squeeze.

"Coffee for the hangover?" he asks.

I nod eagerly. I'd forgotten all about my hangover in that hour, but just thinking about caffeine makes me realise how exhausted I am.

I figured we would leave the hospital to go to a coffee shop, but Ryan tells me there's a café here. I follow him out of the hall and down another long corridor.

Ryan unlocks a large patio door at the back of the building, and the sight sends me into shock. I thought the café would look like one of those depressing, dingy cafeterias you normally get at hospitals, with only a crappy vending machine that pours out a plastic cup of brown slush. Of course, it's nothing like I expected.

I'm met with the sight of a garden terrace filled with white bistro tables and chairs, all facing out towards a huge striped lawn. There are potted lavender plants lining the patio and ivy climbing the outer brick wall. I look up to see a wooden pergola with trailing evergreen plants wrapped around it.

I feel I've stepped into a scene from *Alice in Wonderland*, joining the Mad Hatter for his tea party.

"This place is full of surprises," I say, turning to Ryan as we walk towards one of the empty tables. We settle on a spot closest to the lawn, at the opposite end of the building entrance.

He reaches up to turn on a small patio heater above our heads and I smile as I feel the warmth radiate across my face.

"You didn't think it would be like a prison, did you? Guards on every corner to keep watch over every patient." Ryan smirks.

I swat him playfully on the shoulder. "No, it's just... it's hardly your average hospital, is it? It feels peaceful and... *expensive*."

"It's a private hospital, so it's not run in the usual way." He shrugs. "But it has a lot of donors, so the patients pay next to nothing for treatment. Rumour has it, there was a wealthy entrepreneur admitted here a few years back who now pumps the place full of money. I think he's now a shareholder or something. But I've never actually met him, so I don't know if that's true."

I raise my eyebrows. "That sounds pretty unbelievable."

I know mental health services in this country are limited, you always hear about it in the media, so it seems unlikely that someone would be willing to subsidise a hospital like this and expect nothing in return. Or am I just being cynical?

"I'd like to think it's true. That people care enough to make therapy more accessible. I think so many people would benefit from therapy—without having to pay a shit tonne of money or being placed on the NHS waitlist for decades." Ryan bites his bottom lip as he scans my face.

He fiddles with the ring on his thumb, twisting it around as he stares at me.

I'm not entirely sure how to respond when he talks about this place, but I can feel him studying me, looking for a reaction. I tear my eyes from his and look around at the beautiful scenery.

He doesn't pressure me for a response, he just quietly asks what I want to drink and gets up from the table to order. I watch him as he walks away, slumping his shoulders and looking slightly sad. At least, I think he looks sad, but maybe I'm being paranoid.

It's just, since we've been here, it feels like he's looking for something from me. Maybe I'm overthinking this, but I can't help feeling that my responses are disappointing him. I don't want him to think he made a mistake by bringing me here and showing me his world. I just really don't know what to say.

He eventually walks back to the table, putting two steaming cups of coffee down and taking the seat opposite me. I inhale, filling my nostrils with the rich aroma. It has to be my favourite smell, after Ryan's cotton scent of course.

"Who picks the songs that you sing in those classes?" I ask.

"I make an initial list so that everyone has time to

learn some songs, but others add to it as we go." He takes a sip of his coffee and scrunches his nose as the hot liquid burns his mouth. He licks his lips, placing the mug back on the table.

"But you picked the song Becky chose, right?"

He nods. "Yeah, I did. It was a song I used to sing in the car with my dad all the time. We'd always listen to it together on our way to the beach." He looks behind me with a vacant expression, as if he is imagining being back in the car with his dad right now.

"I wish I could've met him; he sounds like a great guy." I smile, meaning every word. I wonder if Ryan got his gentle personality from his dad. I wonder what mannerisms they shared. Do they look the same? What features did he get from his dad? What about his mum?

"Me too. You would've liked him, and he would've loved you." He smiles warmly. "My dad was actually the one who got me into music, so any chance I get to feel like he's with me, I take it."

I begin to shake my head, smiling, as I look down at my cup.

"What?" he asks, tilting his head with a smirk across his lips.

"I just don't know how you do it, choosing to relive those memories. Aren't they painful?"

"No way, I've found it helps so much." He pulls his hand from his lap and reaches across the table for mine. Despite the cool autumn weather, his hand feels warm as it intertwines with mine.

"If you bottle up those memories because they've suddenly become painful, you won't ever get the chance to enjoy them again," he says. "Of course, they're going to hurt like hell to relive at first, and it'll be tempting to shut them off, to box them away in the back of your mind. But if you stick with them and ride the wave of pain until they don't hurt anymore, you've won. You get to take those memories back from the demons in your head and they become yours again."

He takes a deep breath and leans back in his chair. "That's my experience anyway. Plus, he wouldn't want me to be sad, he would want me to live life to the full." He nods, smiling at me with the confidence that I admire so much.

"Granted, I still have a lot to work on, like how long it took me to be honest with you..." He smiles and quickly looks down at his coffee cup.

"Why did it take you so long, do you think?" I ask.

His cheeks flush a slight pink colour, and he bows his head further. He releases his hand from mine, running it through the top of his hair, shaking his head and ruffling the strands so they fall back into place.

"It was just my fear of losing people, of them disappearing like my dad." He sighs. "But I knew you were different, and I knew if I didn't sort my shit out soon, a team-jersey wearing American footballer was going to take you off my hands." He laughs.

"What made you realise you had that fear?" I ask, ignoring his attempt to laugh his way out of this conversation.

"Uh... good question. Coming here did. Although, it took me a little while to figure it out. Lots of CBT."

"CBT?"

"Cognitive behavioural therapy."

"Oh."

"It's a type of therapy that helps you reflect and change the way you think and behave. It's actually quite practical. Understanding why I react the way I react has really helped." He doesn't take his eyes off of me as he talks, searching my face once again for some kind of reaction.

We sit in silence for a few moments, and I look out at the lawn. My eyes find a girl at the edge of the garden, walking by the hedges with a woman who looks so much like her. I assume it's her mother. They are walking hand in hand, the mother gripping onto her child so tightly, as if anchoring her upright.

"Do you not want to do that?" Ryan asks, suddenly bringing me back to the conversation. I tear my eyes away from the girl and look straight into his eyes.

"Do what?"

"Understand what's going on in your mind. To feel better. To learn how to, you know, cope with the loss of Kady. Maybe if you opened up and spoke to someone about it, you might be able to come to terms with it better." He squeezes my hand with a smile.

I snatch my hand away, placing it back underneath the table. "I have come to terms with it," I snap.

"Zoe, you told me you can't keep food down and you have panic attacks. I thought..."

"You thought *what*, Ryan?"

"I thought that maybe if you came here with me, you'd see that places like this might be able to help." His eyebrows crinkle as he looks at me.

I try my best to swallow my emotions. I take a deep breath, trying to release the growing tightness in my chest.

This was his plan the whole time. To bring me here and convince me that I'm ill. Kady hasn't even been gone five minutes, of course I'm not going to be back to my normal self immediately. I just need time and he's not giving me that.

Is this why he kissed me? Not because he actually likes me, but because he wants to fix me, like his own little project?

I feel restless, unable to sit at this table any longer.

I quickly stand up. Ryan's sympathetic eyes widen with worry. I tell him I just need to use the bathroom. He doesn't seem to think much of it as he hands me his staff pass and points me in the direction of the ladies.

As soon as I walk away, I pull my phone out of my pocket to request an Uber. When I get to the double doors, I look for a sign to the reception area and follow the arrows on the floor. I only glance back once to check Ryan isn't following me.

I can't believe he tried to bring me here for some kind of intervention. Who is he to tell me that I need to go to some hospital to talk about my emotions?

I've been absolutely fine. It's none of his business how I'm dealing with Kady's accident.

He doesn't know me. He doesn't know anything about my happiness or my coping mechanisms.

When I get to the reception area, I check to see my Uber is coming around the corner. I hand Susanne Ryan's card, asking her to return it to him. That way, he'll know I left.

I climb in the taxi and try to focus on calming down. I take a couple of deep breaths, closing my eyes as I clench and unclench my fists.

I turn my phone off as soon as I feel it vibrate in my pocket, not even checking the caller ID before shutting it off.

Chapter Thirty-One

My anger is still overflowing when I arrive at my apartment. My mind is racing. I'm going to explode.

Ryan is just like Alice, so intrusive. They both act like they understand what's going on in my mind when they don't at all.

When I get to the front door, I hear Alice's laugh emanating from the kitchen. Fury erupts inside of me.

Her hateful words from earlier today replay in my head.

I see red.

Before my mind can catch up to my feet, I find myself walking straight into the kitchen. I burst through the door, making Alice jump from her seat at the counter. Jake also spins around to identify the source of the sudden noise.

"Bit hypocritical don't you think, Alice? I thought no one was allowed to laugh or smile since Kady died," I rage. "Isn't that what you said before? How selfish I am for trying to live my life? Excuse me for trying to be positive and make her proud. If you weren't such a fucking... a fucking airhead, maybe you would have realised what I was trying to do, or I don't know... maybe you could have just *asked* me?"

Alice's eyes widen. "Excuse me?"

I take a step towards her.

"Woah! Guys, chill." Jake steps in. "Let's sit down and talk about this."

"Look who finally decides to speak up," I snap. The hurt that flashes across his face makes me instantly regret my words.

"Guys," Jake says again, forcefully. "We're all going through so much right now. Kady wouldn't want us to turn on each other. Come on, we're supposed to be friends."

"We are *not* friends," Alice replies, crossing her arms over her chest.

At that, Jake says nothing. I'm not surprised.

I turn out of the kitchen, slamming the door behind

me.

I make it to my room. My eyes scan the space as my chest beats faster and faster. I clench and unclench my fists, trying to focus on feeling my nails dig into my palms as opposed to the burning sensation in my chest. I walk over to my desk, deciding to pull out my laptop and watch a film to distract me.

Fuck. It's in my overnight bag at Ryan's.

I turn my phone back on but put it straight on aeroplane mode without looking at any calls or texts. I scan through my downloaded movies and pick something I've already watched a million times before. I'd much rather watch a trashy film on this tiny screen than face talking to Ryan, even if only to get my stuff back.

I lean my phone on my desk and try to settle on the bed. My stomach rumbles just as the opening credits roll. I dig through my wardrobe to find my stash of snacks and take them to the bed, lying down as I eat.

Once I unwrap the big bar of milk chocolate, I eat row after row, not wanting to stop until I've eaten the whole thing. I open a second bar and do the same again, inhaling every piece until I'm surrounded by garish purple packaging.

I face the ceiling as the chocolate bloats my body. I wait for the nausea to overwhelm me as I feel every inch of my body double in size.

I don't know why, but every time I eat it's like I can feel the food moving inside me, pushing through my skin like it's trying to escape.

But it can't be freed.

Instead, it expands my body, making my clothes feel tighter and my body larger. I suddenly become aware of how horrifically snug my jeans feel on my legs and how much my t-shirt clings to my stomach.

The only way to stop this feeling is to get the food to escape the way it entered my body.

I walk to the bathroom and turn on the taps, sitting by the toilet, waiting for the nausea to unsettle my stomach. Impatient, I stuff two fingers down my throat. I gag as the heavy chocolate fights to stay put.

Finally, after a few attempts, it empties into the toilet. I smirk to myself and wipe my watery eyes.

Chocolate 0, Zoe 1.

I stand up and run cold water over my face before walking straight back to my room and closing the door. I lie down on the bed. My body already feels smaller than it did ten minutes ago, and the stinging in my throat from vomiting blots out any other pain.

As I continue to watch the film and my body slowly recovers from being sick, the emotions I was trying to suppress hit me like a tsunami.

I'm alone.

I had someone who cared about me, who was worried about me, and I shut them out.

I could have simply disagreed with Ryan's suggestion instead of bailing, especially after he opened up to me about being scared of loss. I didn't have to be so dramatic and walk out, only to come back to this hellhole of an apartment. He probably feels betrayed by me. How could I leave after he was so open with me?

How selfish, how cold can I be?

I hate myself.

I grab my phone and switch aeroplane mode off, racing to call Ryan's number. But it goes straight to voicemail. Has he blocked me already?

I bet he wants me out of his life. I bet he wishes he never met me.

I sink to the floor, wrapping my arms around my knees. I sob into them, letting out streams of salty tears. My body is shaking uncontrollably, but I feel better for it. I need to cry to clear my head.

After a while, my mind starts to slowly unravel into some sense of rationality, and I realise I need to fix this. If he's not going to pick up his phone, I should drive over there, apologise to his face and admit my mistakes. I don't care if he isn't home when I first get there, I'll wait. I'll wait all night if I have to.

I head to my car, dialling his number once more, but it goes to voicemail again. I plug my phone into the sound system and let the loud music fill the car, for once not caring who else may hear. I need it to drown out my thoughts.

I try to wipe my eyes as I pull out of the apartment complex, but the tears continue to spill. I'm able to control my breathing enough to concentrate on driving when the music suddenly cuts out. Ryan's name flashes across the screen. I instantly accept the call, putting it on loudspeaker whilst I drive.

"Zoe?" His voice sounds rushed, panicked.

"I... I..." I try to respond, but my tears are choking my breath. "I'm... coming over," I stutter.

"Are you driving?"

"Uh, y-yeah."

"I'm home. I'll see you when you get here," he says softly. "Just focus on the road, please?"

Why is he being so calm, so gentle? I wouldn't be able to control my anger if I was him. But then again, perhaps he's saving it for when I get there.

Ryan is waiting on the pavement outside his house when I arrive. He's not even wearing shoes or a jacket.

He's stood with his arms crossed, pacing and looking in my direction. He rushes over as soon as he sees me.

I manoeuvre into a parking space and jump out of the driver's seat just as he gets to the car door. He immediately pulls me into his arms. I hear myself gasp, shocked by his reaction. I don't deserve this compassion at all.

"I'm. So. Sorry," I choke into his chest.

"You're sorry? You have nothing to be sorry for, Zoe. It was all me. I pushed you too far. It wasn't fair." He plants multiple desperate kisses on the top of my head, as if it's the first time we're seeing each other after years apart.

"No. I was cruel. I walked out on you... and I know that's exactly what you're afraid of." I start sobbing again, leaving his t-shirt wet with tears.

He squeezes me. "Let's stop blaming each other and go inside and talk. Okay?" He smiles down at me, pulling my chin up with his fingers.

He leans down to kiss me softly, but I place my hand on the back of his head, pressing his lips harder against mine, deepening the kiss.

"Or not talk," he adds, laughing into my mouth.

I keep my hand glued to his as we walk into the house and upstairs to his room.

"So, do you want to tell me why you left?" he asks. I throw him a glance as my heart rises to my throat. He immediately adds, "I promise I'm not angry, Zo. I just want to understand how you feel."

He pulls me across the bed, so I'm sitting in between his legs with my back pressed against his chest. Having my back to him somehow makes me feel like I can truly say what I'm thinking.

"I don't know. I just got really angry. It felt like you were basically calling me crazy or something. You made me feel like I can't handle Kady's death. It hurt," I begin, taking a deep breath. "Then I started to think that maybe you don't have feelings for me, and you just want to, you know, fix me." I shrug.

"No, baby, no. I just want you to feel like you can talk to someone, and that someone doesn't have to be me. You're not crazy for grieving, I just really want you to feel supported through this." He kisses the top of my head. "I'm so sorry."

"I know. But I promise I'll talk to you if I need to talk to someone." I sigh, leaning further back into his chest.

I scan the walls of his bedroom, analysing one of his colourful band posters. It's a holographic poster with a sketch drawing of a man wearing a suit. He has an old-fashioned camera covering his face. I recognise the name of the band, Arcade Fire. Thoughts of Ryan's photographer father enter my mind, and I wonder if that poster reminds Ryan of his dad too.

"What happened when you got home?" Ryan asks, stroking my hair.

I feel my body stiffen. I try to open my mouth to relay everything to him, to be open and honest, to avoid him worrying. But every time I go to say something, my mouth stays shut as if my body is forcing me to secrecy.

"I-I think you can probably guess," I eventually whisper. "I ate... and then I threw up," I say, shame clouding every word.

His grip around me immediately tightens. I feel like the girl on the lawn back at Priory House, whose mother was clinging onto her.

After a few beats of silence, he eventually says, "Zoe, can you promise me something?" I nod slowly as he continues, still stroking my hair. "Promise me that any time you go to do anything like that again, you'll call me?"

I nod and feel him let out a sigh of relief.

We sit in a comfortable silence for a while, letting ourselves digest the heat of the past few hours. He continues to cradle me, mindlessly stroking my hair and planting kisses on the top of my head.

I feel safe again. Home.

"You know, I also called Alice an airhead," I eventually whisper, supressing a laugh.

I feel the tension in the air evaporate as he sniggers. "Good. She deserved it."

He pulls me down on the bed and leans over me, giving me a soft kiss. He puts his hand on my hip and turns me to face him. It doesn't take him long to find the buttons on my jeans.

We both scramble to take our clothes off (leaving my t-shirt on, of course), removing any barrier between us. Our mouths lock together in a deep kiss. I feel the overwhelming desperation to get as close to him as physically possible.

His hand goes to my stomach. I flinch, pulling away for a nanosecond.

I quickly bring him closer, placing his hands on my back, hoping he didn't notice my reaction. I don't want him to think that I don't want him, because I do. I want him so badly.

It's just that my stomach feels like the source of all my pain, I can't stand to be touched there. It's not flat like everyone else's seems to be. I swear there isn't a single member of the cheer squad who doesn't have a washboard stomach.

No matter what I try, or however many sit-ups I do

before bed, it doesn't flatten. It's probably bursting from all the tension and anger it stores inside. It's my enemy and I hate it.

Chapter
Thirty-Two

My alarm rings and I hear Ryan groan next to me. For a moment, I forget where I am. I expected to wake up to the plain white walls of my apartment, but instead find myself smiling up at Ryan's colourful music posters.

He moves half of his pillow to cover his ears, trying to escape the noise. I cut the alarm off and climb out of bed, heading for the shower with some clean clothes.

By the time I shower, change and go back to Ryan's room, it's empty. The bed is still messy and unmade, but Ryan isn't in it.

My phone vibrates on the nightstand.

Nadine: Meet for coffee in thirty minutes?

Nadine: Usual place?

Nadine: I. NEED. GOSSIP.

Nadine: AND COFFEE. Lots of COFFEE!!

I text Nadine back and rush to get ready so I can meet her on time. She's in the year above me and studies politics, but we're both taking the same European Law class this semester. She was allocated to the class after forgetting to submit her preference forms on time. Unsurprisingly, European Law was the only class in the whole of the Law and Political Science department with space left.

As I stuff my books and laptop into my bag, Ryan walks back into the room with two cups of coffee, frowning at the sight of me rushing around. "You're leaving already? I thought your class started at ten?"

"Yeah, it does, but I'm going to meet Nadine," I tell him as I swing my rucksack onto my back and reach for a mug.

"She's not here with Tyler?"

I shrug. "I guess not."

"Shocking. We should alert the news channels."

I laugh, nudging him. "Behave."

"I'll drive you then."

"Honestly, it's okay. You have work today, right?"

"Yes, and a meeting with my management."

"Management?"

"Yeah, for my solo album. But I'm still taking you."

He holds out his set of keys. "Here, take these to the car and I'll put your coffee in a flask." He snatches the mug from me and disappears out of the room.

Why hasn't he told me about his meeting? Come to think of it, he's not even mentioned his solo career once. I only know about it because Claire told me at the gig. Does he know she told me?

I remain silent during the ride to campus, unsure how to approach the topic of his music career. I don't want to rock the boat, especially as we're finally in a good place. If he wanted to talk to me about it, he would.

Once Ryan pulls up to the campus gate, he kisses me goodbye and promises to pick me up after class. I jump out of the car and spot Nadine's bobbed hair in the distance, she's leaning against the trunk of a giant sycamore tree. As I approach, she pulls her headphones out of her ears and stuffs them into her jacket pocket.

"Only you would bring a flask of coffee with you to go and get another cup of coffee." She laughs, rolling her eyes at me and pointing to the cup in my hand. "By the way, do I look different to you?" she asks with a grin, flicking the bottom of her bob with her hand. She loops her arm through mine as we start walking towards the coffee shop.

"Umm... different how?" I hesitate. Her hair looks exactly the same as it did yesterday. I scan her face, but nothing appears different there. I feel like my dad after my mum goes to the hairdressers, he never notices or remembers to compliment her when she gets back.

"Different! Like... I don't know... somebody's girlfriend?" she squeals.

"No way, you guys are official!" I beam at her.

She's so animated as she tells the story of how he asked her out, completely head over heels for him. I don't mind hearing about the mush, I'm genuinely thrilled for her. Although, it inevitably makes me wonder whether Ryan and I will ever be official.

We reach the doors of the coffee shop and groan when we see how long the queue is. I need more than one coffee to get through this torturous class, so I force Nadine to join the line regardless.

"And what about you? We never got to chat yesterday. Spill!" She grins at me.

"I don't know really, there's not much to say other than he finally told me how he actually feels and yeah... it's really nice. So far so good." I shrug.

I decide against telling her about the drama with

Alice and that I'm staying at the band's house this week. I don't want her to panic about my situation or tell me it's too soon to be staying with Ryan. But she practically spends every night with Tyler anyway. She also seems to be the least judgemental person on the planet, so my fears are probably unjustified.

"Look at us with our guys! How fun are gigs going to be now? I mean, they were already fun, but now... I can't wait." She squeals, earning a glare from a redhead guy queuing in front of us. Nadine sticks her tongue out at him once he's facing away from us.

I giggle, shaking my head. "It's not even been a week and you're already marrying us both off in your head!"

"I know, but Tyler was saying yesterday how big of a deal it is that Ryan's admitted how he feels."

My body goes rigid at the thought of them discussing our relationship. "What do you mean?"

"Tyler said he's never seen Ryan like this before." Nadine shrugs nonchalantly. "Apparently, Ryan was always so busy jumping between gigs, work and looking after his mum that he wouldn't let himself get serious with a girl. I think Tyler is really happy that he's putting himself first for a change."

"Yeah, I'm glad he's doing what he wants." I say distractedly.

I shift my focus away from Nadine to one of the baristas as he tries to make an iced coffee. I watch as he squirts a can of caramel syrup too aggressively into a plastic cup, only for it to spurt all over his red apron.

"It's just so sad, isn't it? With his mum and brother." Nadine turns to me, shaking her head. I furrow my eyebrows. It takes me a minute to realise that she's talking about Ryan's family.

"What about them?" I demand before I can stop myself. I know I shouldn't ask. If Ryan wanted me to know something, he would tell me himself. But I hate the idea of Nadine knowing something about him that I don't.

"Well, after their dad died, apparently Ryan's brother went totally off the rails. Got into loads of fights, drank a lot. He even got arrested. Tyler wouldn't say what for." Nadine shivers.

"And his mum?"

"She tried to kill herself." Nadine leans closer to me. Just as she opens her mouth to continue, the barista calls us forward to order.

My mind spins a million miles an hour. My heart feels like it's being crushed in a vice. I can't even begin to imagine what that did to Ryan...

I manage to order my cappuccino and we wait to the side for our drinks to be made. It's pretty crowded, but I'm way too engrossed in what Nadine has to say to care.

"Tyler said that's why the band all moved in together up here."

"I thought they moved so Tyler could be closer to his family? That's what Ryan said."

Nadine shakes her head. "When Ryan's mum recovered and his brother got arrested, she told him to leave, to go and make something of himself instead of clearing up their mess," Nadine says matter-of-factly as she turns to grab our coffees.

I selfishly feel a bubbling resentment over the fact that Nadine has discovered so much more about Ryan than I have. It feels like I don't know him at all.

But I also feel protective, wanting to shield Ryan from his past trauma. I knew his mum struggled with the death of his dad, but I never knew how much. I had no idea about his brother, either. Ryan must have felt so alone, having to be strong for everyone else when he also suffered a huge loss. Now I feel even worse than before about the stress I caused him yesterday.

Thankfully, Nadine changes the subject, happily delving into a story about her recent drama with her flatmate. Usually, I would find the trivial gossip hilarious, but all I can manage is a few simple nods.

When we get to the lecture hall, we take our seats. I

check my messages and see Ryan's name on the screen.

Ryan: I wish I was with you right now xx

Me: Same. I'm not going anywhere btw. I'm here for you too.

Ryan: Babe, stop being cute or I'll have to abduct you from campus xx

Chapter
Thirty-Three

Nadine and I hurry out of the lecture hall when class finally ends. I try to convince her to come and study with me, but (typically) she has a date with Tyler.

When I get to the library, I look around for a decent space. I finally find a desk right in the back corner, next to a large window looking out at the campus clocktower. I let out a sigh as I take in the view and slump down in a chair.

It's hard to concentrate on my mound of class work. In between staring out of the window and slowly reading page after page of my textbook, I continually check my phone for texts from Ryan. I don't get any.

I know he's in a management meeting this afternoon

and had a shift at Jacks this morning, so I don't bother texting him. I can play the cool non-girlfriend role if I want to.

Despite how long it takes me to focus on my studies, I eventually find enough motivation to get me through my scheduled work until the sun starts to set behind the clocktower and most of the other students around me leave for the day.

Ryan's name flashes across my phone screen. I eagerly snatch it from the desk, reading the message. His text asks me to walk towards the south campus gate, so I rush to cram my books back into my bag. I run down the flight of stairs, pushing through the double doors into the cool night air.

As soon as I get clear of the library entrance, Ryan comes into view. He's leaning against the red brick archway under the clocktower, waiting for me.

He has a beige shopping bag in one hand and his rucksack casually swung over his shoulder. When he notices me, a grin flashes across his face.

I want to try to play it cool, but as soon as I see him, my feet have other ideas and I practically run into his arms.

"I thought you were going to pick me up at the gate, you didn't have to walk here!" I gush as he wraps his arms around me.

"I thought I'd surprise you." He kisses me on the cheek and holds out his free hand for me to take. I eagerly intertwine my fingers with his.

"What's in the bag?" I ask, peering at it.

"You'll see. Come on this way," he says smugly.

I follow him towards the lawn opposite the clocktower. The sky has turned a strange bluey-purple colour, making the whole campus look mystical and other-worldly.

Ryan stops in the middle of the grass, laying out a picnic blanket before taking out food and cups.

"A picnic?" I grin, tilting my head to the side.

"Yep. Our first official date," he says, plonking down on the blanket and outstretching his arms. "Now come here."

I crawl into his arms, and he leans over slightly to grab a fluffy blanket out of his rucksack, wrapping it around my shoulders. I pull the material across my body and scrunch it in my hands, inhaling the gentle smell of the fabric. The scent is like a fusion of Ryan's now familiar cotton scent and the fragrance that Claire likes to spray around their house. It instantly calms me.

"This is perfect," I whisper with a content sigh, looking up to the clocktower. The shapes of the individual red bricks are nearly impossible to make out now that the sky has turned dark and moody. The only clearly visible part of the building is the illuminated clock face, hanging in the sky like our very own moon.

Ryan opens a flask and fills a cup with fresh coffee. I immediately grin as the comforting smell washes over me.

"I knew this would be a hit." He rolls his eyes at me, smirking and placing the cup in my outstretched hand. I nestle in closer to him as we both sit and look up at the sky.

"Are you hungry?" he eventually asks. I shake my head. I couldn't think of anything worse than putting food in my stomach right now.

"Can I ask you something?" I begin, shamelessly distracting him.

"Sure."

"Why don't you talk to me about your solo career?" I ask the question that's been on my mind since this morning.

"Oh," he answers, seemingly caught off guard. "It's not that I purposely don't talk about it. It's just all so new and I still don't really know what's happening."

"I just thought I'd be someone you'd want to talk to about it," I say quietly.

"You are, Zo. I know it sounds ridiculous, but from

the moment we met, I was scared to tell you because I didn't think you'd give me a chance if you knew about my music career. I just assumed you'd want to date someone with a more stable career. Someone who would be around all the time."

"You thought about dating me from the moment we met?" I ask with a cheeky grin.

Ryan rolls his eyes. "Of course that's the thing you pick up on." If it wasn't so dark, I know I'd be able to see the rosy colour of his cheeks. "Ask me anything, Zo, I'm an open book."

I smile. "How was your meeting?"

"Good," he begins. "My album's recorded and the team are prepping the artwork and social media side of things." He glances at me out of the corner of his eyes, gauging my reaction. "Management said I should be able to release something in the next few months."

"The band don't have management, do they?" I ask, realising I should already know this.

"Correct. We aren't that big and just play for fun. We'd rather not be tied down with contracts and stuff as a group." He shrugs, leaning across to the bag of food.

He pulls out a box of strawberries and puts them between us. I don't want to seem rude or ungrateful, especially after how much effort he's put in to organise this date, so I pick one up. I hold the bright red berry in my hand, twirling the tiny leaves with my fingers.

"And what's next for you once the album's released? You might be going on a tour, right?"

"Yes. I should be going on a European tour. Management will be booking venues once we see how much attention the album gets." He shrugs nonchalantly, picking at the grass.

"I bet it gets loads, you're so talented." My voice comes out rushed and weird. I realise I'm trying (and failing) to mask my panic with enthusiasm. Ryan must've noticed because he squeezes me tighter.

"You know, the tour will only be over summer. And I figured..." He sits up, looking at me straight in the eye. "I figured you could join me as soon as your final exams are done." He smiles gently, looking slightly sheepish.

I try to hide my grin with my coffee cup, but Ryan pulls it away from my face, tickling my waist with his hand. I let out a scream, spilling my cup onto the grass as I fall backwards.

"Does that sound good?" he asks with a lopsided grin.

I shriek uncontrollably as his hands continue to tickle me. "Yes, yes!" I shout, pushing him away.

He brushes his fingers down my temple, leaning into me, his face is only inches from mine. "Fuck, you're never getting rid of me you know that don't you?"

Chapter
Thirty-Four

Kissing Ryan makes all my worries about summer, his music career, and the distance it might put between us, disappear.

As soon as we pull away, I sit up and grab his left hand, bringing his wrist up to my lips. I kiss his palm softly, noticing an uneven texture to the skin around his wrists that I've never noticed before. His eyes are fixated on me as I lower his wrist to inspect the light scar tissue, gently caressing the lines with my fingers.

"Did you do that to yourself?" I ask, kissing his hand for a final time and placing it on my lap, holding it tightly, not wanting to let him go.

"Yeah." He nods slowly. "A few months after my

dad... it was hectic at home." He looks up towards the sky. The light of the clocktower reflects on his face, highlighting the crinkles between his brows.

"Because your family weren't coping very well?"

"Uh huh. My brother had been arrested for some fucked up shit, and my mum was in hospital. I hated myself for letting it all happen. I felt like I'd failed my dad or something."

Another wave of guilt passes through me as he proves me wrong once again. He was always going to tell me this information about his family, just like he was always going to factor me into his future plans. We just needed more time. Instead of getting jealous that Nadine knew things about Ryan that I didn't, I should've just trusted that we would get there eventually, at our own pace.

"I hope you know that none of that is your fault." My voice strains with all the emotion spinning through my brain. I never, ever want him to feel even a fraction of the pain he felt in the past. The thought of him hurting himself makes my heart tear in two.

"I know that now, after lots of therapy... and music." He chuckles nervously, but brightness quickly returns to his face. I lean across and plant a kiss on his full lips, earning myself a grin.

"Talking of music," he continues menacingly. "What

273

do I have to do to convince you to sing with me?"

"I already sing with you."

Ryan rolls his eyes. "Alright, Little Miss Pedantic. I mean at a gig. Just one. Please?" He looks at me with puppy eyes. God, he's good. "We're playing at a winter festival coming up and, honestly, I can't stop picturing you singing with us. Especially as I don't know if I'll be able to sing with the band next year."

Damn it. He really knows how to get me.

I glower at his shameful tactics "Okay." I sigh. "Fine. One gig."

Despite feeling physically sick at the thought, I love making Ryan happy. It'll be like one huge send off before he ventures into the great unknown.

He beams at me and pulls us down to the picnic blanket, laying me on my side to face him. "You have no idea how much this means to me," he whispers, inches from my face.

He grabs the blanket from around me and lies it across our bodies, covering us like a duvet. He places a hand around the back of my neck and brings his lips to mine. My body practically roars from his touch.

"Shall we go home?" I ask, wanting more, needing more of him. He smirks and starts throwing our empty cups back into the bags.

We walk to the car hand in hand, and I'm on a total high. He makes me feel things I've never felt before. I can only compare it to some kind of weightlessness. It must be happiness but a different, more intense kind of happiness than anything I've ever known. It's all consuming.

I genuinely thought I was happy before I met Ryan, but now I realise I was simply fine. Nothing bad happened in my life, yet nothing extraordinary happened either. Things were pretty simple because I never got caught up in anything other than my studies or hanging out with my sister.

But looking back, I don't think I'd change anything even if I could. Without the life I had at home, I wouldn't be so close to Hannah... and maybe I wouldn't have gone to university, so maybe I wouldn't have met Ryan.

Thinking about my family suddenly makes me realise that I haven't spoken to them for so long. My parents texted me about Kady, but we haven't talked on the phone as much as we usually do.

Maybe it's their uncertainty of how to act after Kady's accident, or maybe I've just been avoiding reaching out because I'm scared to tell them about Ryan.

I know I haven't dated anyone before, and I always thought I would share this sort of thing with them. But if

I'm honest, I just don't know how to broach the topic, and I don't want to lie.

"You're awfully quiet over there. Are you okay?" Ryan asks from the driver's side, breaking my train of thought.

"Sure, I was just thinking about home," I admit.

"Your family?" He glances at me out of the corner of his eye.

"Sort of." I shrug.

"You have a sister, right?"

"Yeah. I do."

"Is she older or younger?"

"Older."

"You never talk about your family much." He glances at me again before turning back to the road.

"There's not much to tell." I sigh.

"What about your parents? They're still together, right?" His knuckles turn white as he grips the steering wheel tightly, his gaze fixed straight ahead.

"Yes. They met in high school and married at eighteen. I swear they get more in love as time goes on. I guess I'm really lucky in that sense." I watch Ryan carefully. I feel bad. His family life is so much more complicated than mine. But Ryan looks over and smiles, his warm hazel eyes holding no sadness.

"Are you close with them?" he probes.

"I guess so. I always want to make them happy."

"Hence the legal career?" He smiles menacingly, reminding me of one of our first conversations.

"Sure. They always wanted me to have good education and successful career."

"Why is that do you think?"

I exhale. "Uh, well, neither of my parents could afford to go to university, and they didn't get many qualifications in high school. My mum left school at sixteen and worked her way up in a fabric store, she's the manager now. Dad was lucky to get into the navy, he told me there's no way he could get in now without any academic qualifications to his name.

"That's why he pushed us to get a decent education, so we don't have to struggle as much as they did just to get somewhere in life." I pause. "Don't get me wrong, it's not like I was ever forced into anything I didn't want to do. I admire their hard work and want to be as driven as them. It just meant that I never explored other options."

"Like becoming a singer?" Ryan teases.

I laugh. "I guess so."

"Your family sound like the total opposite of mine," he says. "I can't wait to meet them one day." He smiles as he pulls into a space outside of his house.

We hear laughter emanating from inside as we walk up the steps to the front door. Ryan groans at the noise, knowing we'll have no way of running up the stairs unnoticed.

"Hey, love birds!" Nadine shouts from the kitchen counter. She's perched on Tyler's lap with a tonne of takeaway boxes in front of them. How on earth could they both eat sat like that?

"It's been a long day, we're going to bed," Ryan shouts back. He tries to make his way up to his room, but I pull his hand to motion him towards the kitchen. He groans and rolls his eyes at me, but I just stick my tongue out at him.

"How was your date?" Claire asks, leaning against the kitchen counter as she dries a plate with a tea towel.

"Really good." I smile.

"So good that she's decided she'll sing with us," Ryan chimes, walking up behind me and wrapping his arms around my chest.

"O-M-G! This is amazing!" Nadine shrieks. "Although, I'll have to find a new dancing partner for your gigs now." She sticks out her bottom lip in a dramatic pout. "Talking of dancing, are you going to cheer practice tomorrow?" she asks.

"Sure am."

Tomorrow is the first session where the team will learn the new routine for the competition season. There's no way I'd miss it—not that Kim would allow any absences anyway.

"You told Kim you're going to the dinner too, right? You gave your food preferences?" she asks.

"Yeah. I submitted them in the library."

"What dinner?" Ryan asks flatly.

"Oh, the cheer squad and football team are going for a celebratory dinner together before sports night at the Guild. They do it every year after the firework event." Nadine shrugs, grabbing a prawn cracker from the bowl on the kitchen counter and popping it into her mouth.

I could've sworn I'd mentioned this to Ryan already, but I've been so busy these past few days that I might've forgotten. His glacial expression confirms this is the first he's hearing of it.

"The football team are going?" Ryan scowls as he unwraps his arms from my waist.

"Chill, Tarzan. We probably won't even speak to them," Nadine says with a playful eye roll. "You guys should meet us for drinks after."

Ryan suddenly storms out of the kitchen, slamming the door behind him. I throw Nadine an apologetic look before chasing after him up the stairs.

Chapter
Thirty-Five

I pause before opening the door to Ryan's bedroom, taking a couple of deep breaths. I know that I need to get to the bottom of whatever is going on, but I'm terrified of what I'm about to face. We were having such a good first date. I don't want anything to spoil things between us—especially not a stupid cheer social.

I lightly knock on the door before swinging it open.

"Hey, is everything okay?" I breathe, trying my best to come across as soft as possible.

Ryan is across the room, stood with his arms folded, facing the window and looking out at the darkness. I can see the scowl written across his face in the window's reflection.

My heart throbs in my chest. The panic eats away at me, pulling the wound in my heart wider as I wait for him to say something.

I step into the room, closing the door behind me. I hover by the side of the bed closest to the door, his mattress creating a barrier between us.

He spins around to face me when he hears me coming closer. His eyes narrow, his face twists into a scowl. I've never seen him like this before. I've never seen him so angry.

"What do you think?" he demands, spitting the words at me.

My ears start to burn and all I can hear is the sound of my heart pounding away in my eardrums, drowning out all my senses. I have absolutely no idea why he's being like this, all because I have plans that he doesn't know about?

"What's wrong?" I ask feebly. I don't know what to say. He always knows the right thing to say to me, yet I can't even figure out what is upsetting him. I just recoil, terrified at the thought of an argument.

"You're not serious? You make plans behind my back to go and have dinner with... with *those* American footballers, and you expect me to be happy about it?" He's shouting as his eyes search my face, looking at me as if

I'm stupid.

I feel stupid.

"Why would you want to put yourself in that situation, Zoe?"

"I probably won't see Dan; their team is huge and—"

"*Don't* say his name," Ryan barks through gritted teeth.

"Okay, sorry. I'm sorry." I hold my hands up. "I'm going to be with Nadine and my team all night, not them." I try to keep my voice calm and level, hoping it will be enough to reassure him. But my words aren't doing anything to alleviate his fears. His fists remain tightly clenched by his side.

He turns away from me, covering his face with his hands as an angry noise escapes him. The sound pierces through me, making me jump. Immediately, tears form in my eyes, but I don't make a move to wipe them away. I couldn't move even if I wanted to. I'm frozen. Stuck.

"Whatever, Zoe. Just go, I don't care. It's where you should be anyway." He eventually turns back to face me, a menacing smirk rests on his lips. "Cheerleaders and American football players. Fucking adorable." His words are bitter and cruel, but I know he doesn't really mean them.

I walk around the bed to get closer to him.

"Nothing is going to happen. I'm not going anywhere." I look into his eyes and reach to put a hand on his shoulder.

He turns away, looking at the bedroom wall with emotionless eyes. "I just... I can't do this, Zoe. It's too much." He sighs and rubs his hands across his forehead.

My heart sinks to my stomach and I take a couple of steps away from him. Tears are fast flowing down my cheeks now, I have no way of controlling them.

"Wh-what?" I squeak. His eyes meet mine but there's nothing behind them, no regret or apology.

Nothing.

I just don't understand how something as trivial as a cheer night out can lead to him giving up on us?

I feel my stomach tighten, followed closely by my chest. I can't breathe. I try to swallow, but my throat closes in on me.

I'm suffocating.

I need some air.

Before he says another word, I walk out of his bedroom and down the stairs. I know the others will still be in the kitchen, so I go out of the front door and sit on the steps, facing the road.

I close my eyes and wipe my soaked cheeks, resting my head in my hands.

I'm exhausted.

Today has been such an emotional rollercoaster. I've gone from a self-inflicted meltdown, to working my ass off in the library, to going on the best date I have ever been on. Only to have my heart shattered moments later.

I hear the front door open, but I don't turn around to see who it is. My guess is it's Nadine, she probably heard everything and wants to check I'm okay. It's so embarrassing to know the whole band would've heard our entire fight.

"Zo, I didn't mean what I said in there. It came out completely wrong, you have to believe me. Come back upstairs, please?" Ryan gushes, taking a seat next to me and putting his arm around my shoulders. I shrug him away.

"What did you mean then?" I ask, unable to keep the anger out of my voice. I'm too tired to bother trying to hide my feelings right now.

He sighs and tries to wipe away the tears that have spilled down my cheek. His touch makes me flinch. He ignores my rejection and continues to gently move his thumb across my face anyway.

"I sound so fucking stupid." He sighs, running his hand through his hair and then ruffling it. "I just meant I can't handle this feeling. This feeling of... jealousy, I guess." He shakes his head and looks out towards the road.

"But what made you jealous? You know Dan completely freaked me out that night, it was horrible."

"No, no, it wasn't even that, which is the crazy thing. Fuck, my mind is a mess." He runs both hands through his hair. "I had a mixture of anger remembering that night, and then I also felt complete jealousy over the fact you're going to a dinner."

"A dinner?" I ask, utterly confused.

"Yeah. You're terrified to eat in front of me." He looks at me with a pained expression.

"I'm... I'm not," I lie. "You do realise university dinners aren't exactly dinners, right? Everyone gets way too drunk to eat anything." I sigh, relieved to finally understand what's going on in his head. "I didn't think I needed to explain. I'm really sorry, Ry."

He pulls me in for a hug. "No, I'm sorry. I know I sound like an asshole." He shakes his head with a small smile. "But I want to be the person you're most comfortable with, just like you are to me. I just feel so... exposed. In this relationship. And I don't want to be exposed alone. If that makes sense. Fuck, I don't know."

I feel all the anger and tension leave my body. The pain in my chest still nags at me, but I push it away, focussing instead on Ryan's amber eyes.

I stand up and hold my hands out to him. "You're already becoming that, Ry. I agreed to sing with you guys, didn't I? I don't even play music out loud in front of anyone else, let alone sing or perform."

He stands up and leans his head down, kissing me softly.

"I'm really sorry, Zoe. I know you're dealing with so much right now and I don't want to sound possessive. I just want to be to you what you are to me," he says.

"You are, Ry. It felt like my entire heart left my body when you said you couldn't do this anymore. I wish you wouldn't say those things."

"I'm sorry. I really am."

"It's okay. At least now I don't have to worry about you running off with some girl during your tour," I joke, trying to lighten the mood. I wipe my face with my sleeve, drying a few lingering tears.

Ryan stops us before we enter the front door. He turns to me and cups my face in his hands, his eyes boring into mine. "No one, and I mean *no one* could ever be what you are to me."

I inhale sharply at his words, smiling. "That rhymed."

He laughs lightly, wiping my cheek with his thumb. "Maybe it's a song."

"About me?" I playfully gasp.

"They do say most songs are inspired by love."

"Or heartache," I quip.

He groans. "Let's just go with love, okay?"

I laugh, trying my hardest not to think about the fact he's used the words *'love'* and *'relationship'* all in one night. I don't want to get ahead of myself.

But I can't ignore what my heart did just hearing those words tumble out of his mouth. I didn't think it would be possible to feel this way about someone so quickly.

How can I be this hooked on him in such a short amount of time? How can the way I feel about him consume every part of me? I can't remember what life was like before we met, and I don't ever want to think about what it would be like without him.

"We're a right pair, aren't we?" he laughs, shaking his head as we head back into the house.

Chapter Thirty-Six

When I run down to the kitchen to meet Nadine, I can hardly meet her eyes. There's no way she didn't hear my argument with Ryan last night. He wanted to drop us both to campus this morning, but I told him no. It would be so awkward.

"Ryan not with you?" she asks from the counter, smiling at me sympathetically. Okay, she definitely heard the fight.

I shake my head, explaining that he's busy and I'll drive us both to class.

"Okay, but you're not driving us to dinner from practice, are you? You have to drink tonight otherwise it'll suck." She picks up the last bite of her toast and stands up, grabbing her shoulder bag from the floor.

"Oh yeah, good point. I hadn't thought of that," I say.

"I'll take you," Tyler's voice booms from the other side of the room, making me jump. I turn around to see him sat cross-legged on the sofa, typing on his laptop. I have no idea how I didn't notice him before.

"Just drive back here after practice and I'll take you to your dinner." He gets up from the sofa and walks over to plant a kiss on Nadine's cheek. "I'd take you right now, but I'm about to leave for work."

"That's okay," I reply.

I start to head in the direction of the front door. If we don't leave soon, I'm not going to be able to grab a coffee before my first lecture. And if I don't get my coffee fix, I'm going to starve until lunch.

Wait a minute.

I throw Nadine my keys and tell her to get the car running. I don't stop to give her an explanation before I bound up the stairs into Ryan's room. He's already out of the shower, sat on his bed with wet hair, scribbling something on a notebook.

"You don't start work until two, right?" I ask, lingering at the door. He throws me a confused look before nodding, staring at me. I smile. "Meet me on campus at twelve. I have an idea."

As soon as my lecture ends, I dart out of the theatre, out of the law building and straight to the clocktower where I agreed to meet Ryan. I eagerly search the crowds of students for him.

It takes me a while to spot him at first, barely recognising him wearing a navy-blue Oxford button-down shirt, black jeans and black suede Chelsea boots. He usually wears baggy shirts, but this one is fitted and hugs his broad arms. I've never seen him look so smart and so... preppy.

"Don't even start." He frowns, holding his hand up as he takes in my expression.

I rush to wrap my arms around him and plant a kiss on his lips, not caring how many other students are around.

"What? You look handsome." I giggle.

"Behave. Emily has me working the shop floor now, so I have no choice." He tugs at the shirt, trying his best to look annoyed, but I can see the corners of his mouth fighting a smile.

"I bet the yummy mummy Jacks customers love you."

I wink at him. He swots playfully at my shoulder.

"Anyway, why'd you want to meet?" he asks as we walk towards the campus gate.

"You'll see." I smile at him as I lead the way towards the main road.

As we get out of the gates and into the student village, I ask if he's hungry. A look of understanding flashes across his face when he realises what I'm up to. He can't keep a straight face, grinning from ear to ear, as he puts his arm around my shoulder, squeezing me closer to him.

After last night, I want to show Ryan that he really is the person I feel most comfortable around. I want to push through these weird insecurities I have over food. For him. I want to make him proud. Plus, it would be nice to be able to actually do normal things like go out for dinner dates without worrying that I'm going to freak out.

I let him pick which restaurant to go to and he chooses the most popular student place, Loco's. We grab a free table, and he passes me a menu. I flip the laminated paper over, my heart rate increasing tenfold. A rising panic moves from my stomach to my throat. The choices are overwhelming.

"Do you know what you want?" he asks. I shake my head, chewing my lip. "Shall I order for us?"

I nod. My mouth feels so dry, I don't even try to speak. Ryan gives me the softest smile, relaxing the tension in my stomach slightly.

Whilst he goes to order, I unzip my rucksack and pull out my water bottle, taking a few gulps. The cold liquid instantly soothes my throat.

I can do this.

I start to feel a little hot in this stuffy restaurant, so shrug off my denim jacket. Ryan comes back and chuckles at me as I finish pulling it off.

"What's so funny?"

He points to the cheer jersey I'm wearing with raised eyebrows. "Cute."

"Shut up! I have to wear it for practice." I move to lightly smack his hand, but he's too quick for me, catching my palm in his and interlacing our fingers. We sit for a moment, holding hands across the red plastic table, looking at one another.

Ryan's eyes scan my face as he continues to draw little circles on the back of my hand with his thumb. "Thanks for inviting me here, Zo. I really appreciate it." He smiles at me, his caramel eyes bright under the lights of the restaurant.

"You're welcome. I've never actually been on a dinner date with a guy before." I attempt a smile, lowering my head as I feel my cheeks flush.

"Well, I feel honoured." He squeezes my hand. "But I find it very hard to believe that you don't have a queue of guys ready to take my place if I fuck up again."

"Absolutely not." I shake my head.

"But surely, you've dated in the past? No angry ex-boyfriends I should be worried about?" He laughs half-heartedly.

"Nope. I haven't had time." I shrug. "The last person I ever dated—if you can call it that—was a guy in the year above me in high school when I was seventeen."

"What happened with him?"

"Well," I sigh. "My high school was very cliquey... the guys were the worst." I shudder at the memory of the huge group of 'popular' guys in high school. All on sports teams, all with rich parents, all entitled. "But Ed was different, he was quieter than the others. We were on the debating team together and hung out a little bit after school. Then, when I finally, you know... g-gave up my virginity after a few months of dating, I ended up on the list." I sit back in my chair, folding my arms.

"The list?" Ryan's eyes narrow in confusion.

"Uh huh." I nod slowly. "The group of guys that Ed was friends with, well, they all kept a list of girls, rating them." I roll my eyes and look at Ryan. His expression hardens, the muscles in his neck tightening.

"What a load of fucking assholes," he replies.

"Yeah. To this day I think Ed was more pressured into acting like one of those guys, instead of truly being one. I mean, I know that doesn't make it okay. But I'm over it. I just swore off guys for a while after that."

"Until you met me." Ryan winks.

I nod slowly, giggling. "Exactly."

"But I don't think you should excuse Ed just because he was more passive. Sometimes not doing something about a situation is just as bad."

Why do Ryan's words instantly make me think of Jake?

"You're right," I begin, my eyes wandering to a waitress approaching our table.

She places a huge tray of appetizers and fries on our table with two cans of Sprite. I'm relieved Ryan picked food that is easy to eat. I was starting to get nervous at the thought of trying to gracefully eat a burger in front of him.

I don't think the food choice was an accident on his part though. I've started to realise he doesn't really do things on a whim.

"You good?" Ryan looks at me as I stare at the baskets of food in front of us.

Surprisingly, I don't feel too bad. I definitely

recognise the nervous waves passing through my stomach, but I trust Ryan. I feel comfortable around him.

"Yeah." I give him a small smile. "I don't feel bad all the time," I admit, reaching for a fry.

"Can you eat in front of other people, or is it just me?"

"Umm... it's complicated," I respond, chewing my fry. "Since high school, I've always had a fear of eating in front of people. Sometimes it stops me, sometimes it doesn't. The people I'm regularly around—my family, my housemates—I never really have a problem with. I think I just have to get comfortable with the person I'm eating in front of. Well... I thought that was the case, but sometimes I have bad moments, even with people I'm used to."

"Have you worked out what triggers the bad moments?" Ryan asks, picking up his fork and stabbing at a piece of chicken.

"No, I don't think any single thing triggers it," I explain, reaching for the ketchup. "Like, take now for instance. I feel okay, whereas tomorrow I might not be. I could be eating the same food at the same restaurant with the same person, but I could suddenly freak out."

Ryan looks at me sternly as he chews his food, thinking about what he's going to say. "You know, it might not necessarily be about who you're with or where you are, but perhaps how you're feeling on that particular day?" He watches me, searching my face. "When I went to therapy, it was all about how your emotions and feelings can trigger certain actions. Like, if I was particularly stressed or tired, I'd get more anxiety attacks that week."

"Yeah... maybe. I'll have to think about it more when it happens," I say. I don't want to talk about the hospital or therapy again and ruin our date. I just want us to take the small victory of me eating in front of him without having to delve into my feelings.

"That would be a good idea. Promise that you'll call me if you get a bad moment again, okay? I want to be there for you." He reaches across the table to take my hand.

"Sure, sure." I shrug, dipping a fry in ketchup. "I already promised you I would."

Chapter Thirty-Seven

Cheer training flew by as quickly as it always does, especially because we learnt the dance section for our competition routine. I know we're aiming for the national championship, but the routine is *impossible*. I have no idea how we're going to pull it off.

After training, everyone stayed in the gymnastics hall to get ready for our team dinner. Once we showered, we all lined ourselves up against the full-length dance mirrors to do our make-up. Usually, I'd run from any forced social activity like that, but there was something kind of nice about being there with the team, especially after last week's performance.

I'm surprised by how much I actually fit in. I'm not as

loud or as chatty as everyone else (like Nadine), but I don't get left behind in conversation either. If I'm silent for too long, someone always asks me a question to bring me back into the discussion. It's nice.

While the rest of the team arranged taxis to the restaurant, Nadine and I dropped my car back to the band's house and grabbed a lift with Tyler. The whole time, Nadine wouldn't stop moaning about how we should have left my car on campus and got a taxi with the others. Apparently, we could get put in random seats if we arrive late.

I rolled my eyes at Nadine's whining, telling her she was being ridiculous. But as we step through the doors of the restaurant and head upstairs to the private dining area, I can't help but panic that she might be right. There's no way I could do this dinner without her sat next to me, even if we aren't actually eating anything.

The floor is packed full of cheerleaders and American footballers, all dressed up and chatting in little groups. The venue is pretty big. It has its own bar to the far side and a long *L* shaped table next to floor-to-ceiling windows overlooking the city centre.

I scan a huge board at the entry way, relieved when I realise it's a seating chart. I'm even more relieved to discover my name next to Nadine's. Kim must've helped put the chart together as everyone seems to be seated with their closest friends.

We walk straight over to the bar and order our first round of drinks, and before too long, Kim calls for everyone to take their seats.

Nadine's high heels click-clack across the floor as we find our places. I'm glad I decided to wear my three-inch heeled boots and not gigantic stilettos. I'm so useless at walking in any type of heel, I couldn't face tripping up and drawing attention to myself. Although, I have to hand it to Nadine, she does look unbelievable in her mini bodycon dress and strappy heels.

Finally, we find our seats and sit down opposite a couple of American footballers I've never met before. Nadine quickly gets into a conversation with them, going over last weekend's performance. I nod and smile along, grateful not to be leading the conversation.

"So, you were the tumbler at the weekend?" one of the footballers asks.

"Yeah, that's me." I politely smile at the preppy brunette. He maintains eye contact with me for a few seconds longer than I am comfortable with, which makes me look down at my black t-shirt dress and start playing with the hem.

"Hey stranger," a familiar, yet slurred voice says

behind me.

My body freezes.

Dan.

He looks even more slick than the rest of the guys in the room. He's dressed in a crisp white shirt, navy chinos and brown loafers, clearly trying to look like he's just walked straight out of a Ralph Lauren commercial. An overpowering waft of his aftershave hits my nostrils as he sits down next to me, the scent laced with a sickly smell of alcohol. It makes me want to vomit.

"Hi," I mumble and glance to my left. Much to my annoyance, Dan's name is clearly written on the place card neighbouring mine. Why didn't I check when I looked at the seating chart earlier? Ryan is going to be so pissed when he finds out.

I turn away from Dan and look to Nadine, whose eyes are wide in horror. She leans into me. "Want to swap seats?" she whispers.

I shake my head. That would be way too obvious.

"Excuse me, I'll be right back." I stand up and turn to Dan with the type of fake smile I would usually save for rude Jacks customers. I shuffle behind the row of dining chairs to make my escape.

As I squeeze behind Nadine's chair, I lean down to whisper in her ear, "Come to the bathroom with me one sec?"

She nods and stands up, reaching for my hand and giving it a squeeze.

"Wanna get out of here?" she asks the moment we get into the bathroom.

"I think I might get Ryan to pick me up. Is that okay?" I bite my lip as I search Nadine's face, hoping she won't be mad.

"Of course." She puts her hands on my shoulders and smiles at me. "I'll come too."

"No, you have to stay! I feel bad leaving but I just don't feel like I can be around him," I explain. Nadine crosses her arms and shakes her head, refusing to let me go alone. "Please stay," I beg. I couldn't bear to cut her night short, especially with the band planning to meet her later on. I know how excited she is for that.

"Okay, fine," she says with a sigh. "But it won't be the same without you."

I pull out my phone to dial Ryan's number and he picks up on the second ring. "Hey, babe. You okay?" he asks. His voice is quick, as if he is trying to catch a breath.

"Yeah, I was just wondering if you would be able to pick me up?" I ask. He pauses for a while so I quickly add, "If you're busy, I can get an Uber."

"No, no, please don't. Sorry, I'm just at the gym," he

puffs, and I think I hear a weight drop to the floor. "Has something happened? I thought we were meeting you out later tonight?"

"I'm good. Just tired," I lie, figuring it better to tell him in person what's happened.

"That's okay, we can just go back to my place and watch a film. I'll be five minutes. Okay?"

"Okay," I agree.

I tell Nadine to go back to the dinner whilst I head outside. I don't want her waiting in the cold in that tiny dress. I already feel bad enough for bailing, she definitely doesn't deserve to catch her death because of me as well.

As I get to the bottom of the stairs, my heart sinks when I see Dan leaning against the wall, smoking a cigarette.

Great.

"Leaving so soon?" he asks, wobbling slightly on his feet. He takes a drag of his cigarette and then throws it to the floor.

I can't find my voice so I simply nod, hoping he will go back inside.

"That's a shame. I was looking forward to sitting next to you." He smirks. "I actually got Kim to put us next to each other. Said we hit it off at the firework night." He laughs and stumbles towards me.

I instinctively take a couple of steps backwards.

He reeks of alcohol and stale cigarette smoke. My nose curls at the disgusting smell.

"Maybe I can take you out some time," he slurs. I shuffle to the side to avoid him getting any closer and he knocks into the wall.

Screw this.

I dart towards the well-lit pavement, away from the restaurant, hoping Dan is too drunk to follow. I'd go back inside but I'm scared he'll manage to corner me on the staircase back up to the dining room. That, and I'm terrified of causing a scene.

I venture further out onto the road, noticing headlights parked up ahead. I'm praying it's Ryan's car, but it's too dark to tell. I make my way towards it anyway.

Within a couple of seconds, the driver jumps out. I let out a huge breath when I recognise Ryan. I run towards him and instantly push myself into his arms.

"Was that Dan?" he asks flatly. His eyes are narrowed in the direction of the restaurant, and I can feel his hands scrunch into fists around my back.

"Yes, can we just get in the car? Please?" I ask desperately. I can feel the tension in Ryan's body, he's stiff as a board. I grab his hands, trying to pull him back towards the car, but his body is so rigid. "Look at me,

Ryan. I'm fine. Let's just go home."

He looks down at me, meeting my eyes. He finally nods as he inhales and exhales deeply. He unlocks the car and I quickly jump inside, locking the door as I settle down on the cold leather seat.

"Did he kiss you?" Ryan demands, gripping the steering wheel so tight his knuckles go white.

"No, why would you ask that?" I gasp.

Ryan seems to relax a little, and his frown turns into a more neutral expression. "He looked like he was trying to," he begins. "No offence, Zoe, but you smell like a mixture of guy's aftershave and cigarette smoke," he says. His sarcastic tone doesn't sound as natural or light-hearted as it normally does, but I'm relieved he's at least attempting to joke instead of getting mad.

"You don't smell so hot yourself, Mr." I smile at him, taking in his gym attire. He looks so good in black thermal leggings, shorts and a hoodie. Part of me wishes I could reach over and take off his sweater, so I could put it over my exposed arms and wrap myself up in him.

"Okay, well I guess we're both showering when we get home." He looks at me with a smirk.

"Only if you join me," I say. Since when did I get this confident?

He seems to like the sound of my suggestion as he

puts a hand on my lap, rubbing my skin and setting my whole body ablaze.

"So, what exactly did Dan say to you then?" he asks, his tone suddenly serious. I feel him gently squeeze my thigh and I start to wonder if he's nervous or irritated.

"He tried to ask me out," I admit, shivering as I recall the encounter.

"You told him you had a boyfriend, right?" he presses.

I try to hide my shock by pretending to cough, but I only end up choking on my breath.

"No... I-I didn't realise I had one," I eventually stutter, staring at the road ahead, unable to look at Ryan after that question.

You told him you had a boyfriend, right?

Boyfriend.

I like the sound of that. And I should probably tell Ryan that I like the sound of that. But I've forgotten how my mouth works. And my brain, for that matter. Oh, and my heart too, because that thing is beating a hundred billion miles an hour.

We sit in silence until we pull up to his house. I think both of us are so stuck in our own heads, we don't know what to say.

Ryan eventually crawls to a stop and dashes around

to my side of the car just as I'm climbing off my seat.

"I think you have one." He holds his hands out for me.

"You do?" I ask, grinning.

"I do."

We stand facing each other on the pavement. He leans down to kiss me softly, placing a warm hand on the back of my neck and pulling our bodies closer.

Holy crap. I have a *boyfriend*.

Chapter
Thirty-Eight

Once we get inside Ryan's house, it's dark and empty. I figure everyone else has already left to meet Nadine in town. I flick the lights on and attempt to make my way upstairs, but Ryan pulls at my hand, leading me towards the basement.

"I thought I needed a shower?" I ask with a grin.

"I want to show you something first," he says.

We walk down the stairs and into the basement. I curl up on the couch, watching Ryan closely as he moves towards the huge sound system in the corner of the room. He pulls his phone out and connects it to the stereo.

Suddenly, music fills the room and I instantly recognise the signature sounds.

"Your album," I say with a whisper, intaking a sharp breath.

I listen to his soul shattering voice; the voice that makes me fall harder and faster for him every time I hear it. Hearing him sing is like cliff jumping into a deep clear ocean on a scorching day. It's like an exhilarating, heart pumping adrenaline rush of sheer happiness.

"I wanted you to be the first person to hear it."

He walks over to the sofa and sits next to me. I'm completely lost for words as I absorb every single lyric.

It's clear that the album is dedicated to his dad, but unlike his other songs, these new tracks aren't full of pain. The upbeat tempo celebrates his memory.

I want to dance, laugh and cry all at the same time.

I close my eyes and picture him in the recording studio, singing for his dad as if he was there with him.

You'd always tell me
Everything happens for a reason
But what reason is there
To say goodbye to you?

Forced into a loss I never expected
Never dreamed I would know
And now all I can do is remember

The places we would go

I'll remember you always
Always and forever
Never forget your lessons
The memories I'll treasure

I'll find hope in tomorrow
Recover from the sorrow, the pain
But there won't be a day
I won't think about you

As I listen, all I want to do is close the gap between us.

I lean across to find his lips.

And time stops.

Our tongues mesh together as our bodies tangle, our hands grabbing at each other with a desperation to say everything that our voices can't.

Each touch is frantic, each moment shows me how much I mean to him, how much he means to me.

I'm lying with my back against the sofa, Ryan on top of me. I tug down his shorts, pushing them off with ease. I grab at the ends of his hoodie, pulling it over his head.

As I undress him, he lifts up the bottom of my dress.

He doesn't pull it off me, he just moves it up to allow his hands to run all over my body.

I don't think I could feel any closer to him than I do right now. Hearing his music as we connect in such a hungry, aggressive passion, I realise how much I've fallen for him, how much I need him to feel my complete, weightless self. How much I... love him.

I grab at the back of his head, brushing my fingers through his hair, eliciting a gasp from him.

"I'm really falling for you," he pants, lowering his head to kiss my neck.

"I want you so bad," I sigh, grabbing at his chest.

"You always have me." He looks into my eyes.

I push my lips to his and place my hand on his lower back, drawing him close to me.

Ryan rests his head on my shoulder, kissing my neck as we come down from our high. We steadily catch our breath before unravelling from one another.

I've never experienced anything like that before, and I can't seem to calm myself.

I sit up and run to the bathroom.

Without thinking, I splash cold water on my face and when I look in the mirror, I realise my mascara has run down my cheeks.

I scan the bathroom for Claire's makeup bag, pulling out a couple of wipes to rub my face completely clean.

When I meet Ryan back in the basement, he's still on the couch—now fully clothed—but his music no longer fills the room.

"That was amazing." I smile at him, and he turns in my direction.

"You're telling me." He laughs, running his hand through his hair and shaking his head.

"No, I meant the album! I mean, yes, *that*," I point to the couch, "was also incredible. But the songs, Ryan. I've never heard anything so beautiful." I sit back down next to him and reach for his hands. He wraps his fingers around mine, tracing small circles on my palms.

"I feel like you're biased," he says quietly.

"No way. Nuh-uh." I shake my head violently.

"Well, we'll see how well it does before I get too excited." He shrugs. I know he's trying to play down how much of a big deal this is, but I wish he wouldn't. He's got so much to celebrate—management, a record deal, tour, everything.

He rests his head on the corner of the sofa, lying flat

311

on his back. I follow his lead, lying down on my side with my head resting on his chest, my whole body curling into him.

We sit in silence for a moment. The stillness is comforting; something you experience when you're so at home with someone you don't need to fill the space with pointless conversation.

I hear his breathing slow. I assume he's drifted to sleep, but then he murmurs peacefully, "I'm glad you're mine."

I look up at him and I realise he's not close to sleep at all. He's staring down at me, alert, watching me with a look of affection I've never witnessed before.

"Me too." I smile. "Although, I thought you were going to flip out when you saw me with Dan," I admit.

"I thought I would too." He chuckles. "I mean, I was angry. Not at you, just the thought of him hurting you." He shakes his head, intaking a breath. "But I realise getting worked up isn't doing either of us any good."

"Well, I appreciate you being there. I mean it." I squeeze him tight.

"I also don't want you to think that I asked you to be my girlfriend because of him. I didn't. I knew from the moment we spent our first night together that this was right. That I was yours."

I nestle into him. "I was already yours too. But I'm glad it's official." I smile and tilt my head towards him.

Our lips touch and our noses brush together as we beam at each other.

He brings me closer to him, our lips crashing on instinct. As we kiss, I feel both our bodies ignite again. He pulls me onto my feet and picks me up, wrapping my legs around his waist as he carries me towards the basement door.

"Shower," he commands.

I laugh, feeling a rush of excitement as he carries me upstairs.

Chapter Thirty-Nine

It's been a couple of weeks since I temporarily moved in with the band, and the house already feels like home. Nobody has asked any questions about my constant presence, instead they've welcomed me like a long-lost family member.

It's like I have an overwhelming ability to just be myself here, to say what's on my mind. For once, I actually want to hang out and be social instead of shut myself away.

The entire week has been a continual state of bliss, like I'm in a safe little bubble. I didn't want to step out of it and go to work this morning. Leaving Ryan in bed was torture, especially knowing he's not on shift today.

I check my unread texts as I walk to Jacks, grinning from ear to ear.

Ryan: This bed is too empty without you xxx

Me: Keep it warm for when I get home ;)

Ryan: Tempting. But you know we'll be in the basement.
Ryan: You're not getting out of band practice after work xx

Me: I hate you ☺

"You're late." Emily glowers at me.

"Sorry."

"You're never late," she observes as she unlocks the shop door and turns the security alarm off. I follow her to the staff room.

"I know, sorry. Traffic," I explain half-heartedly.

We dump our stuff in lockers and get started with the usual prep before opening the store. Neither of us say anything as we move, it's too early and I didn't even have enough time to make a cup of coffee this morning.

"Ryan tells me you guys are getting serious."

"Uh huh, I guess we are," I reply, absentmindedly hanging new stock on the rails.

"Is it going well?" She looks up at me and meets my eyes as she walks over. She grabs some of the jumpers from the pile and starts hanging too. I've never seen her bother with this type of task before, she usually leaves it to the most junior staff members. She must be eager for the gossip.

"Yes, actually." I nod. "It was kind of rocky at first, but we're finally on the same page. I really like him," I admit quietly.

A few awkward beats of silence pass between us as I wait for her to respond.

"Just promise me you'll be careful, okay?" She finally turns to me.

"Why?"

"You know he's like a brother to me. I love the guy. But he's not without his..." she pauses, "difficulties."

"I know," I interject, not wanting to hear the rest. She isn't getting to the point, nor is she saying anything constructive, so I would rather stop talking about him altogether.

"I know he's told you about his family and stuff, but just know that his life is volatile. When the emotions get too much for him, he bolts. You might think everything's

316

good one minute, and the next you're left with radio silence. Let's just say he's made a bit of a habit of it." She sighs, folding one of the jumpers on the table. "He basically did it to you the other week, remember?"

How could I forget those torturous days of silence? But he said it was a total accident, and I trust him on that.

"I know. I promise to be careful," I reply flatly.

I pretend that I've forgotten something in the stockroom and head towards the back of the store. I practically run to my locker and dig for my emergency supplies hidden under my bag.

I'm grateful that it's only me and Emily on shift this early, it means no one will come and disturb me. Not even Emily can leave the shop floor unattended.

I lock myself in the toilet cubicle, rip open the multipack of granola bars and inhale each one without stopping. I then open a large bar of chocolate, ignoring the intense pain of indigestion as I reach the final chunk. I turn on the sink taps, leaning my head under the cold water, taking a gulp to help the food in my stomach resurface.

My actions feel mechanic by this point. I dangle my head over the toilet bowl, waiting for the final step that I know will come.

Once it does, I wipe my mouth, dab tissue under my

watery eyes and hide the empty packets of food in my locker. I take a breath mint and walk back onto the shop floor as if nothing happened.

Five hours later, I'm out of Jacks and on my way back to the house for band practice. There's no denying I'm nervous. The butterflies in my stomach wreak havoc on the drive home.

I listen to music in the car and focus on singing along in the hope of warming up my vocal cords... but I just freak out and turn the stereo off. If I'm this nervous now, how the hell am I expected to sing at a festival?

I pull into my usual spot outside the house and fumble around in my rucksack for the spare key Ryan gave me. My hands are shaking as I eventually unlock the front door.

Music immediately fills my ears as I soon as I step into the house, emanating from the open door to the basement. I try to stall the inevitable by grabbing a glass of water from the kitchen and drinking the whole cup before refilling it and ambling downstairs.

"You made it!" Ryan beams as I pad into the

basement. He rushes over to me, planting a kiss on my cheek.

My heart does a small flip as I take in his outfit. He's wearing an oversized checked shirt, unbuttoned, exposing a black t-shirt underneath. His blue jeans are baggier too. They're nothing like the black slim jeans I'm used to seeing on him. They're straight leg and rolled up at the ankles... and they look *hot*.

"I'm glad to finally have another girl with me in this testosterone-fest!" Claire laughs.

I drop my bag on the couch and take a final sip of water before walking over to the microphone next to Ryan's.

They run me through the set list, explaining which parts of the songs they want me to sing. Admittedly, I've already downloaded their songs and listen to them any chance I get, so I already know most of the lyrics and melodies off by heart.

Given my lack of experience, I'm relieved that they're patient with me as I go through each song meticulously, trying to get it right.

I feel good. *Singing* feels good. Especially with them. The judgement I used to fear over music doesn't exist in this space. It doesn't exist with Ryan by my side.

After a few hours, we're able to run through the set

list without stopping, as if we're on stage at the festival.

I actually feel ready to perform to a crowd.

I'm on a complete high as I sing. I can't stop looking at Ryan. We steal glances and smiles at one another as we go, and I think it might be his smile alone that gives me the comfort and confidence I need to perform.

"So, what's this festival actually like?" I ask as soon as we decide to take a break.

"It's a winter festival, so not as big as some of the summer ones, don't worry," Tyler says, leaning against the wall and chugging down his bottle of water. I stare at him blankly.

"You're maybe looking at a thousand people at max," Adam adds with a shrug.

A thousand people? They've got to be kidding.

"Attending the festival?" my voice squeaks.

"No." Adam laughs. "That'll be the number of people watching us play."

Shit.

Ryan moves closer to me and places a hand on the small of my back. "You honestly won't notice, I swear." He lowers his head and kisses the top of my hair.

Whilst I try to gulp down my internal panic at the thought of playing in front of *a thousand* strangers, the others start packing away their instruments and go upstairs to order pizza. We're all starving after hours of practice, and I know Nadine will be here any minute.

"Zo, can we stay down here a sec?" Ryan asks.

"Sure. You've not made another album overnight, have you?"

"No," he replies with a laugh. "But I did want to ask if you'd record a song with me?" He grins, innocently tilting his head to the side. It's the look that instantly makes me putty in his hands, and I think he knows it.

"Record?" I quietly yelp, watching him dump his guitar on the sofa and walk over to the stereo system, opening a cabinet drawer.

"For my YouTube channel," he continues, pulling out his laptop and various other pieces of recording equipment.

"Your channel or the band's?" I ask, hoping it's the latter.

The band's page is *tiny* compared to Ryan's. I'm pretty sure YouTube was how his management found him in the first place. He has a sizeable following, and rightly so; the videos of him performing are jaw-dropping amazing. And I'm not just saying that because I'm his girlfriend.

"Mine." He smiles up at me.

I'm stunned into silence.

This must be a big risk for him, surely? I know he makes a bit of money from his channel, and I don't want to ruin that for him.

"So, will you?" he prompts me with a cheeky grin.

Ugh, it's the same grin he used a second ago. The putty-in-his-hand grin. Damn him.

"Um," I fumble.

"Please? You can pick the song if you like?"

"No, it's okay. You pick."

"So, you'll do it?" His grin doubles in size. My throat goes so dry, all I can manage is a nod.

Once Ryan sets up the equipment and camera, he picks up his guitar and looks at me excitedly.

"I actually had an idea I wanted to try with you. It's actually two cover songs," he explains. "One of the lines in one song sort of overlaps with a line in the other. I've been messing around with them, trying to mesh them together. I'll show you." He places his hands on the guitar and starts to play.

I instantly recognise the first song, *Forever and Always* by Taylor Swift. As soon as he starts singing the first few lines, he overlaps it with *Cable Cars* by The Fray. I had no idea these were the types of songs he would listen to—or think to cover.

It seems incredible that a few simple, overlapping

words can create such an original blend of two completely different songs. At least, I thought they were totally different... until now.

Ryan's version sounds so seamless, like he's taken the strongest parts of each song and created something so unique. The sound is intoxicating.

Chapter Forty

"That was so cool!" I turn to Ryan, unable to wipe the grin from my face. "How did you get the idea of putting those two songs together?"

We're walking up the basement stairs to join the band for dinner. I'm on a high. I've got *such* an adrenaline rush after filming the cover song mash-up.

Maybe it's my pull to Ryan, maybe it's the overwhelming freedom I feel when I sing. Either way, I'm on cloud nine. Or maybe cloud ten. Is cloud ten better than cloud nine? If so, I'm on it.

"I dunno. I just kind of figure it out by matching chord progressions and stuff." He shrugs nonchalantly.

When we get to the top of the stairs, Claire is at the front door paying the delivery driver for our pizza. My stomach grumbles as I get a whiff of garlic and cheese.

"Are you going to be okay eating with everyone?" Ryan whispers into my ear, stopping at the top of the stairs and clinging onto my waist.

"I... think so," I begin. "I actually hadn't thought about it." I was too focussed on singing to think about anything else, especially food.

"Okay. Well, we can go upstairs by ourselves? Any excuse to have you all alone." He winks.

"No, let's eat with the others. I can do it. I'll have you there." Singing with the band has given me a new lease of life. I feel invincible, like I could handle anything right now, even food.

"God, I love you." He smiles, shaking his head.

The weight of his words hangs between us for a second as his brain catches up to his mouth. I open my mouth to speak, but before I have a chance to respond, Ryan pulls me into the kitchen.

I feel my heartbeat in my throat as my mind unravels. The last thing I want him to do is take my silence for rejection. I'm not rejecting him at all. I feel the exact same way and I want to tell him that, but I want to be sure his 'I love you' wasn't just a casual slip of the tongue and something he really feels. The way I do.

Why did he have to pull me into the kitchen so quickly? It's not like I can say anything to him now in front of everyone.

My eyes follow Ryan as he stomps to the fridge and pulls out two cans of lemonade, pushing one across the kitchen counter towards me with slight force, avoiding eye contact.

"Zoe! Come here," Nadine calls from the couch. I turn to see her waving frantically, tapping the space next to her. I smile and move towards her, figuring I can talk to Ryan later, when we're alone.

Nadine launches into a million questions, asking all about rehearsal. I don't have time to reply before Tyler keenly answers her questions for me.

Nadine squeals with delight as she listens to him, flapping her hands around. I think her animation might be more of a reflection of how she feels about Tyler, as opposed to her genuine excitement to see me perform at the festival. I'm sure she's happy for me, but probably not as much as she's conveying right now. It's sweet though, how much she adores Tyler. They honestly do make such an amazing couple.

"I really do wonder if there is anything you suck at. Besides cheer initiation games," Nadine chimes in, making me laugh.

"Believing in herself." Tyler grins at me as he walks over to the kitchen counter.

My eyes follow Tyler, and then they flit to Ryan. He's sitting on a stool at the kitchen counter, facing away from me, keeping Claire company as she unpacks the food.

Tyler brings two boxes back to the sofa and hands one to me. I keep my focus on Ryan's back as I take the food, silently screaming at him to turn around.

He must sense my burning eyes as he eventually swivels his stool in my direction. He looks down at the unopened box in my hands and back up to my eyes. He then gives me a small, knowing smile and stands up.

Relief washes through my body as he takes a seat next to me and wraps one arm around my shoulders. He uses his free hand to open the pizza box and gives me a gentle, comforting nudge. I guess he's either shaken off his earlier mood, or he's choosing to ignore it for the sake of my food related weirdness. Either way, it only makes me love him more. If he can put his own feelings aside for my sake, that just goes to show the type of guy he is.

I can't wait to tell him that I love him too.

I pick up a slice of pizza and slowly start to chew, feeling uncomfortable, but not terrible. I concentrate on Ryan's arm wrapped around me, the feel of his hand on my shoulder.

I've got this.

Once I've finished my first piece, I feel my phone

vibrate in my pocket. I shift the pizza box onto Ryan's lap and check my notifications.

Jake: Hey stranger. We should talk. Are you home tonight?

I pause and read the text again, unsure of how to feel.

"You okay?" Ryan asks, and the others glance in our direction.

"It's Jake. He wants to talk." I look at Ryan, but he doesn't say anything, his face is neutral.

"That's great! He probably wants to fix things. Maybe you should go speak to him?" Nadine adds with a mouthful of pizza. Ryan's body tenses next to me.

I know that my fear of being back in that apartment isn't really to do with Jake, so I should at least hear him out. I don't know if Alice will be there, but either way, it'll be good to go. I can't hide in this house forever, no matter how much I want to.

I text Jake back, telling him I'll be there within the hour. Ryan's eyes watch my phone as I type. As soon as he sees the message, he gets up, knocking the pizza box to the floor.

I instinctively follow him to the top of the stairs, getting flashbacks to the fight we had just the other week.

"Wait!" I call as he storms into his room. He continues without turning around, but he doesn't slam the door, he leaves it open.

"I don't want you going back there," he snaps, spinning to face me.

"I need to, Ryan. I need to hear him out." I take a deep breath. "I don't even think Alice will be there." I try to reassure him but it's not doing any good, his body is completely rigid.

"I'm not letting them drag you back," he spits.

Anger rises in my stomach. "You mean you don't want them to drag me away from you, don't you?" I shout. I know I need to be patient with him and remain calm, but I can't.

"For fuck's sake, Zoe, this isn't about me!" He waves his hands in the air.

"Well, what is it then?" I demand. "One minute you tell me you love me and the next you're angry with me."

I wait for what feels like hours for him to say something, but he doesn't. He just stares at me, his dark eyes focussed on mine. He turns his back to look out of the window, and by the time he turns around again, I'm no closer to reading him.

"You never understand," he eventually whispers. I can't detect a single emotion in his voice, it's as flat as the expression plastered across his face.

"Ryan, I love you. I'm not going anywhere, I'm not your mum or your da—"

"Shut the fuck up, *now!*" he booms.

My heart jolts. I feel something inside of me tear. It's as if all the pain I've been suppressing since Kady died suddenly reappears again in an earthshattering blow. It crushes the confident exterior I built in the basement only moments ago.

I always thought Ryan walked into my life to stitch that hole of pain back together. But now, he's ripping it open again. And for what? Fear that I might disappear? Fear that I might not love him back?

I search his face for a glimmer of the Ryan I know and love, but I don't see him. His eyes are so dark, his jaw is clenched. This is not how I pictured telling someone I loved them for the very first time.

I feel my eyes prick with tears. I take a couple of breaths to calm myself. "Please, Ryan. Talk to me." My voice comes out in a croaky, desperate whisper, but I don't care. I just want the fighting to stop.

He sits down on the bed and looks at me. His facial expression is still unreadable. I have no idea what's going to tumble out of his mouth next.

"Don't ever mention my parents again," he snaps.

"*Ever.* You understand?"

"Okay, just talk to me. Please," I beg, sitting next to him.

"They're toxic and you'll only end up hurting yourself trying to deal with them." He glares at me, sending a shiver down my spine.

"You don't think I can handle myself with my flatmates?" I ask.

I thought Ryan was the person who believed in me most. I thought he would want me to go and fix things with my housemates, to push myself out of my comfort zone and become stronger. He shouldn't be encouraging me to hide away.

"No, I don't," he admits.

The bubbling anger in my stomach bursts through my entire body and I see nothing but red.

"That's rich coming from you!" I bellow, springing up from the bed. "Yeah, I still struggle with things, but I'm trying," I defend. "Whereas you have a fit every time I want to do the smallest thing by myself! What happened to '*I realise getting worked up isn't doing either of us any good*'?" I mimic his voice. "I'm not the one going anywhere, Ryan. I'm not the one going on a fucking tour for God knows how long. I should be the one freaking out, not *you*," I bark.

I turn away from him, pacing the room back and forth, my sweaty palms holding my throbbing head. I can feel Ryan's eyes following me, but his mouth stays shut. His silence is infuriating

I don't know what more I can do. I'm trying to tackle my fear of singing to spend more time with him. I'm trying to sort out everything in my head so that we can do regular things like go on dinner dates and be a normal, happy couple.

"Why am I still not enough for you?" I finally whisper. Tears have escaped down my cheek, flowing at an embarrassingly fast rate. I wipe them away with the back of my hand.

Why do I always cry when I'm angry?

Ryan tilts his head, looking at me as if I'm speaking another language. He lowers his head and puts his face in his hands, hiding from me.

After a few seconds of silence, I hear a strange noise escape his mouth. He removes his hands from his face.

He's crying?

"Baby, I don't *ever* want to make you feel like that," he croaks, rubbing his eyes. "You're everything to me, *everything*. I just don't want them hurting you. But in the process—" He sighs to steady his breath, "I'm the one hurting you."

He shakes his head and wipes his eyes once again. He reaches out for my hands and brings them to his lips, gently kissing my palms.

After a few moments, he lifts his head, his bloodshot hazel eyes searching my face.

I don't know what to say to him, so I just lower myself onto his lap. I lean closer to him and wrap my hands around his neck, pushing my body against his as our lips touch.

"I love you," Ryan sighs into my mouth.

"I love you," I reply. The tension leaves our bodies, replaced by a desperation to get closer, to be together.

Chapter Forty-One

When I arrive at my apartment, I walk straight to the kitchen to find Jake on the couch, waiting for me. He looks up from his book and smiles warmly. I scan the room just to check Alice isn't around.

"She's not in," he says.

"Oh. Okay. Sorry I'm late," I mumble, taking a seat opposite him.

"It's really no problem." He smiles again. "I haven't seen you in a while."

"I know. I've been steering clear of Alice," I admit sheepishly. Jake nods slowly and rubs his hands over his arms, as if a cold chill has just passed through the kitchen.

"Yeah, she's been..." He sighs and shifts in his seat. "That's what I wanted to talk to you about."

"Okay," I murmur, unsure what else to say.

"I'm sure she doesn't mean it. I think she's just going through a lot right now." Jake runs his hand through his wavy hair.

"Doesn't give her the right to behave like that though, does it?" I snap, feeling more irritated as the words leave my mouth.

"You're right, it doesn't. And I'm honestly so sorry I haven't done a better job at sticking up for you and keeping the peace. That's on me."

"Jake, it's not your fault." I relax slightly, feeling a little bad for the guilt plastered across his face. "Of course, it would've been nice to know you had my back, but the animosity and harsh, unexplainable actions have come from her."

"I know, but still, I played a part. I think perhaps I was trying to cut her some slack."

"Slack for what?" I demand.

"I know the way she's acted out might seem a bit puzzling to you, but I think it goes pretty deep. Moreso than perhaps you realised."

"Right..?"

"Truthfully, I think she just feels a little alone. I think the grief of losing Kady is hitting her more than she's letting on. And I think seeing you with Ryan possibly stings, it reminds her that she's lost the one person she always used to confide in."

I pause, taking a moment to think through my response. "Yeah, I know they were pretty close. But I still find it hard to justify her actions. I don't think she should be taking her anger out on me, even if we've never had a great relationship, it's no excuse. And anyway, there's always been a bit of tension, it's just got worse since Kady, and I literally can't even comprehend why. It's all so juvenile."

"Can I be honest with you about something?"

"Of course you can."

Jake visibly exhales, the weight of whatever he is carrying coming to the surface. "Please don't be mad at me, but do you think that maybe it's not unexplainable?"

"What are you getting at, Jake?"

"I just mean, it seems like her tension with you dates back to first year, but it's not just a case of the pair of you simply not getting along. Because at the beginning of our first year, you used to hang out with Kady and Alice a lot."

"Yeah, but after Christmas break, I came back and Alice would hardly say two words to me. She suddenly changed and it just didn't feel good to be around her."

"Because she needed you and you weren't there, Zoe."

"What are you on about? Jake, just spit it out, please."
I blow out a ragged, frustrated breath.

He groans. "I'm trying, it's just hard when it's not really my thing to tell. You two should be having this conversation, but you're both as stubborn as each other."

I raise my eyebrows, waiting for him to continue.

"Okay." He puffs. "Zoe, do you know what happened to Alice last year?"

I shake my head, staring at him blankly.

"She almost had to drop out of uni because her dad got arrested for fraud. I don't know the full details, not as much as Kady did, but it sounded pretty serious. Their assets got frozen, she had to do a lot of police interviews, loads of their friends and family cut them out. It sounded pretty messed up."

"Wait, how did I not know about this?" I ask, shock rippling through me.

"She tried to tell you. When it happened, she texted all of us, asking for us to come back to the flat because she needed us, she needed to tell us something. You bailed for some reason."

"I... uh... but if she only tried the once, then—"

Jake sighs. "She tried texting you on our group chat so many times after that. Every time she asked if we could all hang out because she needed us, you said you were busy. You didn't make time for her. After a while, she just stopped bothering. She leant on Kady the most, and I guess that's when they started getting really close, and when you started to feel isolated from them."

Shock and guilt surge through my body. I don't understand how I could have been so oblivious to such a huge event in her life.

"Like I said, it doesn't excuse anything. I agree, petty arguments shouldn't have a place in this apartment. But I just wanted you to understand that there was a layer to it you were oblivious to. She's lost her dad to jail, and now she's lost one of her best friends. We're all fighting our own battles, and perhaps if now and then we lift our heads above the sand and check in with one another, this tension wouldn't exist. But I'm not solely blaming you, she could try harder to open up instead of lashing out."

"But I guess I haven't given her a safe space to open up in the past, so why would she keep trying?"

Jake shrugs, confirming my thoughts.

God, I feel terrible... and weird. I'm still so angry at her, yet I feel so much guilt all at the same time. How is this possible?

"Don't blame yourself. We've all got so much going on. And I know her behaviour has been hurtful, so I'm not expecting you to waltz into her room and have a heart-to-heart the next time she's home. I just think it's worth bearing in mind. She owes you an apology for sure, and I honestly don't know if she's ready to give it, or to admit to her behaviour for that matter. I think this is one that'll have to come with time. I just wanted us to have an open chat because I don't want our friendship to suffer because of this."

"I really appreciate it, and I'm sorry to have put you in this position in the first place."

"It's okay." He smiles. "I didn't stick up for you enough. That wasn't fair of me. So long as we can hit reset, consider it forgotten."

"I'll try to be around more," I promise, offering him a smile. "I'm not saying I'm ready to have the big talk with Alice just yet. Maybe in time. I really don't know. But I would like me and you to spend more time together."

"No, I know. There's no pressure." His smile is so genuine, so relieved. I already feel a million times better for coming here tonight.

"Do you want to go for breakfast tomorrow?" he asks. "It's been ages since we last did that."

"Yeah, sure. Sounds great," I agree.

Jake lets out a huge yawn and excuses himself to go to bed.

I pad to my room, immediately calling Ryan to let him

know what happened. I also tell him that I'm staying at my apartment tonight. He tries persuading me to come back to his house, but he eventually gives up, admitting it's what I need.

I thought I'd be able to drift straight to sleep as soon as my face hit the pillow, but I can't. Maybe sleeping alone is impossible because I've gotten so used to drifting off next to Ryan. I don't like the idea, especially as he'll be away for months at a time on tour.

I toss and turn for a while, waiting for sleep to take over. But it doesn't. There's this pulling in my chest that only intensifies as the seconds pass. I have a burning urge to get out of bed and walk down the corridor, towards the source of the magnetic pull.

I stand outside of Kady's room for a second, eventually reaching for the handle, opening the door.

I inhale a breath.

Her room is completely empty.

All I can see is white walls, a white mattress and a plain floor. There's no purple. No pink. No clothes. No makeup. No personality.

She's really gone.

Tears sting my eyes and I go back to my room, closing the door behind me. The familiar pain in my chest spreads through my entire body.

I sit on my bed to steady myself, letting the tears roll down my cheeks as I remain as still as possible.

My mind is spinning a million miles an hour. The pain is breaking me, crushing me.

I want it to stop.

I need to feel something physical instead. I need to feel physical pain.

I take a deep breath to push the terrifyingly dark thoughts from my head.

I find my phone on the bed and dial for Ryan. He picks up immediately.

"I need you," is all I can manage to choke out.

He tells me he's on his way, and before I know it, he's in the car park. I throw my keys out of my bedroom window for him to catch and he lets himself in.

As soon as my bedroom door opens, I collapse into his arms, sobbing. "You were right," I cry into his black sweater.

One of his arms wraps around my waist and the other cups the back of my head.

"It's okay, baby. I'm here now." He leans his cheek on

top of my head and rubs my back, cradling me.

A few minutes pass as I cry uncontrollably. It feels good to let all the tears out in Ryan's arms. He's my rock, the only person to pull me out of the darkness of my own thoughts.

"What was I right about?" he asks when my sobs finally subside. "Did you guys fight? I thought you sorted things. If he hurt you—"

"No, no, it's not like that." I hiccup. "I just got sad again... about Kady."

"Were you sick?" He searches my face. I shake my head and feel his body relax. "Then I wasn't right, Zo. You were. You were strong enough to handle this and I should never have doubted you."

I furrow my eyebrows, confused by his words.

"Zoe, you stopped yourself from doing anything bad. You let me be here for you instead. I'm so proud of you, baby." He kisses the top of my head, placing his hands on my shoulders and guiding us both to sit on my bed. He pulls me onto his lap, rubbing my back slowly.

"I wanted to though, Ry. I really did," I whisper into his shoulder, melancholy lacing my every word.

I want to tell him that, when he's not around, the thoughts of Kady crush me to the point where I want to hurt myself. I want to tell him that, when I'm alone, I can't stop feeling guilty that she's dead and I'm alive. I want to tell him that I never want us to be away from each other again, that I need to fall asleep next to him every night. I want to tell him that he's the one pulling me out of the water when a wave drags me under.

There are so many things I want to tell my lifeguard, but instead, I feel myself drifting to sleep in his arms, the pain in my chest finally dissolving.

Chapter Forty-Two

I jump out of bed, heading for the shower with my phone in hand. I reply to my last message from Jake, confirming I'll be ready in thirty minutes.

I wash quickly and practically race back to my bedroom. When I open the door, Ryan jumps up from the bed, grabbing a spare towel from my wardrobe. As he passes me to go to the bathroom, he plants a kiss on my head.

I smile, enjoying this strange sense of normalcy with him in my apartment. I never thought I'd be the type of girl that wants to stay with their boyfriend every night, but I can't help it. I need him.

"Thanks for staying over," I say once he's back in the

room with wet hair and a towel wrapped around his waist. I could *definitely* get used to the view of him like this in my apartment.

"I'm always going to be here for you," he replies, reaching for his clothes.

As I sit on the floor opposite the mirror, applying my make-up, I ask Ryan about his plans for today. He shifts awkwardly on the bed as he watches me, cautiously explaining that he's doing more work on the new album.

"I thought the album was finished?" I probe, applying another lick of mascara to my lashes.

He catches my eye in the reflection of the mirror. "Uh, it is. I'm... going to discuss the tour." He breaks eye contact and looks at the ground, running a hand through his hair and shaking his head so the strands fall back in place.

I open my mouth to press for more information, but a knock at my door interrupts us. Ryan throws me a concerned look as he gets up from the bed to answer it. I think we're both fearing its Alice.

"Hey. Uh, is Zoe ready?" Jake asks hesitantly in the doorway.

I check my watch. *Damn* that thirty minutes flew by.

I scramble to collect myself from the floor, noticing Ryan towering over Jake in the doorframe, his rigid muscles tensing as he blocks Jake's entry.

"Hey." I smile, pushing Ryan away from the door. "I'm ready."

Despite Ryan's coolness, Jake smiles at him. "I'm Jake. It's nice to meet you properly." He holds out a hand for Ryan, who hesitates for a moment before deciding to shake it.

"I'll see you tonight?" I turn to Ryan as I grab my leather jacket from the hook on my wall.

"You're not coming for breakfast?" Jake asks. Ryan shakes his head. "Well, you should come if you're not busy," Jake offers, stealing a quick glance in my direction for approval. I smile at him, letting him know I'm grateful he's making the effort with Ryan.

"Uh..." Ryan looks at me, also awaiting some kind of guidance.

"Sure, you should deffo come!" I encourage. "If you have time, of course."

"Okay, sure." Ryan smiles, swinging his arm around my shoulder as we all walk out of my room.

"We're still going to study after breakfast, right?" Jake asks, looking at Ryan and back to me. I nod and he rushes down the corridor calling out, "Okay, let me just grab my bag!" as he goes.

"Shoot, I left my bag at yours," I realise, turning to

Ryan. I can't go to the library without my stuff.

"No, you didn't." He smirks. "It's in my car, I forgot to bring it up last night. I figured you'd accidentally left it in your rush to get back here, you didn't even take your purse." He chuckles at me.

"You did?"

He nods and I grin, reaching up to plant a kiss on his lips.

It might sound corny, but in this simple gesture, I know that he loves me. The attention he pays to me, the way he's looking out for me, surely has to be a sign of that.

I never thought I'd experience the type of love my parents have, where two people's worlds are so in sync that neither feels alone or out of place. There's another person supporting me at a time when I often forget how to look after myself.

Jake meets us back in the hallway and we silently amble to Ryan's car. His eyes bulge as soon as they take in Ryan's Jeep, but he doesn't say anything. He hovers for a moment outside of the car, looking a little unsure. I tell him to jump in the front.

"Are you a student too?" Jake asks Ryan as he buckles his seatbelt.

"Nope. I'm a musician."

"No way. What do you play?"

"Guitar and vocals. In a band." Ryan steals a glance at me in the wing mirror. I get the vibe he doesn't want to mention his solo career, so I don't correct him.

"What's your band's name?"

"The Lanes."

Jake's eyes practically pop out of their sockets. "For real?"

"Uh huh," Ryan answers.

"I've seen you guys play! I thought you looked familiar! I went to Green Man last year. You play there every year, don't you?" Jake gushes excitedly and I can't help but grin as I look between them.

"Yeah, we do." Ryan shrugs as he slows down to let a woman pushing a pram cross the road. He continues to stare at them as they cross, perhaps for a beat too long.

"You guys were awesome when I saw you. Do you play many festivals?"

"We try to. Playing festivals is always a blast. You know, Zoe's gunna sing at our next one. It's a big winter thing in a couple of weeks. You should come."

Jake agrees immediately, even saying that he'll invite his rugby team.

Great, more people to witness my failure.

The whole car ride Jake doesn't stop gushing about how cool it is that I sing. I try to tell him I can't, but Ryan doesn't help the situation, bigging me up and setting Jake's expectations sky high.

Regardless of the embarrassment I feel, I'm enjoying the fact that the awkward air seems to have lifted, all thanks to music. I notice how Ryan slowly but surely lets down his tough exterior to engage in conversation with Jake. He even ends up talking about his solo career after all.

"How long do you go on tour for?" Jake asks, continuing his interrogation.

"Six months, over the summer," Ryan answers, shooting me a weird look from the rear-view mirror as he runs a hand through his hair.

"I'm going to join him when my exams are over," I explain, beaming at Ryan in the reflection. His eyes crinkle as if he's possibly smiling, but I can't really see his mouth to be certain.

Once Ryan finds a parking space in the student village, we decide to go to The Oak for breakfast. It's the place Jake and I used to always go to in our first year.

We take a seat at one of the tables in the far corner closest to the window. Jake and Ryan sit on opposite sides and, for a tiny second, I deliberate who to sit next to before plopping down next to Ryan.

I shuffle close to him, our legs brushing.

"So, what's new, Jake?" I ask, picking up one of the menus and flipping it over. I don't feel so nervous this time. I'm not sure why, perhaps it's the fact that I order the same breakfast every time I come here, or maybe it's Ryan's presence.

"Not much. Rugby's pretty brutal." He shrugs. "Do you know what you want?" he asks Ryan, standing up and looking over at the bar.

"I'll order," Ryan insists, but Jake shakes his head.

"Honestly, I've got it." Jake smiles. "Usual for you yeah, Zoe?"

I feel Ryan's hand grip my thigh a little firmer as his body tenses. I ignore him and smile up to Jake, nodding.

"I'll have whatever she's having. Thanks." Ryan passes our menus to Jake, who walks away to place our order at the bar.

Ryan lets out a huge breath next to me, scowling. He lifts his hands, placing his elbows on the table and rubbing his face with his palms. I give his leg a gentle squeeze and lean to kiss him on the cheek. The tiny kiss seems to do something as, when Ryan uncovers his face, I see a gentle smile dance across his lips.

"I know, I'm ridiculous," Ryan says with a sigh.

"The worst," I reply, playfully nudging him.

When Jake gets back to the table, he bows his head

and sits down in his chair, staring at his hands on the table. "There—uh—was actually something I wanted to talk to you about," Jake finally says. "I know I should've mentioned it last night, but after discussing everything we did, it didn't feel right."

"Go on," I reply slowly.

"Kady's accident... the driver. He actually passed away last week."

I stare at him, unable to move. I blink a couple of times and feel Ryan's grip tighten around me.

"What?" Ryan asks. I feel his eyes on me, but I can't turn my head.

The waiter brings over our tray of food, setting down two bowls of granola and a stack of pancakes. Jake grabs his plate and pushes the bowls towards Ryan and me.

"I don't really know the full details, but he passed away last week following a heart attack. Totally unrelated to the accident." Jake forks a piece of pancake into his mouth, wolfing it down before continuing. "It's kind of sad, actually. They do say when someone is responsible for the loss of life, it can break them so deeply that they end up suffering in some form or another themselves. I guess, deep down somewhere, being responsible for Kady's death broke him, and his body just reacted to it. He wasn't that old, late fifties, but I know the accident tore him apart. That's what Kady's family said anyway."

"You've spoken to them?" I ask.

"No, Alice did."

I'm not entirely sure what I expected to hear, but I've had the wind knocked out of me. Is this news supposed to feel like closure? Justice? I don't think the loss of the driver's life is anything of the sort. It's just an added level of tragedy to this already fucked up situation.

The crash was pinned as an accident. Case closed. Boxed away and tied up with a neat, unresolvable ribbon. There was nothing the police could do. No court case. No one to blame.

I didn't even think about the driver and the injustice of him walking around, carrying on his life as normal, because I didn't want to think of him at all. I didn't want to put a face to the person responsible. But does knowing he didn't survive feel any better? Not really.

I feel like I'm beginning to understand what Ryan meant when he described the incompleteness he felt after his dad died, how there will always be a piece of the puzzle missing. How can you move on when so many things are left so broken?

Chapter Forty-Three

My phone won't stop vibrating in my pocket, I can feel it buzzing away every two seconds. I'm trying not to look at it. I want to focus on my assignment, but Nadine won't give it a rest.

I know why she's texting. It's about the video Ryan uploaded, our duet. He messaged me as soon as he got back to his house after breakfast to ask if he could upload it. I know he wanted to do something nice for me, to distract me from Jake's news.

I pull out my phone, figuring if I don't respond to Nadine soon, she's going to track me down in the library and cause a scene.

Nadine: OMFG ZO!!! HE UPLOADED IT!

Nadine: Have you seen how many views it's got already???

Nadine: HELLOOOOO?

Me: Sorry at the library. Not seen it yet ☹

Nadine: FUCK. You can SING. Catch up later, promise?

Me: Sure. I'll see you at the band's house tonight?

Nadine: YES! I'll be there at 7. Can't wait! Xxx

I place my phone back on the desk and put my earphones in, needing music to drown out my thoughts about Kady long enough to focus on my work.

I wouldn't usually listen to music in such a silent space, even with headphones in. I always fear someone might hear a faint beat escaping the buds if I play it too loudly. But today, I don't care.

I scroll through one of Ryan's playlists to find something I'm in the mood for. I like following his account to discover what he's currently listening to. It's like having him with me at all times. It's like peeking into his soul, getting a sense of how he might be feeling based upon the new playlist he makes that week.

Today it's Arcade Fire, *Everything Now.*

The happy song is very much contrasting to my sour mood, but I'm trying to force the sadness out of me and indulge in Ryan's evident contentment.

Most people I know will listen to a song because it makes them feel a particular way, or just because it's in the charts at the time. But I always find myself looking for something a little deeper; studying each lyric to understand the emotions behind the song, to find the reason it was written. I never stick to listening to just one genre either, I meander between artists and stop on a song if I connect with the lyrics in some way. I know Ryan is the exact same, so listening to his playlists is like mindreading.

Out of the corner of my eye, I notice Jake walk back into the study area after taking a lunch break. He goes back to work on the desk next to me and I glance up to the clock on the wall. I've been studying for five hours straight. I could definitely use a break too. I scribble a note to Jake on a piece of paper, telling him I'll be back in ten minutes, and then grab my jacket from the back of my chair, walking out of the silent library.

My music cuts out just as I push through the doors and get out into the fresh air. I pull out my phone, figuring the playlist has ended. Instead, I see my dad's number flash across the screen.

I swipe to accept the FaceTime request and sit on a wooden bench outside the law building. I wince at how cold the bench is at first. Autumn didn't last long this year. Then again, it never really does around here.

"We've finally caught you!" Dad beams, his face ridiculously close to the screen.

He eventually moves the phone away from his face, holding his arm out far enough to reveal Hannah and Mum sat at the dining table in my parent's house.

"Yeah, sorry. I've been so busy with everything," I half-heartedly explain, deciding not to tell them about the band. I doubt they would've seen the video that Ryan posted today anyway. Luckily, they aren't active on social media—even Hannah hates it.

"We're calling to talk about your birthday this weekend. You don't have plans, do you?" Dad asks.

I take a breath and begin to answer, but Hannah cuts across me. "Dad has the time off, so we thought we should come up for dinner! We haven't visited you for soooo long!"

Shit. I still haven't told them about Ryan.

"That would be great. Can I bring someone?" I ask. Better to bite the bullet. I doubt Ryan would want to miss a chance at meeting my family anyway.

"A boy?" Mum teases excitedly.

Hannah beams down the phone and I notice Dad actually has a smile on his face. Maybe they'll take it better than I thought.

"Uh, yes actually. His name is Ryan," I tell them. I chew my lip as I watch Mum and Hannah glance at each other.

"Is he a classmate? That would be excellent for you. Two budding lawyers, you'll be a powerhouse come graduation!" Dad begins.

"Umm no, he's not. I met him at Jacks."

"Oh. Well, you must bring him to dinner," Dad instructs.

Ryan always said he wanted to meet my family, so I hope he doesn't mind me dragging him along to dinner. I haven't actually told him it's my birthday, mainly because I don't normally celebrate it beyond a dinner with my family. I even take a shift at work if it falls on a weekend too.

It's not that I hate celebrating, I just haven't had enough people in my life to warrant doing so. It's weird to think that this year will be different.

357

After cramming in another few hours of studying, I finally leave the library with Jake. It feels strange leaving at six and walking out into the darkness. I miss the long summer nights already.

I say goodbye to Jake as he heads off in the direction of the gym, turning towards the campus gate where I agreed to meet Ryan. I'm a little nervous about seeing him. I know he's going to want to talk about the driver now that I'm over the initial shock of his death, but I don't want to.

Ryan believes in talking everything through, dissecting each detail in order to move forward. He tries to make sense of every single thing in life, but there's no making sense of this.

He leans over to give me a gentle kiss on the cheek as soon as I jump into the Jeep. His eyes scan my face, searching for something readable as we pull apart. I slap on a bright smile.

"How was your day?" I quickly ask.

"Nothing special really." He shrugs. "A few of my songs are being teased next month. We've gone through the release strategy today, it's mad," he explains, twisting his hands around the top of the steering wheel.

"That *is* special, don't be silly!" I beam at him, playfully nudging his shoulder with my hand. "You know

I want to hear about your music career, right?"

"I just—" Ryan fumbles, clutching at the steering wheel. "I know that I'm asking a lot from you, with my career choice. It's so unpredictable."

It's true, his career is so unknown. But I wouldn't change it even if I could. Music is an integral part of his soul, and now it's an integral part of mine... an integral part of *us*.

"I knew that when we met though, Ryan. This isn't news to me." I sigh. "I'm sorry about what I said in the heat of an argument, but it wasn't about you or the tour at all. I just felt like you were being unfair, getting mad that I would leave you when I'm not physically going anywhere and have no plans to, whereas you actually do."

I look out the window as I continue. "But please don't pay attention to me. I want you to talk about your career with me. I couldn't bear it if you didn't." My eyes sting at the thought of pushing him away.

He runs a comforting palm over the back of my head. "Okay, I promise I will." He smiles reassuringly.

He starts to open up about his meeting, placing a hand on my lap as he talks animatedly. I listen as he tells me all about the artist who designed his album cover, the social media marketing strategy his team have put in place, and the plans his management have to record his music videos.

His eyes brighten just talking about his career. I feel so excited for him, he's on the brink of achieving everything he ever dreamed of, and he completely deserves it.

"Enough about me. How was your day?" he asks.

"It was okay. There is actually something I want to talk to you about." I glance at him.

"Shoot."

"It's my birthday on Saturday," I say, immediately raising my hand to stop him talking as he opens his mouth. "I know, I know, I should have said something. But my parents rang and asked if we wanted to go to dinner with them on Saturday night. Would that be okay?"

"I actually knew it was your birthday." Ryan chuckles. I whip my head to look at him. "Remember, my best friend's sister is your manager, she obviously has that information."

Damn, he really is on the ball.

"Whatever happened to workplace confidentiality! I could get her fired for that," I huff playfully.

Ryan laughs. "But dinner with your parents sounds great. So long as I get you in the day?"

"I have a shift at Jacks."

He grins menacingly. "I already got you out of work."

"You did?" I smile when he nods smugly. "But wait, what about band practice?"

"You seriously want to have a band practice on your birthday?"

"Uh huh." I nod vigorously. "Even if we just practice for an hour. I want to be totally prepared for this festival."

"Well, whatever you want on your birthday, Little Miss Pedantic."

>>>>•<<<<

Ryan grabs my hand and pulls me up to his bedroom as soon as we get into the house. I laugh as I stumble behind him.

"Okay! I'm coming!" I chuckle.

He swings the door open and puts his hands on my shoulders, manoeuvring me towards the bed, grinning cheekily.

He lowers me to sit on the edge of the mattress and I expect him to start kissing me, but he walks towards his desk. I cock my head to the side as I watch him walk further away from me.

My smile must have disappeared because Ryan starts

tutting, shaking his head. "Can a guy not just sit his girlfriend down on his bed without her mind falling in the gutter?"

"Not when that guy is you."

He grins and picks up his laptop from the desk before sitting down next to me. He opens the lid and I see the internet page is open with our video on it. I groan, putting my head in my hands.

"Come on," Ryan says with a sigh, lowering my hands to uncover my face. "Fine. I won't make you watch it, but at least look here." He points to the number of views and my eyes widen. The video already has a few thousand views and it's not even been twenty-four-hours since Ryan uploaded it.

I grab the laptop and take a closer look. I can't believe it. Who would want to watch me sing?

I take a deep breath, telling myself the views are all for Ryan, not me. I scroll down to the comments.

This girl can sing!

Who is this girl? She's amazing. We need to see more of her!

I wish I could like it again and again ☺

I feel my cheeks flush as I read the comments. I still can't quite believe other people, besides my closest friends, think I can sing.

Some of the comments make me chuckle, they're from girls asking if me and Ryan are together with several sad emojis next to the questions.

But then I suddenly stop scrolling.

WOW. PLEASE don't tell me that chubby girl is your gf?! You can do better bro!!

My heart drops to my stomach.

Please don't tell me that chubby girl is your gf.

Chubby girl.

Chubby.

I feel sick.

I quickly scroll back to the top of the screen before Ryan can see what caught my attention. I snap the lid shut, passing the laptop back to him. I can feel his eyes watching me, so I try to give him my best smile.

He's not buying it.

"What's wrong?" he asks, searching my face.

"N-nothing. I, uh, just—"

"It's weird, isn't it?" He turns his body to face me,

crossing his legs on the bed. "Seeing yourself in a video for the first time. I bet you never thought you'd get this much of a reaction, did you?"

"Uh huh, exactly," I lie, nodding my head slowly.

"Now do you believe me when I say you're amazing?" he asks, tilting his head slightly with a grin and leaning forward to kiss me.

Chapter
Forty-Four

"But do we *have* to walk?" Nadine sulks, wrapping her scarf around her neck. "It's *freezing*. Like, I literally think I'll die if you make me step outside. I'll freeze like Jack in the Titanic and then what will you do? Who will replace me as your best friend?"

Jeez, this girl is dramatic.

"Well, for a start, I'd actually let you on the huge floating door so you wouldn't freeze and die. Second, we're not drowning in a sea of ice water, we're just walking to town. And third, it's sunny outside so you get to wear your new sunglasses." I point down to the giant pair of designer glasses in Nadine's hand.

She rolls her eyes, sighing. "This is the treatment I

get after you bailed on me yesterday?" she scoffs. I chuckle as she theatrically storms out of the house dressed in a long winter camel coat with the gigantic sunglasses perched on her slender nose. An absolute diva if ever there was one.

Despite her flair for the dramatics, she does have a point. I did completely bail on her last night after promising to catch up with her at the band's house. But I couldn't help it. After seeing that stupid comment on the video, all I wanted to do was sleep.

Ryan didn't even question the fact that I wanted to go to bed early. He even left me alone in his room whilst he had dinner with everyone. I think he thought I was exhausted from the library. Although, he did say this morning that he suffered through dinner without me, unable to dodge a million questions from Nadine about my whereabouts.

Poor guy.

This morning I woke up to hundreds of texts from her, demanding we get coffee and go shopping in town before my shift at Jacks, 'whether I like it or not'. I assume she got my shift pattern from Ryan last night so I couldn't wriggle out of it. Got to love her persistence. Not that I'm complaining, I love my coffee dates with Nadine.

I've never felt like I needed a girlfriend before, but

now I realise just how much I do.

"See, it's not so bad," I say.

Nadine lifts her head towards the sun, still scowling. "Yeah, yeah. Whatever."

We begin our walk, crossing the road to cut through the park. It's much smaller than the one in the middle of town and there's only a couple of dog walkers around. It's peaceful, calming.

"I heard the news about the guy who hit Kady. Are you okay?" Nadine turns her head to look at me, lowering her glasses to the edge of her nose.

"Did Ryan tell you?" I ask, really hoping they didn't spend last night talking about it.

"No, no," she reassures me, waving her hands in front of her. "I read about it in yesterday's paper."

I guess you can always trust a politics student to keep tabs on local affairs.

"Are you okay though?" she asks again. I nod without speaking. "You know it's okay not to be."

"No, I know... but I am." I pause. "His death doesn't really add or take anything away from Kady's. He feels pretty distant from everything, so it's not something that would personally shake me up. I didn't know the guy."

"I guess, but it's still sad." Nadine buries her hands deep in her coat pockets, a sympathetic frown spread across her face.

"Did you watch the video by the way?" I ask to change the subject.

"Yes, yes, yes! I did! It was amazing, Zoe. I hate that you are good at literally *everything*." She grins. "Well, besides—"

"Besides cheer initiations. I know. Thanks for reminding me." I groan, earning a laugh from her. "Did you see the comments?" I press. "The bad ones?"

She pushes her sunglasses to the top of her head, revealing her scrunched eyebrows. "What bad ones? The only ones I saw were positive."

I stop walking, pulling my phone out of my coat pocket to get the video up. It got more comments overnight, meaning I have to scroll even further to find the one in question.

"Here." I push the phone to Nadine. She stands still, grabbing my phone and squinting at the screen.

She huffs and quickly shoves it back to me.

"Of course you'd dig out the one bad comment on the video, Zoe." She rolls her eyes. "Did you even see who wrote that stupid comment? It looks like a fake account. It doesn't even have a profile picture. It's probably some die-hard Lanes fan who has a massive crush on Ryan."

"That's crazy. I didn't think the band were big enough

to have die-hard fans?"

"They're not. That's the pathetic thing about it." Nadine laughs. "Don't take it personally, Zoe. It's a compliment. It means your boyfriend's hot."

"So, you don't think I'm chubby?"

"I'm not even going to justify that question with an answer."

We spend the rest of the walk to town discussing all the outfits Nadine wants to get for the festival and her upcoming dates with Tyler. Apparently, she can't just wear something she already has in her wardrobe and, now that I think about it, I swear I've never seen her in the same outfit twice.

I'm trying not to think about my birthday, let alone the festival, so I haven't given any thought to what I'll wear. The idea of hundreds of pairs of eyes on me as I sing makes me feel sick.

What if they all think I'm chubby too?

I trail behind Nadine as we wander through multiple stores. She parades around, a huge iced coffee in hand, pulling out different blouses and crop tops, eyeing them before throwing them back on the rail with a huff.

"This is useless," she moans as we walk around the fifth store of the day. "Okay, I'm taking a break. Let's find something for you," she says, wrapping her pouty lips around the green straw and taking a slurp of her coffee.

It suddenly starts to feel a lot warmer in the store as Nadine stands still, waiting for me to lead the way around the racks of clothing. I walk slowly, pretending to look at different items without actually touching anything. Maybe if I pretend for long enough, she will quit bugging me to buy a birthday outfit and go back to shopping for herself?

"What about that?" She points towards a black sequin mini dress.

I scrunch my nose, shaking my head.

She sighs. "Why not? You have the perfect figure for it."

I ignore her and continue up the aisle.

Having scanned most of the bottom floor of the shop, we decide to take the escalator upstairs. Hopefully it won't be long until we're done with this pointless exercise, and I can go to work.

My eyes drift to the mannequins gathered around the entrance as the escalator drags us upwards. One in particular is dressed in a black denim boiler suit. It's collared with an elasticated waist and a zip from the waist up to the collar.

"You'd look good in that," Nadine says as I walk closer to the outfit.

"Maybe..."

Nadine turns on her heels, her white Stan Smiths squeaking noisily on the polished concrete floor. My eyes follow her as she waltzes over to the nearest shop assistant, tapping them on the shoulder and pointing in my direction. I quickly lower my gaze to stare at my shoes.

"Here," Nadine says when she finally returns, holding out a hanger with my size jumpsuit hanging off of it. "Try it on."

I don't object, following her across the shop towards the dressing rooms. Instead of waiting outside, she follows me into the changing area, sitting on a round velvet pouffe just outside my cubicle. She pulls out her phone and scrolls through social media as I close the thick black curtain behind me.

Letting out a huge breath, I turn away from the mirror to shrug off my coat.

I can do this.

I peel off my jumper and jeans to slide the jumpsuit on and zip it up, looking down at the outfit before deciding whether or not to face the mirror.

It fits, so that's a good start—it's comfy too. It's much better than the stupid mini dress Nadine wanted me to try. I actually have room to move around without having to worry about tugging any material down past my butt to stop from flashing.

I finally turn to face the mirror and realise that it's pretty flattering. You don't need a flat stomach for this type of outfit, and the slim trousers actually make my legs look pretty small.

"Let's see!" Nadine calls.

I pull back the thick curtain, popping my head around first. She ushers for me to step out of the changing room. I tuck a strand of hair behind my ear and wipe my hands against my thighs as I move towards her.

She lets out a long, slow wolf whistle. "That's the one."

"You think?"

"Definitely. Ryan's gunna have a field day!"

I bring my hands to my mouth, covering my smile as my face warms. Nadine puts her phone down on the seat next to her and swings her legs to stand up. As she walks over to me, she pulls my hands away from my mouth.

"I wish you'd believe it." She squeezes my palms.

"I can't. It's physically ingrained in my brain not to."

"Stubborn ass," Nadine mutters under her breath.

"You did *not* just call me a stubborn ass." I mock gasp.

"I did. And I'll say it again. *Stubborn ass!*" Nadine practically yells the last part of her sentence, causing a shop assistant to run into the changing area. The lady scowls in our direction, tutting and murmuring something disapproving under her breath.

I face Nadine in horror. She has her mouth scrunched together, holding in a breath of air to stop herself from laughing. But it doesn't work. The moment our eyes meet, she lets out a huge laugh and we both lose it.

Once we start giggling, we can't stop. The laughter seems to get louder and louder. I have to hold my hand over my stomach as my muscles begin to ache. This is the kind of pain I could get used to.

In an effort to calm down, I shut the curtain to get changed.

Never in a million years did I think I could try on clothes in a shop and actually enjoy it. It feels good that, in the madness of everything, I can escape the pain in my mind. Even if just for a short while.

Chapter Forty-Five

Ryan nudges my shoulder gently, stirring me from sleep. "Happy Birthday, baby," he breathes into my ear, kissing my cheek.

He's leaning over me, already fully dressed in a black t-shirt and blue rolled up jeans, a smirk playing across his lips.

I reach across the bedside table for my phone to check the time. It's ten. I could've sworn I set my usual morning alarm, I wanted to get some studying done before we did anything today.

"I turned your alarm off," Ryan answers my internal question. "It's your birthday, you deserved to sleep in."

Sitting up, my gaze immediately falls on a line of rose

gold helium balloons tied to the end of bedframe, *'Happy Birthday Zoe'* is written across them. There's also a couple of presents and a huge bouquet of red roses placed carefully next to me. I clutch at the bouquet and hold it close, smelling the fresh flowers.

How did Ryan move all this in here without waking me?

"Open your presents." He smiles. I scoot over so he can sit on the bed next to me.

I reach for two beautifully gift-wrapped boxes and a card with Ryan's handwriting across it. One of the boxes has a number one drawn on it in black pen. Figuring he wants me to open it first, I tear away at the paper.

I find a pair of AirPods inside with my initials engraved on the case.

"Because I know you enjoy music the most when only you can hear it," he explains.

Before I can say anything, he ushers me to open the other gifts.

I rip through the envelope next as it has a number two written on it. It's a birthday card filled with a list of what must be hundreds of songs, all of which I recognise.

"Open your music app," he instructs. I grab my phone, unlock it and hand it to him. He scrolls my library to show me a playlist that wasn't there last night, called

'*Us*'.

"It's every song we've ever played together, or any song that reminds me of you," he explains. His cheeks turn rosy as he hands back my phone.

My eyes start to well as I scroll through the playlist. He really has included everything, from the song we sang in the park with the band, to the one we listened to when I first got in his car. I can't believe he remembered them all, I don't think he's missed a single song.

The final gift is a CD of the same playlist. He tells me that he couldn't resist making me my very own mixtape, even if it's a bit cliché. I giggle and pull him onto the bed next to me, kissing him and ignoring the salty, happy tears that have dampened my cheeks.

We pull away when we hear the band calling my name from downstairs. Ryan yanks me out of bed and I tie my hair in a ponytail before throwing on one his black hoodies, which earns a grin from him.

"You're really making it hard for me to not throw you back into bed right now." He smirks and I glower at him, tutting playfully.

As I open the kitchen door, the others are all sat on the sofas with rose gold party hats on their heads, cheering as I walk into the kitchen. I scan the room to see lots more rose gold helium balloons and a '*Happy*

Birthday' banner on every wall. On top of the kitchen counter is a huge chocolate cake covered in strawberries.

They really did go all out... for me.

My face feels hot, and I'm sure my cheeks must be bright crimson. I shuffle over to the couch and Nadine pats the space next to her.

"Happy birthday, bestie!" She squeezes me tight around the shoulders. It takes me a moment to compose my face into a smile, feeling a lump form in my throat.

"So... we kind of got you something together," Ryan explains, backing out of the kitchen door.

"We? But you already got me something!" I shout as he leaves the room.

A few seconds later, Ryan appears with a gigantic box that comes up to his waist, covered in the same wrapping paper as my other gifts.

"It's from all of us," he says as he sets the box down in front of me.

Ripping open the paper, I uncover a plain cardboard box underneath. I stand up to open the top of the box and peek inside. As I pull away the top flap, I instantly know what it is. My eyes begin to well again.

I pull the guitar bag out of the box and then carefully unzip the black nylon bag. It's not just any guitar, it's a brand-new acoustic Fender. Even between them it must have cost a fortune.

Why would they spend all this money on me?

"I-I don't know what to say." I gulp down the tears and exhale. "Thank you so much." I look around the group, feeling so overwhelmed and so grateful, all rolled into one.

I wipe my cheeks with the sleeve of Ryan's hoodie. The cotton smell envelops me, and I feel a happiness beyond what I have ever experienced before. It makes the joy I felt when I got accepted to university feel like nothing more than mild contentment.

"You're so welcome. It's been great having you around," Adam says, looking towards Ryan as he speaks. I notice he's sat much closer to Claire than usual, and she rests one of her hands on his thigh.

"Does this mean I get my old guitar back now?" Ryan winks.

"Ah! So that's why you did it!" I beam at him, causing the others to laugh. He holds his hands up animatedly and shrugs.

Claire leans forward and hands me a turquoise envelope. I open up the birthday card and pause when I see what is written inside.

Thank you for everything you've done for him. We've

loved having you around. Have the best birthday ever.

I continue to stare at the message over and over. The card is from Adam, Claire and Tyler. I look up at each of them and give them the warmest, most genuine smile I think I've ever produced.

"I was a bit sneaky and also got you something else," Nadine says, pulling an envelope from behind her back and handing it to me. "Tyler helped me with it."

I open the envelope and pull out a folded piece of paper. It looks like a voucher to something, but I can't immediately figure out what it's for.

"It's music lessons with this instructor that used to teach at our music college. She's awesome," Tyler explains.

"She's based in London so I thought you could use them on weekends, and I could come with you. We can stay at my parents' house, make a girly weekend of it or something." Nadine smiles at me.

I snatch her in for a hug. "I don't deserve you," I breathe into her neck.

I don't know what I expected from my birthday, but this definitely wasn't it. It's amazing how you can know people for only a matter of months, yet you can't remember how you survived without them.

Chapter Forty-Six

We spend so long in the basement, practicing the festival set and playing cover songs on my new guitar, that we have to rush to get ready for dinner with my parents. At least I have my new denim jumpsuit to wear, so I don't have to mess around picking an outfit and trying things on.

I can tell Ryan is feeling super nervous about meeting my family. He keeps running his hands through his hair and looking in the mirror at his outfit, tugging at his shirt.

"I know I sound lame, but I just want them to think we suit, you know?" Ryan says as he moves away from the mirror and orders a taxi on his phone.

"They'll know we suit as soon as they meet you. It's

got nothing to do with your clothes. But if it helps, I think you look hot." I smile and kiss him on the cheek.

He looks so good in his oversized black Ralph Lauren shirt and slim jeans. I think it's my favourite outfit yet.

"Says you. I think you might just be the most beautiful girl I ever laid my eyes on, Zoe Jones." Ryan grins.

"Ever?" I ask with raised eyebrows.

"Ever." He traces a cross on the left-hand side of his chest with his fingers. "Now get your ass downstairs, beautiful. The taxi's here."

We bundle into the cab and Ryan puts a hand on my thigh as he stares out of the window.

"Trust you to want to have a damn band practice on your birthday." He chuckles.

"What did you expect? I wanted to test out my new toy!"

"So, despite spending the day locked in my basement, you had fun?"

"It was the best birthday ever. I can't believe you got me my own guitar and all my other presents."

"Was? It's not over yet." He winks at me. "I still have plenty of time to ruin it." He grins, giving my thigh a squeeze.

"I love you." I smile, squeezing his hand.

"I love you too."

We're exactly on time to the restaurant, so I know my parents will already be here. They're always early to everything.

We walk into The Stables, and I scan the restaurant quickly as Ryan pulls my jacket off my shoulders, hanging it on one of the pegs in the entranceway.

I knew Dad would book this place, we come here every time he visits. He loves it. We tend to avoid fancy restaurants, preferring to be able to share pizza and drink cider while eighties music plays in the background. My parents also have a habit of sticking to what they know.

My slightly wet Airforce Ones squeak a little as we walk over to the waitress standing near the entrance to the dining area.

"Reservation for Jones, five people." I smile at the girl, ignoring the flock of butterflies in my tummy. She taps the screen to find the booking information with her long nails.

"The rest of your party are already here. Table fifty-six, next to the bar." She points in their direction.

I thank her, brush my clammy hands against the legs of my jumpsuit and reach for one of Ryan's hands. He throws me a look as if to say, '*should we be holding hands in front of your parents?*' I ignore it and continue to walk towards my family, gripping his palm.

Hannah is the first to spot us, her big brown eyes looking up from the table as she beams at us. She nudges my mother with her elbow and both of my parents turn around.

Ryan wriggles his hand free, just as my dad pushes his wooden chair to stand up.

"You must be Ryan." Dad smiles and holds his hand out for Ryan to shake.

Ryan takes it before running his hand through his hair and ruffling the strands. "Hello sir, lovely to meet you."

"Oh, less of the sir. Call me Keith, please." Dad beams, pulling me in for a quick hug and gesturing for us to sit in the empty chairs.

Hannah won't stop smiling as she looks between me and Ryan. I raise my eyebrows at her and she winks, tilting her head in his direction. I think she approves.

Once we're seated, the waitress comes over and we order drinks, which gives me a distraction from Hannah's gaze.

"So, how's your birthday been?" Mum asks.

I haven't decided if I should mention the band practice or the winter festival. Mixing the two worlds feels terrifying, like it would suddenly become all too real.

"Um... good, thanks. Ryan made a fuss of me," I answer. I look to Ryan, and he nods stiffly, pulling two empty cups from the middle of the table and filling them with water from a jug.

Glancing to the right, Ryan notices Hannah's glass is also empty, so he fills hers up too. Hannah grins gratefully at him. He doesn't notice her though; he doesn't even give her eye contact. Instead, he fixes his sight on the jug of water. He's so nervous it makes me feel terrible. I reach for his leg under the table, giving it a squeeze.

"That's lovely. What did you get up to, anything fun?" Mum probes.

"Uh..." I inhale a deep breath. "We mostly hung out with the rest of his housemates," I answer vaguely, praying they don't ask me anymore questions.

"That sounds lovely." Mum smiles, leaning into her purse and pulling out a slim box wrapped in silver paper. "We got you a little something. You'll have to forgive the lack of card, that was supposed to be your sister's job." Mum shoots Hannah a disapproving look out of the corner of her eye. Hannah just groans in response.

I tear the paper open and look at the bright white box, slightly taken aback. It's an Apple Watch. I didn't realise I came across as the Apple, tech savvy type. I don't even update to the newest iPhone each year; I find it too much for me. Although, this watch will work great with the AirPods Ryan got me.

"We thought it would be good now you're more active with cheerleading. It can track how many calories you've burned in a workout," Dad says.

I feel Ryan shift in his seat next to me. He leans his elbow on the table and covers his mouth with his hand.

"You mean, to encourage me to exercise more," I playfully respond.

"Not at all, sounds like you've been getting plenty with all the cheer training," Dad says, beaming back.

"You're looking good, Zoe. Very slim." Mum smiles at me.

"Oh my god, Mum! Leave her alone!" Hannah swots Mum's hand across the table.

I force a laugh at the terrible compliment, hoping to pierce the growing awkwardness in the air.

The waitress comes back over with a tray of drinks and to take our order. As she sets down the glasses, Ryan leans in, asking if I know what I want to eat. I nod and silently point to the goat's cheese pizza on the menu. He smiles at me, squeezing my hand reassuringly under the table.

I like the newly established, unwritten rule between us that he will always order my food for me. It's one of the worst parts of the whole dining out experience for me. Sometimes, I get so nervous I can barely open my mouth to speak, which only leads to me feeling ridiculously embarrassed.

When I get like that, it makes the actual eating part even worse, so I'm glad this is one internal battle I don't have to fight anymore. Ryan has started doing it ever since our first lunch in the student village. I didn't even ask him to. He just sort of picked it up.

"So, Ryan, I understand you met Zoe at Jacks?" Dad looks at him, taking a sip of cider.

"Yes, that's correct." Ryan wipes his palms on his thighs.

"Is that all you do?"

"No. I work there part time, just to pay the bills. I'm a musician." Ryan picks up his pint and takes a gulp.

"Huh." Dad pauses. "A shame your music doesn't cover your living expenses." He smiles sympathetically.

"Well, he's actually quitting Jacks soon. You've just handed in your notice, haven't you?" I turn to Ryan and then back to my dad.

Ryan nods. "Yeah, I'm finally going full time with music."

"Wow, that's cool," Hannah gushes, smiling at us. Ryan's lips turn up, forming a genuine, warm smile at Hannah.

"Zoe, have you heard that the CEO of AQ Law is coming to your university to do a guest lecture? Rumour has it, he's looking for some paralegals," Dad interrupts.

"Um yeah, I have. I was planning on going," I mumble.

"Good. It sounds like a fantastic opportunity. I'm glad you're on top of it." He smiles before looking between Ryan and me. "Quite the match. A lawyer and a musician." He chuckles. "Polar opposites."

"Well, you know what they say, opposites attract," Hannah responds, smirking. I feel my face flush. Luckily, Dad laughs at her joke and takes another sip of his cider.

"Not entirely opposite, you've been singing with my band a little bit, haven't you?" Ryan turns to me with a proud smile, putting a hand on the back of my chair.

Dad's eyes linger on Ryan's arm, but then he turns his full attention to me. "You have?" he asks.

"Not seriously or anything, just a little bit on the side. I've been trying to learn the guitar too." I take a deep breath, feeling the heat on my face as my family intently stare. "It's fun," I add with a racing heart.

To my relief, two waiters head over to our table and place our food down in front of us, giving me some time to recover from the conversation.

Ryan removes his arm from behind my chair, catching my eye and offering me a smile. He looks down to the food and back up to me. I nod at him, silently letting him know that I feel fine. He squeezes my thigh under the table.

I don't notice both of my parents watching our entire interaction until I lift my head. As soon as I meet their staring eyes, they quickly look away.

"Are you any good?" Hannah asks as she picks up a slice of her pizza.

"At what?" I ask.

"At music," she answers with a mouthful of food.

Damn. I thought I'd escaped the interrogation.

"She's amazing. Best voice I've ever heard, and I've been to music college," Ryan says with an unmistakable air of pride. "She's going to sing with us at a winter festival," he says before taking a bite of his pizza.

Well, I guess the secret is out.

I don't particularly mind the music talk. I like that it relaxes Ryan and I love seeing him get comfortable with my sister, but I'm all too aware of my parents' judgemental eyes on the three of us.

"Woah!" Hannah exclaims. "Let me know the dates and I'll see if I can get it off work?"

"Sure, will do," I say, knowing full well that she won't be able to swap her shifts this last minute.

"I just don't think it's wise." Dad looks at me.

I feel my heart drop to my stomach. I tear my eyes away from his stern glare and look towards Mum. She's placed her hand over Dad's, trying to get his attention.

"What's not?" I ask.

"Playing music. It seems dangerous to be so distracted from your studies. First cheerleading and now this. I just don't see how you can keep up with everything. How is music going to help with your career?"

"Dad, relax. If anyone's going to have it under control, it's Zoe," Hannah says, coming to my rescue and throwing him a warning glare.

"I'm always studying, Dad. I wouldn't let the band become a distraction. I know how important my career is."

"Well, I don't think it's good for you," he continues, looking straight at me. I sigh, leaning my elbows on the table, ignoring him as I pretend to be engrossed in a slice of pizza.

Why does he have to be like this, on my birthday too?

My parents remain silent, refusing to look in my direction. Mum's usually much easier to read than Dad, but she's trying too hard to avoid my eye contact as she eats.

Hannah tries to make small talk for the rest of dinner, but I can barely concentrate enough to murmur out a few responses. My parents stay silent too. The only time Dad opens his mouth again is to ask the waiter for the bill.

I've never brought a guy to meet my parents before, but I never imagined it would go this badly. Well, maybe *'badly'* is a bit dramatic, but it's just so... *awkward.*

I feel bad when I think back to the times I'd spoken to Ryan about my family, how excited he was to meet them. He loved how close we sounded. Tonight must be a total disappointment for him.

"He meant that he doesn't think I'm good for you, didn't he?" Ryan asks as we step out of the restaurant and into the cold air after saying goodbye to my family. The pavement is wet, the sky is grey and dreary. I wrap my leather jacket around my chest to try and warm up.

"No, I think it's just the music," I answer. "My dad is just super protective about my career."

"But I don't agree with him being that way if it means you can't do the things you love. I see what music does to you, Zoe. You come alive when you sing." He exhales, running his hands through his hair. "I honestly wouldn't push it if I didn't think you loved it."

"I know." I sigh as Ryan walks slightly ahead of me.

I reach my arm out and grab a fistful of his shirt in my hand, causing him to slow down. We stop walking and he turns to stand in front of me with a wrinkle between his brows and a frown on his lips. I place both of my hands around his shoulders.

"I'm sorry," I say, pulling him closer to me.

The corners of his eyes crinkle slightly as he smiles. "Zoe, you have nothing to apologise for. They'll get used to me; I'm not going anywhere." He wraps his arms around my waist, lowering his head to press soft kisses along my jaw.

Relief immediately floods through me.

I just want my parents to see what I see in Ryan. I want them to realise how much better, how much happier I am now that I'm with him. Ryan has given me a piece of myself that I never knew was missing. He has lit a fire inside of me that I never knew was out. With him, I'm living my life instead of sleepwalking through it. But maybe my dad can see that, and maybe that's the problem.

Chapter
Forty-Seven

For the past week leading up to the festival, I couldn't decide if I wanted time to speed up or slow down. I couldn't decide if I was excited for this weekend's performance or petrified of it.

As I'd guessed, Hannah couldn't take the time off work, meaning I only have to worry about Nadine, Emily and Jake being in the audience.

The day Hannah called to tell me she couldn't make the gig, I answered hesitantly, pretending to only be able to talk for a minute between classes. I decided that I wouldn't speak to any of them for a little while. I know Dad's reaction at my birthday dinner wasn't Hannah's fault, but I just don't want to put her in the middle.

Even though I've missed talking to my family, I no longer pine for them like I used to. The homesick feeling I used to get doesn't exist anymore. Although, it'll probably come back as soon as Ryan leaves for tour in a few months.

The only thing the impending launch of his solo career has done is make the time we have together go fast. Way too fast.

However, right now, every minute is torturing me as we make the painful journey to London. I don't know if it's the traffic slowly crawling along the motorway that's making me feel nauseous, or if it's the fact that in less than twenty-four hours, I'll be performing on stage for the first time.

I sigh and look out the front window, leaning my cheek against the seatbelt.

"You okay?" Ryan asks softly from the driver's side of his Wrangler. He runs his hand over the back of my head, stroking my hair.

I nod as I continue to look out of the car, watching the vehicles on the other side of the road whizz by, free of any traffic. I sigh again when I look ahead at how many cars are piled up in front of us, barely making any progress at all.

"We'll be there in less than an hour, don't worry. Try

to get some rest," Ryan instructs, stroking the back of my head once more.

I close my eyes, even though I'm far too nervous to sleep. At least if my eyes are shut, Ryan will stop worrying about me. The mixture of nerves and excitement swirls around in my stomach. Butterflies float through my body, too wild to be kept at bay.

I can't stop thinking about the set up for the festival and how many people will be there. I'm relieved that it's not like a normal summer festival, it's far too cold to be camping outside. It's located just outside of London, with lots of different music tents and warehouses.

Everyone plays up to the winter theme too, wearing crazy coloured ski suits and hats. I flicked through Instagram to last year's festival and couldn't believe how eccentric the outfits were.

"We're here," Ryan whispers softly, nudging my shoulders with his hand. I must've dozed off after all.

I blink my eyes open to see my favourite pair of hazel eyes scanning my face. Smiling up at Ryan, I hazily unbuckle my seatbelt before stepping out of the car.

The gravel crunches under my feet as I take in the outside of the cottage. It's pretty dark, but I can still make out the ivy covering the side of the house. The stone building looks so picturesque with duck egg window frames and a matching door. I even spot a chimney on the roof blowing out smoke; there must be a fire lit inside. It's crazy to think this cottage is only moments from busy London.

"Wow." I sigh as we walk closer to the door. A motion detector senses our movements, automatically turning on a flood light, illuminating Adam's red VW camper van and Tyler's blue Honda Civic on the driveway. I smile, realising Nadine will already be here.

"Perks of having rich management." Ryan laughs, watching me gape at the house. I can't believe his manager is letting all of us use this place for free. She must *really* like Ryan already.

Apparently, she owns properties all over the place. I'm not surprised, given that she manages some of the biggest artists in the charts at the moment.

I ignore the brief pang of sadness in my stomach, reminding me of Ryan's impending album release and tour.

This festival is our last hoorah as a team. My first and last performance with The Lanes. Well, The Lanes as I know them. I have no idea if they'll carry on without Ryan or split off and do their own thing. Ryan's management have made it pretty clear that he won't have time to do both after the album is released.

Despite all these changes, he's promised me that nothing will be different between us. I don't understand how he can know that for certain. He doesn't know what his schedule will be like, or how successful his album will be. With a huge management and label backing him, life-altering success is inevitable, I know it.

"Zoeeeee!" Nadine squeals as she opens the front door with a glass of red wine in hand.

She leans against the doorway, her cheeks a little flushed. She holds out her other hand for me and I give her a small hug.

"Go on in, babe. I'll grab our bags," Ryan says.

"Ugh, you two are just *so* cute!" Nadine gushes, pulling me into the house.

I kick off my shoes and shake off my jacket, hanging it in the porch.

For such an old looking cottage, the interior is surprisingly contemporary. The kitchen and dining space is open plan, with floor-to-ceiling French doors overlooking a spacious garden.

I turn my head back towards the hallway at the sound of a door swinging open and murmurs of conversation. I follow the noise and stop just outside the open doorway leading to a dimly lit sitting room.

Claire is perched on the arm of a couch, pouring more

wine into her glass. Emily is next to her, and Adam and Tyler are lounging on two armchairs opposite them. In the middle of the room is a wooden coffee table with a deck of playing cards scattered across it. They look like they're in the middle of some kind of drinking game.

When Claire sees me hovering, she flaps her hand, ushering for us to join her. Nadine runs straight into the room and onto Tyler's lap. I hesitate, glancing back towards the front door.

Ryan is pulling the last of our bags into the porch, I excuse myself to give him a hand.

"Come on!" Tyler shouts, just as Ryan gets into the hallway.

"Just a sec!" he answers. "You need to eat first," he instructs softly, placing his hands on my shoulders and guiding me towards the kitchen.

I shake my head. "I'm okay, honestly."

Ryan scowls, ignoring me as he leads us towards fridge.

"Please, I don't think I could," I beg.

I feel so sick, I'd rather go hungry than throw up. I don't want to deal with stomach pains, especially when I already have butterflies floating around my entire body. It'll be a struggle to ban myself from throwing up this whole weekend as it is.

Ryan sighs, seeming to understand. He holds out his hand and pulls me into the living room.

"Sit. Come play." Claire waves her arm.

"Sorry, I'm so exhausted. But you stay, Ryan. Please," I insist, knowing he'll want to make the most of this weekend with the band.

"You sure?" he asks, his eyes glistening with the reflection of the fire that burns on the nearest wall.

"Of course," I reply.

As I say goodnight to the others and turn out of the room, I'm surprised that Ryan is following me. I throw him a confused look.

"I need to show you which room we're in." He chuckles.

In my tired state, I nod and follow Ryan as he picks up our bags and leads me up the wooden staircase to our room. I don't even notice how beautiful it is, I just stand at the end of the four-poster bed whilst Ryan rummages through our bags.

Eventually, he pulls out one of his t-shirts and hoodies, handing them both to me. I take off my clothes and replace them with his, immediately climbing into bed.

He kisses me gently, telling me he won't be downstairs too long. I fall asleep in a matter of seconds, his fresh cotton scent surrounding me.

Chapter Forty-Eight

I can't focus. I mechanically repeat the motions of getting ready, applying my eyeliner and lipstick, trying to make myself look good enough to sing in a band. I feel like I could pass out at any moment.

How am I supposed to sing if I can't even breathe properly?

The rest of the house is electric. Music blares through all the speakers and laughter floods the kitchen. Everyone is drinking downstairs, but there's no way I could join in. I'm struggling to drag myself out of the bedroom as it is, I'm too nervous.

I check the time on my watch. Only three hours until we perform.

"You can do this," I mutter to myself, placing my hand on the doorknob. I take a few seconds, closing my eyes and inhaling deeply before turning the handle and walking downstairs.

Everyone is sitting around the kitchen island when I enter, eating breakfast and drinking champagne. Nadine and Ryan both lift their heads from the table and beam as they see me walk in. Ryan scoots over so I can sit in between them.

"Fuck, you look beautiful." Ryan kisses the top of my freshly curled hair. My butterflies settle momentarily as I take a seat between two of my favourite people.

Nadine is dressed in her all-black outfit as planned, with a bright blue ski jacket draped over the back of her chair. She even has glitter all round her eyes.

"Are you nervous?" she asks, leaning into me and smiling. I nod as she squeezes me around the shoulders. "I'm *so* proud of you. Just remember, this is supposed to be your fun."

Nadine's right, this is supposed to be my fun. I don't sing to be famous. I don't do it for money or a career. I do it for fun. I do it to be closer to Ryan. But most importantly, I do it for myself.

Besides, people coming to this festival are coming for a good time and to make great memories, just like we are.

I'm sure no one will notice me.

I turn to Nadine. "Thanks. I needed to hear that."

Ryan watches me, smiling proudly, as I reach for a slice of toast from the board in front of me.

Okay, his smile alone just transformed the butterflies in my stomach into bubbles of excitement.

"Vans are here," Tyler calls, looking out of the window at the two black vehicles pulling onto the enormous drive. "Instruments in," he instructs.

Ryan gets up from the table, following the rest of the band out to load the cars. Before he leaves, he places a hand on my back and kisses the top of my head.

"I love you," he whispers into my hair.

I watch him all the way until he is completely out of sight. My body yearns to be close to him, I don't know how I'm going to make it through today if he's not constantly by my side.

"Are you excited?" Emily turns to me once it's just the three of us alone in the kitchen.

"I wasn't, but then Nadine made me realise, this is my fun. I need to relax."

"You're only realising this now?" Nadine laughs.

"She's right though, you're going to be great. Tyler won't stop banging on about how talented you are. I can't wait to watch you perform," Emily says warmly, reaching across the table and giving my wrist a squeeze.

"Thanks." I smile through the nerves.

I'm so grateful my friends are here today. I thought I would hate having extra people to witness this performance, but now I realise how much their support means to me. I need them like I need Ryan.

"Will you guys put glitter on my face too?" I ask, looking up at their bright, adventurous make-up.

"Of course." Emily leans across for a pot of teal-coloured glitter and starts dabbing it onto my temples.

Once Emily has finished her magic, we hear the others calling from outside. I take a quick, final bite of toast and throw on my platform Dr Martens, tying the bright yellow laces. I grab my vintage purple and sage ski jacket from the peg and swing my cheer backpack over my shoulder.

After climbing into the van and buckling myself next to Ryan, he grabs my hand. I lean my head on his shoulder, feeling his lips press against my ear as the driver pulls away from the house and towards the venue.

"Don't we need to go that way?" I ask Ryan, pointing to the queue of traffic on the opposite side of the road.

He smirks. "No, we're going to the artists' entrance."

I text Jake to ask where he is. He replies instantly, letting me know he's walking from the nearby train station with his friends. Ryan stares at the screen and holds his hand out, asking for my phone. I hand it to him, and he dials Jake.

Ryan starts chatting away animatedly, telling him to walk towards the entrance we're heading for to save him queuing. I give Ryan my warmest smile, happy he's making so much effort with Jake.

When we arrive at the entrance, the driver pulls into a field turned parking area. We hop out of the car and Claire hands each of us an artist wristband.

A guy dressed in green, driving a golf buggy, pulls up to our parked vans. The band seem to know him as they all go over, bumping fists with him and chatting away. He explains that the festival crew will take our instruments to the stage so we can go into the event.

I check the time on my watch again. Two hours until we perform.

As we stand at the entrance waiting for Jake, I hear the loud pumping of music radiating from the fields behind. A wave of panic strikes through me.

I close my eyes, remembering the advice Nadine gave me only moments ago.

This is my fun.

"Zoe!" Jake's voice booms. I snap my head up to see a group of heavy-set guys walking towards us, all dressed in different animal print ski suits, laughing away to each other. Their outfits make me chuckle. They look amazing.

My eyes wander down to the cans of beer they have in their hands. I wonder how much alcohol they've already consumed.

"Cool outfits." Ryan smiles at them.

I'm surprised when Jake actually puts an arm around Ryan's back, patting him. They both look genuinely happy to see each other. Maybe it's the alcohol, or maybe it's the excitement of a party.

We continue towards a row of security lining the artists' gate and Ryan manages to talk them into letting Jake's friends come through with us.

Once successfully past them, we march across the pathway towards the event. The space is filled with so many groups of people stood outside various performance tents and warehouses. They're all wearing ridiculously vibrant winter coats and jackets, drinking beer and dancing despite the chilly air.

The atmosphere is so much better than I imagined. More friendly somehow?

"We'd better go warm up," Ryan says to the band.

Nadine and Emily squeeze me tight, wishing me luck before running towards one of the warehouses with Jake and his friends.

I follow the band to a barrier with a flag pinned across it reading, 'Artist's Corner'. We flash our wristbands, and the giant security guard lets us through.

We head down the field until we reach a large beige tent. A laminated piece of paper is pinned to the outside with 'The Lanes' written on it.

I duck into the doorway to find a relatively unimpressive space. It's pretty bare, minus both Tyler and Ryan's guitars and Claire's bass in the corner next to a plastic table with a crate of beers on it.

Adam immediately darts for the crate, handing out the bottles. As he pushes one towards me, I shake my head, pulling a bottle of water out of my bag instead.

Everyone reaches for their respective instruments whilst Adam casually sits on top of the plastic table, swinging his legs, drinking a beer.

"Wait, where are your drums?" I ask him, suddenly panicked.

He chuckles. "They're already by the stage. They're too big to bring here."

"Oh," I reply.

I glance at a smirking Ryan. "Amateur," he sniggers.

"Give over," I groan, shoving his shoulder gently.

Ryan laughs, shaking his head as he turns his attention back to his guitar. He finishes tuning it before delving into one of our songs.

It's hard to hear his guitar clearly over the thumping music playing all over the festival, so I move closer to him. Claire and Tyler join in with their instruments too. As soon as they start to play, nerves jolt through my entire body.

But then Ryan opens his mouth to sing, and his voice alone does something to my core. I intently listen to his velvet voice, allowing it to send a wave of calm through me.

I join in on the parts I'm supposed to, singing quietly at first to gain control over my shaking voice. As soon as my throat feels clearer, I begin to sing louder.

Ryan smiles up at me proudly, and it's enough to melt my soul.

We all start messing around as a group, singing and trying to pump ourselves up to perform. I completely forget where I am, totally lost in the moment, until a petite woman dressed in a black polo top with a wired earpiece dangling on her shoulder asks us to follow her to the stage.

We shuffle out of the tent, and I'm surprised to be following her to a warehouse, the second largest performance area after the main stage. I thought we'd be in one of the small tents...

"You never told me we'd be performing in there!" I turn to Ryan and Tyler, pointing at the giant warehouse.

Ryan smirks, shrugging casually.

Tyler lets out a loud laugh. "We didn't wanna freak you out." He gives me a playful nudge with his elbow. "You got this, Zoe. I'd even go as far to say you're better than Ryan."

"Dick." Ryan scowls. They both burst into laughter. Meanwhile, I'm barely able to crack a smile.

I can't do this.

The walk to the warehouse seems to take forever. We're eventually led through some barriers to the side of the stage. I try to scan the audience to see if I can spot Nadine, but it's impossible.

The venue is absolutely packed full of people clustered around the front of the stage. The crowd reaches all the way back to the bar area. It's got to be at max capacity.

The audience are pretty loud too, singing along and cheering for the band currently on stage. I just pray they have the same energy when they listen to us.

As Ryan, Tyler, Claire and Adam all assemble backstage, checking their instruments and waiting for the go ahead, I turn my attention to the act on stage. The singer is good—amazing in fact. Her voice is so unique and raspy as she sings, not to mention she's devastatingly beautiful. I can see why so many people have crammed in to watch her.

Not only is her voice incredible, but so is her body. She's nearly as petite as Claire, with tattoos lining her arms. Her long curly brown hair shines under the stage lights. Her lips are full, painted a deep red, and I notice she has a nose ring in her nostril. She couldn't look more indie if she tried.

If you told me to describe what I thought would be Ryan's type, it's her. I don't even want to think about how plain I'm going to look on stage in comparison.

Why did I agree to this?

"Are you ready?" Ryan walks behind me and whispers into my ear. He places his hands on my shoulders and then wraps them around my chest, so my back is pressed against him.

Even though my heart is racing a million miles an hour, I manage to nod.

"I love you," he says into my ear, planting a kiss on it.

"I love you, Ry."

Our moment is interrupted by Claire pulling us closer to the side of the stage. "It's nearly time," she says with less brightness than usual. She's nervous for sure.

Adam must sense her jitters as he reaches his arm

across her shoulders, pulling her in for a bear hug and a kiss on the temple.

We hear the band on stage wind down their set and say thank you to the crowd. We huddle together in a tight circle whilst the stage is reset with our instruments. I can't help peeking out at the crowd. I didn't think it was possible to cram anyone else into the space, but it seems even more people have gathered for our set.

"We've got this, guys. Let's make this one count," Tyler says.

Suddenly, the MC walks on stage, standing behind the main microphone, confidently addressing the huge crowd.

"I'd like to introduce to the stage a very special band, who I know you're all eager to see. Please give your loudest and warmest welcome to The Lanes," he booms, holding out his hand towards us.

Before I have time to register what's happening, we're rushing onto the stage and taking our positions. The crowd's cheers are overwhelming.

My heart continues to pound. My ears feel hot as the tsunami of noise from the audience fills my body. I feel completely outside of myself as I shuffle to my place beside Ryan.

I look out to the sea of people and then back at him.

He steals a glance at me and winks as he places his hands on the microphone. As I watch him, I gulp down the butterflies that threaten to escape my body.

"You guys are looking epic tonight," Ryan says to the eager crowd, who whoop and holler in response. He introduces the band, continuing to hype up the audience for our first song.

I scan the faces in front of us and finally spot Nadine and the others. Nadine waves dramatically, flailing her arms around. I grin at her, letting her know I've spotted them. How the hell did they get so close to the stage? It's packed in here.

As soon as they recognise the opening of the song, the crowd clap along. I close my eyes to allow the beat to take over.

Finally, I forget where I am and drown in the music, delving into the upbeat sounds blaring all around me. It's as though I'm back in the band's basement, singing and dancing like nobody is watching.

I turn to Ryan during my first solo, feeling his energy pounding through my entire body. He doesn't even look down at his guitar as he plays. Instead, he keeps his eyes locked on me, keeping me safe, anchoring me.

Before I know it, I'm clambering onto the huge amplifiers dotted around the stage, waving my hands in the air as I sing.

I can't believe I'm performing in front of an audience.

I can't believe I'm dancing this freely onstage.

I can't believe I'm having fun.

This is a high I have *never* experienced before, and I never want to come down.

Chapter
Forty-Nine

"That. Was. *Amazing!*" Ryan shouts, spinning me around as we run off the stage. He picks me up and I wrap my legs around his waist, kissing him with force. "That's my girl." He grins, leaning in for another kiss.

We stay like this for a couple of moments before he places me back on the floor. I look around and notice the others have already left, they must've gone to put their instruments back in the tent. Ryan keeps his hand locked in mine as we head out of the warehouse to catch up with them.

We run as fast as possible to join the others, embracing in a huge group hug as soon as we reunite. I look around to see everyone's eyes welling up, including mine.

"Dude, if that wasn't the performance to bow out to, I don't know what was." Adam beams at Ryan, leaning across the table and handing us all a beer.

"We're gunna miss you, man," Tyler gulps.

Ryan pats him on the back. "Guys, I'm not going anywhere," he begins, but the band roll their eyes at him, groaning. "Looks like you might've found a new lead singer anyway." His eyes dart to me and the band follow his gaze, looking at me expectantly.

Strangely, I don't immediately reject the idea, but it's definitely not something I could think about right this second, my adrenaline and mind are pulsing way too much.

"No more serious talk, please? Let's go have fun!" I reply.

"Yeah, let's go find Nadine," Tyler says quickly.

"And your sister?" I add, smirking.

"Yeah, yeah, and her annoying ass." He rolls his eyes.

When we get back to the warehouse, a DJ is already on the stage and the venue is still just as packed as it was when we performed.

When *we* performed.

That has a nice ring to it.

Lights flash across the stage and dance music booms

from the speakers. I watch everyone locked in a trance, eyes closed, dancing.

Adam points towards a group of animal ski suits in the crowd. Ryan grabs my hand as we push our way towards them.

As soon as we are within reach, Jake and his friends start chanting, pulling me in for a massive hug. I can't stop giggling. I control myself long enough to steal a quick glance at Ryan. He's staring each of the guys, eyes narrowed. When he notices me looking at him, his expression changes into a smile.

"*Tarzan,*" I mouth at him. He waves his middle finger at me, stifling a laugh.

Jake hands me a bottle of vodka. "Drink," he demands.

I take a gulp, shuddering as the liquid burns the back of my throat. I shake my head and pass it back to him. He gives it straight to Ryan and the group start cheering as Ryan practically downs it.

I look across the group to see Nadine pulling out of a long kiss with Tyler. I reach for her hand, and she catapults into my arms.

I'm immediately hit by the smell of vodka on her breath. These guys must have been drinking quite a lot during our set, not that I blame them, I'm ready to party too.

"You were amazing. Like, *unreal*," Nadine slurs into my ear before leaping back into Tyler's arms.

I laugh, looking around at my friends, wondering how I got so lucky.

Suddenly, a sting pierces my heart. My mind and body are on a total high, but I can't help thinking about Kady. She would be so proud of me and Jake, living our lives to the full and becoming genuine friends. I'm no longer hiding in my room alone. I'm leaning on other people, opening up to them and allowing myself to experience things just for the sake of enjoyment. I feel free, but *heavy* all at the same time.

"What's up?" Jake turns to me, shouting in my ear.

"N-nothing," I stutter. "I was just thinking about..." I trail off, unable to finish my sentence.

"Kady?" he asks softly. I nod as he continues, "I know, I get like it too when I'm out, having a good time. The guilt suddenly hits me, knowing she should be here. I know we weren't that close, but it doesn't stop how shit it feels."

My eyes widen as I listen to Jake. I never knew he felt her absence in the same way I do. It makes me feel like less of a freak for getting so upset in such a happy moment. I actually feel comforted knowing I'm not alone in this.

I always assumed that Jake was completely fine, that he was handling Kady's death so well. I thought I was just being dramatic and selfish, feeling the weight of grief so strongly. I realise now, we all probably feel the same way, we just don't know how to show it.

"But we have to remember, she would want us to party like freaking mad for her." He smiles, wrapping his arms around me and pulling me into the biggest bear hug.

I lift my head and catch Ryan's warm eyes. He smiles and walks towards us. I'm not sure how much of that conversation he heard over the music, but the look on his face makes me feel like he can read my mind somehow. That he knows.

"Come on, let's get a drink from the bar," he says, putting his hands on my shoulders to usher me away. I wave a small goodbye to Jake and let Ryan lead me out of the crowd.

He doesn't take his hands off me as we weave through the mass of people. He tells me to wait at the edge of the warehouse as he bustles to join the queue for the bar. I'm relieved to finally be out in the open space, it's so much quieter.

I watch several people begin to stare at Ryan as he joins the queue. I'm surprised when a few people start eagerly chatting away to him, I assume congratulating him on our set.

If he's going to be this popular now, I have no idea what it'll be like when his album is released.

"You're the new singer from The Lanes, right?" a male voice asks. I turn around to see a guy with brown, preppy styled hair and striking blue eyes. He offers a polite smile and I answer his question with a small nod.

"You were amazing. I'm Austin." He holds his hand out.

I shake it whilst looking down at his outfit. He's wearing an olive wax jacket, a blue oxford shirt and black chinos. He looks too smart to be at a festival, and very out of place amongst the eccentric, colourful costumes in the crowd.

"I'm Zoe." I smile, stealing a glance back towards the bar.

"Apologies for the random introduction, I noticed your university backpack. It's my alma mater," he explains. "What do you study?"

"Law."

His eyes widen. "Okay, I may sound like a complete stalker, and I know Zoe is a common name—no offense—but is your last name Jones by any chance?"

"Uh... yeah? How come?"

"I know your professor, Dr Jenkins. I'm doing a guest lecture with his class next week."

Wait a minute...

"You're the CEO of AQ Law?" I ask. Of course he is, I should've recognised him the moment he said his name was Austin.

He's the entrepreneur of one of the largest tech law firms in the country. His first office opened in the Midlands a couple of years ago. I remember reading about it in some law journal. I'm pretty sure he's planning to open a new office in London as well. I wonder what a guy like him is doing somewhere like this.

He nods his head. "What a small world."

"But wait, why did my professor mention me?" I ask, horrified at the thought.

"Because you're top of your class, Zoe."

"Oh." I blush.

Austin grins and nudges my arm. "No need to get all shy about it. He sang your praises, and I didn't think Dr Jenkins had any emotion beyond distain."

"Right? He's *so* stern." I laugh. "I didn't even think he knew my name, let alone where I ranked in the class!"

We both laugh until Austin's expression becomes serious. "I hope you'll come to my lecture? My firm is using it as an opportunity to recruit. I'd hate for you to miss out."

"I wouldn't miss it for the world." I beam.

"Hey, babe," Ryan calls from behind. I turn to face him just as he puts his arm around me.

"Hey, Ryan. This is Austin," I immediately introduce them. "He's a guest lecturer at my law school," I continue.

Austin shoots out a hand for Ryan to shake, but Ryan doesn't take it. His only free hand is on my shoulder, the other is clutching the recently purchased bottle of wine, and he makes no attempt to move out of the territorial embrace.

"It's nice to meet you, I'm a huge fan. I've actually watched The Lanes loads of times. You guys are awesome," Austin gushes, dropping his hand quickly, completely ignoring Ryan's hostility. "Is it true you're going solo?"

"Yeah."

"That's awesome. I'm gunna have to keep an eye out for your gigs." Austin pauses, shifting awkwardly when Ryan doesn't respond. "Well... anyway, I'd better get back to my buddies. They'll be wondering where I am. See you in a few of weeks, Zoe." He rushes off quickly and I turn to Ryan who has a menacing smirk on his face.

"*Buddies,*" he scoffs. "What a tool."

"That was rude." I scowl.

"Whatever. He was hitting on you," he says into my ear, leading me back towards the noisy crowd with a hand still on my shoulder.

I sigh and roll my eyes. "No, Ryan. He was talking about his company. He's that CEO my dad mentioned at dinner," I shout over the music, even though my explanation really shouldn't matter. Ryan should trust me by now.

Ryan continues to scowl, closing his eyes and taking a couple of deep breaths.

I stop walking and turn to face him. "I love *you*, Ryan," I shout, grabbing his wrist and shaking him.

My stern voice seems to trigger something in his mind because he smiles, his face softening and the corners of his eyes crinkling.

"Fuck, you drive me crazy," he breathes, running a hand through his hair and ruffling the strands. He then runs his hands over his face, trying to hide the smile playing on his mouth.

"Come on, we're supposed to be celebrating." I grab the wine bottle, twisting off the cap and taking a large gulp. I pass it back to him and he takes an equally large drink.

We walk back to the group, our hands intertwined, all tension evaporated.

421

The DJ set has gotten louder, at least I think it has, but maybe it's just the alcohol.

As soon as I see Jake in the crowd, he puts an arm around me, pulling me to dance with him. We both jump and dance to the music, dragging a now buzzed Ryan along with us

Whilst we dance, I switch between taking shots of vodka from Jake and chugging the wine Ryan bought. It's no surprise when I begin to feel more than tipsy.

"Don't leave my side tonight, okay?" I shout to Ryan.

"I promise." He grins as he watches me dance. He pulls my hand, tugging me closer to him. "With a girlfriend like you, why would I go anywhere else?" he says into my ear, the feel of his breath on my skin sending shots of electricity through me. Every hair on my body pricks from the chill.

I lean up on my tip toes and crash my lips into his. He grabs the back of my head, running his fingers through my hair as our kiss deepens.

"Come on, love birds," Nadine shouts, tugging my shoulder. "We're going to the main warehouse."

We race to the main stage in time for the headline act, Flume. I'm excited to see him live, Ryan plays his songs all the time in the car, meaning I'll actually know the lyrics to a set. I'm pretty sure he's the only act I've actually heard of that's playing this festival.

Once we're in the warehouse, we bustle through the mass of people to get into the middle of the crowd. Everyone is buzzing, smiling at us as we pass. I figured people would get aggressive at our pushing to the front, but everyone seems happy to let us by.

The space goes dark, and the crowd start to roar as we wait for Flume to come on. Nadine and Emily shuffle next to me and start to squeal in excitement as the build-up intensifies. My heart begins to race. I feel a chill rush through my body. I physically shiver from anticipation, yet my palms feel sweaty at the same time.

Ryan notices me shake, so moves behind me, wrapping an arm around the front of my chest so the back of my body is pressed tightly against him. It feels as if he is protecting me, whilst opening us up to the stage at the same time. It's like he wants us to feel the set together, to enjoy the music as if we're one person.

Suddenly, the opening line of *Holdin' On* plays and the crowd erupts. I raise my hands in the air, swaying gently.

The lights are flashing so brightly. The bass of the song pulses through my entire body. I wait impatiently for the beat to drop, anticipating its crash as my heart pounds like I'm on a rollercoaster.

"I feel so good," I say to Ryan, leaning my head back to rest on his shoulder.

He squeezes his arms tighter around my chest. "Me too," he replies, kissing my ear.

Finally, the beat drops, the sound igniting my body like an explosion.

I drop my hands and start bouncing around, singing the familiar lyrics with the rest of the crowd bobbing around me.

Nadine leans over and grabs my hands, pulling me closer to her and Emily. I reach my spare hand out and pull Ryan with me, unable to bear the sudden disconnect from him.

We dance in our circle. I'm sandwiched between Ryan and Nadine, who have completely lost themselves to the performance. Tyler, Emily, Adam, Claire and even Jake and his friends are right with us, losing themselves too.

I now get why people love going to festivals and gigs. Live music does something to the inner core of your soul. You don't just hear the songs; you *feel* them. The bass shakes your entire body and makes you feel on fire. It's a drug.

I nestle back into Ryan's arms as we dance. We face the stage, my eyes transfixed on the bright lights. We keep our bodies locked against each other and dance to the set like we're in our own world.

Ryan leans down to kiss my ear, sending my whole body into a frenzy. I tilt my head to his chest, closing my eyes as I feel his tongue swipe across my ear lobe. I let out a tiny moan and open my eyes, turning to face him.

His eyes are bloodshot, his pupils are so large that the hazel colour is barely visible. He grins at me, biting his lip before pressing his mouth to mine. I put my arms around his neck, bringing him close to me, letting the bass of the music pulse through me as we stand together, clinging to each other as if our lives depended on it.

Chapter Fifty

"Fuck," I hear Ryan groan. I slowly flutter my heavy eyes open.

My head is pounding, my throat feels completely dry. I try to ask him what's wrong, but nothing comes out, not even a croak.

Propping myself up on my elbows, I search for my bottle of water. I reach down, finding it on the wooden floor next to the bed, and gulp back the entire bottle.

Two days of partying at the festival has left me feeling like total crap.

Once my eyes refocus, they immediately land on Ryan sitting by the bay window, staring down at his phone with a scowl on his face.

"Is everything okay, Ry?" I ask. He doesn't look up from his phone.

A few more seconds pass before he sighs and puts it in his pocket.

"Yeah. Sorry, babe." He smiles, standing up and coming to sit on the end of the bed. "You don't mind if I go home for a bit, do you?"

A million questions suddenly dance through my already spinning head. I bring my hands to my forehead, hoping to physically stabilise my thoughts.

"Uh, as in now?" is all I can think to respond.

"Yeah. I just texted Tyler. He said you can catch a ride home with them. They're not leaving for a while, so why don't you go back to sleep for a bit, you must have one hell of a hangover." He tries to sound casual, but his words fall flat.

"Wait, you're already packed?" I say as I notice his bag and guitar by the door. How did I miss him getting his stuff together?

He doesn't answer, instead shooting me an apologetic look. I take a deep breath, rubbing my temples with my fingers. "Don't you feel too hungover to drive?"

"I'll be fine, I didn't really drink yesterday, and it's gone midday." He shrugs. "It makes more sense for me to go home from here, rather than drive north just to come south again."

He does have a point. But what I don't understand is

why he hasn't asked me to go with him? Wouldn't he want that? I'm already skipping some classes to be here, and cheer training isn't for a few days.

"Is everything okay at home?" I press.

"Yeah, I just haven't been back in a while. My aunt said Mum's feeling a little lonely," he explains, picking distractedly at the hem of his sweatshirt.

I sit up, disentangling myself from the bedsheets and shuffling closer to him. I slide a hand behind his back, holding him tightly.

"It won't be like last time," he whispers. "I swear."

I lean my forehead onto his shoulder. "I know." I sigh, trying to hide how panicked I feel.

"I promise I'll be back in a couple of days, and I'll call you every night," he offers.

"No, don't make any promises. Just go and spend time with your mum. Do what you have to do. Don't worry about me, I'll be fine. I'll just miss you." Attempting to give him my best smile, I squeeze him close.

"Okay. I'll let you know when I'm coming back, it'll be before your cheer competition. It's two weeks on Saturday, right?"

"Yeah." I smile.

He lifts himself off the bed and picks up his duffle bag, turning to look at me. The pain spread across his face makes my heart drop to my stomach.

"I love you, always," he says, disappearing out of the door.

I wait until the bedroom door shuts before I bring my hand to my mouth.

Alone, in this huge bedroom, I no longer try and hide how I feel. I lie back in the bed, pulling my knees to my chest, letting the tears stream down my face.

A light knock at the door startles me. I quickly wipe my eyes, terrified Ryan has forgotten something. I don't want him to see me like this.

"Come in," I croak.

A tangle of messy jet-black hair walks through the door. I let out a relieved breath.

"Hey, Tyler just told me about Ryan. Are you okay?" Nadine asks, rubbing her tired eyes. She takes one look at my face and hops into bed next to me, getting under the bright white linen sheets and pulling them over us.

We lie down, facing each other. She strokes the top of my head with the palm of her hand and rests her other hand over me in a bear hug. I can't stop myself, I let out a loud sob.

"It's okay," she tries to sooth me. "The comedown from partying won't be helping things right now, you'll feel better tomorrow. He'll be back soon, I'm sure."

If this is caused by the alcohol, I'm never drinking ever again. I feel *terrible*. It's like my body is out of balance. The depth of sadness I feel today must be a way to compensate for the total bliss we experienced over the weekend. Although, I'm pretty sure, even without this foggy hangover, I would still feel this low today. Because I need Ryan. I don't have any happiness without the other half of my heart by my side.

This is the first time we've been apart for weeks, and I already don't like it. I'm never going to survive his tour.

Ugh, why didn't he take me with him?

I don't even know when he'll be home.

The uncertainty makes me feel physically sick. I bolt upright as bile rises in my throat. I run to the toilet, throwing up whatever is in my stomach and gasping for air as I finish. I take a gulp of water from the taps and climb back into the bed with an unsuspecting Nadine.

Now my stomach is settled, I need to think.

There's no point crying over the fact he left me here, I can't change that. Instead, I need to figure out if he's really changed, if this isn't just one of his old tricks again. Emily already warned me that, when the emotions get too strong, Ryan disappears. Is that what's happening here?

I shake my head. His mum needs him, that's all. I shouldn't be so selfish. This isn't about me.

And maybe spending quality time with her will make him realise he misses me. Maybe it'll make him wish he invited me. Hell, he might even call and ask me to join them.

You don't walk out the door saying, '*I love you, always*' if you don't mean it. I should trust Ryan. He's given me no reason not to, not really.

I wipe my damp face and reach for Nadine, cuddling her close. "Thanks for being here for me," I whisper.

"You got it, bestie."

I grab my bags from the boot of Tyler's car and stare up at my apartment, pausing for a moment.

My feet feel heavy, like the sadness I feel is weighing my entire body down.

"Are you sure you don't want to come back to ours?" Tyler asks, rolling his window down and calling out to me.

I shake my head. The last place I want to be is in Ryan's room, alone.

I take a deep breath and push through the heavy door, trying to walk without dropping my guitar or duffle bag. Once I reach the apartment, I make my way straight to my bedroom, dumping everything in a heap on the bed.

My eyes start to well up as soon as I enter the room. I try not to think about the fact that waking up next to Ryan has become second nature to me. I don't crave the cheap bedsheets in this apartment the same way I crave the cotton smell of Ryan's navy duvet.

This apartment isn't home anymore. I don't think it ever was.

I go to the kitchen to get a glass of water, only to discover Jake sprawled out on one of the sofas with glitter all over his face. I didn't think he'd be back from the festival so soon, I thought he was staying in London to party with his friends this week.

"I. Am. Dead," he announces as soon as I enter the kitchen. His voice is croaky, practically non-existent.

I grab two glasses and fill them with water before sitting down on the couch and handing him one. He gulps the whole thing down in a matter of seconds.

"Thanks. I needed that." He smiles.

I cast my eyes down his outfit. *Yep*, he's still wearing his animal ski suit.

"How come you're back so early?" I ask.

He sighs, brushing his hands through his hair. I watch as clumps of glitter fall from his scalp. "I just couldn't hack another day of drinking. I wanted to come home."

"I get that." I smile at him.

"Do you want to watch a movie or something?" he asks. I pause for a moment, worrying about bumping into Alice. "We can watch it in my room if you like," he adds, reading my mind.

"Sure. But I think you might be due a shower first." I point to his outfit.

He laughs, hopping up from the couch.

As Jake showers, I refill our cups with water and check my phone. My heart leaps when I see a text from Ryan letting me know that he made it to his aunt's house. I smile and immediately text him back, telling him to make the most of his time at home and that I love him.

Chapter
Fifty-One

Two weeks have passed since I last heard from Ryan. Two long, miserable weeks.

I get up. I check my phone. I don't hear anything.

I call Ryan. It goes to voicemail.

I head to class (if I can be bothered).

I go for a run until I burn five hundred calories.

I go home. I go to my stash. I eat my stash. I vomit.

I call Ryan again.

I go to cheer.

I come home. I eat. I vomit again.

Oh, and I remember to smile when I'm around other people.

And then I repeat.

"He'll be here, try not to panic," Tyler says from the driver's seat of his car, looking ahead as we slowly roll through the traffic surrounding the competition arena. I can't work out if he is trying to reassure me or himself.

Nadine turns around from the passenger seat and shoots me a sympathetic smile.

I know I need to focus on our cheerleading competition today, but how can I after the two weeks I've just endured? I need Ryan.

As soon as we pull into the car park, our eyes scan for Ryan's Jeep, but it's nowhere to be seen. Tyler decides to go and look for him in the arena, telling us to prioritise the competition. He kisses Nadine goodbye and I feel a bitter pang of jealousy watching them.

Nausea hits and fear washes over me. I tell Nadine I'll catch up with her as I run to the nearest toilet to empty my stomach. My throat burns and a now-familiar pain shoots through my body. The pain has become worse in the past couple of days, but I know as soon as Ryan's back, it'll stop.

I begin to walk towards the rest of team, scanning the

faces of every person that walks by, searching for him.

We eventually head backstage, where a room is set up with a sprung floor for practice runs. My mind races, but I still manage to execute every tumble and stunt without any issues.

I don't feel nervous for the competition, not even as we head to the edge of the performance mat. I don't feel anything as I look out at the huge crowd.

The arena has a giant audience space, like a concert hall, but the chairs are mostly filled with other teams, all waiting for their turn to perform. A panel of judges sit right at the front of the audience at a long table, looking like something out of a TV talent show. Not even they intimidate me as we step onto the mat.

I force my mind to focus during the routine.

The crowd starts to cheer as I flip and twist and tumble all the way across the stage.

But I feel nothing.

There's no adrenaline, no rush, no wave of excitement like I had performing with The Lanes. I don't even feel the way I did when I performed at the cheer firework night. Maybe the emptiness is simply down to the fact that I've used up all my energy worrying about Ryan, or maybe it's because all of this means nothing without him here.

I look to Nadine as we finish the routine. Excitement floods her face, and she bounds over to me, squealing. "That was *unbelievable*! There's no way we haven't won!" She loops her arm through mine. "Come on! Let's go find the guys. Tyler would have found Ryan by now; I just know it!"

I can't help but feel a tiny bit of optimism as we wander out of the performance area, down the stairs and out to the spectator stands.

The hope is short lived when I see Tyler sat alone on a row of empty seats, staring at his phone.

"No Ryan?" I ask quietly, trying to stop my voice from cracking.

He shakes his head. "No, but something doesn't feel right. I tried calling his number and it didn't even go through to voicemail. I think the number's been disconnected." His eyes are glossy as he looks at me. His worry for his best friend suddenly makes my fear valid. I'm no longer just a needy girlfriend yearning for her boyfriend. Something is wrong and we both know it.

"What do we do?" the words tumble out of my mouth in a rush. My eyes are wide, alert, as they scan Tyler's face. He stays silent for a moment, as if contemplating how to answer me.

"He's done this before, but..." he trails off, looking at

Nadine and then back to me. He shakes his head, biting his bottom lip.

It looks like he's about to cry, but then he suddenly looks at me with a newfound smile on his face. "Look, there's nothing we can do right now. Don't let this spoil today. You guys were amazing, and the results will be announced in ten minutes, right?" he asks and both Nadine and I nod. "Okay, so go down with your team, try to enjoy it. I'll call Ryan's brother," he says matter-of-factly, still forcing a smile.

I hesitantly agree and follow Nadine back through the rows of spectator chairs to where our team are huddled in the corner. They are so high from performing, they didn't even notice that we slipped off in the first place.

Suddenly, an unbearable pain flashes through my stomach and beads of sweat form on my forehead. I instinctively reach for my stomach with my hands and wince.

"You okay?" Nadine spins to look at me, placing her hands on my elbows. I focus on breathing in and out until the pain settles and I can stand up straight.

"Yeah, just cramp or something." I shrug nonchalantly, which seems to satisfy her concern. I'm not due my period for another couple of weeks. Although, now I think about it, my periods have become so irregular lately. Maybe it is period cramp after all.

I shrug it off, putting it down to nerves, and follow the team back to the stage.

Every squad in our division walks onto the sprung floor and each team huddles together. We all hold hands, sitting in a group circle, waiting for the results to come in. I feel like this whole day has been a huge blur. I've gone through the motions, my mind totally outside of my body. I barely even remember getting out of bed this morning and getting dressed for the competition, let alone performing only moments ago.

After what feels like hours, the MC announces that our team has won. I do my best to play my part by plastering on a big smile and hugging the rest of the team. As soon as Kim collects our trophy, I nudge Nadine, asking if we can leave.

She pulls out her phone. "Tyler's just text me. He asked us to meet him out front."

"Did he say anything about Ryan?" I ask. She shakes her head.

My heart is racing as we scan the arena for the nearest exit. Spotting a bright green fire escape sign, I pull Nadine towards it. I'm practically running as we get to the car park.

My heart instantly sinks when I see Tyler sat on a

wooden bench with his head in his hands. Alone.

I practically run to him but stop dead in my tracks when I look at his face. His eyes are puffy and bloodshot, tears streak down his blotchy cheeks.

I brace myself for what's coming.

"His mum died," he croaks, lowering his head.

I exhale deeply, Ryan is safe. I feel like I would have sensed it somehow if something had physically happened to him.

But that doesn't stop the pain in my chest as Tyler's words sink in.

Ryan's mother is dead. Ryan has lost another parent.

Nadine immediately rushes to Tyler's side, pushing his head into her chest and rubbing his back, comforting him in a way I long to comfort Ryan.

"What happened?" I whisper. My brain feels like it's frozen along with the rest of my body. This can't be happening. This can't be happening. Not to Ryan. Not to *my* Ryan.

"She killed herself," he mutters. His eyes stay transfixed on the floor as he talks. "He found her when he got back from the festival."

"He found her?" I croak.

I feel sick. My mind flashes with images of what he could have seen, what he walked into. I turn my head and rush towards the nearest bush, throwing up hot acid into the leaves. My stomach roars with burning pain.

I stumble back to the others, feeling droplets of icy rain hit my face. I look up at the dreary sky; I'm pretty sure it's going to hailstorm any second.

"Am I still insured to drive your car?" Nadine hastily asks Tyler, and he nods. "Okay, I'll drive us home then. Come on." Nadine heaves him upright and tries to keep him steady as they take small steps towards the car.

"Shouldn't we drive to Cornwall? Go and get him? We can't just let him deal with this alone," I yell as I catch up to them.

There's no way I'm letting him push us away, he needs us. He can't cope with losing his mum by himself. I shudder at the thought of him in an empty family home, alone with no one to comfort him. I can't even begin to imagine how this could scar him.

I won't let him drown in the grief. *I can't.*

"I spoke to his brother, apparently, he's not there. He seems to think Ryan has driven back to our house, so maybe he'll be there when we get back."

My heart soars at the thought of seeing Ryan when we pull up to the house. I know he's learnt from his past. He'll be there when we get back. He'll talk to us, open up. We can be there for him like I know he must want us to be. I'll be able to put my arms around him and give him all the love he needs to get through this.

Chapter
Fifty-Two

But Ryan's not home. He isn't waiting for our love.

The car isn't parked out front, and the house is dark and empty.

Neither Claire nor Adam are home, they've gone away somewhere for the weekend.

As we push into the empty house, Nadine murmurs to me that she's going to check the basement. I nod and rush upstairs to Ryan's room.

I stand outside his door for a couple of seconds, praying to whoever is listening, asking for him be in his room, sat on his bed with his guitar, scribbling lyrics on scraps of paper.

But he isn't here. The room is empty. The white,

empty walls mock me in the same way Kady's room once had. All his belongings are cleared out, there's absolutely nothing left. No navy duvet, no Arcade Fire poster, no skateboard, no guitar. Nothing. There's no sign that he ever lived here. The only thing left is the Ryan-shaped hole punched through my heart.

I bolt downstairs to the basement, praying I'm dreaming.

But I'm not.

All of his instruments are gone, all of his recording equipment, everything. Even the pictures of the band pinned up on the wall are taken down.

He's gone.

And so is my heart.

PART TWO

Chapter Fifty-Three

The memory of white walls flashes through my mind, tormenting me as it has done every time I've opened my eyes and allowed reality to drag me under. As usual, the memory makes bile rise to my throat. I reach for my bin, emptying my stomach into it.

Pain.

Relief.

Pain.

The physical pain in my stomach burns my body and I let it wash over me.

I call his phone once more and get nothing, nothing but an unbearable pain through every inch of my body. I wait for unconsciousness to take over once more.

Chapter Fifty-Four

I don't know what day it is. I don't even know what time
it is. It could be early morning or the middle of the night.
My curtains are shut so tight, I have no way of telling.

I could check the time on my phone, but I'm not sure
where it is. I'm pretty sure I left it to die somewhere in my
bedroom, and I have no energy to find it.

I sit up and lean on my elbows. Every part of my body
aches.

My eyes go to the end of the bed where a pile of food
used to lay. It's now covered in empty wrappers,
reminding me that I finished the last packet of chocolate
yesterday. I remember inhaling it, much in the same way
I have with every other piece of food that's entered my

mouth since he left.

I've not eaten much, but when I have, I've consumed it as quickly as possible before lodging my fingers down my throat to bring it back up again.

It's the only thing that momentarily stops the unbearable pain in my chest. It's the only thing I have control over right now. The only thing I can be certain of. The only thing I can depend on.

But it's never long before the pain in my heart overtakes and I'm back to wishing he would save me.

I close my eyes, waiting for sleep to come so I no longer have to think about him.

I'm so exhausted that I've finally stopped dreaming. The first couple of nights were torture, my unconscious mind would take me back to happy times with him. He would feature in every single dream I had. The image of him would be so vivid that I could swear it was real. I'd forget all about the fact that he's gone.

But then I'd wake up, and his absence would hit me as if it was the first time I was experiencing it, shattering me all over again.

Now my mind has finally given up on me, it's abandoned all hope of seeing him again. Sleep has finally become a black void of nothingness, allowing me to escape from the nightmare I'm living.

A loud knock at my bedroom door stirs me awake, startling me from my daze.

Why is someone knocking on my door?

No one knows I'm here, not even Jake. I'm pretty sure he's gone on rugby tour; I haven't heard him in the house for a few days. Alice wouldn't be knocking either; she's gone to visit her sister. It's reading week, so I've had the whole place to myself.

"Zoe!" a male voice yells. Ryan?

"Zoe, open this door right now, I mean it!" Not Ryan, *Tyler.*

A few seconds later I hear a key turn in the door. How does Tyler have a key to my room? Maybe Ryan left the spare key I gave him at the band's house. I suppose he doesn't need it anymore.

The door swings open and Nadine and Tyler stand in the doorway, gawping at me.

"You told us you went home to stay with your parents!" Nadine shouts. At least, I think she's shouting. Her voice pushes against my throbbing head. I cover my ears with my hands and close my eyes.

They move in silence, looking down at my bin, then to the wrappers on my bed and then at each other. A look of fear seems to flash across Nadine's face, but she turns her back to me before I can be sure. Tyler puts his hands on her shoulders and their eyes meet. They seem to be communicating silently with their eyes, just like Ryan and I once did.

The thought of him sends a fresh wave of agony through me and I groan, clutching my torso with my hands. I curl up on the bed and face the wall. I don't want them to see me like this.

Nadine sits down on the bed and tries to pull me to face her. "Zoe, are you okay?" she cries, but I can't say anything. The pain is too intense.

I sit up and quickly move for the bin, throwing up nothing but sticky, acidic bile.

"Tyler, there's blood in here!" Nadine shrieks and I have to cover my ears again, closing my eyes.

I feel a cold hand on my head before something moves under my body. And then everything turns black.

Chapter Fifty-Five

"How are you feeling?" Tyler asks once I open my eyes. He's barely left my bedside since I got admitted to the hospital, neither has Nadine.

I look to my left and see her sat in her usual chair by the window with a stack of politics books piled next to her. Guilt crashes through me knowing the end of semester exams start next week, yet she's here every day without fail.

"Fine," I croak. I lean over to grab a cup of water, gulping it down in one. I wince as my stomach lurches in pain. The doctor said it would take a couple of days after surgery to feel better.

Tyler glances at Nadine and she closes her textbook,

walking over to perch on the end of the bed. I feel both pairs of eyes staring at me.

"Zoe, we haven't wanted to pry whilst you've been so poorly, but please talk to us. We're so worried," Tyler begs, his voice cracking at the end.

"The doctor said the stomach ulcer has been the result of months of vomiting. How did we not know?" Nadine raises her hands to her face as she lets out a tiny cry.

"I'm so sorry. I-I just, I swear I didn't know what was happening." I couldn't feel the pain of the stomach ulcer, not when my heart was so shattered, so broken. No physical pain could compare to that unbearable torture.

"Does he, did you, is he—" I begin.

Tyler shakes his head and closes his eyes, a frown etched on his tired face. "No, Zoe. We haven't heard from Ryan." I swear I can hear venom in Tyler's voice wrap around *his* name. He raises his head and places one hand on Nadine's and the other over mine. "But we're not going anywhere, Zoe. You have us, always," he says.

The word *always* sends a dagger through my heart as I remember the last time I heard that word leave Ryan's mouth. '*I love you, always*' he'd promised. Oh, how naive I was to believe him.

A lump forms in my throat. I look up at my friends

and stare into their dark, tired eyes. I can see how much pain they're having to endure, having to bear, because of me.

They didn't deserve to be dragged into this mess. They didn't deserve to have to carry me out of my apartment after I passed out, unconscious. They didn't deserve to have to witness me being whisked from the emergency room into surgery. They didn't deserve any of this. They still don't.

What's worse is that I know they're blaming themselves. I've overheard them so many times whilst they think I've been sleeping, asking each other how they didn't notice my problems, how they didn't see what I was doing to myself, how they could have stopped him from leaving. The blame they're putting on themselves kills me, and it's killing them. Their suffering is written all over their faces.

"I'm sorry I've put you through hell. I feel terrible. I know you're both so busy with your own lives." I let a tear roll down my cheek, not bothering to catch it with my hand.

Nadine scrunches her face and lets out a deep breath. "Zoe, our love for you isn't conditional," she begins. "It doesn't matter what I have going on in my life, you're my sister. If you need me, I'll be there. No matter what. I want to be your safe place, because from the moment I met you, you've been mine."

She moves around the bed to hug me. Tyler follows, wrapping his arms around both of us. The embrace feels slightly uncomfortable on my raw stomach, but I don't care.

"I love you guys," I whisper, loud enough for them to hear me.

"Do you think you could eat something? The nurse sent you in some yoghurt." Nadine points to the food on my side table.

I hesitate and Tyler playfully glares at me. "If you really love us, you'll eat."

I chuckle, sticking my tongue out at him as I reach for the yoghurt. Before pulling the lid off, I quickly flip Tyler off, which earns a laugh from Nadine. Hearing the beautiful sound of her laugh is enough to get me to force down the yogurt.

It feels surprisingly good; the cold, thick liquid settles the burn in my stomach.

Once I finish, I pick up my hairbrush and begin to comb my hair. My head feels tender as the brush touches my scalp. Noticing me wince, Nadine takes it from me and gently untangles my hair, brushing slowly until my wild waves are tamed.

I run my hands through the strands and sigh at how thin it feels. I used to love my thick, wavy hair, but now I barely have enough to put it in a ponytail. So much of it had broken or become weak during the past couple of weeks.

"Have you heard from my parents?" I ask and watch Tyler's face drop, his lips forming a tight line as he slowly shakes his head.

"Not much. Only when I call them." He bows his head and touches my hand, giving it a gentle squeeze.

It hurts that they haven't actively called or turned up to the hospital. I thought they'd be there for me no matter what. But maybe I just pushed them too far.

I didn't stick to the plan, and I only have myself to blame. Or maybe they think it's Ryan that's to blame.

It wouldn't be right to pin this on him though. I know what's happening to me goes deeper than him simply walking out on me. Ryan was just keeping me afloat, holding me above water so I wouldn't drown in the chaos and grief of losing Kady. But a crashing wave was always inevitable, whether he was in my life or not. I was always going to end up this way, Ryan just delayed the process.

And with my life jacket gone, I need to learn to swim.

Unlike my parents, Hannah's been texting and calling every chance she gets. I won't let her visit though. I don't want her to see me like this. Not yet anyway. It'll only make her panic more. Promising to see her once I'm better is another motivation to actually recover.

"Have you thought about what you're going to do once you're discharged from here?" Nadine asks.

"Yeah, I discussed it with my doctor. I think I'll go to Priory House," I tell them. They smile proudly, relief flooding their faces.

"Let me see her!" a familiar voice booms.

Am I dreaming?

I slowly open my eyes to realise I'm not.

Nadine is wide eyed, staring out at the door of my hospital room.

I don't move. I force my eyes shut, pretending to sleep.

I hear Nadine bolt up from her chair and rush to the door.

"You're not going anywhere fucking near her. I mean it, Ryan," Tyler spits, his voice thick with threat.

"*Shhhhh!* Please! She's sleeping," Nadine begs.

I hear footsteps and the sound of a door clicking. I

don't move in case one of them has come into the room.

"Why are you here? Why now?" Tyler asks. His voice sounds muffled, so I assume they're talking just outside my hospital room.

"I just want to know she's okay," Ryan pleads.

"How the fuck do you think she is, *buddy*?" Tyler snaps. "She's got a fucking eating disorder and none of us had a fucking clue about it." I wince at his words. It's unbearable to hear the anger between them. They used to be brothers and now their relationship is in pieces because of me.

No matter how broken my heart is, I can't be angry at Ryan for walking out on me. I was too much, too selfish at a time that should have been all about him. He needs to focus on the loss of his mum without his complicated ex-girlfriend obstructing his healing. I just wish Tyler would see it that way and choose Ryan instead of me.

"Did you know she was sick, or were you too busy running away from all your problems to even notice what was happening?" Tyler presses.

I strain my ears to hear Ryan's response, trying not to move. I remain facing the opposite wall. I don't want to see him. It would hurt too much.

"I—I... I knew," Ryan stutters, exhaling in what I can only assume is defeat. "But I swear, I didn't know it was this bad. I thought she got past it. She always called me before she ever did anything, and just before the festival it was so infrequent, I thought she wasn't doing it anymore. Please, just let me see her," he begs.

"She called you every time she needed help, and you didn't think to at least mention this to us when you decided to fuck off?" Tyler yells. "No way are you getting near her. I don't care what's going on with you. Leaving her like this, leaving us to clean up your mess, is out of line. Nadine has exams and she's here every goddamn day, when it should be *you*. I won't have you do this, not while she's this way."

I'm grateful for Tyler, but I can't help but feel a sting at his choice of words. *Leaving us to clean up your mess.*

Me being the mess he is referring to.

It's times like this that my mind goes dark. I start to wish that my eating disorder got the better of me.

I don't want to drag those I love down with me. I just want to disappear from the world, disappear from the heartache and pain without leaving a trace of hurt and destruction behind. It would be easier that way.

An impossible wish.

I internally laugh when I realise that's exactly what Ryan has tried and failed to do. The irony.

"Please," Ryan begs.

"Are you here because you actually love her? Or are you here because she's ending up like your mum and you feel guilty about it?"

"Don't," Ryan warns.

I hear a few footsteps and shuffling outside of the room, but luckily the door doesn't open.

"Woah, woah," Nadine interrupts. "Less of the toxic masculinity. We're in a hospital for Christ's sake, not a boxing ring. Let me handle this," she says with an air of unwavering authority.

The door clicks open, and I snap my eyes shut again.

"Zoe, are you awake?" Nadine asks.

I don't respond.

I hear her walk around to the side of the bed my body is facing. I don't risk moving, hoping she'll give up.

"Girl, I know your fake sleeping," she says, a smile in her voice.

I curl my lips together to hide my own grin. How does she have the ability to make me smile at the weirdest, most heart-breaking time?

"Ryan's here, shall I let him in?" she adds softly.

That does it.

My smile vanishes and I can't hold it in any longer. A huge sob spills from my mouth. Before I know it, I'm clutching my stomach, screaming from the pain, screaming from the tears, screaming from the thought of seeing his beautiful face again.

I push the emergency button to call the nurse and scream and scream and scream. Until finally, I see darkness once again.

Chapter Fifty-Six

I stare at the pale green wall in front of me, counting the cracks in the paint as I wait for my therapist to call me into her office. If I don't keep myself occupied, the pain in my heart rips through, clouding my thoughts and making me think of *him*.

My chair squeaks as I shift my body to get a closer look at the wall.

I have no idea how much longer I have to wait for my session. I'm not even sure what time it is. They took my watch and phone the moment I stepped through the doors of Priory House, and there isn't even a clock on the wall of this waiting room.

I have to say, after almost two months of being here,

the silence in my head without my phone and social media has been absolute heaven. I hated sitting in my hospital room during recovery from surgery, scrolling through Instagram and seeing my housemates and cheer friends having fun, celebrating the end of the first semester.

The security door behind me unlocks with a click, making me spin my head round to check if it's my therapist... but it's not.

"Fancy seeing you here," Austin says, smiling and walking to sit in the empty chair opposite me.

He's dressed in navy chinos and a crisp white shirt. The clothes are different colours to the ones he was wearing at the winter festival, but they look identical. I bet his whole wardrobe is filled with pristine Oxford shirts and chinos.

"What are you doing here?" I demand, my tone too sharp to be considered polite.

"I have a therapy session."

"Oh." I nod, feeling ridiculously silly for even asking.

Why else would he be in a mental health hospital, dumbass?

"Sorry," I mutter.

Austin chuckles. "Don't worry about it. After eight years of therapy, there's no way you could offend me."

463

"Wow, eight years." I let out a pained breath.

Will I still be going to therapy in eight years' time? God, I hope not.

"Uh huh. Therapy isn't anything to be ashamed of, you know. I think it shows we're self-aware."

"I guess that's a nice way to look at it." I shrug, returning my gaze to the wall.

"Are you in here overnight or are you an outpatient?" he asks, penetrating the momentary silence.

My cheeks instantly heat. I press my cold hands to my face in an effort to cool down.

"Sorry, you don't have to answer that," he adds.

"No, no it's okay." I smile weakly. "Overnight. Not sure when that'll change though." I shrug.

"Well, that's okay. You're in the best place. They did so much for me here, still do. I remember a time when I didn't want to be alive anymore." He pauses. "But you have to tell yourself the pain is only temporary. You'll get through it, I promise." He smiles again.

"I take it you're an outpatient?"

"Yeah. I travel up from London every week especially."

"London? Why would you travel all this way just for therapy? Can't you see someone down there?"

Austin shifts uncomfortably. "I—" He lets out a

cough. "Well, actually, I'm a donor here."

"*Wait*," I practically spit. "You're the entrepreneur who helped fund this place?"

Austin nods sheepishly.

"Talk about an overachiever. Let me guess, you're not even thirty yet?" I joke warmly and nudge him with my elbow. He seems to relax a little at my mocking him.

"Correct. Twenty-eight-years young, thank you very much." He smirks, his eyes fixed on my face.

"Figures."

He chuckles, his laugh sparking something inside of me that I thought was dead. For the first time in what feels like forever, I let out a small laugh, the unfamiliar sensation sending a shiver down my spine.

But it's not long before my laughter fades and the pain in my chest takes over once more. I let my eyes wander back to the cracks on the wall behind Austin.

"I'm really sorry you're unwell," he finally mutters.

"It's okay." I half-smile.

"Do you like it here?" he asks.

"Do I like living in a hospital?" I ask slowly, glancing at him out of the corner of my eye.

"Sure."

I sigh. "Uh, it's okay. Everyone is nice enough. It's still a hospital though."

Austin smirks, nodding understandingly.

"But they do let me study so I don't fall behind," I add, unsure what else to say. I'm not sure if he's asking me as the owner, or just to make conversation.

"Why haven't you been going to music therapy? I would've thought you'd be the first one there, but I haven't seen you. It's a shame your boyfriend—"

"He's not my boyfriend," I snap, watching as the expression on Austin's face falls at my rude tone. Guilt rushes through me, so I quickly add, "I didn't think they ran the sessions anymore."

"Sure, they do. I run them now." He smiles proudly. "Not quite as talented as Ryan, but I play the piano and saxophone."

"Did you know him?" I ask, refusing to meet Austin's eyes and clutching the edge of my chair. This is the first time I've spoken about him since he tried to crash the hospital after my surgery, and I'm not sure I like it. I'm not sure my heart likes it either.

Austin crumples his brows and turns his head. "Did I know Ryan?"

"Yeah. If you own this place, wouldn't you have met him before?" I press.

What is wrong with me? Why am I still talking about him?

"No, actually. The festival was the first and only time I've met him. Our paths just never crossed. I was never here on the days he ran the sessions, and I didn't even realise the Ryan that came here was the lead singer of The Lanes, or I would've made sure to come to music therapy. I felt like an idiot when Susanne told me who he was just the other week."

"Oh right," I mumble.

"Sorry. That was awfully tactless of me," Austin responds.

"It's okay."

"You should come," he suggests. "To music therapy."

The thought makes me want to vomit.

I haven't picked up my guitar or sang since Ryan left. I haven't even been able to listen to music because it makes me feel everything I'm trying to run away from. I'm not strong enough to take it. I don't tell Austin any of this; I simply agree to go to the session, even though I probably won't go.

My name flashes on a TV monitor above us, notifying me that my therapist is ready to see me. I say goodbye to Austin and walk into Dr Locke's office, taking my usual seat on a brown leather armchair.

She gets up from her mahogany desk and sits on the identical armchair opposite me. I look behind her head of pixie brown hair, my eyes wandering to the row of blue and red books stacked on the shelf behind her. She has quite the impressive library of psychology books.

She lets out a cough and my eyes dart back to her face. "Do you think we could begin where we left off yesterday?" she asks, opening her clipboard and crossing her legs. Pressing a pen to the blank sheet of paper, she scrawls something across the top of the page.

"Sure."

"Okay, so we started to talk about loss. You told me about Kady, but then you mentioned there was one other loss you suffered recently."

"Uh huh," I respond slowly, looking to the floor.

"Do you think you could tell me what this second loss was, or do you still not feel ready to talk about it?"

I gulp. "I suppose I could talk about it." I inhale sharply. "R-Ryan. His name was Ryan." I take another breath to steady myself. "We met just before Kady's death. He was my rock throughout the whole thing. But his mum recently died—she killed herself—and so he disappeared. He left me and didn't even say goodbye. I went to his house and found he packed up all his stuff and just left." My voice is rushed, and I know I've skipped over so many details, but my throat feels tight. Tears sting my eyes.

"And how did you feel when you realised he had gone?"

My mind flies back to that blurry day, pleading with Tyler to help me find Ryan as I ran down the stairs, hysterical after finding his room empty. I won't forget the look on Nadine's face as she passed me the note that he'd left on the basement coffee table.

Zoe, please don't look for me. I have to move on. This isn't what I want anymore. I need to focus on my career. I'm sorry you're caught in this mess, but I can't be there for you in the way you need me to be. It's too much. I need out.

"Betrayed," I admit.

Dr Locke scribbles more notes on her page. She then raises a carefully plucked eyebrow, ushering me to continue.

"I think we all felt that way. Initially, we thought he was just hurting and needed to come to terms with the death of his mum, but I understand now that he wanted a fresh start. A clean break.

"I think maybe he realised he was spending too much time away from her, and I think the guilt crushed him. So, I guess now he's on a mission to make her proud, and I don't think I can blame him for that."

"That's quite the prediction," Dr Locke adds, not looking up.

I shrug. "It's just a guess. It's how I would've felt if I was him." I bring the sleeve of my hoodie to my mouth and chew at a hole in the stitching. "I think I also remind him of her, in the way I struggled to cope after Kady died," I whisper, feeling the weight of the admission on my chest.

"I don't think you can blame yourself. You can't help the way your mind has reacted to loss. In the same way you are cutting Ryan some slack for his reaction to the passing of his mother, you need to cut yourself some slack too," Dr Locke continues, clasping the pen on the clipboard and putting her hands together.

"I know, but I didn't help. If I was normal, maybe he would have wanted to stay." I sigh and bite at a fresh piece of my sleeve, nibbling another small hole in the fabric.

"What is normal, Zoe? And do you honestly believe that he would have stayed if you hadn't been sick?" she presses.

After an intake of breath, I shake my head and wait for her to continue.

"I don't want you to think of your illness as something to apologise for. It's human to need the help of others to cope with huge events in your life. It is entirely 'normal' to turn to a loved one when you are trying to cope."

I shrug. "I think it's just hard when everyone around me seems to be able to cope with things. None of my housemates took time out of their classes when we found out about Kady. They continued to go about their daily lives, whereas I became a mess, and I didn't have a right to be. I wasn't her best friend; I wasn't her family. And yet, I coped worse than anyone." I sigh and lean back into the chair, already feeling exhausted.

The memory of a piece of advice Ryan once gave me floats through my head. 'Grief affects everyone in different ways, and to take a measure is cruel.' I shudder at the memory.

"Zoe, think of your mind as a phone battery. Everyone's batteries are different. And sometimes, when big things happen in your life, the battery depletes at a faster rate than others; in the same way that your phone battery would deplete faster if you downloaded an entire film or spent the day scrolling through social media.

"Your battery took a huge hit when you found out about Kady because you'd never experienced loss before. And then, when Ryan left, it took another hit on an already depleting charge. It's okay to need to take time to recharge the batteries, and it's okay for them to have depleted in the first place. The most important thing is that you recognised it."

"I don't think I did recognise it," I admit with a sigh.

"But you do now." She smiles kindly. "And how do you currently feel about Ryan's disappearance? Have your feelings evolved at all do you think?" she predictably circles the conversation back to Ryan. I knew she'd want to make the most of my sudden openness.

"When I got back from the cheer competition, I was utterly crushed when I realised he deleted and blocked me on everything. I was stripped of all contact. It made me feel like I was drowning. But now, I'm glad he did it. I'm glad I can't see what he's up to. I'm glad I'm in here too, it shields me. But I'm scared I'll break again when I get out of here."

Ryan's career is so public, it's going to be hard to escape when I'm home. When Nadine last visited, she told me that his tour sold out within a couple of minutes, and he's now got millions of followers on social media. Apparently, magazines have featured him in so many articles. He's even been nominated for 'Best Up and Coming Artist' at some big awards show. It's crazy to see how much both of our lives have changed in the space of a couple of months. His for the better, and mine—well,

I'm here.

"Is that why you wanted to come here? To escape?" Dr Locke probes with a neutral face. "I fear if you use a similar coping mechanism to the one that you say Ryan is using, by running away, you will never learn to conquer your true demons."

I pause for a moment, pondering her words.

"I'll be honest, at first I was sceptical of how much being here would actually work. I didn't think I could get better without Ryan. I just agreed to it to appease everyone else, to stop them worrying about me... and to stop burdening them."

"Do you still think that now?" she asks, her lips press into a thin line.

"No, I don't. The most important thing I've realised since being here is that the only person who can save me is myself, and I deserve to save myself."

"Go on," she probes.

"I always thought that Ryan walked into my life to save me, to make me whole. Our love was addicting, maddening, but I now realise it was also toxic. It consumed me. He was my every coping mechanism, my every thought. I didn't realise at the time how dangerous that was. It's no surprise that I broke when he left. I was an addict on the biggest comedown of my life.

"I eventually realised, if I'm going to survive, I've got to learn to love myself, because it's not Ryan's soul I'm connected to forever—it's my own. Could you imagine what I could achieve if I poured the love I gave him into myself?"

Chapter Fifty-Seven

.

We sit in silence for a moment, and I know Dr Locke is waiting for me to say something, so I just admit what's on my mind. "I know it's great and all, that I've finally discovered that I need to look after myself, but I still feel so lonely without him."

"What do you mean by that?"

"Ryan seemed to be the only person who understood why I was the way I was. He never judged me, he always made sure to be around to stop me binging and throwing up—not that I always told him when it happened—but still, he tried to be there for me when I did need him. And now he's gone, I feel alone in this mess. Not even my family want to speak to me." I rub the sleeve of my hoodie over my tender, damp cheeks.

Dr Locke puts down her clipboard and leans over the side of her leather armchair, picking up a plastic box filled with small rocks and stones. I furrow my brows as she empties the box onto the mahogany coffee table.

"Humour me?" She smiles. "This rock symbolises you." She picks up the biggest rock and places it in the middle of the table. "I now want you to pick up different rocks, each symbolising different people in your life. Place them next to your rock in relation to how close you felt to them before you got really sick."

"So, the closer I was to them, the closer they should be positioned to my rock?" I ask and she nods.

I pick up a rock. "This is Ryan," I explain, placing it right up against my rock, so close that they are almost touching.

"These are my parents." I pick up two more stones and put them close to me. "And this is Hannah." I put another small stone next to my parents.

I then pick up various stones symbolising Nadine, Emily, Tyler, Adam and Claire, putting them a bit further out. I smirk as I pick up rocks for Jake and Alice and put them all the way to the edge of the table, as far away from me as possible.

"Okay, I want you to remember how this looks. Now,

please move them to where they sit today," Dr Locke instructs, watching my hands move the rocks around.

I remove Ryan's rock from the table completely, replacing him with Hannah, Nadine and Tyler. I also move Jake and Emily a little closer. I move my parents' rocks further away and leave the others where they were.

"So, what do you think when you look at this change?" she asks as we both study the new pattern.

I thought I would feel sad looking at the new image, but actually, I'm pretty surprised.

"I have more people close to me now than I did before I got sick," I observe and she nods, smiling.

Nadine and Tyler have visited me every moment they can get, and I know my sister is going to join them next time they come, she's booked the time off of work especially. I even think Jake and Emily may join them as well.

Despite never meeting, my sister talks to Nadine all the time, calling her every day to ask for updates on my recovery. They've weirdly formed a pretty close friendship. I guess Nadine felt like a sister from the moment we met, so it's no surprise they get on so well. Now both my sisters have each other for support.

"And how do you feel about the other rocks?" Dr Locke asks.

I bring my fingers to my lips, lost in my thoughts as I study the table.

"Fine, actually. I always thought I'd be close with my parents, but I've started to realise that as you grow, you have to find your own way. I need to stop seeking their approval and start thinking for myself," I admit to my therapist, but also to myself.

"And your housemate, Alice?"

"Well, I guess despite never fixing things with her, I learnt a lot. The relationship breakdown with her made me realise how oblivious I can be to people around me, how self-absorbed I can be sometimes." I shrug, exhaling deeply.

"I'm sad I didn't understand why our relationship was as tense as it was until it was too late, but maybe that's the point. Maybe we don't have to fix things. Maybe I just accept it for what it was—a learning curve. We don't have to fix things in order for us to get something from the relationship. I was able to identify a flaw in myself, and hopefully I won't ever make the same mistakes again." I cross my arms and sit further back in my chair, leaning my head back to look into Dr Locke's eyes.

"Exactly. Not every relationship has to work out. It's very admirable and brave to be so self-aware that you can learn from the past." She smiles reassuringly. "So, circling back to the wider image in front of you, what do you think now when you reflect on the statement you made earlier, about feeling alone?"

"I guess I'm not." I smile.

She beams and tells me our time is up. I rise from the chair, feeling a headache form. These sessions always exhaust me, I can't wait to get back to my room and sleep.

As I leave her office, I walk towards the only window in the waiting room and look out at the gravel driveway. I spot Austin walking out of the front door, heading towards a black and blue BMW i8. The door flies up as he unlocks it before scooting into the driver's side.

As I watch him, the realisation hits me that he's gone from wanting to end his life to becoming a really successful entrepreneur with his whole life ahead of him. I guess he's right though, if he can do it, perhaps I can too.

Chapter Fifty-Eight

"I didn't think I'd see you!" Austin beams from the stage as I walk into the music hall. I tighten my grip on my guitar bag as I feel a sting of pain flash through my chest thinking about the last time I was here.

"I didn't think you would either." I sigh, sitting down on one of the empty chairs.

I let the absence of Ryan and the memories of his music therapy session hit me. I know that I need to face the painful memories in order to feel better.

I internally chuckle, remembering Ryan giving me the same piece of advice the last time we were here together. Instead of running from the thought, I embrace it.

We sit in silence as I pull my Fender from its bag and begin to tune it. As I fiddle with the strings, I hear notes on a piano. Austin is messing around with the keys on a grand piano perched in the corner of the room. I hadn't noticed it when I first walked in here, and it definitely wasn't in here when Ryan was teaching. Maybe Austin added it when he started leading these sessions, I wouldn't put it past him to do something so extravagant.

As people begin piling into the room, Austin moves to the front, standing on the stage and pacing around, smiling at us.

"As you know, I've very much kept to the same structure you always had in these classes. I want you to lead them." He looks in my direction. "I also want to welcome Zoe back." He stands still, motioning towards me. "Did you want to pick a song today?"

I gulp, feeling my heart pound violently. I try to embrace the nerves, welcoming them back into my body like an old friend.

"I actually had a slightly unusual request," I begin, watching Austin smile encouragingly. "I've written something. I was hoping we could maybe turn it into a song?" I ask, my voice tight. "But we don't have to. If that's not how you do things."

Austin's smile grows into a huge beam. "Absolutely,

we can. Have you written music before?"

"No, but last night I couldn't get these lyrics out of my head."

I don't know what came over me yesterday, but I finally found the strength and motivation to open my heart back up to music. I spent the entire evening sat on the tiny single bed in my hospital dorm, scribbling line after line on the back of a law textbook, messing with a melody stuck in my head.

"I have an idea of how I think I want the song to sound, so maybe everyone could help me with the rest?" I suggest.

"That sounds great! We'd be happy to help, wouldn't we?" Austin asks the rest of the class. A sea of nodding heads and murmurs of encouragement flow through the room.

He gestures for me to get up on the stage as he walks to the piano. When I jump up and look out at the rest of the class, I notice Becky at the back of the room. She's wearing a plain white t-shirt this time and doesn't have any bandages on her arms. My smile grows as I look at her.

"Do you think you could sing a Capella until we figure out how to add our instruments?" Austin asks.

"Sure," I murmur, looking at the floor.

I close my eyes to drown out my surroundings and

steady my breathing. I open my mouth and begin to feel
the electricity in the air as I sing unaccompanied.

Thinking back to before
I was told to want more
Stability, comfort
A place to call home

But the safety I sought
Only left me caught
In a cage of self-destruction
A prisoner, alone

So, what do I want?
To be free like a bird
Migrating south for the promise
Of a warmer tomorrow

Looking for my mind to escape
Break free and never take
The expectations, reality
A toxic society makes

I'm hungry to feel alive
Escape the corners of my mind

Stand tall, never fall
I want it all, a life I can really call
My own

The room stays silent for a few moments. A humming, static tension fills the air. All eyes are on me.

"It's all I have so far." I shrug and jump down to sit on the edge of the stage. I begin to panic; fearful I made a huge mistake.

My fear is short lived as the room erupts into applause. I even see Becky wiping her cheeks with her hands. I meet her eyes and she smiles before quickly dropping her gaze.

"Does that song have a name?" Austin asks once the room goes quiet.

I shrug. "Not yet."

"And you can probably guess my next question." He smiles. "Why did you write it? Where did the inspiration come from?"

I pause for a moment. I already know the answer to his question, but I'm scared to say it out loud, to risk the pain in my chest magnifying to a point more unbearable than it already is. I take a deep breath.

I can do this.

"Yesterday, for the first time since coming here, I felt

an overwhelming drive to recover for myself, and not just for the sake of everyone around me. I want to build a life to be proud of, not just one that pleases others. I want to feel happy and alive. I don't want to rely on other people or toxic coping mechanisms to get me through." I stare at Austin, waiting for him to say something, but he just beams widely.

He stares at me for a moment too long, nodding and then rubbing his hand across the bridge of his nose.

He asks everyone to take out a pen and write the lyrics down on an empty space in their song binder. I call out the lyrics slowly, citing them line-by-line whilst they write. Austin runs his hands over the keyboard, playing with different keys to find the perfect fit for my song.

The hour goes by in an instant, and in the end, we have the start to my very first original song. It's a weird feeling, hearing everybody singing along and playing their instruments to something I thought of last night. I didn't expect it to sound so good.

"Do you have any other sessions this afternoon?" Austin asks as I finish stacking away my chair.

I shake my head.

"Would you like to go for a walk?"

"You mean on the grounds?"

"No, I mean at a local park. You are allowed out

y'know."

I hesitate. "Okay."

I thought I'd be too scared to leave this place and the comfort it brings, but instead, I'm intrigued.

Before I know it, we're out of the front door and into Austin's ridiculous car, driving towards—actually, I have no idea.

Even though it's winter, the sun is shining brightly, melting away the morning frost that covered every inch of the grounds when I woke up this morning.

"I still can't get over your talent," Austin says over the purr of the engine.

I feel my face blush and murmur a small, "Thank you," before turning to look out the window, inhaling the strong smell of leather inside the car.

"How do you have time for everything?" he presses. "There's no way I could fit in practicing music to the level you can perform, plus law school... and you say I'm the overachiever." He flashes a grin at me, and I can't help but laugh. "Any other hidden talents I should know about?"

"Uh... well, I'm a competitive cheerleader—I mean, I

was—I *was* a competitive cheerleader." I shrug. "Before all of this."

"Ah yes! You had the backpack on at the festival. I remember now. You really are something else, Zoe." He shakes his head, laughing.

"You say that, but I've kind of started to realise that I maybe did all those things as a way to compensate for never feeling good enough."

Austin sighs heavily. "You have no idea how much that resonates with me."

I start to wonder what he means but decide not to probe.

Austin turns up the radio and I hear a familiar song blare through the speakers. OneRepublic, *I Lived*. The irony is, the lyrics *'hope if everybody runs, you choose to stay'* flow through the car just as the memory of singing this song with The Lanes crashes through my mind.

I tell myself to let the pain in, let the memory burn. It's the only way to move past it. I'm not going to run anymore, I'm not like Ryan. I'm stronger.

We turn onto a quiet road leading up to a small car park. The wet, sandy ground sprays up the side of Austin's pristine car, but he doesn't seem to care.

"I'm sorry you were too ill to make my lecture the other month." Austin smiles sympathetically as we pile out of the car and begin walking in the direction of a footpath up ahead.

"I'm sorry too. Did you find a paralegal in the end?" I ask, genuinely intrigued.

"Yes, I did," he begins. I feel a knot of disappointment form in my tummy. "It was a lot more stressful than I thought it would be. I interviewed what felt like a hundred students in your class."

"Yeah, my university's law school is filled with eager, high achievers," I agree with a knowing laugh.

"You can say that again." Austin shakes his head, grinning widely. "It was exhausting. Now I have to do it all over again for the London office. I'm dreading it."

"I didn't know you were hiring in London so quickly."

"Yeah, I've found the office space, so now I really want to get moving on it."

"Where's the office?"

"The west side of Fleet Street. Have you heard of it?"

"Yeah, it's near The Royal Courts of Justice? And Somerset House? Right?"

Austin nods in response.

"Wow." I exhale a gush of air. "That sounds amazing. Right in the middle of all the city's most beautiful sights."

"Not to mention all the restaurants and theatres. I might be biased, but it's the place to be." Austin smiles proudly.

Something gnaws at me in the pit of my stomach. It's my gut, shouting at me to listen to it.

For once, I'm going to.

Before I can overthink, I blurt out, "But what if you didn't have to do the search again?"

"What do you mean?"

"What if I put a really great case forward as to why you should hire me as a paralegal?" I don't know where this confidence has come from, but I'm going with it.

A new start. In London. Away from this place. Away from this city. Away from the memories of Ryan.

I want it. I want it *bad*. I didn't even realise how bad I wanted it until five seconds ago.

"Go on," Austin replies slowly.

"Okay, so I know that my current situation complicates things, but I was planning on going to your guest lecture and applying for the paralegal job before I messed everything up. So, if there's another opportunity going, I'd love to apply. I promise I'm more than my illness. Before all this," I say, waving my hands in front of me, "I was top of my class, even whilst I was a competitive cheerleader. Remember, Dr Jenkins mentioned me?"

Austin nods, staying silent.

"And my attendance record was near perfect before

this year, plus I've gotten over eighty percent in every assignment so far. I promise you I'll work damn hard. You won't regret it."

Austin remains quiet, keeping his cards to his chest. I almost wish I could put all the words back in my mouth.

"Look, don't worry about it. I'm sorry I overstepped. I know there's no way you could hire me. I mean, I currently live in a crazy hospital," I add with a nervous laugh.

Austin snaps his head to look at me, his face coming back to life. "Zoe don't use that phrase. You are *not* crazy." He almost spits the words and I'm slightly taken aback by his harsh tone. He's not being rude; he sounds more protective than anything else.

"Your illness doesn't matter to me, Zoe. And it shouldn't to any employer. We can make adjustments and make it work. Your health comes first. Why would you think I'd care about that? I already told you I have therapy myself; I mean—I *own* the place for God's sake."

I guess he has a point.

"So... you don't think it's completely out of the question?"

"Not at all. I don't mean to come across as patronising, but I'm *so* glad you asked. It's so brave. I just can't believe I never thought of the idea myself."

"Really?" I beam so wide my cheeks hurt.

"Of course. You'd have to go through an interview process with a couple of other people on my team, but I don't see why this couldn't happen. It saves me going through a hundred other interviews at another law school."

Despite my overwhelming joy, my insecurities creep back in. "But please, don't do this because you pity me. I wouldn't want to enable any form of nepotism just for a fresh start. I wouldn't want to take the opportunity away from someone who truly deserves it."

Austin chuckles. "Zoe, you do deserve it."

I flash him a questioning glare, as if to say, '*but how would you know I deserve it?*' He raises a warning hand to keep me silent.

"I don't pity you, Zoe. I'm impressed by you." He takes a deep breath and exhales loudly. "You even said so yourself, Dr Jenkins mentioned you by name, not just for being top of the class. He said I should talk to you about the job because you have so much potential. You clearly have a lot of drive and ambition. It has nothing to do with you being sick, I really do believe you'd be a great fit for my company, mental health battle and all.

"If your interview with my team goes smoothly and you get the job, I would want you to monopolise on the company's flexible working policy to accommodate for your recovery. You could finish your degree here and work from home, or you could transfer to a London university and come to the office when you felt like it. I actually know a professor at UCL who I could put you in touch with. We can figure this out."

My mouth hangs open, agape, and I make no move to close it. "I... uh... don't know what to say. Wow."

"You don't need to say anything, you still need to ace the interview," he jests.

My mind is racing a million miles an hour, it's a surprise I can even get my feet to carry on walking. My first thought is about Nadine's plans to move to London in the summer once she finishes her degree. Perhaps her pipedream for us to live together in the big city could actually become a reality.

My second thought is: maybe this could work. Maybe I can I get my own version of a clean break, a fresh start, without running away from my problems. I'd still tackle them head on, taking weekly trips to therapy, just like Austin does. I'd still get the help I need alongside the opportunities of a huge city. Maybe I'll even get some clarity on what I really want from life.

Chapter
Fifty-Nine

We walk in silence for a while as I mull over the potential London opportunity. It's ironic that my parents were so disappointed by my interest in music, lecturing me about how it would be distracting from my law career. When in actual fact, without music and this battle with my mental health, I wouldn't have connected with Austin in the same way. I wouldn't have had the confidence to ask him for the job in London. At best, I would've just got the job here and never moved out of this city, out of my comfort zone.

We continue to walk up a steep hill towards a viewpoint overlooking the city. I follow Austin towards a worn-looking wooden bench, sitting down next to him and admiring the breath-taking scene.

"Can I ask you something?" Austin asks carefully, searching my face.

"You've just offered me an interview for a dream job in London; you can ask me anything you like," I say with a laugh, watching as dimples form on his cheeks as he smiles.

"I just wanted to ask what happened? How you got sick?" He looks at me. "But please, don't feel obligated to answer," he adds, his breath forming misty clouds in front of him.

"No, it's okay." I half smile. "I think it started when my flatmate was killed. A bus knocked her off her bike. I'd never had to deal with anything so serious before, I didn't know how to handle the pain. I felt guilty that she died, and I didn't." I inhale a large breath of cold winter air. "So, I think I maybe binged and purged as a coping mechanism. After the first time I made myself sick, I couldn't stop. I would purposely buy so much food just to go through the process of inhaling it and chucking it back up."

I turn to face Austin, reading his expression. It remains neutral as he intently listens to me.

"The scary part is, it felt like a trance, a total out of body experience, so I guess that's why I never noticed how bad it got."

"Why do you think it manifested with food?" he asks.

"I'm not sure. I never thought it was about weight. I mean, I've always hated how I look, but I didn't do it to be skinny. I think it was more of a control thing for me. It got worse when Ryan left because I think I was trying to give myself something to have control over when so much around me was changing." I sigh, feeling somewhat relieved to get that off my chest to someone outside of the therapy room.

"I get that," Austin says, letting out a deep sigh. "Loss is a hard thing to experience."

"And so is recovery. Having the motivation to decide to get better is one of the biggest hurdles I think."

"I know. Mental illness is something we'll have to battle with for a long time, and simply deciding you are worthy of that lifelong battle is challenging enough," he replies.

I stare at Austin. I can't believe how much he understands. It's amazing how this illness is a secret in our own minds. We go through it feeling so alone, like no one could possibly understand. But when you finally open up and talk to someone else who has gone through it, it's surprising how many of your experiences overlap.

"How do you feel now, about Ryan, by the way? It

can't be easy seeing how much fame and attention he's getting. I'm really sorry about your break-up." Austin bites his lip.

"It's not easy, no, but there's nothing I can do about it." I shrug and try to act as casual as possible while a twang of pain shoots through my chest.

All I ever wanted was to be a part of his life, his goals and his dreams. I trusted him to let me be there for him and he broke that trust like it meant nothing.

"It's not fair that he gets the success and comes out of our breakup unscathed. But I wouldn't be able to look at myself in the mirror if I wanted him to fail, I'd hate myself. And I think I've gone through enough self-loathing for one year." I laugh lightly, and Austin smiles sympathetically. "It's just funny, he'd done so much work on himself. He'd gone to so many therapy sessions before we met to deal with his fear of losing people. He seemed so self-aware and so confident in his own recovery from grief. But when it came to it, none of that mattered and I wasn't enough for him."

"I think it's more complicated than you not being enough, Zoe. If you of all people weren't enough, no one ever would be." Austin stands up and holds out a hand, gesturing for me to follow along the rest of the trail.

"Your turn. What's your story?" I ask.

496

"Uh... where to start?" He chuckles. "It was during my final year of university. I'd been dating Josh for coming up to a year. It was the first relationship I'd ever been in. I was lucky; when I came out to my friends and family, they were all so supportive. But they weren't the problem.

"One night, Josh and I decided to go into town for a date. On our way home, on the train, we got attacked by this group of guys. We weren't even holding hands or anything, I guess they could just tell we were a couple. I think they were younger than us, they had to be around eighteen. There were so many of them, we didn't stand a chance."

Goosebumps begin to crawl up my arms and I shiver from the sensation. "Shit. That's awful."

"Neither of us were seriously hurt. We both had black eyes and needed some stitches, but we recovered. We just didn't recover together... Josh distanced himself from me, and I can't say I blame him for ending our relationship. At the time, I understood, but I just felt so lonely afterwards. He was the only one who knew exactly what I was going through. I was terrified every minute of every day, constantly looking over my shoulder. It was scary to be born into a world that didn't want you to be *you*."

"I... I don't even know what to say."

"It's honestly okay." Austin exhales deeply. "At the

time, I knew my mum was worried for me, so I just put on this brave front and hid what I was feeling. I wallowed in my self-hatred, blaming myself for not conforming to a version of myself that society would accept, not harm. So much was happening in my head, but I couldn't understand why I felt so low. I didn't lose anyone, I had amazing support in my friends and family."

"That doesn't mean you didn't have the right not to be okay, just because no one died. You can't help who you love, Austin, and no one should have ever laid a hand on you. It was none of their business."

"I know that now." He shrugs. "I also think depression is something that guys aren't expected to go through." He kicks at a small rock on the gravel path with the toe of his brown suede boot.

A moment of silence passes between us before he turns back to me. "But the thoughts kept getting darker and darker until I didn't want to be around anymore. And that's when I turned things around. The thoughts sort of scared me into recovery. I immediately got help, and I'm so glad I did. After a while, and a lot of hard work, I used my low as motivation. I started focussing on my ambitions, my passions in life, instead of behaving the way I thought everyone else wanted me to."

Listening to Austin's story, it's funny how the facts of

our experiences are so different, yet the feelings are so similar. I thought I was alone in the prison I had built for myself, trapped by my worries, trapped by other people's expectations. Just like he was.

"Thanks for telling me that." I smile at him.

"You're welcome. I have every faith that you'll get through this recovery battle too," he says, giving me a gentle nudge with his elbow. "You know, there was also another reason I wanted to ask you on this walk today," he adds, looking at me out of the corner of his eyes.

"Okay," I reply slowly.

"I've been toying with the idea of doing a fundraiser event for the hospital. My firm would sponsor it and use any proceeds towards supporting the hospital, perhaps by expanding music therapy sessions to other cities. I figured if my company backs it, that may draw people in. I'm sure I could get a lot of clients and corporate bodies to attend. It could be a great way of raising awareness."

"I think that's an awesome idea," I agree.

"Hearing your song today made me realise that the fundraiser should be a concert, perhaps a summer one. I was hoping you could perform too," he says coyly.

I raise my eyebrows at him, and when I don't reply, he continues. "Your song today was amazing, Zoe. I could help you finish it, or we could create a few new ones... or

we could get your band involved—minus Ryan, of course."
He laughs awkwardly.

"How about doing a music therapy performance with everyone?" I suggest.

Austin smiles, nodding eagerly. "That would be incredible."

A concert. A live performance. Without Ryan.

Could I do it?

I want to.

SIX MONTHS
LATER

Chapter Sixty

Ryan

I had to come. There was no way I was missing the chance to see her again. The last time I saw her she was lying on a hospital bed, fixed up to an IV, frail and lifeless. I'll never forget her piercing cries when she found out I'd come to visit. It fucking killed me.

I feel the raw pain in my chest every damn minute of every damn day. I know I fucking deserve it. I walked out on her. I abandoned her when she needed me. When I needed her.

Instead of pulling each other out of the darkness, I dragged us further into it.

I realised the weight of what I'd done the moment I saw her in the hospital, but I still didn't come back and fight for her. I ran away. Again.

I let the success of my album distract me, pull me away from her and my grief until I could barely recognise the shape of my own life. I told myself it was for the best. I told myself she needed to stand on her own two feet. She was already trying to take on so much, she didn't need to deal with a grieving boyfriend on top of everything else.

I also lost every member of my family the day I decided to clear out my stuff from the house. Sure, I still technically had my biological brother, but he wasn't a sibling in the same way Claire, Tyler or Adam were. And yet, I left each one of them for a clean start, or my 'big break' as I tried to convince myself it was.

I thought, with a new team around me and fans screaming my name every night, I wouldn't notice their absence, but the loneliness crept in further each day.

Once I realised the gravity of what I'd done, it was too late. She needed them and I had to let go. The only thing that made the loneliness bearable was knowing she was getting better.

I'm grateful that Adam eventually took pity on my selfish heart, giving me a few snippets of information about her every now and then. He told me when she got out of hospital, he told me about her new job, he told me that she moved to London, he even sent me the event link to the concert today.

I didn't hesitate to tell my manager to clear my schedule. I was determined to get a glimpse of her, and there wasn't a damn thing that was going to stop me.

I push my baseball cap lower on my head and weave through the crowd with my bodyguard, Patrick, in tow, trying my best to go unnoticed. The last thing I need is someone recognising me. This concert is about Zoe, and I don't want anything to ruin her perfect day. Especially me.

I find a spot in the corner of the courtyard and steal a glance around the setting. I can't believe Austin managed to book Somerset House for this fundraiser. I knew he had connections, but fuck, this is impressive.

I spin my head to take a quick peak at the high stone walls that surround the space, blocking out the rest of central London. My eyes move to the hundreds of string lights overhead, running from building to building.

The venue is epic, and they've managed to get some of the biggest new artists to perform. I'm not surprised how quickly the event sold out.

As the crowd grows, I move closer to the stage whilst making sure to be on the edge. I need to be able to dart for a quick exit if someone recognises me.

I stand near one of the two projector screens that hang on either side of the stage. It looks exactly like the type of set up you'd get at the main stage of a music festival; Austin must've spent a fucking tonne of money.

I grab my phone to text Adam and tell him that I'm here, but suddenly decide against it, placing my phone back in the pocket of my jeans. I don't want to text him in case he's with Zoe. I can't risk her knowing I'm in the crowd. It'll just distract her.

Music starts to blare from the speakers and the crowd grows animated as Austin walks onstage. He hasn't changed one bit since I last saw him. He still looks like a complete tool dressed in navy chinos and a white shirt. At least he's decided to roll his sleeves up this time, making him look slightly more relaxed but still like a total asshole.

Deep down, I know it's me who is the asshole, and a jealous one at that. I know he must be pretty close to Zoe by now. I bet he's become everything to her that I never could be, and damn, does it sting.

"I want to begin by thanking everyone for coming out this evening and supporting this wonderful cause. It looks like the weather has even decided to support us tonight," Austin begins.

I roll my eyes. Austin cracks a joke like someone's dad at a wedding. He earns a laugh from the audience though. And he has a point, the venue looks even more impressive in the mild summer heat, a pink and purple sunset just visible behind the stage. It's fucking beautiful.

"We have a few incredible and talented acts for you tonight, and I want to thank the lovely Zoe Jones for helping me to organise this event." The mention of her name pierces my fucking soul, ripping me in two. I scan the stage eagerly, hoping to catch a glimpse of her.

"Mr Walker, fancy seeing you here," a voice says from behind me. I instantly spin around. Claire launches into my arms and my baseball hat flies off my head. Patrick takes a step towards us, but I hold my hand up to let him know it's fine.

As soon as Claire releases me, I quickly duck to pick up my hat, shoving it back onto my head and looking between Claire and Adam. I glance down at their entwined hands and smile through the burning jealousy, happy that at least one of our relationships has worked out.

"How did you find me?" I ask. I didn't expect to see anyone in such a huge crowd, I figured they'd all be with Zoe backstage. Claire shrugs, not giving anything away.

I feel a spike in my throat as I look between two of my closest friends. It's been eight months since I last saw them. Eight. It's the longest we've ever gone without seeing each other. And yet, they're acting as if no time has passed at all.

I don't deserve them.

"She's on next you know," Adam says, and my stomach does a backflip. "She's doing good by the way, nervous as hell, but I think you'll like her songs."

I fucking hate that they still get to hear her sing. I hate that I've missed out on so much of her life, especially her song writing. Adam told me she started writing a while back. I couldn't believe it at first, but then again, she always had more talent than the rest of us put together.

I lift my hat off my head and run my hand through my scalp, shaking my unruly hair. I slide my cap back on and turn my focus back to Austin, who has just finished rambling to the audience.

Austin holds one arm out to the side of the stage and the crowd erupts again.

A sudden rush of heat hits me.

I watch as Zoe, *my* Zoe, runs on stage and into Austin's arms.

I've been dreaming of the moment I would see her again, how I would feel, what I would say. But seeing her now, in the centre of this giant stage, is nothing like I ever imagined.

Her soft wavy hair is longer now, it looks thick and

healthy. Her big brown eyes are the same, but the face that holds them is fuller, more vibrant. Alive. She's wearing high-waisted black combat trousers with her favourite pair of white and lilac Nike's and a sparkly teal bodysuit. Every curve on her body has been brought back to life.

She radiates.

She's damn beautiful.

I think I also spot a tattoo on her wrist. I look to the big projector to get a closer look at the design. It looks like a small flock of birds taking flight up her arm.

No way did she get a tattoo.

She takes the microphone from Austin and brings it to her full lips. "Thanks Austin," my favourite voice says, my heart crumbling at the sound. "Thank you everyone for buying a ticket to come and support us tonight, you have no idea how much it means to us."

I bite down the growl in my throat at the word 'us'. She must mean everyone at Priory House, not just her and Austin. They aren't an us, Adam would have told me, surely.

Or maybe he wouldn't.

The crowd begin to cheer and Zoe's perfect cheeks flush crimson as she waits for the crowd to quieten. She brings the microphone back to her mouth and my heart aches to hear her voice again.

"I can't tell you how much Priory House has helped me and so many others find our way out of the darkness and back into the light. When I was fighting an intense battle in my own mind, they gave me a safe space to find myself again, to rediscover my love for music and, most importantly, love for myself."

I rub a hand across my face, wiping away the tears pricking my eyes.

"We wanted to open tonight with an incredibly special act—and I'm not just saying that because I'm in it." She laughs along with the crowd. I find myself laughing too, even as now-thick tears threaten to escape my eyes.

"At Priory House, we have a music group. It's a safe place for us to be creative, to sing songs that we can identify with in that moment. The money we raise tonight will help expand these sessions to other hospitals across the country, providing instruments and teachers to run the classes." The crowd cheers again. I have to remind myself to snap my jaw shut as I stare in awe at this confident, sweet girl.

Claire rubs my back and stands on her tip toes to launch her arm around my chest, bringing me in for a hug. I wipe my eyes and shake my head, laughing awkwardly at being caught acting like such an emotional wreck. I've not even heard her sing yet, how the hell am I going to cope with that?

Zoe introduces the rest of the group to the stage. I'm surprised by how many people run on to join her, old patients and new, all coming together for this performance.

I notice Becky, wearing her usual purple knit jumper and blue jeans. She pulls at the sleeves of her jumper, wrapping them over her hands to hide the bandages. My heart throbs for the girl and her uphill battle of recovery.

In this moment, I realise I not only abandoned Zoe, but Becky and the others too. Fuck, I'm an asshole.

Zoe opens her mouth again, twisting the dagger already lodged in my heart. She introduces the song they've all decided to sing.

Adventure of a Lifetime.

I almost choke. I can't believe they picked this song and Zoe didn't object. Surely, she would have wanted to distance herself from being reminded of me.

I have so many questions I want to ask her, so many unknowns, but I know I lost the right to ask them so long ago.

Austin moves across to a black piano to the left of the choir and Zoe runs to the back of the stage, out of view.

The ache in my chest moans at the loss of sight, but I look at the screens to find she has moved to join the event band. She stands next to Tyler who passes her a guitar.

Her *Fender* guitar.

I'm shocked that she hasn't smashed it to pieces.

She kept it. She kept the reminder of me, the reminder of us.

Austin counts the group in, and the familiar song fills the space. Tyler's electric guitar plays the opening lines and I so desperately wish I was up there with them.

Chapter Sixty-One

Ryan

Once the choir finish singing, Zoe jumps back onto stage with an air of confidence I've never seen. She looks so at home, so comfortable running this enormous show. I never imagined she could climb these heights of peace; I wish I could take a slice of it for myself.

She takes the microphone from the stand at the front of the stage, bringing it to her face and looking out at the audience. As much as I ache to meet her gaze, I force myself to bow my head, not wanting her to spot me. I brush away the nagging hope that she's looking for me. That would be damn impossible.

She takes a deep breath. "I've written a couple of new songs and I hope you don't mind if I play them for you tonight," she begins. "I'll admit, the first one is a little sad, but I'll make sure we shake it off with something more fun afterwards."

Her stage presence is so captivating. I can't believe this is the same girl that was too scared to even sing along to music in the car with me when we first met.

She walks over to the grand piano and places her microphone on the stand hanging above it.

She learnt to play the piano? In a matter of months?

Jealousy washes over me just picturing Austin teaching her a new instrument, one that doesn't remind her of me.

Tyler remains on stage, ready to play one of Zoe's original songs with her. Austin stands next to him, saxophone in hand. She looks across to them and they both flash her comforting, encouraging smiles, spurring her on.

"I wrote this at a time of loss. I hope the song resonates with some of you. You might be mourning your former self or mourning someone you loved and lost. Either way, I hope we can all find peace one day."

Her words hit me like a tonne of bricks. I feel as if she is talking directly to me. Her words dig into my soul, ripping at the stitches struggling to hold my broken heart together.

"It's called *The End*," she adds quietly, looking down at her hands on the piano.

As her fingers press down on the keys, I feel a punch right in my gut. I bow my head again, bringing my hand to the bridge of my nose. Claire keeps her arm tightly around me, stabilising me. I close my eyes as the music plays and I let Zoe's voice cradle me.

Even if I wanted to,
I could never forget your golden eyes
The way they stared into mine
Like we were forever

You set my soul on fire
Set my heights higher
Kept me dreaming
Kept me wanting more

You were my best friend
A love till the end
A fire, a spark
A claim on my heart, I'm yours

But you pulled the trigger
Your pain so much bigger
Than the love you felt for me

And I couldn't breathe

I listen carefully to her words, knowing that every single lyric tumbling out of her mouth will be deliberate, precise to the way she felt when she wrote them.

Whenever she used to listen to music, she was always so intent on analysing the lyrics to understand their meaning. And as I listen to her words, I can't help but do the same.

You were supposed to fix me
Stop me drowning in a sea
Of reality and shame
But now you're to blame
For walking out on me

You left me broken, a mess
Surrounded by white walls, emptiness
No way to forget
And I fell off the edge

You were my best friend
A love till the end
A fire, a spark
A claim on my heart, I'm yours

But you pulled the trigger
Your pain so much bigger
Than the love you felt for me

And I couldn't breathe

But just so you know, I'll never let go
I still feel every touch
I just wish it was enough
To start over again

The words spin around in my head. I bring my hands to my face, trying to cover the tears as I remember where I am.

I just wish it was enough
To start over again

Am I foolish enough to think that she is singing about me? Does she feel the same way as I do? That she would die for another chance to be together?

Could she really feel this way after I betrayed her?

How could she, when I shattered both our hearts into a million pieces?

Before my mind can catch up to me, I turn to my friends. "I need to see her."

They glance a sceptical look at one another before nodding and leading me out of the crowd.

I follow their every step as we weave through the audience towards the backstage entrance.

Claire pulls out two spare passes for me and Patrick. I wrap mine around my neck, not giving myself time to question whether Claire had the pass for me all along. I don't think about whether this is the right thing to do. All I can think about is *her*.

I'm grateful for the epic sound system at this concert, I can still hear every single word as I walk through the gates and up to the side of the stage. I continue to listen as she talks to the crowd, getting them hyped for her next song.

When we get backstage, I hover at the back of the space in the darkest corner, not wanting her to see me yet. I ignore the gasps and murmur of voices coming from the side of the stage. Nadine, Emily, Hannah and Jake are huddled right by the edge. Their eyes burn my whole body as they stare at me.

Not giving a shit what they think, I meet their stares

and look a little closer to see another guy stood with them, but I don't recognise him. I swallow down the jealously that rises through me just thinking about Zoe's new life. There's so much I don't know.

Adam, Claire and Patrick flank me as we face the stage and watch Zoe jump around, climbing and scaling the speakers like she did when she performed at the festival with us.

Her confidence is even greater than before. I watch in awe as she waves her arms in the air and the crowd join in, mirroring her and clapping along to the beat of the music.

And then she finishes.

The set ends and I'm struck with the reality that soon, she will walk off the stage and I will be in front of her once again.

I pull off my baseball cap, gripping it tightly in my left hand. I brush my other hand through my hair several times. Claire rubs the small of my back, trying to comfort me.

I watch as my beautiful girl skips off the stage and into the arms of her closest friends. Her smile wild, her confidence infectious.

This was what I wanted when I left.

I wanted her to embrace every minute of her life and

do the things she loves, without me holding her back.

This was what I wanted, but I thought I would feel better about it.

Nadine leans into Zoe's ear, whispering something. Zoe nods her head slowly, her eyes widening in shock. She slowly pivots to face me.

Her big chocolate eyes lock to mine.

I search her face for a hint of emotion, any sign of hatred or anger or upset, but I don't see it.

I just see... curiosity?

My brain finally catches up to my body and I take a step towards her. Zoe does the same.

In a mere moment, we are face to face, inches apart.

"Hi." I inhale the electricity between us, lapping it up with a hunger I didn't know existed.

"Hi," she replies.

Zoe's Most Played Songs

"Wings" by *Birdy*
"Hold Me Like You Used To" by *Zoe Wees*
"Closure" by *Sarcastic Sounds, Birdy & Mishaal*
"One Day" by *Tate McRae*
"Heaven" by *Amber Run*
"Last Call" by *Jamie Miller*
"Control" by *Zoe Wees*
"Disco Wings" by *Plastic Mermaids*
"Growing Pains" by *Alessia Cara*
"Weight of Living Pt I" by *Bastille*
"I Lived" by *OneRepublic*
"Worst of You" by *Maisie Peters*
"Sweet Melancholy" by *Amber Run*
"Adventure of a Lifetime" by *Coldplay*
"Come Home" by *OneRepublic*
"Icarus" by *Bastille*
"Castles" by *Freya Ridings*
"I'm Tired" by *Amber Run*
"Feel Like Shit" by *Tate McRae*
"Forever and Always" by *Taylor Swift*
"Over My Head (Cable Cars)" by *The Fray*
"I Miss You" by *Amber Run*
"Laura Palmer" by *Bastille*
"Trouble" by *Coldplay*
"Someone To You (Acoustic)" by *BANNERS*
"Rich Love" by *OneRepublic*
"A Sky Full of Stars" by *Coldplay*

Resources

If you are experiencing mental health problems or know someone who is, please visit: www.time-to-change.org.uk/mental-health-and-stigma/help-and-support.

For every book sold, Florence will donate to Samaritans, registered charity 219432.

About the Author

Florence Williams was born and raised in Bristol before moving away to pursue a history degree and corporate career. She also has a beautiful working cocker spaniel, Lola, who is Florence's (much loved) little shadow. Although working in the corporate world,

Florence always turns to books as a solace when life gets a little bit complicated. During the pandemic, that love of reading naturally shifted to a love of writing. Once she wrote the first sentence of this book, she couldn't stop.

Writing gave Florence the opportunity to open up about the mental illnesses that have occupied her mind since she was thirteen. She's suffered with depression for fourteen years and developed an eating disorder whilst at university. Although *Complicated You* is a product of fiction, the mental health battles somewhat mirror her individual experience. She hopes that this book may comfort others going through similar struggles in the same way that it comforted her when she wrote it. Florence also hopes it can be educational, to show people that there is no one size fits all approach to dealing with mental health.

Florence would love to interact with you on social media, so please give her a follow and say hello!
Instagram: @florencewilliams1
TikTok: @flosfiction

Acknowledgements

Wow. Okay. Where do I start? There are so many people to thank that I think my acknowledgments would become longer than the actual book, so I'll rein myself in as best I can.

Firstly, thank you to the people who have helped me turn this book from a secret hobby, buried on my laptop, to a real-life book. I couldn't have done it without you —Tom, Annie, Rachel, Rozzi, Chelsea, Sophia and Felix. You have no idea how much your boosts of confidence, voice notes, creativity, edits, love and friendship have helped me believe in myself enough to put this book into the world. Thank you thank you thank you.

Thank you to my amazing parents and sister; your patience and unwavering support for me and my unpredictable mind never ceases to amaze me. Also shout out to Mum and Dad for being the complete opposite to the parents in this book!

Thank you to all my girlfriends (you know who you are!!) for being my real-life Nadine. I love you endlessly.

Sue, thank you for being a wonderful mentor and a listening ear throughout all my career and life highs and lows! Your amazing advice and encouragement rivals some of the best life coaches out there!!

Finally, to my depression, anxiety and eating disorder... thank you. Thank you for making me stronger every time I kick your ass. Thank you for creating the most challenging and scary situations I have ever had to deal with. Because without you, I wouldn't be who or where I am today. You will never win. I will.

Oh... and one more 'person' to thank. It would be criminal not to acknowledge my beautiful puppy dog and best friend, Lola, who has helped me out of more dark situations than she will ever realise. You really are a gal's best friend.

Printed in Great Britain
by Amazon